WHERE ARE WE?
lower
MONKLAND
SHERBROOKE STREET WEST
MADISON
WILSON
TRENHOLME
DE MAISONNEUVE
UPPER LACHINE
ST JACQUES
LEE
JOHNNY
$112,600
in ill-gotten rewards
YOU
comma
Idiot
Ack!

YOU comma Idiot

YOU
comma
Idiot

a novel by
DOUG HARRIS

Edited by Bethany Gibson.
Jacket design by Julie Scriver, with a nod to Akoulina Connell.
End leaf thoughts and squiggles courtesy of Doug Harris.
Page design by Julie Scriver.
Printed in Canada on FSC certified paper.
10 9 8 7 6 5 4 3 2 1

Library and Archives Canada Cataloguing in Publication

Harris, Doug, 1959-
You comma idiot / Doug Harris.

ISBN 978-0-86492-630-2

I. Title.
PS8615.A7477Y68 2010   C813'.6   C2010-902415-X

Goose Lane Editions acknowledges the financial support of the Canada Council
for the Arts, the Government of Canada through the Book Publishing Industry
Development Program (BPIDP), and the New Brunswick Department of Wellness,
Culture, and Sport for its publishing activities.

Goose Lane Editions
Suite 330, 500 Beaverbrook Court
Fredericton, New Brunswick
CANADA E3B 5X4
www.gooselane.com

For William, and in memory of Gary

One

You're the kind of guy who falls in love after one date.

You're the kind of guy who rehearses a conversation fifty times in your head then blows it when it's for real. You're the kind of guy who washes your hair three times in a single day because you're meeting a chick at a restaurant that night. And then gets caught walking in the rain to get there. You're the kind of guy who's kind of stupid that way.

You're the kind of guy who's always feeling sorry for yourself. You're the kind of guy who takes it personally every time a girl walks by with barely a glance over. The kind of guy who likes to think of yourself as sensitive. The kind of guy who confuses sensitive with pathetic.

You're the kind of guy who still thinks about the pretty girls you were afraid of in high school, girls who never even knew your name. The kind of guy who can't stop wondering what it would be like to meet one now. Maybe she's not doing so well. Maybe things are tough. You're the kind of guy who's attracted to women having a hard time.

You're the kind of guy who thinks you can save them.

=

You are not, it's fair to say, a good-looking guy. You were given a look too dreary and drawn, skull too thin, face too long. Forehead too high. Cheeks hollow, chin weak. A nose that points oddly, breaking down and away like a difficult putt.

In the mirror in the morning, you often stare at yourself for long periods of time. Sad, extended moments. You wonder what you did wrong and whom you angered. You wonder what you're being *punished* for.

You find yourself contemplating a face that is angular and gaunt, yet with skin curiously loose and fleshy. Jowly. If you ever traced your family tree it wouldn't surprise you to come across the name Flintstone. Unlike Fred, though, you are skinny and tall. Very tall. Which makes you look, well, very skinny. Jeans fit you like a twelve-year-old girl. You haven't worn a pair of shorts in a decade. Jackets hang off you like they're sopping wet and sweatshirts engulf your laughable shoulders. The average tie covers half your chest. Clothes hate your guts.

As soon as you set foot outside your apartment you feel as though you're on display for all to cringe at. You're forever glancing at your reflection in every store window you pass, checking your face, your hair, your shirt, your legs, obsessing with a vanity only the truly dismally endowed can appreciate.

Strangely, you don't do well with women.

You are, more accurately, the kind of guy who gives other men the confidence to approach them. You're the kind of guy plain girls practise their dismissive looks on. You're the guy at the bar who's always going off to sit and mope in a corner by yourself, whose friends always have to come and get you, cajole you back to the table. You are what the periphery of the group was made for. When a pretty girl tells a funny story and everyone laughs, that's you in the everyone part. A voice that matters only in that it rounds out the chorus.

You are, of course, an entirely necessary element of your species. You are what balance must have. A low end.

Or maybe it's not as bad as all that. Maybe you have a tendency to exaggerate. Maybe it just *feels* that way some days. Mornings are hardest. The waking-up-alone thing. In the evening it's not so bad. You go to bed maybe having done something, hung around with your friends, gotten high. Watched a movie, or some TV. The night is over and now you can go to sleep.

But in the morning the whole rest of the day is waiting. You get to be ugly, and with a whole mess of hours ahead of you. It's why the first thing you usually do once you're up is go back to sleep. Also because you have no job.

You're lying in bed now. You can hear the TV talking from across the apartment. You keep it on almost all the time. There's a commercial playing. It's the one with the two detectives on a stakeout late at night. You can picture it from memory. They're slouched in a car, both handsome guys with chiselled jaws and cool expressions, exchanging clever, clipped dialogue. One guy is black and the other is white and they make it clear that even though the white guy has been driving his partner crazy lately because he's always sneezing and his nose is running and he should just take the cold medicine, they're the kind of partners that deep down really like and respect each other.

It's a good spot. They sure know how to make them, you have to admit. It seems like a wonderful product and it's fun to sort of bond with these rugged dudes, even if just for thirty seconds. And the whole black-white thing is good too, them being good friends, reminding us how far the world has come, that we now live in a perfectly harmonious, racially integrated land only TV seems to truly endorse.

Finally, the white guy takes a pill and the black guy is happy because he won't have to listen to his sniffling all the time. It looks like maybe they can even get some sleep. But then at the end the black guy sneezes and now it looks like *he's* getting a cold. Uh-oh. His buddy gives him a knowing look and reaches for the box of medicine.

Fantastic!

Actually, it's amazing that you can recall all this. You, with the short-term memory of a week-old puppy. You, who half the time can't remember what you came into the room to get. You, who this very moment are wondering, What was that thing you were supposed to do today? Something important, you think. Although with you that doesn't necessarily mean anything. Not a lot happens. A guy like you, it could just mean you're out of milk.

Honey came over this morning. To kill a few hours. She does that after a night shift sometimes when she's not ready for bed yet. Wakes you up at eight-thirty in the morning buzzing from downstairs. It's all right, you've gotten kind of used to it. She brings breakfast that she buys on her way over. Those greasy egg-cheese-bacon-on-a-croissant heart attacks they sell at doughnut places. Honey's a nurse but she's got the worst health habits you could pick. Smokes, drinks, eats garbage. She's a coffee freak, too. And she never exercises. It doesn't matter. She'll be gorgeous until she's ninety. She's just one of those chicks.

Honey's been with Johnny a long time. Johnny Karakis is your best friend. Everyone's always known you're crazy for Honey too. Johnny knows, Honey knows. Your friends know. People make jokes. Fuck them anyway, they all lust after her too. You have nothing to hide.

Your life's regret has surely been rooted in the way you look. It bothers you to have been so shortchanged in this department. It angers you. What a *gas* it would have been to walk through life as attractive as Johnny. And other lucky pricks you can think of. And so, a certain cynicism has set in. You believe that everyone but you is dumb. Or some degree of dumb. You believe that you're accountable to no one. You believe that people waste their lives doing whatever they think will sound good when they tell it to their friends. You believe that all friendships are fleeting. That if it means enough, anyone will betray anyone. You believe that people will pay to be entertained by just about anything. You're convinced that video ruined music. And then music ruined movies. You've downloaded the soundtracks to some of the stupidest movies ever made. You believe that all handsome men are simpletons. And that the problem with attractive women is that they're too shallow to look beyond the obvious in order to see the real you. Myopic bitches. You believe that only you know what's really funny. You believe that no one else brings any real perspective to the table. You believe that computers are just a fad. Relatively speaking, that is. A hundred years from now everyone will be busy being revolutionized by something else. You believe that knowing all this, that being burdened with this much vision, is paralyzing, that it would paralyze anyone, and so it's not your fault if you've never really done anything in your life.

You believe that you have the right to say whatever you feel. As well as the right to say nothing. And on the whole, lying is easier than both. You've slept with friends' baby sisters. You've been with desperate women. You've had relations *with a cousin*. It's been rough. You've had to watch year after year as lesser men than yourself escorted perfectly good chicks through shopping malls while you had to shop for some shitty gift for somebody's shitty birthday all by yourself. You believe the world's against you. You believe that you're entitled to whatever you can get.

You made it with your best friend's girlfriend this morning.

You're an idiot.

two

"You're not sleeping," Honey says.

It's not quite a question, but the way she says it makes you feel obliged to respond. It's maybe nine o'clock.

"I think I'm going to get up," you say.

You've been lying here, the two of you, post-coital, for the past twenty minutes. Longer than it took you to screw her.

Her head is tucked into the crook of your armpit, a strange posture. You wonder if she does this with Johnny too, or is it just for you, today, her snuggling in like this? You're dying for a cigarette.

"I'm dying for a smoke," you say. Low, almost a whisper.

"Get one, then."

But you don't. You just lie there some more. She just lies there some more. There's nothing to say. You think to yourself, How weird is this?

You've thought about sex with her almost *daily*. For years. About seeing her naked. About touching her body. About just basking in the glow that is her relentless beauty. About slowly sliding her panties down off her hips, over those perfect thighs, tiny blond hairs on her leg glistening, standing up straight as you go. About your hand worming its way up into that tight T-shirt, softly cupping one of what you've always considered to be two of the finest breasts ever grown. About grabbing a fistful of that ass, rolling it around, feeling it between your fingers.

And you did that today.

So how do you feel?

She throws an arm over what little chest you have, pulls herself in closer to you. "You're gorgeous," she says, kissing your neck. "You're a beautiful guy. You're too much man for me."

"Really?"

"No."

"No?"

She smiles. "Well, you're alright. You're *okay.*"

"I don't care," you say, pretending to pout.

"Don't. It doesn't matter."

A beat goes by.

"It was weird," you say.

"It *was* weird," she allows.

You slide the comforter off her. Expose some of that beautiful flesh, look at it again.

"You know something?" you say. "You're really how I thought you'd be. Naked, I mean. Really something."

"Just how you thought I'd be? Not better?"

"Yes. Better. Even better than I thought."

"Really?"

"No."

Actually, yes.

Better than you'd ever dared to imagine. Better than you've ever seen. That's the truth. The kind of body that belongs in the movies, belongs up on a screen. Belongs with somebody else. Like Johnny.

She came on to you.

She made the first move, got into the bed. Climbed on you.

That's also the truth. It couldn't be anything but true. You'd never have had the courage to do anything on your own.

She enjoyed it, you think. Joking aside. Reasonably so. As in, it wasn't like a complete failure or anything.

You enjoyed it. It was amazing, an amazing thing.

It wasn't great.

It's impossible for it to have been great. It could never be as great as you'd built it up to be. And you'd have had to go at it with her a lot heavier than that to compete with the jillions of scenarios that used to flutter through your head during those relentless off-the-wrist sessions she's starred in for you over the years. You'd pretty well have to be shooting a porn flick too, given that you used to picture other babes in there with her. And a lot of it in slow motion.

This is not the beginning of an affair.

This is not something that will ever happen again.

You have no illusions about *that*.

It went by too fast.

You were too nervous.

She never kissed you.

These are all facts.

You kissed *her* a few times. More or less pinned her mouth down. Like when you read that hookers don't kiss their clients. It felt like that sort of thing.

You don't even have a clear idea as to why it happened in the first place.

Another fact.

"I'm so tired," she says. "Let's sleep a bit. Let's crash for a couple of hours."

"I don't think I can sleep, Hon."

"But I worked all night, Lee."

"I know. I'll go read the paper or something. Tell me when you want me to wake you."

She ignores this, snuggles in tighter. "Close your eyes, my little watermelon seed."

Her little watermelon seed. Her little potato chip. Her little cucumber salad. Her little guacamole dip, her little eggplant. These are pet names she's always called you by. Names that make you smile. Make Johnny smile. It's always seemed so cute to everyone how she does this, how this stunning creature takes it upon herself to bestow these affectionate little monikers upon you, you who everyone knows couldn't in a million years end up with a girl like her. And how she knows how much you like it, though you pretend you don't. How she always picks the right moment to do it, make you feel a little better about yourself even if you're determined not to. Say it when she knows other girls can hear it. In a bar, at a party, a barbecue. Bring you just a little closer in from the periphery of the circle. Her little kumquat. Her little pie crust.

"Honey?"

"Sleep, Lee."

"No, I want to ask you something…"

"I don't want to talk about *this*. If that's where you're going."

"No, no. That's not it."

But it was.

Later. At the door. She's looking for her keys. She's always looking for her keys. Keys to the ancient Firebird she loves so much. Like her other nurse friends, she's always dug old muscle cars.

She finds them. They were in her pocket. It always ends up they were in her pocket. "Lee, don't say anything to Johnny, alright? Okay?"

You don't answer. Try to think of a good lie.

She picks up her jacket, purse, slings them both over her shoulder. She says, "I'll see you on the weekend. You're still coming over."

This is a question.

"I don't know," you say. "I guess so."

She reaches up, strokes your cheek. "I'll see you on the weekend."

She kisses you on the chin, releases you with a stern look. Opens the door, turns back to you.

"Don't get weird, Lee."

"I won't get weird."

"You're already weird."

"I'm a bit weird."

"Just take it easy."

"I'll take it easy."

"Okay."

"Alright."

Pause.

And then you say, "But I don't understand."

Audible sigh. Hers.

"What?" she says finally.

What? Why she got into bed with you this morning, that's what. Why she didn't just wait for you with the food in front of the TV like she did all the other times. You were just trying to get a few more minutes' sleep. Honest, Ma. Why you woke up to her tongue on your stomach. Why she *wanted* to. After all these years, she picked *today* to cheat on Johnny? After all these years, *you* suddenly got sexy to her? A thousand different guys could've been you. And now she's splitting like it's no big deal. Telling you to take it easy.

It is a big deal. It means it's over. You've thought about this since forever, and now it's over. The two of you went at it like alley cats this morning — okay, not really — and now it's over.

When something like this is over, it's time for the *consequences*.

You turn to her. "Well, what do you mean, don't tell Johnny?" You don't exactly stammer, but it doesn't come out smooth either. "Ever?"

She walks to the elevator, pushes the button. She could be there a while. This is one slow elevator.

"No, I just meant don't tell him," Honey says again. The door opens. For once in its lifetime the stupid thing is there. She steps in, turns back to look at you. "It'll be better if I do it."

Oh.

And with a smile, she goes.

Man, is she beautiful.

three

Where you've lived your whole life, in Montreal, in the city, in the buildings below Sherbrooke Street West and in the ones on the other side of the tracks too, where the streets get a little shabbier and the block apartments and postwar housing all seems a little jumbled and lopped on top of itself, the arrow's not necessarily pointing up, baby. There's a lot of blue-collar, a lot of part-time, a lot of people dropping unemployment cards into the mailbox on Friday afternoons. People still go to sad little restaurants with ancient signs out front that say *Jimmy's* or *Steaks* or, more popular still, *Restaurant.* They still go to laundromats and sit there all afternoon with a magazine in their lap and one eye on the machines, making sure no one's stiffing their towels. They still line up in banks to make deposits and withdrawals, some of them, because using a bank card or a computer seems like such a hassle. The passwords and codes and everything. Standing in line isn't so bad when you know the people and have the time.

Unlike many big-city neighbourhoods, here time treads water in a way most urban areas aren't used to. People planned to leave a lot earlier but just never did. There's almost too little change. Too much continuity. There are still streets where generations endure, friends and family still around to remember and be remembered, people's stories that have beginnings, middles, and even ends, entire lives sometimes wrapped up into what turns out to be not much more than an overly long anecdote.

You're driving with Henry. Henry has a car. You don't have a car. Henry is a poor driver, he never knows where he's going. Even when he's been there many times, each time for Henry is like the first time.

"Left," you say between slightly gritted teeth. Already you're on edge. You adjust your shades, glance over at him.

Henry sails straight through the intersection.

"When?" he says.

You look over at him again. "Then."

"There?"

"Yes, there."

"I didn't think you meant there." He approaches another cross street. "Anyways, isn't it here?"

"You can't turn here."

Henry looks over, sees that it's one-way the wrong way.

You say, "Alright, forget it. Make a right and we'll go up and around."

Henry edges over to change lanes but there are cars there. "Right?" he says weakly.

"Yes. Get over."

"I can't. There's cars."

"So slow down."

"There's guys behind me."

"Speed up then."

Henry nods. "I see."

But he doesn't, and you miss this turn too.

"That was sad," you say.

"It's not my fault."

"Alright, just stay in this lane. Go straight until the lights."

Henry squints up ahead. "Hey, *that's* where you turn left. *That's* where we turned last time."

"Because we did it *wrong* last time."

"Are you sure?"

"Flicker. Put your flicker."

When he's made all his rights, then a left, then a right again, and he's finally got you within walking range of where you're going, you see a place to stop.

"Alright. Let me out here."

"I'll go up a bit further."

"Here!"

"I see."

Henry swerves violently towards the sidewalk then yanks the steering wheel away at the last instant before he runs up on the curb. A girl and her dog yelp in terror, scramble onto somebody's lawn.

"Dump the car and I'll meet you later," you tell him, hopping out.

"Don't be forever."

"I won't."

"Please, Lee. Last time was long."

"Last time someone else was there. I told you."

"Well, even if there's someone, don't be so long."

"I'll be fast."

"I don't want to wait forever."

"Alright."

"Don't forget."

"Go. Now."

Man, it's like a husband-and-wife thing. Enough. You'll be as fast as you can. It's not like you want to be there any longer than you have to.

You wince watching Henry pull away, careening into the oncoming lane, swerving back to his side. What makes you bring him with you, anyway? Well, he's tough. And a little crazy. And you get nervous going alone. Even after all this time. It's why you go through this stupid ritual. Henry drives you close, you walk the rest of the way, go in the front. When you leave, you go out the back of the building, through the basement door, cut through the alley there, and walk to where you're meeting back up with Henry, who has dumped the car.

If everything is cool, you grab a cab together. Henry comes back for his car the next day.

If they're watching the front door, they never see you come out again. If they're watching Henry's car, you never go back to it. It's parked on a side street all night long. And of course if they've got a half a brain, they catch you anyway. Easily. It's a pointless manoeuvre. It makes you feel better just the same.

Your long legs carry you quickly. The streets are nicer here, the sidewalks clean. It may be lower Westmount, but it's still Westmount. Somebody's sure paying some taxes. When you get to the building, you give a cursory look around, scanning the entrance and lobby to see if anything looks out of the ordinary. Other than that, what're you looking for? To spot an undercover cop? As if. It's impossible to make those guys. You just want to make sure that no one's looking to jump you. That there's nobody hanging around whispering into their cellphone. Nobody that looks like they're there to let somebody else know you're on your way. You heard of a guy who got robbed in an elevator on his way up. Not here, somewhere else. They got in with him on the ground floor, beat the shit out of him, and were gone by the fifth. The guy never even bothered going the rest of the way up. What was he going to do there without any money?

Another guy you heard about, you're thinking this as you open the heavy glass door that leads into the names and buzzers, showed up at his dealer's place right during a bust. Imagine that. This guy *knocked on the front door* as the narcs were combing through the apartment. Hello! And the guy's name, this is the best part, was Lucky. Ha! Come on in, Lucky. Beer, Lucky? He did three months. For a while after he got out he was The Dealer Formerly Known As Lucky, but it never really stuck.

A lady's leaving through the interior security door. She's having trouble, struggling to squeeze two big bags through as she braces the door open with a hip. You hold it to let her out but then allow it to swing locked again without you going in. She looks back at you, wondering why.

Because that's how Lucky got in.

"I'm not sure if my friend's home," you say. "I'm going to ring him first."

She moves away, gives you another look as she goes.

Schmuck. *Ring him first.* What're you, British? Just say nothing. You walk over to the listings, trace a finger across the glass panelling. Pretend like you're looking for his name, searching for the code. Behind you, bag lady has heaved herself through the outside door. You press the tiny rectangular button beside 6060.

"Yes?"

"Lee."

"Lee?"

"Lee."

"Alright."

Buzz. Click.

In the elevator you're reminded of Honey and this morning's fiasco. Yipes. You're going to pay for that. It's still so fresh in your mind, you haven't even had a chance to freak out about it yet. Just forget it for now. Concentrate. Stay sharp.

You get up to fifteen, slide out the doors, and turn right. No one robbed you on your way up. This is a good thing. If they had, they would have run off with two thousand bucks. Not a bad ten minutes' work. You make your way down the long carpeted tunnel. You're going to the very end. Two thousand bucks. That's peanuts in a place like this. You pass door after door, rich, dark wood. Pretentious little gold plates with the apartment numbers carved in. Thick locks. Stylish door handles. You keep waiting for one of them to turn and open, put you face to face with somebody coming out of their place, the once-over they'll give you, look you up and down wondering who let you in the building. Or maybe they know who let you in the building.

You keep walking, staring straight ahead. Chest tight. Heart pounding. Still. After all these years.

Nobody's door handle turns, nobody's door opens. You let yourself relax a bit, breathe out, breathe in. Funny how even in expensive buildings you can still smell what people are having for dinner. You get to the end of the corridor, push the buzzer, and listen as the footsteps arrive.

Your Dealer opens the door, steps back from it. "You're fifteen minutes late."

"I'm *five* minutes late."

You file past him and make your way into the living room. There are more plants here than you've ever seen in one room. Regular plants, not pot. Floor plants, shelf plants, rows of potted flowers. Mini trees. Bushes, even. Pots in waiting, filled to the brim with dirt. You sit down at one end of a leather couch, not far from a skinny cactus.

"So, what can be done for you?" Your Dealer asks, following you in. He's sipping through a straw at some murky-looking shit in a tall glass. "Juice? Tea?"

Your Dealer is one of those guys who's trying to live forever. He's over fifty, always on one kick or another. He doesn't drink or smoke cigarettes or eat anything that doesn't have fibre and grain and sprouts and whatever else you're supposed to need. He lifts weights and runs and reads health magazines and avoids the sun like the plague.

He sits down at his fancy antique desk.

"No," you say, "I don't want anything. I just dropped by."

He opens a drawer, pulls out a little book, and flips through several pages until he comes to your name. "What'd you bring?"

"Two."

"Two," he says, studying the page then reaching for a pen to write this number down. "And you don't want anything?"

"No, I still have." You stand up and pull your jean jacket off, turning it around to find the double-sized pocket sewn inside against the back. You open it, take out the thick envelope that's been gnawing at your spine the last half-hour. You walk over and hand it to him.

He pulls out the money, unwraps the elastic bands, and sighs. Begins counting.

"I've got to go in the shower," he says. "You can't stay long."

You shrug. "You're going out?"

"With Sharon."

Sharon is his ex.

"Where?"

"Restaurant. Did you count this properly?"

"Yeah."

"Properly?"

"Sure."

"Mmn." This comes out as a bit of a grumble. Is it all the little bills? You watch him count.

After a bit he looks up at you. "You know what the problem with growing old is, Lee?"

You don't answer.

He stares at you like there's an obvious reply.

"I don't know," you say finally, fiddling with a stack of coasters on the table in front of you, nervous, anxious to go, watching as he returns his gaze to the money and continues counting. "Your eyesight goes?"

He shakes his head. "No."

You say nothing. He says nothing. You wait. He waits you out, keeps counting. Christ, how are you supposed to know? He's the one that's old.

You guess again anyway. "All the time wasted with the little details in life?"

"No." But a faint smile comes to his lips, a softened expression has worked its way into those pale little features. He likes these little discourses.

You think a little more, wonder what he's getting at. And then it occurs to you that he's referring to Sharon. Of course. She of the shrill, lispy voice. You've met her a couple of times. Ugh.

"Old relationships," you say. "The tangled webs we've woven."

He smiles again. "We weave. No."

He slides a couple of piles away from him, starts on the rest. You watch him. He's careful and practised, slipping each bill out from the one underneath it, feeling it to be sure there's not another one hidden. Deliberate, unhurried. Precise and methodical. Slow. You could bash him over the head with a heavy pot of dirt.

Your Dealer decides to explain. "The problem with growing old" — he reaches over for his anti-aging serum — "is that your ass itches constantly." He presses the straw to his lips and sucks in some goop.

You pick at your jacket, toying with the buttons. It's always a little tense over here. The bizarre little conversations. The fear of a sharp knock at the door. The desire to leave as soon as you arrive.

"That's fascinating," you say.

"Itching, burning," he says. "All the time. There's always an irritation of some kind. It can drive you nuts. Sometimes it goes away for a bit, maybe a week. But it always comes back. Itching, tingling."

He finishes a pile, starts another.

"It's on fire right now," he says, actually squirming. "*On fire*. My own asshole. It's killing me. I could cut it out with my apple-paring knife. That's how I feel. Like I could gut it right out. Or grate it raw with a great big vicious piece of sandpaper. Rub it raw. Or freeze it. Pack it with the coldest, driest ass-numbing ice I can lay my hands on. You know what I'm saying? It's to that point. I dream of spiking my ass with a giant syringe full of cortisone. Can you imagine? It's a curse."

He takes another long, thick sip of that murky shit and pushes a small stack of money to the side.

You say nothing once again, remind yourself that you've heard this kind of stuff before. He goes off on tangents sometimes, Your Dealer. This isn't the first time. This time it's a bit incredibly stunningly astoundingly disgustingly freakishly weird, but what the hell. Maybe he had to tell somebody. Maybe he's allowed. Maybe it's good that he finally told somebody. He said it. Now it's over and done with. After all, if his ass is that bad.

"You ever try that cream?" he wants to know. Oh God. You settle back against the couch. "That clear stuff in a tube? Useless. It does nothing. It's for idiots. I've bought a ton of it. It never works. I smear it on me like icing on a cake. It does nothing. Within ten minutes I'm digging my fingers back in, up to the knuckles. I wouldn't show you my underwear at the end of the day if you begged me."

"Really?" you hear yourself say. "Not even if I begged?"

He finishes the last pile, pushes it by the rest. Counts the piles. Then one by one he places each of them in his bottom drawer and gently slides it closed.

He looks at you. Where is this going?

"The problem with getting old is that everything starts to go," he says. "Your body starts to wear down. Like any machine, part by part. Piece of junk. Your back goes. Your ass goes. Your feet go. Your hair falls out, your joints get stiff. Your skin starts to loosen and turn colour and dry up. Your brain doesn't want to learn anything anymore. It's shrinking. In fact it's getting so small it's trying to get rid of things. It's throwing stuff out. It's why you can't learn new things or remember old things."

He takes another grotesque guzzle of his lumpy potion.

"Everything starts to hurt. Not a lot, just in little bits. When you're young and you get hurt, you get better. When you get older, nothing ever comes back a hundred percent. An ache here, soreness there. Everything lingers. Just enough to make you wonder. Make you wonder what you're getting. What new ailment. What sickness. What cancer is lurking behind the sore throat you had this morning? Why does one of my arms feel dead lately? What's just a sore chest muscle and what's a chest pain? Is one of my arteries about to collapse? Do I have a tumour in my head from all those hours on the cellphone?"

"I never use mine," you say. Pointlessly.

"They'll kill you. I had one when they first came out. Back then. You should've seen the size of it. Carrying a fucking brick around with you all day would've been lighter. Think of all the radiation that must have melted through my skull. I could have a brain tumour right now. I get headaches, you know."

"Maybe you just exercise too much. Maybe you should take it easy a bit. Eat a pizza."

A faraway look settles into his eyes, an expression he affects whenever he's speaking with someone of obviously limited scope. He says, "Getting old forces you into decisions. First you have to decide to learn to live with it. The aches, the pains, all of it. The adjustments. The compromise. All of it. Then you have to agree to accept death. Not as hard as you think. You're older. More tired. When you're young, the inevitability of death drives you crazy. It makes everything pointless. What's the point if we're all going to end up dead one day anyway? That's what stumps you. Why try hard? Why get rich? Why sacrifice? When you're older you're looking back on everything. A done deal. You did and he did and she did, and they did and life did. And that's what ended up. Everything *was* pointless. And yet not. But it's not so frustrating anymore. Death is closer, yet not as daunting. Fatigue has set in. Do you think I'm rich?"

You look up. "What?" You sort of nodded off there during the he-did-she-did bit.

"How much money do you think I have now?"

"I don't know."

"Guess."

Again with the guessing. "I said I don't know."

He raises an eyebrow, glares at you, giving you what he thinks of as his stern look. "Guess," he says.

"No."

"If you had to say."

"I don't have to say." But it's a lot, you think.

"Conservatively," he prods you.

You shrug.

"C'mon. Conservatively."

"Conservatively?"

"Right."

"How much you have?"

"Yes."

"Now?"

"Yes, now." His eyes light up, anticipating your answer.

"No...I don't want to say."

"Say!"

You glance over at his desk drawer. "Two thousand bucks."

He stares at you. Smiles a tiny smile, the one he thinks is enigmatic. "Bright boy," he says quietly.

The buzzer goes. From downstairs. Lord! It catches you completely off guard. Very loud. You actually gasp. How cool of you.

He laughs, picks up his remote, and turns the TV on. A grainy lobby shot of Sharon appears, squinting into the camera. She of the big purses and silly hats. Even in black-and-white they look gaudy. He clicks it off, goes over to the phone on the wall by the door.

"I didn't shower yet," he says into the receiver.

"What have you been doing?" she crackles back. "We're —"

He stabs at the button to let her in, cuts her off.

You get up. The leather of the couch makes a slurping sound, glad to be rid of you. You flex your knees, unglue your jeans from the backs of your thighs, re-blouse your shirt.

"I better take off," you say. "*My* ass is starting to itch."

"Ah. Humour. I'm a big fan." Your Dealer walks back across the room, burrowing into the back of himself as he goes. At his desk he opens a different drawer than the ones previously, pulls out a black slab, and flips it at you. "Here. Fabulous stuff. Let me know what you think. Twenty-four hundred."

You catch it, unwrap it, smell it, seal it back up, and stuff it into the inside pocket of your jean jacket. Put the jacket on. Feel the bulge against your spine. You walk across the room, sidestepping bushes and trees much of the way. You hear him drain what's left of his drink, hear the straw sucking at air, the bubbles cackling. You arrive at the door, turn back to look at him.

"You know, Lee," he says, waiting for you, "I was born poor. Dirt poor. Less than auspicious beginnings, I assure you. But you know what? Do you know what I quickly realized? That it was only in relation to those immediately around me. That I was, in actual fact, very lucky. Privileged. To be born in North America. In the twentieth century. Like you. I was in no danger of starving to death. There were no flies hovering, looking to infect me with virus. I was not under threat of genocide. My country was not even at war. Both hands worked. Both legs worked. I could see and hear and think. Lucky indeed. At first I understood very little, of course, but as time went by I discovered that most people understood very little. Luck again. I worked hard. I made the most of my opportunities. I made the most of the opportunities of others too, on occasion. But that's not to say I became rich. I didn't get *rich*. I just ended up with a lot more than I started out with."

You watch as he crosses back towards you, picking his way nimbly through the jungle. Not so bad for a guy whose machine is winding down.

"I have more now," he says. "It's true. More money. More clothes. More things. More taste. More expensive taste, certainly. More knowledge. More experience. More insight into what this world asks of us mere mortals. More lines on my face, more wrinkles, more grey, more worry. More problems. More aches, more pains. More self-doubt. More memories."

Your Dealer opens the door for you.

"And so what is left can only be less. Less energy. Less desire. Less life. Less hair." He smiles, runs a hand lightly across the front of his scalp, across the wispy strands that curl there. "Less time."

His other hand rises to your shoulder, escorts you through the doorway. The touch is soft and friendly, but it's telling you to go.

"At least you have your wealth," you say.

He ignores this, bids you farewell. "Next time, not so many small bills. Okay?"

Without waiting for your reply, he closes the door. You retrace your path along the corridor. When you get to the end the elevator doors open and Sharon elbows her way out, sweeping the door aside with one arm and you with the other. She barely looks at you. You watch her barrel down the corridor, she of the flat feet and waddling hips. With each stride her purse bounces against her side and her hat struggles not to fall. Every time you've ever seen Sharon she's been pissed off at something. She makes you think now of a very large, very angry duck.

You step in and punch for the basement. The doors slide shut and erase her image. You're thinking of just one thing: get out of the building with your dope, out the door and through the alley in back to the next street over. Without anyone so much as looking at you. That's all you want. That's what must happen.

The elevator starts its descent. You make several vague, hasty promises to God, forgetting them as soon as you've thought them up, hold your breath, and start counting floors.

f○ur

Later now, back home, and you and Henry are walking familiar sidewalks that will lead to the park where you so often gather. You pass a building you used to rent in. You lived there for a while in a basement apartment you shared with a bunch of different people, something like eleven roommates in three years. What a place. Long, like a submarine, and dark like one too. A window at the front, a window at the back. That was it. You used to come outside and sit on the steps all the time, just to get some daylight. Try to talk to chicks. Say hello to people you knew. With stores nearby, there was often a steady stream of pedestrian traffic. A lot of females. And if you counted the number of girls you managed to lure down those steps into that apartment over the years, if you counted them all, including the girls that happened to walk by *and* the ones that already lived in the building, if you counted every chick, daytime and nighttime, and then rounded it off to the nearest five, you'd get, um, zero.

"Remember that place?" you ask Henry, gesture over.

He picks his head up, looks over. Thinks. "Oh, sure," he says.

"That place had rats," you say. "Big rats that used to run through the apartment at night."

"I know."

"I know you know. Whenever I walk here I think of them."

Henry drops his head back down, staring at the sidewalk going by beneath his feet. "It's a good thing you moved."

"They used to scare the cat to death, those rats. I mean, which you can understand, but still. He was so useless. He used to sleep on top of the fridge. Eventually we made a bed for him up there. What a nervous cat."

"You needed a dog."

"I don't think a dog would've helped."

"Well, they're bigger."

"Rats are vicious, my friend."

"Dogs are vicious."

"Dogs are big. Rats are *vicious*."

"Oh, no. Dogs can be very vicious."

"Sorry, but I believe you're confusing them with *rats*."

Henry says, "I got bit once by a dog."

"I remember," you say. You think, So what?

"I've got a big scar."

"I've seen your scar."

"It's a good scar," he says, worried you've never been impressed with his scar.

"It's a terrific scar."

"Fuck you. It hurts when you get bit. More than you think."

"No dog's going to kill a rat. A dog runs away every time."

"You can't be sure."

"We had rats tough enough to rip any dog to shreds."

"I don't see how you can be so sure."

You're watching him now. Closely. The funny pattern of his steps. The uneven gait. You realize that he's concentrating, measuring his strides. He's trying not to step on a crack. *Henry doesn't want to break his mother's back.*

Yeesh.

"Anyways, that's not why I moved," you say. "It was a good place.

I don't know why I moved. I just moved. I wanted to change. There were all these arguments after a while."

"What you wanted," Henry says, "was a snake. You have a snake, you don't have a rat problem."

"No, you have a snake problem."

"A *pet* snake."

You're trying not to pay attention to the way he's walking. It's not working. You feel like yelling at him. Or hurling him forward so that his whole face steps on a crack.

"Who's going to keep a snake for a pet?" you say. "Besides you, I mean."

This pre-empts him. He can't say "I would," which is what he wants to say. That he'd gladly have one. Because he's such a wild man. So unpredictable, so living on the edge. He's into cultivating this If Everyone Thinks I'm A Bit Crazy, Maybe I Am sort of aura around himself lately. Going with the flow, trying to milk it for something. Danger Boy.

"Well, if you've already got *rats* running through the place," he says, "I don't see what you have to lose."

"What does that mean? So you let a snake loose at night? Think for two seconds."

"I've been bitten by a snake too. A bunch of times. Paul Berubé had snakes. In a cage that took up half his bedroom."

You sigh. What kind of answer is that? What kind of conversation is this?

"We called *exterminators*," you inform him. "Professionals. That's what normal people *do*."

"I see."

You walk in silence again. His gaze settles back down on the ground. The sidewalk rolls by. You suddenly realize now *you're* trying not to step on the cracks. Goddamned Henry. You stop. See that you're in front of the Korean place. You go inside and buy cigarettes.

When you come out, you continue along with Henry. There's an intersection with lights up ahead. You walk towards it.

"Did it work?" Henry wants to know.

"What?" you say. But you know what he's talking about. You've been waiting for him to ask, the suck.

"The exterminators."

"Oh," you say. "No."

"No?"

"No, it was worse. After they left we could've sworn there were *more* rats."

"Really?"

"Oh yeah."

"Well, what did the exterminator say?"

The light changes, you cross.

"He told us to get a snake."

You give him a shove, laughing. He pushes your arm away angrily. You don't care. Man, you're funny.

You've known Henry a lot of years. Johnny too. Honey, a few less. Henry's father was a prison guard at Bordeaux who was strangled to death during a riot when Henry was fourteen. *Strangled to death.* Which inmate actually did it, they never even found out. Henry says that one day he went home for supper and the phone rang and his mother answered and just like that his father was dead. He says the phone rang many more times that night but his mother wouldn't let them pick it up. He says they ate in front of the TV watching the same news again and again and that he remembers his mother letting him drink beer in the living room with her, and that he'd never had more than one beer at once before that night. He says he caught a huge buzz. He says that he liked the feeling, and it was secretly thrilling to drink one beer then another, waiting for his mother to tell him to stop. He says that he remembers thinking the whole time about how everyone at school must be seeing his father's picture on the news and that his father dying on TV seemed very humiliating. He says he got giggly after a while and had to go into the bathroom and laugh into the towels. He says that it's a shameful way to remember your first drunk. He says they fell asleep on the couches.

And he says that in the morning the newspapers and radio recounted the story of the riot at the prison that raged six hours until it was brought under control but not before two guards and four prisoners were killed and an inquiry was going to be held and they said how they're going to get to the bottom of it damn quickly and *How did so many inmates have so many weapons anyway?* and it raises a number of questions about what's going on in our prison systems, we may just have to "overhaul the whole damn thing" by the time this thing is over.

And by the time the whole thing *was* over, and everything began to be just a little less fresh in everyone's mind and other atrocities began making newer news, and friends and strangers had settled back into their own lives, Henry saw the world return to how it had been before, but of course his didn't.

And that, he said, was a strange sensation. As though every problem he'd had in his life up until then had been so ridiculously petty and temporary and now here was something that was *permanent*. And you asked him — like a jerk — if he thought he became a man that day and he said no, he just felt as if he was no longer a boy.

Henry was never the same again, of course. No siree, Bob. Never ever. To be the same, he would tell you later, his father would have to be *living*. Which he clearly *wasn't*, seeing as an *animal* had choked *every last breath* out of his *fucking lungs*. Crushed his windpipe. And whipped him with his own belt. He would recite this at every opportunity. Which pretty much made it clear where Henry stood on the subject.

Henry didn't *want* to be the same again and he couldn't give two shits what any of you thought about it. And then it wasn't long before none of you were really seeing much of Henry anymore anyway. By the time he was twenty he'd surface only in the most obscene, obnoxious moments, all stupid and dopey, usually with these freaks he got to know, bizarre behaviour that drove everyone crazy. On and on like this for literally years until he sort of blew out all of his brain cells at once, collapsing finally in a taxi outside his mother's house and getting dragged out and dumped on her porch by the driver, taken in by her and not really let out again for what amounted, incredibly, to two years.

And when he did come back out to play, he came back changed. Once again. This time to the person you meet today, give or take. Twenty-nine years old and sad and apologetic and lost and out of touch with even the simplest of tasks much of the time, another drug casualty left behind to live with his mother. The poor man's Syd Barrett. Few friends, hardly ever a girlfriend. A nothing job. A beaten man. Shine on you dull diamond.

And the thing is, people *forget* what happened to you in life. Eventually they just shrug at your hardships and dismiss your bad luck, they've had their own. People expect you to *move on*. They want you to *put it behind you*. People have their own problems, Henry. It doesn't matter what was unfair or what could've been, you're the only one counting those chits now. If you act stupidly long enough, people come to think of you as stupid. And if you behave weirdly for long enough, they think of you as weird. And that's how you end up a stupid fucking weirdo. That's how it works. People don't *set out* to be losers. It happens when you're not paying close enough attention. Your father's dying is just a footnote now.

And so that's Henry's thing. Everybody has a thing. Henry's is that he's the guy whose father got strangled in that prison riot years ago. Or, if you knew him a little better, Henry's the guy who was never the same after his father died. Or, to others still, Henry's just the guy who blew his head out on tequila and acid and coke and mushrooms. It's all pretty much the same.

You glance over at him now. Study the perennially bewildered look on his face. Doe-eyed, defensive. Caught in the headlights, like Honey always says. You, Johnny, Honey, Cuz, Aaron, and Mo. That's pretty well his whole galaxy right there.

By now you're almost at the park, about to turn in, but a strange scene has been forming and it seems now to be asking you to watch it. It's different people — too many people, strange for this time of day — suddenly in the street, spilling out onto the street from out of the park, out of stores, out of cars. Even the traffic has paused, you notice. You pause too. This catches Henry by surprise and he stutters to an awkward stop beside you, stumbling to control his footing, his mother's spinal column briefly in jeopardy.

You see that a mob has created itself, though it doesn't seem to know why. Everyone is straining to see, pushing forward to get a better look, a slow-motion surge of curious faces and craned necks, gathered together, slowly pressing forward. There's a Blockbuster on the next corner and it's as though that's where everyone is aiming. Fifty, sixty bodies have collected. Someone, a man's voice, is shouting.

Beside you, people are walking more quickly now, shouldering themselves past you and up to the next set of dawdlers then thrusting their way through them. You look over at Henry, who's looking at you.

"What's happening?" you ask him, wading cautiously in towards the herd.

"I don't know," he says, following. He looks around him, his trademark squint appearing. Unlike you, Henry is short and thick and there is nothing for him to see.

You press your toes into the tips of your boots, arch yourself to greater height. This vantage point gives you a fuller sense of the commotion but you can see only that the eye of the storm is agitating, growing.

A freak with blue hair and three rings through his nose abruptly emerges from out of the bodies in front of you, elbowing his way against the flow.

"There's something going on up there," he says to the both of you.

"Whoah!" Henry says excitedly.

"What is it?" You raise your voice as he disappears. "What's going on?"

"I don't know," he calls back. "But it's been like this for like twenty minutes."

"Twenty minutes!" Henry is impressed.

You survey the scene for several seconds and when you turn back the guy is gone.

Henry says to you, "We have to find out why."

"What for?"

"Everyone's wondering."

You're inclined to leave. "Forget it."

"No, we have to."

"Why, what do you think is happening?"

Henry's eyes shine. "Something!"

So together you press ahead, mingling, looking for avenues of advancement, until finally you are forced to veer left, away from Henry, then cut between several parked cars to reach the other sidewalk. You continue along the outside for a bit and then begin angling back in towards the front of the flock, squeezing between couples, almost stepping over several kids, feinting past the elderly, manoeuvring yourself through increasingly small openings. For five minutes you're the skinniest, most devious halfback the NFL has ever produced. Eventually you get up far enough that you can sense whatever everyone's trying to see is just ahead, but the wall of bodies has become too great and there is nowhere left to move.

"What's happening?" you say to a guy next to you. He has only two nose rings and bleached blond hair. A conservative.

"There's a naked chick walking around," he says. "In front of Blockbuster."

You lift up on tiptoe once again, peering above the sea of heads. "Really?"

"Totally naked."

You pan left, right. Notice nothing. Every woman within your field of vision is, sadly, clothed.

"Why?" you ask him.

He turns to you like you're from outer space. Like this is the strangest question he's ever been asked. "Why?" he repeats.

"Yeah, why?"

"What do you mean?"

"I don't mean anything. I just want to know why."

"Does it matter?"

"I'm not sure."

"Then why do you want to know?"

"Why not?"

"What do you mean?"

Sweet Jesus. If you needed a conversation like this you could've just stuck with Henry.

"I'm just wondering why a chick's walking around naked, that's all."

He stares at you a while more. A bit thick, this one.

"Why is she naked?" he asks finally, eyeing you like maybe you're a homo. "Or why is she walking around?"

"I don't know," you say, losing interest. "You choose."

Suddenly everyone takes a single, simultaneous step backwards. It catches you by surprise. You teeter helplessly for an instant, rocking back against some poor twit behind you. A voice from up ahead shrieks something unintelligible. The same voice as before. Another massive recoil follows. You're having trouble keeping your balance. You take two steps sideways, crushing your pal's feet. He shoves you off him. Not far from you a woman stumbles, bringing several others down around her. Which causes a larger ripple in the crowd as people sway unsteadily.

And at that instant a sudden glimpse of flesh winks at you from an opening more than thirty feet away. Just the slightest wink of pink. But you see it. A tantalizing rosy sliver of what can only be naked female derma. As a guy, you immediately know this. You're immediately excited. Even though you don't know what it is you've just seen — it could've been her *arm* — that glorious wisp of pink has spoken to you. And eighty other people, apparently. The crowd surges forward now with renewed will. You get tangled up with a pair of teenagers in front of you. You look up, spot her again. Red hair. Short. A bit stocky. Not naked actually, wearing boots. Walking quickly. You see all of this in maybe two seconds.

For some reason the mob suddenly parts. People go left, others go right. Once again you can't see anything. You choose right. Your group tramples up onto the sidewalk, past Blockbuster, past Pizza Hut, and then around the corner. You keep your arms flexed and away from your body, protecting your ribs from the errant elbows and shoulder blades of shorter people, namely everyone. A pretty girl falls into step with you. There is more shouting now, more than before.

Somehow the notion of a woman walking through a crowded street without a strand of clothing on — except boots — breasts free, maybe gently swaying from side to side, full, heavy breasts, your mind is starting to go a little wacky by now, her pubic hair just out there like that, curled and crawling up against her inner thighs, everybody looking at it, *pubic hair*, just the words excite you, you're a bit of a freak that way, you'll be reading a book or a magazine and if *pubic hair* or *nipple* or *penis* is written on the page your eyes will dart down to find it, seek it out paragraphs early, you wonder sometimes if there's isn't something a little wrong with you, how the simple notion of a wandering nymph gets you all frothy like this. But then the girl beside you is pretty intent on getting a glimpse of her too, and so are a bunch of old ladies and kids and other guys too, so what're you, all sickos?

And then you notice a camera, on top of one of the buildings. And another camera, on top of another building. Cameramen. Recording. You crane your neck up and see a big fat light arcing down from atop yet another building. And you get it. They're shooting this.

Your group has closed in on the girl now, coming up behind her. The other part of the mob is coming towards her, head-on. She breaks into a run, dashes across Sherbrooke towards the park. Everyone follows. You notice now a third guy with a camera at street level, and another guy with a microphone at the end of a pole. They run after her too, equipment swinging wildly from side to side, cables and cords jangling in time with her chubby, bouncing ass, alternately recording her escape and the crowd's moronic frenzy.

five

And that just ruins it somehow. Them shooting it. Everything being faked. There's no story to that girl now. That girl has no history to know about, there's no *reason* why she was walking down the street like that. She was being paid.

And all for some shitty movie or TV show or commercial someone's making. Everything's on TV now, what a fucking drag. Everything's a commercial for something else. Everyone's plugging something.

You scan around, look for Henry, but he's nowhere, so you split and go to the Burger King further down. On the way in you meet the sister of a girl you know. You talk with her at the door for a while. She tells you how she's going on a trip soon, to Europe. To see all these great cities. Describes what she's planning to do in each place. She's a fairly good-looking girl, especially if you're not too particular in the face department, which you're not.

Eventually you have to make a decision about staying and trying to hang out with her or taking off. The conversation hasn't been award-winning up to this point, and you find yourself confronted with a somewhat familiar equation, in this case what to do after already having spent fifteen minutes of your life talking to a twenty-year-old chick about a ten-thousand-dollar trip she saved up for for two years in order to travel to six countries in three weeks, divided by the fact that you were only listening to her in the first place because an hour or two from now, if you can get her to go downtown with you, three or four clubs later, seven or eight drinks, a couple of joints, some cheap food, probably around a hundred and fifty bucks all told, there'll be maybe a five-to-one chance that she might go home with you. And those are shit odds.

Not that it's stopped you before. But this time you blow her off and go buy your burger. Someone else can do the math.

Instead you go to Stacy's. Single mother, two-year-old kid, always sweating it out, good person, trying to be über-mom, on and off lately with a guy she met last year, Graham, you sometimes drop over and help her out if you can, yap with her a bit, she's witty in a remarkably humourless way, and for whatever reason you'd told her you'd be by today.

The first thing you notice is how loud it is. The Boy is howling, the TV's on, music's on, she's on the phone, trying to talk above it all. People have kids and suddenly it's like they went deaf. You go over to the couch and pick up the remote, turn the TV down so you can hear yourself think. The Boy looks over at you, looks like he's going to holler louder but then instead shuts up. Stacy gets off the phone.

It's suddenly quieter.

"You said this afternoon," she says, lobbing the phone underhand at you. "I've been trying to reach you since suppertime."

You catch it, lower it, and give it to The Boy, who's come teetering over and is holding on to one of your legs. He takes it and stares at it in that cross-eyed way kids look at something's when it's too close to their face. This makes him lose his balance and plop down directly on his ass, punching buttons the whole way down. Like he can stop his fall if he can just find the right combination. The Boy is a gas.

"Can I make coffee?" you ask her. "You want some?"

"I want to go out. I need you to watch him. But I'll have coffee, too."

She talks fast, Stacy. Garbled thoughts and mixed-up meanings. Everything comes out like it's rushing through her brain. Inconsistent and unedited. Part earth mom, part fascist. You have to watch yourself around her though, she's very bright.

"Where do you want to go?"

"Nowhere. I just want to walk somewhere, or buy a magazine. I haven't been out."

"I'll go too. We'll take Ack! with us," you say.

"No, Lee. It's to get away from him, too, for a little while. And it's too late." She's followed you into the kitchen, starts putting on the coffee you were supposed to make. "Can you give him a bath and read to him? I really haven't been out *all* day."

"Put him to sleep?"

"Can you?"

You reach up and get the filter she needs. "I guess. How long are you going for?"

"Not long. Make sure he doesn't go to bed past eight, though. I mean it."

There's a clock just next to her on the wall. "That's in half an hour, Stace. I won't even get Ack! out of the *bath* by eight o'clock."

"Yes, you will. Okay, eight-fifteen. But I mean it." She leans out of the kitchen. "Zachary, Mommy's going out. You have to take a bath in five minutes. Five minutes, Zachary."

You wince when you hear the name. Zachary Chelsea Tara Brittany Meighan Dylan Brandon Rory Bullshit Trendoid Names That You Just Fucking Hate. It's why you refuse to use it.

"Ack!" says The Boy.

"I won't be out long, honey," Stacy reassures him.

Graham suddenly comes through the front door. Graham, whom Stacy's still kind of seeing after all these months and no one even knows if he's even kissed her yet. Graham, Mr. Straight-Up-The-Corporate-Ladder Guy, swears he doesn't mind sucking dick, it's just what you have to do these days, don't you get it? Financial Planner Graham. Just like that, here he is.

"Hey!" you say, louder than you mean to, eager to argue. "How's money these days?"

"Money's great," he says, walks past you, and kisses Stacy on the lips. Okay, there goes that theory. "I'll tell it you said hi."

"Market's dow-own…" You say it in a lilting, lyrical way.

"I'm sure your twenty bucks is sa-afe…" he sings back, turns again to Stacy. "Can you go?"

Stacy clicks the button to turn the coffee maker on. "I'll get my own coffee while we're out, Lee. Don't forget, eight-fifteen. Zachary, come here so Mommy can kiss you." She passes you then turns back. "Oh, there's no milk. For your coffee. Graham, make sure we get milk while we're out. Zachary, come here, honey. Thanks, Lee!"

You watch as she smothers his belly with kisses. "Ack!" he says again, his eyes shining.

"Lee, start running the bath. Graham, let's go."

You watch them leave, then close and lock the door and walk into the bathroom to start the water. The Boy follows you in. You fiddle with the taps to get the temperature right and watch him as he fiddles with everything he can get his hands on, provided it's dangerous. He's still not very solid on his feet and you have to worry about him slipping. A bit slow that way, in your opinion. You see other kids his size and they seem so much more sturdy. Stacy's too soft with him, you think, and that's a big part of it.

You lead him out. He has a toy in his hand, a squishy frog that squirts water. When he gets to the couch he puts it down in the middle of a cushion. You crouch down, reach in, pick the toy up, and move it over six inches.

This makes him look over at you, then pick up the frog and move it back to where it was.

You reach across, put it back the same six inches over.

He moves it back.

You move it back.

He picks up the frog and clutches it to his chest.

You try to snatch it from his hands. A light wrestle ensues. It ends with you being thrown horrifically to the ground. Lying on your back, you hoist him into the air, holding him above you. He drools directly down into your eyes. You wince, sputter. Can't see, need to wipe your eyes. He falls on top of you. You groan in anguish under the sheer weight of him. As he lands, you hug him and feel that gorgeous warmth against your chest. The tiny heel of his hand lands against your nose, pushing it up like a snout. You oink, he grins. The frog falls to the rug, bounces away.

You turn and reach across the floor for it. He scrambles over your arm to reach it first.

"Ref!" you yell. "Penalty!"

"Ack!" he cries. "*Blick!*"

You see people sometimes and they just don't know how to be around kids. Being around kids is simple. It's those other people that are hard to take.

Stacy returns just before ten. She looks perky and tired at the same time.

"How was he?" She closes the door softly behind her.

"Good. Not a problem."

You see that Graham isn't with her. You're glad of this.

"What time did you put him to bed?"

"Eight-fifteen," you lie.

She contemplates you for several seconds. "With a bath? And you dried his ears and did his bum properly? With powder? And gave him water and put his cream?"

"All of the above."

"What *time*?"

"Twenty to nine." Another lie.

"I'm going to go look at him."

She disappears down the hall. You pick up the remote, click it over to sports news. Before she gets any ideas. You don't want to get stuck watching the lifestyle channels again. They're mental, those people. They actually *do* watch paint dry. Someone's got to do a joke about that one day.

When she gets back, she settles on the couch at the end opposite you.

"Where'd you go?" you ask.

"Nowhere. Just coffee."

"All that time?"

"One of my shows is coming on," she says. "Can't I just watch it?"

You say nothing. Opt out of arguing. She snakes the remote back from you, wanders from station to station. You can tell from her expression they're all repeats, though. You stare at her eyes, her mouth, the shape of her head. She's pretty in a big-girl way. Not slim and sexy like Honey, but not unattractive either. It dawns on you that she's been out more or less on a date while you were home watching The Boy. Whatever. It's none of your business anyway. You're suddenly exhausted. How does she do it? Day in and day out. Man. You see Stacy differently after an evening like this. What with his bath and teeth and books and butt cream, Ack! is a regular shift at the office now, isn't he?

"Oh, I forgot," she says. "Johnny called for you."

You do a tiny double take. "When?"

"Before you came over."

"Why?"

"He was looking for you."

"Why?"

"I don't know."

"Looking for me? What does that mean?"

"He wanted to speak to you."

"About what?"

"He didn't say."

"Something specific?"

"I dunno — did he want something specific the other thousand times he called here for you?"

"Still. You should've told me."

"*I forgot.* Don't be such an asshole."

She gets up, walks towards the bathroom. Some girls, when they throw a swear word in, they knock you over with it. It's fresh, funny. They catch you off guard in a way that makes you like them more than ever. Stacy, sadly, is not one of them.

You look for your jacket. Get your smokes from the balcony. The sound of brushing and gargling comes floating down the hallway. Her teeth, you know, are your cue to split. You've been dismissed. Ah, screw it anyway. If that's what she wants, you will. You'll go. You thought you'd hang around with her awhile but you won't. You think of Johnny. You think of Honey. You wonder, was it inevitable? Sleeping with Honey? Is it just basically unavoidable if you spend enough time around somebody that attractive? That you'll find a way to get to her? No matter how long it takes?

This new vantage point suddenly makes everything seem a little clearer, adding a twist to the story of Honey and you. Putting forth the theory that for you, then, it had simply been a question of opportunity. How sad. The only thing stopping you was that you hadn't yet had the chance. That you'd always been biding your time to make it with her. Waiting for her to slip, stumble.

How long have you known Johnny? Since you were twelve? Wow. What can you say? That's long. And how long has he been with Honey? Six or seven years? This could change everything. For them. For you. Sometimes life feels like it'll never change. Things have been the same way for so long they feel permanent. And then sometimes it feels like change is *imminent*, that you're so due for it.

You stand completely still for a moment. Breathe in, out. Slowly. Consider what has gone down. Concentrate. Force yourself to face up to what it is that you've done. And yet, try as you might, you can't seem to make yourself feel that badly about it.

Before you leave you take the remote and punch in the numbers to your best sports station, hide it under one of Ack's trucks. Why not? Make her go looking for it. But you must have hit a wrong number. One of the local stations came up instead. You can tell because they're finishing one of their tacky news updates. There's a shot on the screen of an apartment building, wobbly as if the cameraman wasn't using his tripod. The image is under-lit and a bit grainy. A chintzy gold graphic slides in, and it reads SEARCH FOR MISSING GIRL. The voice-over, a woman, finishes up in an overly sombre tone.

"Police…have not yet…ruled out…violence."

You look down towards the bathroom. Stacy is studying herself in the mirror, still foaming at the mouth. You consider calling her to hurry back, insisting that she rush over to see this.

It's the building they're showing. You recognize it.

It's Henry's.

You're sure of it. Right there, on TV.

But you hesitate too long and Stacy's got her floss out, and when you finally turn back to the screen it's already over. A commercial comes on. The cold medicine dudes again.

six

With Henry you have to be delicate. You have to be careful. You have to be calm. You have to approach him in a diplomatic manner, gingerly and without immediately giving away your full intent. You never know what he's thinking. A lot of rewiring has been done up there and not all of it by a certified electrician.

"Henry?"

"Yes."

Hmm. How to put this exactly? You've been trying to reach him on the phone all day. You finally have him. You give it thought, want to phrase it just right.

"Are you retarded?"

You hear the breath go out of him. Picture those wide, rattled eyes.

"No."

"Are you completely demented?"

"No…"

"So you're just…" — and again you want to get this just right, make the proper word selection — "…traditionally stupid then?"

"I'm not. Stop it."

In the paper they said she was Henry's girlfriend. That she was a dropout and an addict. Who sometimes lived on the street. Or with her alcoholic mother who barely came home herself most nights. Then on TV there was a report that she'd last been seen five days ago, as she was leaving the apartment she sometimes shared with another girl. Possibly headed to Henry's neighbourhood. And then on the radio you heard that police had already questioned Henry several times about her disappearance, and how he rarely left his apartment now, hunkered down alongside his mother.

The missing girl's name is Darlene Dobson. Seventeen years old.

You say, "Henry, what are you *doing*?!"

"About what?!"

"What're you *getting involved in*?"

"Nothing!"

"Your 'girlfriend' is missing? Girlfriend? Are you sick? Who is this chick?"

"She's not my girlfriend."

"You were fucking her."

"*Everybody* was fucking her."

"Are they going to arrest you?"

"For what!?"

"You're in serious trouble…"

"No way, man. You think I was her boyfriend? Yeah, like ten other guys were."

"In the paper it says you're being uncooperative."

"I *am* being uncooperative!"

"They said you haven't told them anything."

"I don't *know* anything."

"They want clues."

"I'm clueless."

"You're not helping."

"I'm *helpless*. What do they want me to say?"

You say, "You're supposed to tell them anything you can think of. About anywhere she might be."

"Then they should check the stalls at Club Oxygen for a chick giving out blow jobs for lines of coke."

Wow. You cop an instant visual off this.

"Really?" you say. "That's how you met her?"

"No. That's not what I meant."

"Hang on while I undo my pants…"

"No, no—"

"So you're saying that if I go into the can at the Oxygen—"

"Okay, get away from me, you freak."

"I'm just *asking*…"

"Look," he says, "I got to go."

You stop fucking around. Time to serious up.

"Alright, Henry. Now listen to me—"

"No, really. I have to go."

"Henry—"

"I have to go."

"Henry, don't be so *nervous*—"

"Dude!" he says. "I ordered food. There's a guy standing at my door with a pizza."

"Oh," you say, taken aback. "Alright, call me after he goes."

"Okay. Later."

"No. Soon."

"Okay, soon."

"Don't forget."

"I have to go!"

"Click," you say. "That's me hanging up."

You putz around for five minutes. Start gathering dirty clothes from around your apartment. You have an enormous place. You live in an old warehouse semi-converted into living spaces. Ancient wood beams, walls of exposed brick. Old factory-style hardwood floors, beaten in and scarred over the years by everything from heavy machines to high heels. Floors that go on and on. Huge. Big spaces. Half the top floor is yours.

You don't pay rent. You collect it from others. A bunch of years ago there was a big investment push in some of Montreal's southern boroughs to snap up many of the older buildings and divide them into hip loft-style units. Some projects flourished, some stalled. Then the tech bust came and the money really started running out. A lot of the buildings ended up getting auctioned off to bargain hunters. One was a young mover and shaker who loved smoking dope. Your dope. You got along. He found you interesting. He promised you could stay here until he flips it someday. It's a great deal. You keep an eye on the place. You administer general upkeep. And, as it is generally acknowledged that you are completely useless with an operator's manual or a power tool, you are asked only to organize the solution to any problem. A simple call to an electrician or a plumber. Or reimbursing tenants for repairs they've done on their own. As easy as that. There aren't many things. It isn't exactly a palace. Compared to working for a living, this doesn't exactly take a lot out of you. You couldn't live cheaper.

Your apartment is the kind of place they shoot movies in. The kind of place where the main character supposedly has no money but they give him a big, cool space so they can film his hanging-around-at-home scenes, the worn-out, neglected warehouse look. Except that this place has seven-foot-high ceilings. And you're six-three. And the roof is starting to go, so it leaks in places. And in the winter it's freezing. No matter how high you put the heat. And a lot of the floorboards are rotting and weak, and the brick needs pointing, or whatever that's called. And there's a faint but persistent odour of mechanical oil that you still get whiffs of sometimes, depending on where you walk. To this day. And you've been here for years. So nobody's really shooting any movies in here. But it is big. And you like it.

An old man lives across the hall, the other half of the top level. He's lived there forever. His wife died a few years ago. He's gotten worse since then. There are increasingly frequent moments when you eye each other awkwardly at the elevators, or ignore one another in the lobby. Meet in the laundry room in the basement, circle each other warily. He gives you the shivers. And of course, he knows what you do. He's creepy, the way he's short and wiry with those hairy arms that old guys always have, the knotty wrists that look like they're just dying to grab you by the shoulders and shake some goddamned sense into you.

Most of the people on the floors below are students or part-time students. They've crammed themselves into these spaces three, four, and five to an apartment, coming and going at all hours. But they've always been a surprisingly tidy group. Proud of their meagre surroundings, loath to disturb. Very Canadian. A couple of the kids like to smoke dope. You lay free grams on them periodically in exchange for lawn mowings and snow shovellings, or the garbage properly removed from the bins in the basement. A good arrangement. You've had it for a number of years.

You see your laundry basket lying on its side. Throw some jeans and T-shirts in it, carry it near your bed to fill it more. The underwear on the floor, the sheets from your bed. Which feels vaguely like you're destroying evidence. And a memory. You see another pile of laundry on a chair. Clean stuff. Sitting there for days, all bunched up, still waiting to be folded. Towels in frozen poses, like giant potato chips. You have a lot of towels. You dated a girl named Maral for about a few months, a long time ago. She bought you a lot of towels. Beautiful ones. Not because she really liked you, she just took a lot of baths.

You sigh. Survey the mess around you. It all seems like such slave's work.

Fuck it. You grab the phone and redial Henry.

He answers with a full mouth. "Oh, hey. What's up?"

"You didn't call back."

"Me?"

"Yeah, you."

"Was I supposed to?"

You shake your head. They leave bruises sometimes, these conversations.

"It's alright." You pause. Gather patience. Make sure, once more, no kidding this time, that you have the right words. "Look, Henry—"

"*Did I kill that girl?* Is that what you want to know?"

Whoah.

"What? No."

He says, "You think I'm slow and don't get all the jokes all the time and so maybe I'm also a killer and a raper? Right? Don't you?"

"It's rap*ist*."

"Is that what you think?"

"Henry, no—"

"Honey called me today. And Aaron and Mo. And Johnny wanted to come by. And Cuz phoned. And now you. Suddenly everyone's calling me. Wouldn't you think it was weird if it was you?"

"Not if my name was in the papers."

"My name's not in the paper! *Her* name is in the paper."

"Check again, dude."

A silence.

"Do you know how embarrassing it is?" he says finally. "What it's like when your friends wonder this about you? Do you think I'll *forget* this? That this is what you think I could do?"

"It's not why I called."

"Oh, fuck you. Even my mother's freaking out. Everybody's freaking out. But they're full of shit. How do *I* know where this chick is? She could be anywhere."

"Did you tell the police that?"

"I *tried* to tell them that."

"Well, when's the last time you saw her?"

"Everybody asks that! What does it matter? The day before they say she went missing. Okay? That's what I told them. What does it matter? Even if I'd seen her that day, so what? Do you have any idea how wacky this broad is?"

"Well, she was letting *you* do her on a regular basis. So how stable could she be?"

He thinks about this. "Yes! *Exactly*. Thank you."

What a goof.

"Okay, but listen," you say. "Answer their questions and get rid of them. Nobody needs cops around all the time. Right? Don't be stupid."

Another little silence. This time it's Henry controlling it.

"And," he says, "pray for the safe return of the girl, right? That she's okay?"

"Yeah, that too."

He waits a beat. Says, "Her safety being of great concern to you, of course."

He's actually mocking you now. A weird sensation, in that it's coming from Henry.

"If you say."

"Because it's true," he says, "you *didn't* call because you think I did something. Did you?"

"No." You make sure he hears the sincerity in your voice. "I didn't."

"Johnny and Honey and Aaron and Mo and Stacy and Cuz. Everyone thinks that maybe, possibly, you never know, maybe I could do this. Don't they? Like, I probably wouldn't, but if one of us had to be the one that might do it, I guess they would pick me. Right?"

"You'd have to ask them, man."

Another beat.

"But not you," he says.

"No."

"No..." You can hear the gears grinding in his head. Finally he says, "No, you're worried because there's cops around."

Pause. Yours this time.

"I'm just saying don't make extra trouble, Henry."

seven

Johnny Karakis. John K. On Sherbrooke Street West he is known this way. Younger brother of George and Peter Karakis. Sons of Kostas. Of local restaurant notoriety. Decades' worth. From concession stands and cafeterias to chains of theme bistros throughout the city. The latest theme being waitresses in tight black T-shirts with young tits pushing out against them.

George is the eldest, the lawyer. The one who rescued the dad's business. The one who *thought modern*. The careful one and the quiet one, the one *who knows how things work*. The one who's *building a legacy*. Peter is less clever but more outgoing. The talker. The dreamer. Peter knows many, many people. He needs to be flamboyant and works hard at it. The clubs bear his name on the registration, and his face is the one that's attached to their image.

Of course, his face is also known for a very messy zoning bribe and damning hidden-camera footage posted on YouTube that cost them caravans of money before it would finally go away. And not long after that there was the discovery of his affair with a well-known singer who was still married to the father of her two daughters. A well-publicized saga. Which only helped in the end, naturally enough. No such thing as bad publicity and all that. Everything these two brothers touch seems to work out. There's a swagger to these boys.

It's beyond confidence. It's a faith that everyone else is a lesser being than you.

John K. Johnny Kay. Cute, handsome, adorable, ruddy and cuddly and dashing all at once. He never disappoints. You've seen him groggy and dishevelled and barely able to wake up at five in the morning to get the coffee going so that the two of you could get your asses out the door and over to whatever shitty job you had together that summer. And you've seen him fucked up and strung out of his head and hardly able to walk down the street, arriving home at an entirely different five o'clock in the morning. And you could still take a picture of him in either scenario and tack it to the bedroom wall of most teenage girls.

He's that appealing. Manly face, manly physique, and yet an indeterminate feminine side subtly tucked into each feature. The slightly long eyelashes. Stubble so smooth and even that it could be painted on like make-up. Ethnic but guy-next-door. The kind of face TV and the movies have taught us to love. Prominent features, but rounded at the edges. Thick lips. A heavy voice yet a soft, raspy way of pronouncing words. When he's done something stupid he looks lovably dumb. And when he's done something wrong he seems rakishly guilty. But when he's done something right or funny or occasionally even nice for somebody else, his eyes get a liquid shine that lights them up and a sloppy, self-satisfied grin comes out to play. And everyone just seems to be willing to hang around with that. That he's so into himself is part of the charm. When your two older brothers are George and Peter Karakis and you look like *that*, everybody wants to be your friend.

Unlike you, Johnny's days are not spent comparing himself to others, wondering how he can get a leg up on the guy in front of him. He doesn't have to. He never has a bad day, he just has some days that are not as wonderful as others. He'll tell you so himself. Johnny Karakis loves himself to death and believes everyone else does too. When Johnny Karakis attends a family gathering, aunts and uncles fawn all over him. They could eat him up with a fork and a knife. Nieces poke each other every time he draws near. He's one of those boys whose mother doted on him and spoiled him and bathed him in a constant glow of adoration from the moment he was born. Johnny is her star. You've seen the way she looks at him. Mrs. Karakis loves all her children, but she wants to *dance* when this one is around.

Johnny Karakis is the youngest and best-looking of three very good-looking Karakis boys. And all three own pretty much every room they walk into. George, because he has so much power. Peter, because everyone knows his name. And Johnny — even though he's never done a goddamned thing in his life — because he's got the brash styling of his brothers and he's so pretty to look at.

You're at Johnny's brother Peter's newest place. It's called Q, or sometimes The Q. Pool tables and upscale waitresses. A good spot, near Concordia University. You get a free shot when you walk in. Management's way of saying please get bombed and spend all your money. The girls are knockouts. Legs up to here, twitching in their minuscule skirts. *So* friendly. And always smiling, you could almost swear it's for real. An unspoken contract exists between you and them. That they'll pretend to wish they could be your girlfriend for a few hours and that you'll slither back home alone when the night is over. It's not such a bad arrangement.

You come in at Johnny's side. Watch everyone gather Johnny in as he walks through the gaudy entrance. You spy even the waitresses ogling him. It's as though someone has clicked a small spotlight on. If you've never seen him before there's a tendency at first to be *entranced*. Being along for the ride is one of the best things about being Johnny's pal. And probably the worst.

Eventually you drift off to the side, fading several steps back. Taller but less significant. You know your role.

Johnny sees his brothers. They see Johnny.

"Bro!"

"Bro!"

"Bro!"

Bro is a popular word. They exchange several more of them.

"What are you doing here, Bro?"

"I'm here, Bro!"

"Bro, where you been, man?"

"Where the fuck *I* been?"

Eventually they *bro* you too. You *bro* back. You've learned how to do it. It's rare that George and Peter are here at the same time. Rarer still that Johnny would be here to join them. A reunion of sorts. John Peter George and Ringo. You being Ringo. Someone decides that a celebration of shots is in order. And more *bros*. Followed by additional shots.

At the door to the terrace a couple of girls have started dancing with each other. Another, even prettier, is lighting a cigarette directly under a sign that says she's not allowed to. You pick out the light aroma of marijuana nearby. Peter sure knows how to run a club.

It's a while before you see Johnny again. You're itching to leave, hadn't planned to stay. You've had too much opportunity to drink. Too many beer. Useless beverage. How is it you drink four and piss eight? Plus the doobs, your energy is really waning now. Alcohol and dope combined has never been a winner for you. They work much better individually. You need food.

If you could get Johnny alone, you could be gone in minutes. George and Peter are deep in conversation with a couple of heavy-looking dudes. Everyone's head is bowed, they talk in quiet shouts just above the music. Johnny is at the edge of the discussion. You grab a pool cue leaning against the wall, lean over, and nudge him with its rubber-tipped butt.

He comes your way, grabs a stool.

You say, "You're allowed to talk to me too, you know."

"What are you, a chick?"

"I'm going to split."

"Quelle surprise."

"I'll call you tomorrow."

"It's nine-thirty. Where you going?"

"There's nobody here."

"There's chicks everywhere."

"I'm starving."

"I'll get you wings and shit. What do you want?"

You hold up a hand, wave the idea away. "Please. I'm ready to toss already."

"What's wrong with you?"

"Nothing."

"Why such a long face?"

"I don't know. Part Ukrainian ancestry?"

Two beer and two shots arrive via Morgan Fairchild *circa* 1986. You lean back, away from the table. Can't stomach the idea of another drop.

He looks at you, purses his generous lips. Rubs the sandpaper stubble at his jaw. Christ, if *you* were a chick, you'd swoon.

He says, "When did we last see him? A week ago?"

You exhale. Overplaying it. As if it pains you just to think of Henry.

"At least."

"Before all this shit."

"For sure."

His turn to sigh. "It's always something."

"It is," you agree. "It's always something."

The song changes. More girls get up to dance. What a place.

He asks you, "Did you talk to him?"

"Yes."

"What did he say?"

"You know what? I'm not sure. What did he say? Fucking gibberish. Does he know anything? No. Did he do anything? No. But then I ask him what kind of thing he had with her and I get a nervous answer back. And when I ask where she is, he can't say. He seems more interested in what people are thinking and saying about him. He's Henry. It's hard to get more than that. Did you?"

Johnny says, "I call, no one answers. Or I get his mother, she says he's not there. But then I turn on my TV and they say he hardly leaves his place."

"They said no one's seen the girl in a while. Not a trace."

Johnny nods. Downs a tequila shot, starts his beer.

You ignore yours. One more sip and the room will begin to rotate. Careful, here. You feel vulnerable. All this chatting. You remember Honey. Feel like one single, pointed question from Johnny about her and you might spill every bean in the bag. You feel like the sooner you get moving, get out of here, the safer it will be for everyone concerned. By everyone, of course, you mean yourself.

"What's her name again?" Johnny asks, though you're sure he knows.

"Darlene Dobson."

"Darlene Dobson. You ever meet her?"

"No."

"Me neither." He takes another swig, motions in front of you. "Drink."

You look down at the shots, shake your head. "I'd rather stab myself in both eyeballs."

He nods, like this explains something. "You know," he says, "the annoying thing is, she'll turn up. Somewhere. Soon enough. And it'll just be another dumb story about Henry getting caught in the middle of something."

You smile. It's true.

"There's a reporter on TV," you say, "trying to do a story on it. I guess she couldn't get any interviews with Henry. She was asking other people what they thought. If they believed Henry could do it."

"Asking who?"

"People. Guys from his work, from the shop. And the ladies in reception. You know what Mrs. Fernandez said?"

Mrs. Fernandez is his boss. Henry started working at the Sears depot a few months ago, tagging and stacking and brooming up. It's not a great employer–employee relationship.

"No, what?"

"That it isn't so much the killing she has trouble believing," you tell him. "She said it's the *planning.*"

"The planning."

"Yeah, that he could plan it. Hide the body and everything."

"She said that?"

"She did."

"Ooh, that's a shot…"

"It *is* a shot."

George and Peter's tête-à-tête breaks up. The gangster types move away. George motions at Johnny to come over and join them. Winks at you. It's friendly but it means stay where you are. Like a command signal you flash to your dog.

"Stick around," Johnny says to you, moving off.

"Okay."

"I won't be long."

"Alright."

"Let's *do* something tonight. Think of something."

"Okay."

"Something cool. When I get back."

"Alright."

"As soon as I come back."

"Okay."

Sixteen seconds later, you leave. It'll be tomorrow morning before he even remembers you were here tonight. You stroll out the front door, bill unpaid. It's all right. They don't expect you to pay it. It's always on the house, you're inner circle with the Karakis boys. Though you have to wonder how long *that's* going to last.

eight

You drift over to one of those bar restaurants where they do the retro sports thing. To death. Old jerseys hang from every rafter. Ancient golf clubs, baseball mitts, and hockey sticks are tacked everywhere. It's also the kind of place that encourages patrons to toss their peanut shells all over the floor. Even to the point of the employees scattering them around themselves on slow nights, you suspect. The kind of cheesy spot you sometimes eat at with the guys after playing hockey. Peter and George K. hound you and Johnny about it every chance they get. It drives them crazy that you'd spend your money here. Outside of the waitresses there's maybe three women in the whole place. Everyone else is a variation of geek hunched in front of a plastic chicken dinner on a Wednesday night.

You ask the girl to sit you out on the upstairs terrace. Order a club sandwich and a beer, reach for your cigarettes the instant she takes the menu away. Five left. You pick one with a twisted end and light it, all the while watching two guys play a drinking game using bottle caps. They're older than you, well into their thirties. Not young guys. Old enough that it looks ridiculous. They're also talking too loudly. In your opinion. About movies. Everyone's always talking about movies. This particular conversation is centred on special effects. The relative merits thereof, versus the tendency towards overuse. You hear one of them say, "A movie used to seduce you. Now it rapes you." Ooh, heavy. You swallow a big gulp of smoke, blow a stream of nicotine exhaust in their direction, watch it billow softly away. Ahh. Now that's nice. How do people ever give these things up? What do they do with all the extra time?

You remember how you quit once. You got to a point where you just felt so bad. You felt like you were rotting from the inside out. There were days your chest simply ached, that's how serious it was. So finally you stopped. Amazing. You felt better so quickly. The throbbing stopped immediately. Your throat and chest cleaned out like you'd never been a puffer in the first place. You were so proud of yourself. In just a few weeks you felt like a new person. Incredible. Then, after a while, your lungs felt so good, so recovered, you just had to try it again. It was as though a penance had been paid and you were being taunted to do it all over. And of course the sensation of the smoke going down — into what once again felt like virginal territory — was fabulous. Delicious and irresistible.

TVs are mounted on walls. From where you sit you can see a couple outside and several more inside, through the glass. All but one of them are showing sports. You watch everything, glancing from one to the other. You can't help it. It's stronger than you. Highlights are your thing. Even if you watch an entire game it doesn't feel complete to you until you've caught the recap. It's the poetry you enjoy. The singular plays, not the final scores. The scores are an excuse to show the plays. The plays are in *slow motion*. Everything looks good in slow motion. You get off on the bulge of the twine as a puck explodes into the back of a net, the ricochet of the ball as it leaves the bat, the hypnotic spiral of a football as it knifes through the air. The putt rolling then dropping from sight. The rotation a basketball takes spinning off a player's fingertips, the hoop shimmering, teasing, soft-focus in the background. They score with superhuman grace, these demi-gods, whirling and pivoting as though dancing to a secret music, all the while straining with such agonized strides. Frame-by-frame fantasy feats. Even colliding and crashing into each other, hammering each other open ice, open field, there is an elegance that makes the violence on the screen beautiful. The pain ethereal. The way sweat trickles down a forehead in extreme close-up, in super slow motion, makes an athlete glisten like a movie star.

You watch so much of this shit it's unreal. And you know there are millions of other dumb goobers just like you, glued to these images as though they actually mean something. A truly colossal band of losers, all of you.

The meal is over. Your skinny belly is bursting. The dishes have been whisked away and she's brought you a coffee and a fresh ashtray. You light another fag. Four left.

The bottle cappers have left. In their stead are two minions and a girl they have pinned down with constant banter. Who cares, she's a mutt anyway. You're not sure what the point is. Minion One is one of those guys with an overly big head but tiny, scrunched-up features. And a radically receding hairline that only makes it worse. It's like he doesn't have enough face for his huge, gleaming skull. Too much time spent at The Giant Forehead Store. Beside him, Minion Two is dull-eyed, head shaved, both elbows anchored heavily into the table in front of him, like a sloth. A pair of short-haired freaks. *Ecch.* You feel yourself shudder. Guys like this always get to you. So utterly disconnected. So uncool. It makes you wonder sometimes, what might have been. There but for the grace of dope go you.

On the screen closest to you, soccer, of all things, is on. You tend to find soccer somewhat dull. You normally think of soccer as a somewhat slow game to watch. Tonight, however, observing it this past hour or so, actually concentrating on the play of these two teams, breaking it down, analyzing it, studying this taut 0-0 duel while chewing patiently through your club sandwich, you've come to realize that soccer is, more accurately, the most crushingly dreary spectator sport on the entire planet. It has no peer. It is beyond numbing. They just punt the fucking thing back and forth all night long.

You finish your smoke, down your coffee. You're not sure what to do with yourself. Going back out is an idea, but where? Not back to The Q. And Henry seems out of the question. You could hang over at Aaron's, which would be okay, but with the kids in bed and Maureen finished cleaning up and getting everything ready for the morning, eventually she'll come and sit in with you and that'll just kill it, her going on and on about everything.

You could go to the Elbow Room but that's a younger scene and you know Cuz is there. And his buddies. And if there's a guy who's bugging you lately, it's Cuz. So not that.

You need to piss. You go to the back. They have a pool table there. Not fancy like at The Q. Coin-operated, with the huge pockets. There's two guys playing and other names waiting on the blackboard. You pass them, enter a stall. Drain the beast. When you come out you see the resident hotshot has won again. He does the white man's strut back to his drink, impressing no one. His girlfriend sits tableside, just waiting for them to leave. The hotshot thinks she's digging him but actually she's bored. It's not hard to tell.

You pass her slowly. She looks like deep down she thinks he's a dunce. She looks like a smart girl. Who could do better. With you. And yet you know that if you caught her alone for a moment and tried to talk to her, she'd cut you down and go running right back to him. Now why is that?

You get back to your table. To catch the waitress's eye you give her the international sign for bringing the bill, an imaginary pen in one hand scribbling onto an imaginary pad in the other. She nods and looks away. You're pretty sure you see her give the international roll of her eyes that means she can't wait to get rid of you and everyone else and go the fuck home.

You sit back, watch everybody. Think of Johnny. Has he missed you yet? Think of Honey. Picture Honey. Beautiful Honey. Think of

Henry. Think of Aaron. Think of Cuz. Think of Cuz more. Really mull over Cuz. And then, as though it's been trying to fight its way to the front of your mind for the longest time, a realization abruptly comes to you. That Cuz has his eye on your business.

More than that, actually. More than his eye. His hands. His dirty paws. He's begun his move, he's after your business. It's that simple. You start fiddling with your lighter, rotating it end over end. You picture him at the Elbow Room. Holding court. Selling pieces. You better wake up. Not that Cuz is so smart or so calculating. But still, that's what he's doing. He's *horning* his way in. He's moving as much product as possible to as many people as possible. At cheaper prices. At stupid prices. You've been seeing it for months. And he's always around, always available. Unlike you. Especially lately. You just can't seem to bother. To care enough. And so that's what he's doing with all these side deals to everyone. And some of these people are supposed to be yours. *Are* yours. Yet they're getting their dope from Cuz now.

Not good.

And the problem with Cuz is, he's not a guy you can talk to. He'll tell you anything you want to hear. He'll tell you bullshit. He'll tell you anything but what's actually going through his crazed brain. And then go out and just do it again the next day. Wily little ferret. Selling it for next to nothing.

And so what are you supposed to do? *Give* the shit away?

You remember when he used to fight people all the time. He'd get his brains kicked in constantly. Absolutely murdered. And then want to go fight again. You can think of guys that pounded him out two and three different times. The thing is, he just had to get his licks in. Had to. It didn't matter how many fists rammed themselves into his face, if you got Cuz, he had to get you too. Even just once. Even if only to say he had. It would make him boil over to think that you got the better of him and he got *nothing*.

You've seen him go after someone who'd beaten the shit out of him three years earlier. *Three years*. He hasn't seen the guy in three years, suddenly he sees him. Bang! Mindless attack in the middle of a restaurant. Just dove at the guy while he was eating, flailing at the poor fucker as they fell to the floor. Getting his shots in. He had to. Naturally, it didn't take long for the guy to start tattooing Cuz's eyes and mouth with big meaty fist prints, but to Cuz he'd done what he had to. The guy you're thinking of actually broke Cuz's cheekbone, if you remember right. As usual, you and Johnny had to pull him out of it. You and Johnny have hauled a lot of people off Cuz over the years. Such a drag. Cuz's blood everywhere. Every time. If you're always pulling a guy out of scraps, it's better to be friends with someone who wins occasionally.

You never could trust Cuz, and you knew that from the beginning. Cuz isn't even really your cousin. He just went out with Irene, one of your cousins, for a really long time. Charles is his real name, and that kind of became Chaz, and then he was always involved with whatever family things they were doing, always around, and so he sort of became a cousin too, and between that and calling him Chaz, which nobody ever really liked mostly because it sounded so stupid, he became Cuz.

Why did you ever get involved with him? You remember at first you and Johnny thought he was a gas. Dating Irene but hanging out more with all of you. Always looking to get into it with somebody. It was like owning a young Rottweiler. What a scene. What a show. And you and Johnny abused him for the hound he was.

But of course he ain't no puppy anymore. And Irene kicked him out long ago. Now he's older and thicker and a lot meaner to look at. No one scraps with him anymore. It's not worth it. Everyone's gotten older and mellowed, but he still wants to fight to the death.

And in that way — you're thinking this out loud to yourself for the first time ever — in that way you're all a little afraid of him now. That's the truth. And so if that's what he was after all along, well, maybe for once he's won.

You glance up at the TV. They've gone to a local news break. They put up an image of Darlene Dobson. They're calling this the most recent photo of her. You see an extremely pale face. Creamy white skin. Almost translucent. Super-bleached blond hair. Dark, obvious make-up for contrast. Tattoos and piercings. Face bling. Blond goth, if there's such an animal. But with good cheekbones and eyes that hold your attention. A nice long neck. White trash, but not hopeless.

Despite the outdoor music, you follow bits of an interview with the roommate that last saw her. She is dumpy with mean eyebrows and has her hair done in that frizzy rock star perm that overweight girls seem to go for. She's insisting harm must have come to her friend. The last time she spoke to Darlene was the morning she disappeared. Darlene left their place in The Point and headed over to your neighbourhood. Where she was supposed to meet Henry Miller. For coffee. Where Henry had asked to meet her. Possibly. The girl's forehead scrunches up at these memories, the caterpillars of thick hair below knitting themselves perilously close to the dreaded unibrow.

While she yaps on they dissolve to another photo of Darlene. This shot head-to-toe with friends. You'd never seen this chick with Henry, that you're sure of. How many times could he have been with her? Then again, how often have you seen him lately? They zoom in slowly on the photo. It gets grainier and grainier as they crop past the others and isolate only her, and then in further until finally the screen is just a series of giant dots. By the time the effect is finished, she feels dead.

A spokesman for the cops comes on next. They're still cautioning people not to assume anything. A phone number slides in, for people to call. Or for Darlene Dobson to. She's just a wild, young seventeen-year-old who could return home at any time, he reminds everyone.

Yeah well, good luck. You can't help but think this. Watching these chicks on TV, they look like the kind of sad girls who show up for auditions on those talent shows then swear and spit at the cameras on the way out. Who cares if one vanishes from the face of the earth? There's a million other contestants.

You look around. No one else is watching. No one else gives a shit. And neither would you if it weren't for Henry. You consider the possibilities in the coldest possible light. He did something to her. He didn't. Someone else did. She ran off. Someone took her. She's hiding. She's lost somehow. She's about to reappear. Henry knows where she is. Henry doesn't.

The waitress comes to your table. "You done?"

"Yes."

"You're watching that story," she says to you. "I hope they cut his balls off, that guy."

You look up at her. "Whose balls?"

"The guy. Her boyfriend."

"You think he did something to her?" you ask.

"Of course."

"Why?"

She tears your bill from her pad, places it in front of you.

"Because they always do, sport."

She turns on her heel, moves off. Okay. Time to lay your bills down and blow this Popsicle stand. And that's what you're about to do when Minion One — who's been sneaking little glances at you since he arrived — suddenly gets up and starts walking towards you. Good Christ. You push away from your own table, get to your feet.

"Hey, what's going on?" he says in that minionesque way. They have no presence at all, these people.

"I don't know. What's going on?"

"My friend and I are just out, you know." He gestures back over at Mini-Me, who hasn't even noticed his counterpart has left. "To have a bunch of drinks."

"Yeah."

"You know. Whatever."

"Right, whatever."

You tower over him. But then you tower over most people.

"You?"

"Me? What?"

"Anything going on?"

"I told you, no."

"Nothing? Nothing going on?"

Uh-oh. This sounds familiar.

Minion One suddenly softens his voice and affects a conspiratorial tone, one you've heard a million times before. "I was wondering if I could, uh, get something. You know? For my friend and me."

You look around. Like you're bored. Take your time. Then look back at him. Say nothing.

He says, "Just a gram? Couldn't I?"

"I don't know what you're talking about, man."

"C'mon."

"No."

You look away again. Around, curious to see if anyone is watching the two of you. How sad is this? Even when you're just out eating dinner you look like you're dealing. Is it *that* obvious? This screwball thinks you're holding, right here in the middle of the restaurant. Note to self: haircut this year.

"I *know* you," Minion One says now.

Or, a second theory. He knows you from somewhere.

"No, you don't," you say.

"Yes. I was with another guy. We met you at a park once. He knows Johnny and Aaron. You wouldn't remember me. I didn't say anything."

You look at him. "I *don't* remember you. And I don't know what you're talking about."

"Just sell me a little piece," he begs. They always beg. "We can go outside if you want."

You pocket your cigarette pack and lighter. "I am going outside. But you're staying here. Go back and sit with your buddy. And that mutt."

"C'mon, don't be a prick," he says. Then drops his voice back to an urgent whisper. "Really. It's cool in here. You can sell me something. No one cares. Please."

You walk towards the door.

He scampers over ahead of you. "Let me give you my number then. You could call and I could see you another day."

In the time it takes him to say this, the same amount of time it has taken you to readjust your gait and brush past him, in just that infinitesimal moment, you make a decision. Clench a fist, put a snarl at the edge of your lips. If this guy keeps it up, he's going to get it. If he doesn't back off, you're going to back him off.

You notice the waitress staring from the other end of the terrace.

"I'm leaving now, dude," you say, low.

"Please."

"Go back and sit with your friends."

"They're not my friends."

"Neither am I."

You walk down the stairs to the level below, navigate your way past the tables to the main entrance. Minion One trails a safe distance behind. You open the front doors, descend the short set of steps to the sidewalk. Turn back. See him hesitating at the doorway, lacking the courage to follow. You wait for him to plead once more, a chance for you to cut him down a last time.

Instead he says, "I didn't mean to bother you. Forget it. I'm sorry."

You're taken aback. Not sure what to say. Scowl at him, though you're not actually angry.

He says, "I'm sorry. I apologize."

"Alright."

"I'm sorry. Sorry."

You walk out into the middle of Ste-Catherine Street with your arm out to flag a cab. Intercept one that's about to pick up another couple. Get in. You're a little rattled. Not even sure what address to give the guy. Finally you say the Elbow Room. Why there? Why not? Where else? The fresh air has given you a sudden surge of energy. Minion One has awoken something in you. You'll go to the Elbow Room, see if Cuz is there. And if he is, maybe it's time you set things straight. *Explained* things. Gave him a smack upside the head if necessary.

Or not. Is this a good idea? Maybe not so much. Perhaps the fresh air has also given you a sudden surge of delusional thoughts. You're in no condition to get into a scrap. Not tonight, not against Cuz. Not with all his friends around, not even an argument.

"Elbow Room?" the cab guy says now, in some kind of delayed reaction. "This is only four streets from here."

"Yeah, so?"

"Four streets? Why do you stop me for this?"

"Why? Because I want to *go there*." What's with this hombre?

He grunts. Doesn't budge.

You say, "C'mon, pal."

Cab Guy glowers at you. "There was a couple on the street also that I could have driven. Farther."

"Hurry up then. Take me and then go back."

"Obviously I cannot. They will find another."

"Fine. So let's just stop talking about it then."

Cab Guy looks at you in the rear-view mirror. Stares a couple of seconds. Says nothing. Finally turns back to the road, moves forward. He pilots you through several intersections then pounds on his brakes. You lurch forward, catch yourself before slamming face first into his headrest.

You watch as he slaps at the meter and stops it at four dollars even. "Okay. Out."

Through the window, you look at the entrance to the Elbow Room. It seems suddenly ridiculous to think of going in there. The instinct to flee is strong. You picture all the losers that are likely to be there. Picture confronting Cuz. That moment. The tension. Your throat is dry but the last thing you need is a drink. Though you're hours from being able to fall asleep you feel suddenly fatigued. Listless. Nauseous.

You turn back to Cab Guy.

"I think you better take me to the hospital," you say.

nine

"Oh, no," he says.

"Oh no, what?"

"You go out."

"Take me to the hospital."

"Which hospital?"

"Royal Victoria."

"You are not sick!"

"I don't feel well. My head hurts."

"Out!"

"Hey, man!"

"Your head hurts? My buttocks hurt! What are you thinking of that?"

"You know, there's a cream they sell."

"Come! Out, please."

"Just drive. What's your fucking problem, man?"

"You are not to fool me!"

"Dude, I want to *hire* you."

"If I must call the police."

"What?"

"If I must."

"What? Call the police about what?"

"They will make you go."

"No, they'll make *you* go, Chief. You're a fucking cab driver! They'll *make you* take me."

Cab Guy folds his arms in front of him. Glares straight ahead.

You glare back, finally throw a twenty-dollar bill into the front seat. "Don't you think I have money? Is that your problem? C'mon, let's go."

He unfolds his arms. Looks down at the twenty, picks it up. Puts the car into gear.

Apparently it was.

He takes you, muttering his way through the city.

At the lights in front of the Vic, he pulls up. Lets you out.

You take your change, walk away. Once you're a safe distance from his vehicle he calls at you through his window.

"Go get a big X-ray of your head then!" The way he says it you know he's been working on it the whole trip.

"Thanks. I might."

"Yes. Do it!"

"I probably should. You're right."

"Check it then! Immediately!"

"Okay, I will."

"Yes, ha! You will!"

"Wow, you're really stinging me with these zingers, man."

"I am!"

You enter through the doors at Emergency, passing the guard and making your way across the Registration waiting room. It's a zoo, as usual. Shrieks and roars and cries of mayhem. The chairs are crammed with creatures of all colours and sizes. At one end a semi-conscious cow moans, bulging over the edges of her stretcher. Two jackals behind desks type frantically at their keyboards, ears pricked to gather information that's being bleated at them above the general din.

Another pair of doors hisses open and a chimpanzee in a white uniform wheels an aging elk through the opening. When no one is looking you walk through these same doors and into the back halls.

Inside you walk briskly, looking for a corridor that will lead you to other wards. The hospital is built into the mountainside, with structures adjoining at different levels. This means that if you leave one building at ground level, you may connect with the next building on the third floor. Or you can take an elevator up in one, cross over, and actually end up *lower* in the next.

In other words, it's a fucking labyrinth, this place. And ancient. Everything is falling apart. The paint is old, the pipes are older, the air is musty. The lighting is poor. There are areas where the air conditioning system is a fourteen-inch fan. It's shameful. It needs its own surgery. And it's not the only hospital that's been treated this way.

You negotiate your way along several corridors, eventually arriving at a passageway clearly marked HOSPITAL PERSONNEL ONLY. A good idea this, big signs to keep the riff-raff out.

You enter it, walk towards the elevator waiting at the end.

At this moment a door swings open and a big brown rhino in housekeeping togs steps out, stops when he sees you.

"Where are you going?"

"Just up a few floors," you say, breeze by him and straight into the lift. "I'm going to see one of the nurses there."

"Who do you know there?"

"Honey Zamner."

He turns clumsily to look at you, the big horn jutting up from the middle of his forehead. "You're not supposed to take these elevators, sir."

"Yeah, but now I'm here."

The door tries to close. He lifts one of his big hooves to block it.

"You're really supposed to take the ones from the lobby."

"Yeah, but now I'm *here*."

"Yes. But really you should be taking—"

"But it's *straight up.*"

He doesn't reply. Stares at you instead. You can see him weighing the options, labouring through the process. Not many people know this, but rhinoceroses rank in the bottom twenty percentile intelligence among mammals. A fact you made up just now.

The door begins its slide again. This time he allows it to close.

You get up to Honey's floor, instantly block your nose and begin breathing through your mouth. The acrid smell of shit that fills the air will be with you your whole time here, will even be in your clothes when you leave. This you know. It's not your first time here. You know this territory, worked here for almost two years. There are people in this hospital who remember you.

You walk over to the nursing station. It's deserted. You look around, see no one. There are chairs inside the office but you're hesitant to go in and sit down. Depending on whom Honey is working with, it might not be cool.

You hear noises coming through the open door of a room nearby. A scuffling sound, then bumping. A light goes on inside the room. The bumping stops, the scuffling continues. The sound, you know, of slippers slithering across the hard floors on a late night trek to the toilet. A perennial event with these golden oldies. One of these trips can take ten minutes or more. Sometimes they get there and sit down but then have to call for help to get back up. Or doze off on the seat.

Of course, the worst is when they fall. Old like this, frail and confused, it happens. The sudden noise of one of them slapping down hard against the floor is a sickening sound you don't easily forget. That's how they break their hips. And breaking their hips is how they die, shrivelled up in bed month after month. They waste away, drips in their arms and meds in their heads. Even the pretence of recovery quickly becomes a distant memory.

Honey arrives, with Margaret in tow. Margaret likes you. You like Margaret. Margaret's older, close to retiring. She likes to bum cigarettes off you whenever she sees you. Margaret still likes to think of herself as naughty. She smiles when she sees you.

"Well, look who's come."

"Hey, Margaret."

Honey seems less thrilled by your presence. "What're you doing here?"

"I just came for a few minutes. Want to go for a smoke?"

"No, I don't want to go for a smoke. It's almost midnight."

"As in, it's too late? Or too early?"

"As in, what're you doing here?"

"*I'll* have a cigarette," Margaret says, extending her hand. "Don't talk so loud. Go inside and have a coffee."

You reach into your shirt pocket, hand her your pack and lighter. When Margaret leaves, you and Honey go inside the station. You make yourselves coffees. In the background, a radio plays softly.

"You sure do a lot of night shifts lately," you say.

"It's my last one."

You haven't seen her since the morning she arrived at your place, days ago. She works rotation of shifts, usually five or six in a row then several days off until the new ones. Day evening night.

"So you're off after this?"

"For three days."

"That's great."

"It's good. My parents want Baby and me to go out and see them." Baby is her sister. The youngest of three. The eldest is back in Europe. Honey's the middle girl. Their parents live in the Eastern Townships.

"They have a nice place, your parents," you say. A big, beautiful house with many rooms, it was a bed-and-breakfast before they bought it. "You took me there once."

"I remember. There was a bunch of us." She sips from her coffee. "Who were you out with tonight?"

"No one."

"At all?"

"Johnny, a bit. But not long."

She drops her eyes, chews on the plastic stir stick from her coffee. "You shouldn't have come."

"I wanted to."

The phone rings. Honey moves over, answers it. She listens then puts the receiver down and goes over to her charts. When she returns she speaks in a low tone, precise and business-like. It's always a buzz for you to see this side of her.

She talks for several more minutes. In that time Margaret returns. At night everyone smokes outside the same building, a forgotten little patio not far from here. Barren until morning. Just put a rock to keep the door from locking behind you and then puff away all you want.

Margaret gives you back your smokes and lighter, plops herself down. Honey puts down the phone at the same instant, closes the folder.

No one says anything. The song on the radio ends. For some reason the DJ starts talking about a kind of insect that mates constantly. The three of you listen, unsure of what conversation should follow.

After a time Honey says, "Alright, we'll be back." She pushes her chair back, gets to her feet. "If Linda calls again, the chart is there."

She motions and you get up. Margaret gives you a smile.

You walk in silence alongside Honey. You remember the nights when you used to patrol these halls, beeper on your belt, white shirt, white pants, white shoes. Yes, you used to be a monkey too. Cleaning shit, running bloods, turning bedridden patients. Flapjacks, you used to call them. You had that fake nameplate you wore for a while, *Jerry Attricks*. Fuh-nee. You used to buddy around with another orderly named McIntyre, who always wanted to take everyone to 7 West because there was this lady there, Mrs. King, that would yell out "Taxi!" every time you passed her door. What a laugh she was. McIntyre used to take all the new guys there.

You pass an empty waiting room and then a set of glass-pane doors that lead to a grungy stairwell. You are about to turn the corner and continue on to the smoking door when Honey suddenly takes your arm and steers you towards a room next to her. She pushes the door open, angles you inside. Closes the door behind you and positions you up against it. You are surprised but know better than to speak out.

Inside it's dark, but she doesn't turn on the light. You make out that you're in a semi-private room, empty, with two freshly made-up beds. The parking lot lights perched outside the window bathe them with a soft glow.

"So, why did you come?" Honey leans in close to you, her forehead just inches from your chin.

"I just came," you say.

"Because you miss me?"

"No!" It comes out petulant. High school.

"Come on. You can say it."

"Say what?"

"You've been thinking about me."

"I have been thinking about you. Does that mean I missed you?"

She moves in closer, cuts the distance between you in half. Now it's centimetres.

"It's so cute that you needed to see me," she teases.

"I just thought we should talk. You know."

Her hand is at your belt now. She's fumbling to unhook the clasp. Holy Jesus. Is this really happening? Again?

"What did you think we needed to talk about?" she asks, making you look right at her eyes, making sure you don't look down.

"Well, I'm...a bit confused."

"Confused?"

"Sure."

"About what you want?"

"About what *you* want."

She backs you against the wall. You offer no resistance.

"I *have* what I want," she says huskily.

"Wow. You know, you're really playing around with my head."

Wow. Did you really just say that?

"Am I?" She unbuttons you. Unzips you.

"Um…"

"Are you worried about Johnny?"

"Yes…"

"Good. So am I."

"What do you mean?"

"I'm not sure."

"But you just said it."

She's grinding herself against you. By now, it's fair to say, she has your full attention. You reach in to kiss her, consider veering her towards the beds. She pushes you back with a forearm. A surprisingly strong forearm.

And then crumples to her knees.

Gadzooks!

Your head snaps back, your eyes go to the ceiling. You feel her hands tugging your jeans and underwear down to your knees. You feel yourself straining, anxious for her fingers to release you.

Instead they pause, and you hear her ask from below, "What would it be like to be your girlfriend?"

A question. She's asking you a question.

What would it be like to be your girlfriend? Is this to you, or is she just musing? Are you supposed to answer this?

Because it's a toughie.

Like, for you, it would be great. And sad. And something else. But for her, you're not so sure. Maybe not so great. She'd better like hanging around doing nothing an awful lot. It would be different for her. To be the homely guy's girlfriend.

But then maybe it would be hilarious. And cool. And fun and sexy and everything else. Everything would be new again. Because when you're with a girl like Honey, everything is new again. Everything is fun again. Just driving along in a car is fun. Doing groceries. Or just walking down the street —

Oh.

Oh God.

And she's gotten down to it now. And this is embarrassing but you can feel already that it won't be long until you spill yourself. It feels so warm and her mouth is so hot and you shouldn't look down but you do, damn you, the image of her hair splayed across her uniform that way, soft and satin and white beneath you, one of her shoes has come off, the way her hands cling to your hips as her head pushes you back against the wall, the way it feels like she has complete power over you —

Oh.

And there you go. Unbelievable. You tense and jerk. Bwit bwit. Ah. Then again. Bwit. Your eyes are back up now, trained on the ceiling. You thrust more, a last time, sensing that she has subtly unglued herself from you somewhere along the way, pulled her head back, though you feel just as smothered in her grasp as ever, the utter physical sensation of it is already cross-fading with an all too immediate sense of sinking heart, like a high that has peaked and broken and has nowhere to go but down. How fast this all was, how swift. *Swift.* Good word, that. Is swift bad? Hard to say. Not that it feels terribly manly for you, having given up the goods in less time than it takes the average person to comb his hair. No, this is not a terribly proud moment.

Unless, you never know, unless it's all right. Perhaps it is. Could it be? Certainly in bed, taking long is good. But here? Maybe as fast as possible is good here, maybe she's *grateful*. Maybe it's expected. But then you don't have a wealth of experience getting blown in hospital rooms.

Honey stirs beneath you, you hear rustling. You look down again, see her holding her hand out in front of her, see that somehow she's wearing a glove, one of those white plastic hospital gloves that leave powder on your skin after you take them off, that somehow she's slipped one on back there when you were counting ceiling panels and got all the way to three, and she's *caught you* in it.

And, oh boy, it's not a pretty sight.

Good Lord. Is this woman completely mad?

She gets up, delicately strips the glove from her hand and lets it fall into the wastebasket a few feet away. You shudder, watching. She turns back to you. You are standing there in full ignominious splendour. These are never great moments for you, but this one feels like it belongs in its own special diary of shame. All your years of lust for her feel right now as though they're being held in contempt against you.

She comes forward and takes your wrists in her hands, places them down at your knees where your pants are waiting.

You pull them up. She caresses your cheek, patchy with teenage stubble though you are twenty-eight.

"Now I feel like a smoke," she says, quiet and matter-of-fact. "Don't you?"

You arrange yourself, buckle up. Nod dumbly.

She goes to the door and opens it, walks out. Straight out, no looking around, no neck craning around the door frame first to see if anyone is there.

You take your own steps, tepid, in another direction, to the trash container by the bed. You peer inside. It's lined with plastic, also white. Shiny and industrial. The glove lies there, propped up, held aloft by the folds of the bag, your ardour prominently displayed in its palm, white on white on white. Ugh. Are you going to just leave it there like that? Well, what's the other option? Pull out the bag and tie it up. Stuff it somewhere. Where? In your pocket. Hold on to it until the opportunity arises to stash it somewhere. Secretly carry it around until then.

Uh, no. Not in this lifetime.

Instead you grab the bag, twist and tie it in a single terse motion, then, holding it like a vial of bubbling plutonium, spirit it into the adjacent bathroom. There you bury it into the bottom of the garbage basket, tear off a few strips of toilet paper to crumple, and garnish a light topping. If someone goes to the trouble of removing it and opening it up, they deserve what they find.

You leave the room, burrowing down the hallway head down, breath held. In a hospital there are many airborne dangers, not the least of which is gossip. Just because Honey doesn't care doesn't mean you don't. You keep your eyes on the floor until you reach the door to the outside, the rock already jammed in place.

"Do you think I'm mad at Johnny?" she asks as you light up.

You watch her pull her cigarette from her lips, notice the fine powder that has collected along the edges of her slender fingers.

"Well, I think something."

She says, "You think I'm getting back at him for something? Is that it?"

"Are you?"

"*Do* you?"

"Maybe."

"For what?"

"I don't know."

"For what?"

"How would I know?"

She flicks an ash into the filthy tin box screwed to the wall. "That's such a guy thing to think."

You flick an ash into the filthy tin box screwed to the wall. "Well, I'm a guy."

"Guys think that if you sleep with someone else there has to be, like, a plot. A big reason for it. I've known you a long time and I know you like me. You don't think I've ever thought of kissing you before?"

You say nothing. Sometimes it's best not to answer. Even you remember this from time to time.

"You're so full of shit," she says now. "How many years have you been staring at me with big, sad eyes like you'd give anything if I looked at you the way I look at Johnny? From even the earliest days, Lee. You always did. Watching me when you thought I couldn't see you. Staring at Johnny like he was so lucky. Like you wished so hard you could be him. So, if one day I kiss you and show up at your place and get into bed with you, suddenly it's only *me*? Am I the only one with courage? What have you ever done, Lee? Nothing. You never even *said* anything, ever. Guys are the biggest chickens."

"I came to the hospital. Tonight. *That's* why."

"Well, I thought you'd be here before now."

"I wanted to."

"I waited for you."

"I should have."

"When I went home in the mornings, I couldn't believe you hadn't come."

"I guess, because Johnny's my best friend…"

Her eyes flash. "Lee, Johnny's *my* best friend."

"Well, I —"

"No, you aren't. Don't you know? Are you that naive? You're *one* of Johnny's friends, Lee. The one that always has hash for him. The skinny one. The one he looks so good standing beside."

You say nothing, look away. *Skinny* is not something Honey would say without knowing what it means to you. She's hurt you, saying this. It's on purpose. She must know.

Honey moves back inside. You follow.

When she gets to the elevators she stops. To bid you off.

"I waited, Lee. You didn't come."

"I know."

"It was kind of a test. You didn't do great."

You don't answer.

Another guard passes in the corridor. He slows, wants to be sure this nurse and the guy in the civvies are not in a situation. His reptilian eyes appraise you until finally he slithers off into another corner of the jungle.

"Go," Honey says, pushing the button on the wall for you.

"Tell Margaret I said bye."

The doors open. Thankfully, no one is inside. You enter. When you turn back, she's no longer there. The doors close. Your blurry reflection gapes back at you.

What would it be like to be your girlfriend? That's what she wanted to know. Like at this rate you'll ever get there. Such strange behaviour. Weird scenes inside the chick mine. You think of Johnny. Picture him, see him in a different way suddenly. A guy whose girl is fucking around on him. A guy who can't hold on to his woman. Just like a whole lot of other guys. Less of a deity. More one of you. Wow. Awful thoughts. What a shit you are. What a weird broad Honey is. Who would've thought?

So many questions. Unexpected answers. If you could ask her one more question, what would it be?

What's the one answer you need most?

Hmm.

Just one question?

Okay.

What was with the glove?

You make your way down, over, across, all the way back through the hallways to Registration and the freak show in the waiting room. Then out the Emergency doors with a nod to the guard you've been nodding at since forever without ever exchanging a single word and across the parking lot to where the taxis park. Pick one, get in one.

The driver smiles at you. At least this guy, you're pleased to note, is not having a meltdown. He pulls out onto Pine Avenue, speeds away from the hospital. Like most everyone else who came here tonight, you're going back home not much more healed than when you first arrived.

ten

You sit back in almost total darkness as the taxi knifes down the side of the mountain. It's not far to where you live. Within ten minutes the gorgeous old greystones will be replaced by smaller, undernourished homes, attached duplexes, and blocks of condos.

Each time you pass a street light the inside of the cab brightens then falls black again. You stare out the window. Even these lesser gems are in demand. Signs are everywhere announcing that they've just been sold or soon expect to be. Places that used to go for pennies are selling for three times what they're actually worth. People with money are crazy to live in the city. They'll buy anything not to get into traffic in the morning. By the middle of summer, half these neighbourhoods will be in renovations.

You're almost home when you realize you have exactly two smokes left. You allow the driver to overshoot your stop, dropping you a couple of lights later near the only store open this time of night. You wrestle your wallet from your back pocket, pay him. He takes your money without even a decent thank you. Another thirty-cent tip wasted.

You start walking, sparking what's left of a spliff you've snaked from the bottom of your pack. Ah, yes. Everything gets just a little milder this way. The edge comes off, the walk becomes a *stroll*. Store lights twinkle, front doors glow. Your mind meanders as you drift past the buildings. Such a warm feeling, this old friend. You'd have to go back to when you were fifteen years old to find a time when you weren't getting high every night. It's why you've always been careful to monitor yourself so you don't end up hooked.

You take it slow, easy. Where are you in a rush to, anyway? Nowhere. You slide your hands into the pockets of your jeans and make your way.

When you get to the store, you glance down the cross street before going in. This is Madison, Henry's street. At the bottom is Henry's place. He and his mother live in the same apartment building.

At this same moment a van glides up, slows down in order to turn the corner, gently passes in front of you. Also in no hurry. You recognize the call letters on its side. It's a production vehicle for one of the TV companies that shoots in town. Soft news, local celebrities, documentary bits when something unusual happens. Probably on its way home after a long day at the fame and fortune factory.

You're about to enter the store, hesitate once more. Wait, watch. As the vehicle parks outside Henry's building. Through the darkness you can make out the back doors opening and equipment being loaded out. It's parked under a single street lamp.

You toss your roach, exhale, and start towards Henry's place instead, still keeping your pace calm. That naked chick outside Blockbuster, you remember they were shooting it that day. Was it the same van? Does it matter? What a lot of nothing. Everyone's filming everything now. But like every other simpleton, you can't bring yourself to just ignore it and move on.

Eventually you make your approach. A woman walks briskly out in front of the van to intercept you, a microphone held at her side. You recognize her. The name escapes you.

"Hi, what can I do for you?" She smiles at you. Stares at you right between your eyes. Her free hand is perched on her hip.

Behind her a young guy, short and thick-shouldered, mounts a camera onto a tripod and then clips a small light atop it. There's just the two of them.

"Nothing," you say. "What're you doing?"

"Nothing. A shot."

"A shot."

"Right. No big deal."

"No big deal."

"Nothing to see." She smiles again. It feels more like a threat now.

"I see," you say.

"Great. Okay? So you can go."

"Yeah, alright. Thanks."

But you don't move.

Camera Guy turns to face you. "There's nothing to see, man. No glamour." He says it oh-so-cool, like he wants you to know right away that he's not the kind of guy who thinks there's anything special about him being a cameraman.

"Wow," you say. "You're sure?"

"Yeah, I'm sure."

"Really? Because it *looks* so glamorous."

He squints at you. Unsure.

"Carry another big, heavy box out of the van for me," you say. "Would you? Just one. And do it real glamorous-like."

Camera Guy turns to the woman. "You want me to call someone?"

She shrugs no.

Liz Hunter, it suddenly hits you, is her name.

"You know, there really is nothing important going on here," Liz Hunter says.

"I don't doubt it."

"We're just working."

"Sure. I know."

"You do?"

"Yeah, I know you." You say it real cornball, lay it in there. "You're, like, a movie star."

"I'm a reporter," she says in a tired way. "See the microphone? That's the clue."

"And a *funny* one."

They both stare at you. Liz Hunter's phone rings. She answers it and swivels away in one practised move.

Camera Guy says, "It's just that it's tough for us to do our work with you here. It's late, you know. We'd like to go home too."

"I'm sure you would. Anyway, don't you, like, need a permit or something?"

Camera Guy scans the immediate area around him, lifts the camera and tripod up, walks it over several feet, and puts it down. He wears a heavy belt of battery packs at his waist and a sound machine is slung over one shoulder. "For what?"

You follow him the few steps over. "Shooting. Here. At night."

"Forget it. No. We can do anything. Don't worry."

You look on as he adjusts his frame. "What're you shooting?"

"The building."

"The building? The building's all dark."

"It's not that dark."

"You're not going to put a light up?"

"No. It's fine."

"I saw them shooting something the other day, they had four big lights up. And it wasn't even night."

Camera Guy takes a disc out of the black leather bag lying at his feet and loads it into the side of the camera. "Do you see any *electricity* around here, friend? Where do you want me to plug the lights? My ass?"

Ah, the delicious arrogance of the unionized employee. You reflect fondly on your own halcyon days as a workee at the hospital. The unspoken impunity that governed your actions. The way you treated people like pure shit knowing your local loved to fight anybody over anything. You get misty just thinking back.

"You could string a couple of extension cords out of the lobby of the building," you suggest.

"What do I look like? Five guys? It's the news."

"What news?"

"*The* news."

"What's the little light on the camera for?"

"For her."

"Oh. She's going to talk?"

"Why else would she be here?"

"Well, what's the point? So she can say what? That the girl's still missing? That's not news. Why are you wasting everybody's time?"

Liz Hunter ends her call. Walks back over.

Camera Guy snaps the camera light on. She blinks in its glare. You instinctively take a step back.

She looks at you. "Weren't you leaving?"

Before you can answer, Camera Guy gestures towards you. "No, he's staying."

Liz Hunter smiles, a curious look on her face now. She studies you.

"He knows what we're doing," Camera Guy tells her. "He knows whose building this is."

You feel yourself getting all hot, your cheeks and ears starting to burn. You feel ashamed. Cornered. Why? Because you've been caught, that's why. Though you're not sure at what.

Liz Hunter reaches her hand out for yours. Inexplicably, you take it.

She guides you into the warmth of the light.

"Speed," Camera Guy says. "We'll do the intro after. In three, two, one..."

She lifts the mike to her lips, slides her hand out of yours, and begins talking.

"And so, here we are... in the dead of night... while inside this building, behind these walls... Henry Miller, presumably asleep... still refusing comment... the young girl, Darlene Dobson, still unaccounted for..." She takes a breath. "Beside me now, an interested observer...

or perhaps a friend…" She turns to you. "Is that right? Are you a friend of Henry Miller's?" She flicks the mike over, just below your chin.

By now your face is on fire. Your ears are baking. Your nuts are melting. You have drymouth from the hash. You gape directly into the camera. For five, ten seconds. Mother of God. How moronic. You're going to make people think *you* killed her. Johnny and Honey are going to laugh themselves sick when they see this.

Liz Hunter tugs your attention back towards her. "What's your name?"

"Lee."

"Lee what?"

"Goodstone."

Hmm. Is it okay to say this? You remember Your Dealer. What will he think?

"You're a friend?"

"I guess I am."

"Surely you must have something to say then…"

You take a deep breath. Consider the question. Something to say? Surely you must. Henry's seventeen-year-old girlfriend is missing. These two saps seem convinced he's done something. But they don't even *know* him. You know him. Henry could never hurt anyone. Wouldn't. You believe this a thousand percent. Well, okay, sixty-five percent. Kidding. You're kidding. So what should you say? This feels oddly like a defining moment in your life. There's a camera, microphone, lights. Or at least one tiny light. How lazy is this guy anyway? *Quelle* joke. What a job. Maybe he can get you a part-time gig. It looks easy. You look at the camera. At Liz. Back at the lens. Something needs to be said. You seem to be the one who has to do it. After all, it's not like you volunteered. You're being *asked*.

You smile. Clear your throat. Look straight ahead.

"I'd like to thank the Academy. I'd like to thank my fans. I'd like to thank my high-school drama teacher, Phil McCracken. Because without his input—"

Liz Hunter pulls her arm down, lets the mike fall and point at the ground. Looks at Camera Guy. He clicks the camera off. Thirty seconds pass wherein they look at each other, then at you, then you look at each of them, and they look back at each other. No one speaks.

Finally, Liz Hunter lifts the microphone back up. Camera Guy rolls again.

"Three, two, one…" he says softly.

"I'm here… with a friend of Henry Miller's… who, as many of you know, has been questioned as to the unexplained disappearance of young Darlene Dobson… and so, Lee Goodstone… people are puzzled… the police are frustrated… perhaps you can help…"

You consider this request. A fair one. Maybe you *can* help.

You look past the lens, catch Camera Guy's available eye. "Hey," you ask him, "how wide is your shot?"

You give your balls a big scratch.

"Can I do this? Do you see this?" You scratch them again. Exuberantly.

You see Camera Guy reach up and twist the ring around the lens. Reframing. Is he getting wider or tighter?

"Whoah, dude. Are you getting wider? Or tighter? Ixnay on the ose-ups-clay." You look around, call out to no one, "And let's get some make-up over here…"

Another silence.

Boy. They sure know how to use the pregnant pause, these people.

The camera continues rolling.

You see Liz raise one eyebrow. To let everyone know what a tool you are. You've always wanted to be able to raise an eyebrow like that. It's so effective. Is that something you practise, or just a thing some people can do and others can't?

She turns slowly back to you. Painfully. "How long have you known Henry?"

You stroke your chin. For pensive effect. "A long time."

"Did you know Darlene Dobson?"

"No."

"You've never met her?"

"I've never even *seen* her."

"Until lately."

"Right. Pictures. On TV."

"Is Henry ever violent?"

"No."

"Never?"

"No."

"Are you sure? How can you be sure?"

"Then why do you ask?"

"Have you ever seen him strike a woman?"

"No. But I've seen him throw up so much beer on the street that it flowed twenty feet until it found a sewer."

A beat. Then, "Why won't he talk with us?"

"Why should he?"

"To clear his name."

"Is that what you're offering?"

You try to raise an eyebrow at her. Instead, your right nostril flares open and your lip rides up, baring your teeth. You're pretty sure it looks like you've just been stung by a bee.

Liz says, "Does Henry know you're here?"

"Yes."

"He does?"

"Sure."

Her eyes light up. "Because there's something he wants you to tell us?"

"Yes."

"Really?"

"No."

"Try to focus."

"I will."

"You're making it harder than it needs to be."

"Sorry."

"So, Henry...didn't send you here?"

"No."

"He doesn't know you're here?"

"Well, unless he's looking out his window."

You glance over. Liz glances over. Camera Guy pans over.

Nothing moves in the darkness.

"I don't see anything," Camera Guy tells her.

You say, "Maybe if you'd put up a light."

Liz sighs. Strokes her forehead with her fingers. Cleans the make-up powder from her fingers. You think back to the hospital and Honey.

She says, "You understand a girl is missing? Seventeen years old."

"If you say."

"You're denying it?"

"Well, no..."

"She could be dead."

"I guess..."

"You realize the police are keeping close tabs on your friend's every move?"

You roll your eyes. "He hasn't left the house in three days. He moves from the sofa to the toilet and back. Mostly because of you. What's to watch?"

"The police consider him their prime suspect."

"Really? I haven't heard that."

"Trust me."

"Uh, I don't think so."

"You think I'm being unfair? You think this is a joke? You think I'm wrong to be worried about this poor girl?"

You look directly into the lens. You've been watching her, and this is how she makes her strongest points.

"I think that you're going to be one disappointed chick if it turns out Henry didn't chop her up and stuff her into little Baggies."

She lowers the microphone again. Brings her fingers to her forehead once more, smudging herself.

"Okay," she tells Camera Guy. "I've had a headache all day. Now it's really hurting. Let's take a minute here. Cut, will you? Let me think for a bit."

You couldn't agree more. "Good idea." You give your nuts another giant scratching. "And I'm itchy again. If you have to know. So if we're going to keep shooting, I might need some ball powder. If you have some. I can't help it, I'm nervous. Do we have any Clammy Balls Powder? And, like, one of those big, puffy make-up brushes?"

Camera Guy wraps his gear. He did a stand-up with Liz. By herself. *Sans* you. Then he took the shot of the building by itself. You offered to help, in case he'd changed his mind and wanted to run a couple of lights. He hadn't.

In the meantime Liz Hunter received several phone calls, made several more. One of them was to call a taxi for herself so she could leave and let Camera Guy finish up and take the van. So maybe they're not that tight.

You light your second-to-last cigarette. Camera Guy asks for the last one. For some reason you toss it over to him. He catches and lights it, sucks at it like he's got a minute to live, wolfing the smoke down.

You see the cab's glow coming up the street. You call over to Liz before she can dial another number. "I thought it went quite well…"

She turns, stares at you. Like you're already a distant memory.

"You're a very good interviewer," you say. "Very professional."

She scowls. "Aren't you *ever* going to go?"

"No, really. I feel like you got me to bare my soul."

"Mmn. A big moment for all of us."

"We should have dinner together sometime. You can pay."

She flips her phone shut, tucks it away. "You know what? I think maybe you're a sicko too. Just like your friend."

"You don't even know my friend."

"Don't be so sure."

"Don't be so arrogant."

"Listen, darling. I don't do stories on *the ones that didn't do it.* Understand?"

"Wow. So cool."

"Maybe this is just too hard for you to deal with."

"Don't worry about what I can deal with."

"He's hiding something."

"Everybody's hiding something."

"He's a very odd person."

"It's his best character trait."

She gives you the eyebrow again. "Violence against women is a serious issue."

"I've seen the posters."

She shakes her head sadly. "You could have helped tonight. Instead you were stupid."

"Helped what? Your career?"

"The story."

"*What* story?"

"Keep watching."

"Ooh, so cool," you say again, disappointingly. Nice comeback, Potsie.

She turns away. The cab is there. You watch as she opens the door.

"Call me any time!" you say too loudly, using the international thumb-and-finger sign for telephone. "I'm ridiculously available…"

"Go home, Lee Goodstone."

The taxi pulls away. You look over at Camera Guy. He's almost loaded up, he'll be leaving soon too. You start back up the street the way you came. Forget the store. Forget the smokes. Time for bed.

Somewhere, in the distance, a child is crying.

At least, probably.

eleven

Aaron's van hurtles into the tunnel at seventy miles an hour at six-thirty in the morning carrying your motley-looking foursome off to play eighteen holes of golf on a grey, sticky morning that's been threatening to rain since the light came up. Johnny is in front beside Aaron, Henry is in the back seat next to you. A tune from The Reluctants floats from the speakers.

Your brain is still foggy at this ungodly hour. For some reason the words CLOSED CAPTIONED RADIO are spray-painted on the inside wall of the tunnel. The letters are thick, gold with a black contour, shaded as though in 3-D. Very stylish. They've gotten much better, the graffiti people.

Aaron looks over, his hand steady on the steering wheel. Reads it, goes back to the road.

Henry sees it too, frowns. "I don't even get that."

You say nothing. Johnny says nothing. You sip at the coffee you've been holding between your knees until now. Maureen always makes a Thermos of coffee for Aaron to serve on mornings like these. He keeps mugs in the van, and sugar and extra milk if you need it. Somehow it always manages to stay ridiculously hot.

"Nakedly clad women," Aaron says now, to no one in particular.

You and Johnny give him a tight smile. NAKEDLY CLAD WOMEN. This used to be written outside the Amazon club. In those big black plastic letters on those high white signs where the person has to go up on a ladder to change the message each time. Always clumsily spaced out, raggedy, like alphabet soup. It stayed there for a whole winter.

You look over at Henry. A gloomy expression has been etched into his face from the very first. The idea was to get him out of his apartment. Your idea. It wasn't easy. Henry didn't want to. His mother didn't want him to. It was a lot of effort. She's not an easy lady to convince. You had to agree not to talk about the girl. You had to agree to bring him straight back home. A lot of negotiation, you think this as you watch him cradling his coffee between his fingers for warmth, pouting and staring out the window, for something that isn't looking like the greatest of notions so far.

"And I don't see why we're going golfing in the rain anyway," he says. "What's the point?"

Aaron looks back at him. "So grumpy."

"It's going to be all wet."

Johnny says, "It's not even raining. Shut up."

"Right. It's going to wait until we get there."

Johnny sips, doesn't bother to reply.

You say, "You'll feel better once you've hooked a few balls into the woods. And splashed a couple. And played a bit at the beach."

Aaron nods. "You'll be alright once you write that first nine on your scorecard. You're just anxious to get started."

Not that Aaron's such a great golfer. You're better. And Johnny's better than you are. That's why the teams are always Johnny and Henry against you and Aaron. And where Henry is a terrible golfer, Aaron is a terrible cheater. And it's actually harder being partners with the cheater. The day is long. Your rare victories are tainted. When Aaron says his score, often you can't help but wince and Johnny will always glance over at you before writing anything on the card. Then you have to decide if you're going to suggest Aaron count his shots again or point out the proper penalty strokes he's chosen to omit. It can be a drag.

You and Aaron are getting your asses kicked. Johnny's playing great while Henry refuses to blow up, instead taking only sixes and sevens and even three bogies in a row at one point. You and Aaron probably owe thirty bucks each by now, and have just pressed. They then double-pressed to quadruple all bets. Suddenly the balance of money and bragging rights hinges on one hole. Eighteen.

Par four, 414 yards. Long. With a big fat creek running across at 170 yards. This hole plays like a par five to a lot of people.

Henry is not one of them. It usually plays like a par eight to him. He squints down the fairway now, licking his lips and blinking his eyes repeatedly. His brow is furrowed. There is tension. Golf is a game that essentially asks its players to develop, practise, perfect, and then repeat the same action over and over again. It demands that its participants be focused and disciplined. It rewards mental toughness. Why you, Aaron, and Henry even own clubs, then, is something of a mystery.

But today he stands at the tee with a five-wood in his hand.

"Ooh, I smell lay-up," Aaron says.

Henry nods. "That's right."

"I can't believe it."

"Believe it."

"You, afraid of the River of Death? But you *always* go for it."

"Not this time."

Instead of trying to fly the water, Henry's plan is to knock his first shot close and then go over with the second.

"That's smart," Johnny says. "Stay out of the River of Death and we'll take this hole."

You try to dissuade him. "But Henry, beyond the River of Death are the Plains of Sanctity. You've *been there* before. Off the tee. Think of the glory."

Henry shakes his head. "Nope. I'm just going to *bunt* it down the middle."

Aaron removes the cover from his driver, waves it in the air. "Hit the *big stick*, man. It never works when you don't swing full. You know that. You'll pull it or something. You're the kind of guy who has to swing full. You're a *man*. And you definitely don't want to pull your ball on this hole. Reconsider, I beg of you."

"Aaron's right," you warn Henry. "If you pull it on this hole you could end up in the Trees of Perdition."

"I can hit it three-quarters," Henry says, "and still keep it straight."

"Are you sure?" Aaron asks. "The Trees of Perdition are very unforgiving."

"Actually, they're not so bad once you get to know them."

"Henry, you've *tasted* the fruits of the Plains of Sanctity," Aaron says, appealing to him one last time. "They're calling for you. You can do it. Show us."

"No, no. I'll just hit my five-wood," Henry says, bending his knees, extending his arms, and drawing his club back.

He swings. The ball takes off. It's a well-hit ball. Not pulled, like Aaron suggested, but blocked a bit right instead. More of a line drive than Henry planned to hit, surely. It flies about 120 yards then lands and starts to roll. You can see that it will stop safely short of the creek.

That's not the problem. The problem is that if you go that far right on eighteen, there's a strange, ugly growth of a bush before you get to the water. It's big, at least twenty feet around, with leaves and vines and all kinds of shit hanging down in ball-eating fashion. Even if you *see* your ball when you get there, hitting it out is an entirely different matter, and it often leads to even worse second and third shots. Shots that can destroy your whole round in a matter of minutes.

"Uh-oh," Aaron says quietly as Henry's ball bounces towards it. "Not the Bush of Doom…"

"Good God, not the Bush of Doom…" you say in an even more hushed tone.

Henry's eyes are bulging out of his head now.

"Not the Fucking Bush of Doom!"

He screams as his ball disappears into it, throwing his club violently to the ground. It bounces once, twice, ricochets, and ends up leaning against Johnny's pull cart.

You look over at Johnny. He reaches over, picks it up, hands it back to Henry without a word as they cross on the tee box. Henry keeps his eyes on the ground, not at all keen to meet his gaze.

You watch as Johnny addresses his ball. Johnny is the rare athlete who plays everything well. Everything. Johnny *moves* well. Just walking down the street, Johnny prowls like a panther. On a ball field, Johnny moves the way other guys who play sports *think* they move. It's from good genes, two older brothers, and being careful never to let his passion for sports be derailed by any of the other pastimes of life, like getting educated or finding gainful employment.

He coils, unleashes, follows through. Finishes high, like you're supposed to. Watches his ball take flight. Even while it's still in the air, still carrying over the creek, drawing into the left centre of the fairway, he's already bent over, pulling his tee out of the grass. The truly talented don't have to watch like the rest of you plebes do. You guys watch your nice ones all the way to the very last revolution of each ball. Because you have to, because there may never be another. But Johnny knows that his next shot will likely be just as pretty.

"The Plains of Sanctity," Aaron coos, striding up to the tee. "Nice. And here comes another one."

You find yourself grimacing as Aaron rears back, transferring every pound of his huge frame onto his back foot. Something here will go wrong. There are too many moving parts. The club comes forward, a vicious swipe through the air. It's a brutal hook that doesn't even get thirty yards in the air before it dive-bombs back to earth, bouncing a million times on its way towards the Trees of Perdition, exactly what he'd warned Henry about. Mercifully, the ball comes to a stop with less than ten yards to spare.

You walk over, pass him. "Beauty," you say, clapping him on the shoulder.

"Thank you," he says, grateful just not to be in hell.

You take a good long look at where Johnny's lies, set up, and then, after a deep breath, swing for all you're worth. Watch as it launches itself down the centre of the fairway, soaring high up into the air, floating lazily over the water, and then dropping and coming to rest just short of Johnny's. Wow.

Coolly, you walk down off the tee, aware that they're all watching you. You don't crack a smile, you don't meet their eyes. Like all of a sudden you're Joe Serious Golfer, too intent on your game to be distracted by their attention, by their awe at the incredibly fluky fact that on the eighteenth tee, *with the game still on the line*, in a pressure situation where your partner had just drilled a bag of shit into the rough, you actually didn't choke. You too have reached the sacred plains.

You start to walk, Johnny falls into step with you. Aaron hustles past, hurrying to reach his ball before the rest of you, eager to nudge it out of an impossible lie without the weight of your scrutiny.

Henry catches up as well, his old set rattling his arrival. "Nice ball," he says to you as he passes.

"Thanks."

He peels off to face the Bush of Doom.

"Be brave!" you call after him.

"Suck my dick!" he calls back.

Johnny lights a cigarette, offers you one that you wave away. You're into smoking less lately. You trek across the grass in tandem, the walk that guys who hit bullets down the middle get to walk. No dodging trees. No poking around ponds. It's a good feeling.

You squint up ahead to where your balls are, notice that his bullet is actually a good twenty yards beyond your bullet. Man, even when you smack it with all your might. That's what guys like Johnny do, hit it on the screws almost every time. To beat him you have to really bear down and make every single shot. An almost impossible task.

"I was talking to Honey," Johnny says now, in a low voice. Looking directly at you.

Your heart leaps. Lands in your mouth. Instantly you feel your fingers begin to tingle. Droplets of sweat that have been streaking down your back freeze in mid-descent.

"About what?" you croak.

Holy fuck. All day, even from the drive in this morning, even from in bed last night, you'd been wondering if he knew anything. Suspected anything. You were dreading spending all of this day with him. What a rotten thing to say. Your best friend. But by now, who knows what Honey might've said to him. Was she joking when she said she'd tell? Maybe not tell him exactly what happened, but some version. No?

But then if she had, wouldn't Johnny have said something by now? Wouldn't he have done something? Like kill you with his bare hands? Strangle you by your rooster neck until there was nothing left but a gurgling mess? Like Henry's father ended up. Again, maybe not. Johnny's not like that. Someone else would come plowing through your front door. But that's not Johnny's style. Johnny's so fucking cool, isn't he?

"About Baby," he says.

"Baby? What'd Baby do?"

"Baby and me."

Baby. The conversation is about Baby. You fight back a huge sigh of relief.

Honey's sister, Baby. Wispy blond and waif-like. Flighty and selfish to the core. Forever flitting from one melodrama to another. Vain. Dim. And yet irresistible. Especially to you. Honey is taller, fuller, stronger. Prettier. Baby is blonder, paler, thinner. Sillier. The younger sister. But boy, there's something about her. Tiny hips, astonishingly round ass. Apple-firm tennis ball breasts. Where Honey is the magazine ad, Baby is the comic book. You began chasing Baby with your eyes the first night you met her.

"Why were you and Honey talking about Baby?"

"*She* was talking about Baby. About how flirty and everything she is. Easy. You know…"

"No, actually." You fucking *wish* you knew.

"Yeah, but…" He sighs. "But you *know*, you know? What she's saying. Right? Anyways, and then I just, I don't know, *told* her."

"Told her?"

"Yeah."

You both turn towards Aaron, searching for his ball. He doesn't look happy. On the other side of the fairway Henry has parked his pull cart and is poking around the perimeter of the bush with his club. He also looks as though he may have to drop a new ball.

"Told her *what*?"

Johnny says, "You remember when Honey went away that time on training? That whole week? For the nursing thing?"

"Like, three years ago?"

"Right. And you remember how Baby was always around me? Around that time? I mean *always*."

"Uh, I guess."

"Well, she was. Believe me."

Johnny looks at you, raises an eyebrow to emphasize his point. Jesus Christ. Can *everybody* do this?

"Alright, I believe you."

"Right. And, well…there you go."

You look over at Johnny. "Sorry? Where exactly did I go?"

Henry takes a drop and hits a wobbler that gets over the water but not much more. Then Aaron suddenly finds his ball, or at least *a* ball, and before anyone can question it, hits an uncertain liner that also barely makes it over.

Johnny looks at you.

You say, "What do you mean? What're you telling me? You're saying—you and Baby?"

"A few times. Maybe a bunch."

"A bunch of times?" Fuck! When you think of how long you chased her, how hard you worked her. All for nothing. And here's Johnny now, feeding you this shit. "Three years ago?"

"Right."

"And Honey just found out now?"

"A couple of weeks ago."

You look at him. Search his eyes. Though how surprised can you be, really? Now that he says it. Actually. It kind of makes sense. Thinking back.

You search him too for signs of pride. Anybody else, there'd be a smug look, a flash of ego, dropping a bomb like this. Banging a chick like Baby. No matter how dumb an idea it might have turned out to be, any other guy has a glint in his eye when he gets to this part. But not this guy. It's just matter-of-fact here.

In single file you and Johnny walk across the narrow bridge that takes you over the creek, towards your drives.

You shake your head. "How'd she find out? Baby told her?"

"No. From me. Baby doesn't even know."

"From you?"

"Right."

"*You* told her?"

"Yeah."

"That doesn't sound like a good idea."

"It wasn't a very good idea."

"It sounds like a terrible idea."

"It was a very terrible idea."

"I can imagine," you say.

"No, you *can't*…"

And he starts to laugh. Just a bit at first. Then more. Then a lot, to the point where you're grinning and then chuckling along with him. Though you don't why.

"Why," you ask him, "would you do that?"

And of course he just laughs some more. Tears in his eyes. Because he doesn't know. Because he was stupid. Or angry. Or just had to finally say it. Spill it. Trying to prove something? Who knows? Who the fuck knows? What carnage this will bring, what possessed him, where this will go. Just exactly how stupid it was.

But you've got a pretty good view of it, don't you?

You arrive at your ball. Johnny positions himself off to one side.

You choose your club, slide it from your bag. Glance at him once again. He wipes his eyes, laughter subsiding. Smile fading.

You turn away, look down, suck in your breath, and swing. Five-iron. Contact is solid, and the ball takes off on a line. Slowly it rises, climbing, travelling stronger and higher than you expected, though leaking a bit right.

Johnny starts walking. You continue to watch your shot. It's tailing away, but because you've aimed left it's still going at the green. It looks like maybe it even has enough juice to carry the sand trap and land on the right-hand side.

It does, rolling to the back and stopping on the fringe.

As in, you're putting.

Good Lord! A wonderful sight.

You walk over, slide your club back into your bag. Suppress the urge to run naked across the fairway. Instead you pull your cart down to where Johnny is standing.

"So, what're you going to do?" you ask him.

"Do? There's nothing to *do*."

You watch him sizing up the challenge. He is a warrior. There is no doubt. If you could bet on *him*, you would. You think of Honey, wonder what she's doing now. Is she thinking of you? See Aaron and Henry, observing from the edge of the fairway. Is Henry in trouble? Are *you* in trouble? Everyone traces his or her roots back to the friendship between you and Johnny. You go back the longest. Two decades? Almost. Yet in a way, you and Henry are closer. You know everything about each other. Johnny is more secretive, more solitary — but all of you seem to measure your self-worth according to how highly Johnny regards you.

He takes out a seven-iron.

You squint at it. "A seven?"

"That's right."

"You're never going to make it with a seven."

"You don't think so?"

"No."

"Watch then. Behold."

You look over at the flag. "The wind's against us. You know that, right?"

He takes his stance, ignores you. You watch him. There's an absolute elegance to the way he sets himself. The way he fills his golf shirt, chest broad, arms taut yet loose at the same time. Thigh muscles gnawing at the fabric of his black pants. The way Johnny looks in clothes, even fucking golf pants, you'd die to look that good for one day.

He pulls back. Steady, slow, but with purpose. Then whips right back down and completely through the ball, hands continuing up and around, right heel twisting off at the end. The ball shoots straight up at the green. It hangs in the sky for several seconds and then begins its descent, down towards the flag, straighter, well inside your shot, almost directly above the hole, dropping, dropping, then suddenly — *you said* he didn't have enough club — falling short, in front of the green, hopping backwards, and disappearing into the Trap of Despair.

twelve

The way things are in life, at least the way you see it, every single encounter involves a confrontation on some scale. Big ones, medium ones, small ones. Subtle ones. *Mostly* subtle ones. Buying bread at the store. Ordering a meal in a restaurant. Meeting a friend, approaching a stranger. On some level, each act of human interaction evokes an innate decision as to whether to dominate or be dominated. Impose or acquiesce. You either lift your eyes to meet the other guy's or you don't.

And that's just the way you see it. In your lifetime there have been 72,910 confrontations. So far. Of which you have, in your estimation, lost 41,694. And won 31,200. Sixteen draws. A success rate of 38 percent. Based on numbers you're making up right now.

Still, you figure you're not doing that badly. Not everybody's won more than they've lost. Though there's certainly room for improvement in your case. Perhaps if you didn't try so much *less* than everyone else.

Music pounds. Bodies circulate. You watch as the door to the bathroom opens, revealing Johnny. It's Aaron and Mo's bathroom. In Aaron and Maureen's lower duplex. At yet another of Aaron and

Maureen's barbecues. It's only midsummer and already there have been a half-dozen of these.

Johnny clicks the light off and ducks out without even a glance in the mirror as he passes. The door closes lazily behind him. Johnny never looks at mirrors. You've known him enough years, been with him in almost any situation you could name, to know that this is the truth. Not just something you say about someone. He barely checks himself before he goes out of the house in the morning. Stop him in the middle of the day and ask him what colour T-shirt he's wearing, he can't tell you without looking down.

You watch as he saunters into the kitchen, slows down when he sees Honey standing with her hands on her hips, leaning belly first against the counter. Atop it are two bags stuffed full of groceries. Which, based on the look on Honey's face, you're getting the distinct impression Johnny had been entrusted to put away.

"Johnny, why're these bags still sitting here on the counter?"

"I don't know, Hon. Gravity?"

He floats past her on his way to the fridge. Pulls a bottle of beer out for himself and one for you, though you don't need one.

She turns and follows him. "Well, put them away."

Maureen pads into the room, slides in beside Honey. "Here, I'll do it."

Johnny shrugs and smiles at her. "It's just that I don't know where everything goes, Mo."

Honey puts an arm up to ward Maureen away from the bags. "Yeah," she says, "Johnny doesn't know where the *lettuce* goes. Or tomatoes. Or meat. Or the milk." She's lifting one item after another from the bags. "The answer is *in the fridge*, Johnny." She opens the fridge, stacks them inside. "Cold Stuff, in the fridge. Not Cold Stuff, not in the fridge." On this, she pulls open the pantry door next to her and slides bags of buns and chips onto a shelf. "But Maureen understands, of course. Right, Mo? It's just confusing for *him*. We understand. That's where these things usually go, but here, I guess, he thinks maybe it's different. Here, he's not sure, he says. Maybe here, the meat goes in the oven. Or in the sink. Maybe cheese goes in the dishwasher. Is that what it is, Johnny?" She's emptied one bag entirely, folds it, swipes the palms of her hands against it to flatten the edges, a loud sound. "Or maybe here they just leave the groceries in their bags, sitting on the counter in the middle of the kitchen all week long. And everyone just comes over and gets whatever they need. Maybe here, that's the system. A combination of practicality and conservation of energy that you, Johnny, have somehow stumbled upon. Could that be it? Maybe it's *good* that you left the bags here like this. Do you suppose?"

Honey holds his gaze for a last beat then glances at the rest of you. Starts emptying the next bag.

"Nurses on Drugs," Johnny whispers to you. "It's frightening."

Honey stops, squints at him. "Or maybe it's just that face. Maybe he thinks that face is so pretty everyone will just forgive him everything. Could that be it? Could he really think he's that cute?"

"Here," Maureen says, calmly sliding the second bag from Honey. "I'll do it. Sit."

"No, I can do it. But he should be doing it."

"I love you, doll," Johnny says to her. "You're the reason I breathe."

"It *is* the face," you say at this point, inexplicably. "I agree with that."

Aaron comes in, begins digging through a drawer for the tools of the flesh-grilling trade. He pulls out his prongs and flipper, and the long-nosed lighter thingy. He also takes a half-burnt oven mitt, a knife, a fork, and a 7UP.

"Gabrielle's in bed waiting for you to read and Danielle's watching a video," he says to Maureen.

"Aaron?" Honey says. "Should Johnny have to help? Or is he too good-looking?"

"Someone should make patties," Aaron answers, "and bring them to me in about five minutes. And someone else should cut tomatoes and onions."

"Do you need someone to stand beside you smoking and making fun of everybody?" Johnny wants to know.

"Yes."

"Okay, me."

Honey says, "Oh, so now you're going outside?"

Johnny prowls over, eases in towards her, blocks her path of escape. "No, wait. Hold on. I've changed my mind. Instead, everyone go outside with Aaron so Honey can have sex with me here in the kitchen."

She backs up. "Get away from me."

"C'mon, babe — you're always saying you wish we could have sex in Maureen's kitchen."

"I am not —"

"Yes, you are. So let's just do it, then. Now's the time."

Honey rolls her eyes at Maureen. *Don't believe him.* Johnny circles her with two strong arms, guides her in towards him, tries to lick her neck. Maureen barely glances back at them, like this is a TV show she's seen before. She's occupied, pushing a jar of freakishly yellow mustard onto a shelf. Aaron is impatient to go, has what he's come for. He scoops a long box of stick matches into his shirt pocket, paying little attention. You, of course, are enraptured.

Honey wrestles herself free. "Let go of me, you pig! You're spooking me."

Ha! You almost laugh out loud. *Spooking me.* A very Honey thing to say. Perfect.

"But it's what you've always said." Johnny turns now, pleading his sincerity directly at Maureen, flashing big soft eyes. "She's *always* saying it, Mo. How she'd like to get into a hot one right here on your counters. She loves your counters. It's a wood thing, I think."

Honey gently rotates him away from her. "Go now," she says.

"You know, if Honey and Johnny are going to have sex in the kitchen," you say even more inexplicably, "we should be allowed to watch."

Ick. What's *with* you tonight? Maureen glances quickly at Honey. Honey looks at you as though you too have spooked her.

Aaron addresses Johnny. "Besides, I think screwing on our counters is *your* idea, man."

"That's a very sick thought, friend."

"But you've said it to me lots of times."

"Well, I'm a sick guy."

"You've said the same thing to me," you add.

Maureen says, "And me."

Aaron turns to Maureen. "You too?"

"Oh, so what? So have *you*, Aaron. You said you wanted to do the exact same thing." She turns to the rest of you. "He did."

Aaron blushes. Or does he? It's hard to see against the brown skin. He says, "Yeah, but I'm *me*. I'm *allowed* to tell you. We live here. They're *my* counters." He turns to Johnny, wincing at the sight of him now. "Why are you telling her stuff like that, man?"

"I tell anyone that asks."

Aaron slowly turns to glare at Maureen. "You *ask*?"

"No, I don't ask! For God's sake, Aaron."

Johnny says, "Although I have told her tons of stuff. A crazy amount of inappropriate material."

Maureen nods, acknowledging this.

You watch Aaron steady himself against the counter, wipe his brow. It's always hard to know how much he's pretending.

Honey turns to Maureen now. "It's not that I don't like your counters, that's not what I meant. You made a nice choice. But do I want to get naked on them? That's not what I was saying. You know?"

"I understand," Mo says.

"I mean, maybe I have a bit of a wood thing. But did I mean that? Are they that sexy? I don't think so."

"*Let's find out,*" Johnny says, "is my point." He's edging back in towards Honey.

"I understand," Mo says again.

"I mean, I see Johnny and I think, in the bedroom is enough, thanks very much," Honey says to her. "You know?"

Mo giggles. "And I see Aaron and I think, what's on TV?"

You glance at Maureen. Wow. This is about as *go with the flow* as she gets. And usually it takes quite a few more nips of red wine, and it's much later in the evening. Maureen's not your easygoing type. She's not much *into the banter*, not the one usually to help *keep the ball rolling*, or *riff off* anyone, if you will. Doesn't usually *partake of the repartee*. As such. Not really into the *inanity thing*.

Johnny suddenly reaches out for Honey's hips and spins her a half turn so that her back is to his front, and then pulls her into him, against his loins, clamps his greedy hands against her belly, sliding upwards, swelling her breasts full from underneath and nuzzling at her neck.

"What're you doing?!"

"Relax. It's okay."

"Uh, you know what? I don't *think* so." One of her elbows smashes backwards savagely against his chest. He lets her go, dodges a second blow right after it.

"You see?" He grins at all of you now, a safe distance from Honey. "How did I know she was going to do that? That's being a couple. *That's* a bond. It's a special thing we have. We just know each other. It's that simple."

"Don't come near me, you cretin."

"*Cretin!* You see? How did I know she would say that? It's amazing."

Honey folds her arms in front of her, abruptly looks at you. "And what about you, Lee? Are you just going to stand there?"

You try to look cool, buy a few seconds to think of something manly to reply. Johnny is positioned to the side of her now, where she can't see him. Grinning at you like a fool.

You say, "Why, where do you want me to stand?"

She looks at you with that look. Okay, not funny. It's your turn to blush. Because you're thinking, *Now?* You look at her hard. Does she think that you're going to make some kind of stand here, right here? *Now?*

Is she nuts?

Why should you? Why would you? You lower your eyes. You're also feeling weird about Johnny seeing this exchange. Whatever it is that's going on between you and Honey is hard for you to even contemplate at this time. You try to think of anything else, scared to meet Johnny's gaze for more than a second. You begin picking the soggy label from your beer bottle. And these are dangerous thoughts to be having, a tiny part of your brain calls shrilly. You get this way sometimes, wonder if others do too. As though you're suddenly willing to entertain the idea that the person across from you can actually read your mind. Just by the way they're looking at you. It happens to you on buses and in subways, a tickly feeling at the back of your neck that makes it actually seem bizarrely plausible for the briefest of instants that others can hear your thoughts. Which sometimes makes you think obscene thoughts in order to test the person. Like, *What if I smashed my fist into your face?*, or, to a woman, *What if I just leaned over now and kissed you?* Almost shouting it in your mind, to see if they hear it. But of course they don't.

Or they pretend they don't. Right? That's the thing. How can you really know? If they know what you're thinking then they'd know that too — that you're waiting to see what they'll do. Right?

You watched a girl and her boyfriend on the ride into the city a couple of weeks ago. A beautiful girl. Maybe fifteen. Mulatto, if you're still allowed to say that. One of those astonishingly graceful mixtures, a face from heaven. Fully featured yet exquisitely lined, a white woman so clearly black. A soft dimple in the middle of her perfect chin. Light, caramel colouring. Blond, kinky curls spilling from underneath a funky cloth hat. You kept stealing looks every chance you got, finding excuse after excuse to glance towards her. She was with a guy, holding hands and sitting in the seats at the very rear of the bus. Fooling with each other behind the backrest of the seat in front of them. Hands playing, legs wrestling gently. The guy was probably sixteen or seventeen. A skinny guy, like you. Better hair though. Actually great hair. All thick and spiky. And better eyes. And he didn't have a funny nose, the way you do. All right, better-looking all around. But not like *her*. She was a knockout. She was stunning. If you were that guy you wouldn't be able to look at that girl without wondering when she was going to leave you, knowing that you were fated to wake up alone one day and then spend the rest of your life in pathetic remembrance of the angel you once knew.

But this guy didn't seem to be that kind of guy at all. And she seemed happy enough to be with him. For now. What a chick. And then they sort of caught you checking them out and you couldn't really watch anymore, until the bus arrived at the station. When they got out and went inside, you hung back and looked a bit more, at them just walking, not all lovey-dovey anymore, not even holding hands anymore, just casually standing and talking as they took the escalator down, and it came to you once again the incredible difference between your generation and the one that took over from yours, how early they grow up now and how mature they are in a way you never were.

When you were that age, simply being friends with a girl was something you still hadn't figured out. And your buddies were the same. Except Johnny. The rest of you were all geeky and intimidated. Horny and clumsy. And so hopelessly inarticulate that it was best to just stay home with your favourite songs and action movies and Net porn.

Now the two sexes hang out as actual friends, if you're not mistaken. Boys grow up surrounded by push-up bras and bare bellies belonging to girls who are sophisticated and fashionable, coltish young women by the age of fifteen. And yet each of them, both genders, somehow stays in controlled possession of their hormonal rages, interacting with ease, poised, unpanicked. Occasionally engaging in a simple, emotionally indiscriminate sexual release and then getting back to the business of being friends.

Or does it just seem that way to you?

The mulatto girl and the boy eventually separated, exchanging no more than a few words. He, you could see already, heading towards another group of kids at the other end of the platform. She walked alone, passing in front of you, several yards ahead. After a few seconds she turned and looked straight at you, stride unbroken. You stared back, too guilty to avert your gaze. What were you, in her eyes, at that moment? A loser? A pervert? You hoped neither. *I'm not,* you tried to tell her with your eyes. *You might like me if you knew me.* Read my mind.

And then the girl, this teenage goddess, smiled at you. At that very moment. As though she really did know that you meant no harm. Like she understood. That you fell in love with girls on the bus all the time. Girls like her.

Which has nothing at all to do with the way Johnny is looking at you right now. Or anybody reading anybody's mind. As usual, just another derailed train of thought. Where were you? What was the question?

And what's also a bit creepy is, when you first got here this afternoon you distinctly remember yourself staring at this very same large expanse of counter surface right in the middle of the room — one of those island jobs with the pine finish that Aaron installed himself when they pulled down the wall that used to divide their kitchen from the dining room, a five-weekend job that he did with his brother Alex, and even Johnny a bit, with exactly no help from you, an impressive, major undertaking, though a kind of a stupid one too when you consider that they don't even own here, they *rent,* but one that certainly made their place much more fun to hang out at — and so there *you* were an hour ago thinking what would it be like to somehow be alone with Honey, naked and spread out on that giant, erotic chopping block as you suckled and savoured her very deepest culinary delights.

You look at Johnny. Maybe you should bring that up now. Just *work that right in there.* As a segue. *Throw it in the mix.* Go ahead. *Stir the pot.* As it were.

But Johnny has lost interest and is drifting away.

And Honey is looking at Maureen, who has walked over to the doorway where little Danielle now stands. All six-years-old of her.

"I think somebody better come read to Gabrielle," Danielle says, already in her pyjamas, using her big-little-girl voice to refer to her four-year-old sister.

Maureen says, "Okay. I'm coming, darling."

She leaves with Danielle while Aaron leaves for the backyard and that pretty well breaks it up, everyone splitting to do their thing, yours primarily being to stay the hell away from Honey, whom you just don't *trust* tonight. She has that sadistic look about her.

You move down the hallway. The doorbell rings, announcing Stacy and Graham. Then Baby and a red-headed friend, a heavily freckled guy you've never seen before. And finally, Henry.

thirteen

You're handing out dope left and right. Free barbecue dope. Half-gram pieces from a so-so batch you got stuck with at the beginning of summer. You do this sometimes, on nights like this. It's no big deal, you sell to these same people week in week out. And their friends. And their friends' friends. You make a whack of money from all of them. It's public relations. It doesn't really bother you. You don't mind. You do it happily. Though, of course, they could at least *offer* to pay once in a while. Fucking mooches.

You watch Henry as he sets up a small spliff-rolling lab on the picnic table, his baseball cap propped on one side to provide shelter from the light wind, his cigarette pack serving as an operating table. He burns the dark lump quickly on one edge and then scratches flakes and dust down onto the tiny sheet of rolling paper. He adds clumps of tobacco squeezed from the end of a cigarette, twists it closed, and puts it behind his ear. With the tip of his finger he mixes the black and gold together, then takes the paper between his fingers, balancing it like a canoe on water, until his practised thumbs roll it into a tiny white cylinder, tobacco bits poking out at the ends. With a quick lick of his tongue he seals it along the glue strip and then folds one end closed.

Finally, as Johnny watches and Aaron salivates, Henry picks up his cigarette pack and tears a tiny rectangle of cardboard from the inner flap, where it will not show. He curls this into a spiral filter which he fits into the open end. Lights the spliff and draws in, passes it. Johnny takes it from him. Henry leans back and slowly exhales, the thick smoke gradually escaping from his mouth the way steam wafts up from a sewer.

It will only be seconds before it takes hold. Because Henry is the most far gone he will seem the least affected. Henry can ingest enormous quantities without it visibly altering his manner. He no longer needs drugs to disconnect, as Honey likes to say. He has only to wake up in the morning. There is permanence.

Johnny is different, stronger mentally. He'll smoke every day and never lose control, going toke for toke with whoever's around, and then suddenly refuse to touch it for a week straight. Bark at you for even offering. This is his idea of discipline.

Aaron is a different animal altogether. Father of two, married to Maureen since they were eighteen. A big hombre, like two-fifty. Exhausted at the end of the week after forty hours loading and unloading produce trucks. Grimy from the pallets and jiggers, reeking of putrid tomatoes and rancid berries. And on the weekends he and his brother have a small moving business driving a cube truck they co-own. Small moves, local moves, midnight moves. They'll work both days during the busy season. Leaving Aaron exhausted and sore at the end of the weekend too. And still he and Maureen never have enough money. The girls need clothes. The house needs fixing.

Aaron is also a recovering alcoholic. Reluctantly so. Since he was twenty-two. A huge bummer, really. Because if you're going to spend the rest of your life pining for something, you should have at least spent a large part of the front end enjoying it. Aaron blew it way too soon. It seemed like overnight it was a choice between a very pregnant Mo and the debauchery, violence, and blackouts. And not that it wasn't a pretty close call, by the way. But at least he made the right one. Except now, at the end of a sweaty day, there's no cold beer waiting. It's carefully gritted teeth and a kiss on the top of the head for the kids. Fall asleep in front of the TV. And the knowledge that he has to go out and do it all again the next morning.

And, of course, dope. Of which he is a *sincere* fan.

The joint arrives with little left. Enough for one last set of lips, yours. Perfect. Where Aaron is militant about always getting off like a herd of turtles, you've always been a nibbler and a dabbler. You appreciate the mind expansion, don't dig the loss of control. This will do you fine for many hours. Unlike everyone else tonight, you haven't smoked yet. You've been *saving* it. The first hit is the deepest. As everyone knows. The rest just chase the first one. The first one, that's where the *joy* is.

You inhale. Swallow. Feel it burn.

This hash is better than you remember it. A good taste. You recognize the quick rush. The world, just a few degrees to the left of where it was a second ago. The molecules come out. Everywhere. This is what you see. Air suddenly filled with a million quintillion infinitesimal agitating dots. All around. In every direction. In every beam of light, every open space. In the air. Dancing specks of matter. Suddenly you can actually *see* the molecules of life. Friendly, warm. You bask in them. You've asked others, in the past. If they see them too. Do you see the dots? Several have said yes, they see them. But you don't think they have. Not the way you do.

"Lee. Dude!"

If you're not mistaken, that's you.

"wHAt?"

"You alright?"

"i'M fiNe," you say too quickly.

Aaron gives you a look. A quick surge pulses through you, with just a hint of paranoia. Funny how it still gets to you. Sometimes. After all these years. The brief panic, the utter loss of confidence. Getting too high too quickly. Unsure what to say, convinced everyone is staring at you. You glance from Aaron to Henry, too chicken to check if Johnny is watching you.

"NoTHinG," you say to Aaron, answering a question that hasn't been asked. "WhEN do wE EaT? eVERyOne's hUNGry..."

He pays no attention to you. Moves back in front of his barbecue. Next to him is a platter of bumpy little burgers. Overcooked and ready way too early, as always. A mound of little black discs. Only the NHL logos are missing.

On the grill, one of his steaks has caught fire. You see him sizing up the situation. He lights a cigarette, preparing to do battle. Henry is watching, and Johnny too. Aaron suddenly seizes the metal spatula and begins jabbing at the meat, chiselling at its edges, wedging one side up then the other. Over and over until the flames snuff out. A second later the one beside it is ablaze. He punishes this one as well, hacking at it, grinding beneath it, tearing meat from metal until the fire subsides. Precisely as the one next to it lights up. With a visible sag in his shoulders he shifts his attention there. As the one beside it catches fire. And then the first one sparks up again.

The three of you observe this without comment. Through it all Aaron is smoking, his eyes glazed, constantly mopping the sweat from his face. Finally, Henry reaches up and pulls the cigarette from between his lips. It seems a small act of mercy. Ashes have been tumbling down onto the meat. You look away. It's hard to watch.

Johnny turns away as well. He is scanning the yard. Looking for a better class of person to hang out with. It reminds you suddenly of being at concerts with him. Specifically of one show. Several years ago. You remember the music vaguely, some sort of glam-band reunion. Getting together to play the old hits. One of those shows that always sounds like such a great idea until you get there.

There were people wall to wall. Besides you and Johnny, there was Aaron and Maureen and Henry and Cuz too. Honey wasn't there, but Baby was. You'd begun seeing a girl named Dagmar and she was there too. A real weeper that one, she'd cry over anything. Together you'd tried your best to make your way through the corridors and stay intact, a tiny gauntlet of friends struggling its way past the throng of bodies. Johnny led the way. It seemed like every single person in the stadium held a plastic beer cup in their hands, the relentless slosh of suds splashing all around you. People shifted like cattle from one waiting point to another. The dull metallic roar of the opening band bled through the walls. Maureén held tightly on to Aaron's arm, as you remember, the whole time you moved along. Really tugged on it. This was before Aaron got dry and these could be long, hard nights for her.

You'd angled yourself to fall in step with Baby, eased yourself in beside her. "I don't even know why I'm here," you'd said casually, or something equally cavalier. "Why does everyone come to these things? These guys haven't written a new song in ten years. They're going to play four tunes we've heard a million times on the radio, and about twenty others we couldn't care less about. And make all that money. How does that make sense?"

"I'm going to buy a T-shirt!" Baby said, pressing ahead of you.

Inside the arena it was dark. You were at floor level when you hit the final wall of bodies. There was no choice but to split up. General-admission mayhem. Cuz took off. Aaron and Mo moved in one direction. Henry and Dagmar huddled briefly on another side. Unable to locate you, each scared to end up alone. You should have rejoined them but didn't. Instead, under cover of darkness, you hugged the boards and moved off in the direction Baby had taken. But when you caught up with her, Johnny was there. And it felt uncomfortable. You'd interrupted them with your presence.

You feigned innocence at bumping into them, then pretended to be surprised that Dagmar was not with them. A surge of bright white light and a deafening explosion jolted the building at that moment, as the first act launched into its final tune. You remember the look Baby gave you before she turned away to watch. Nothing short of disgust, and a desire to see you go. And Johnny's. He could read your mind.

He looked at you in such a pitiful way. Annoyed. Mad at you for being stupid and obvious. Embarrassed that you'd ditch your girlfriend so cruelly to chase after Baby. It went through you like a knife.

There has always been an unspoken understanding between Johnny and you. Girls like him. A lot. You, not so much. It isn't debated. And there is no posturing otherwise. You try not to complain about it much and he never lords it over you. That's the deal. And whenever he can, he steers something your way. If it makes sense. This is the arrangement. It keeps the relationship on a quasi-equal footing, and the friendship endures. Of course part of the deal is also that you behave with a certain amount of dignity.

Avoiding situations like that.

There was nothing to do but slink away, hide yourself in the masses. You can still recall the ache of shame in your chest. The way you'd had to jam your fists into your jeans, backpedal the first few steps, and then teeter off. Knowing they were watching you, exchanging looks. You've thought of it a thousand times since then.

During the intermission you caught up with Dagmar, but by then she was mad and crying and the night was ruined. She sobbed again on the way out, refusing to speak to you. Then together you came across Henry in the parking lot in an awkward situation with a girl he'd met who wanted now to leave and rejoin her friends — with Henry not accepting this news terribly well. Not meanly, but insistent and clingy, desperately hanging on to the girl's arm. You'd had to walk over to where he'd cornered her between two cars and gently pull his hand from hers, set her free. Keeping Henry at bay with soothing words. It was then that Dagmar had cooled off, managed to see you for what you truly were. A jerk, of course. But less of one than Henry. God bless him. So, maybe you could be salvaged. And in fact it straightened you out for a bit. You'd had a hard time mistreating Dagmar for a good while afterwards.

You remember it like it happened yesterday. Can only cringe a last time, expel it from your mind. Try to think of something else.

Purge it. But not before you realize — this time — that this is what Johnny was talking about on the golf course. Johnny and Baby had been *together* that night.

=

You spy Honey inside, near the kitchen. Make your way up the back stairs. Against your better instincts. Sidle up to her. You can tell right away that she's had a few. She slurs a smile your way and steals closer.

"Hi sweetie," she says.

"What's up?"

"I was looking for you."

"Were you looking hard? I was here."

"I was waiting till you were alone."

You nod. "I was with others."

"Mmn. You were."

"But not now."

"No."

Stacy and Graham pass nearby. Neither of you speak until they have moved away.

Honey asks you softly, "Are you going to leave with me tonight?"

"Leave with you?"

"Yes."

"Go back to your place?"

"Yes."

"You're not working?"

"No."

You look around. "Even though Johnny's here?"

"Especially because."

Your breath catches at the top of your throat. You swallow, displace it. "Really, tonight?"

"Yes."

"Together?"

"Yes."

"Sneak back to your place?"

Her eyes snap back in her head. Her expression clouds. "Not sneak back. Walk back. Walk out. The front door."

"With you?"

"With me."

The challenge. Again with the challenge.

She waits, watching you.

You collect your thoughts. Formulate your rebuttal. And then, in a measured tone, say, "But I can't, Hon."

"You could."

"I can't."

"You don't want me?"

"I do."

"You don't care."

"I *do*. That's why."

"*What's* why? Are you afraid of Johnny?"

"No."

"That's not what it is?"

"No — it's for you."

"I don't think so."

"It is. It's...to protect you."

"*Protect me?* Are you joking, Lee?"

You've surprised yourself. Hadn't thought you would do this tonight. Fuck with her like this. But how else to get out of it?

And so in a teasing voice you say, "But Honey, darling. Please. Listen to me. I couldn't bear to see you get hurt...again."

She looks at you. Smart enough not to speak right away.

"I mean, if I left...and you left..."

She's watching you closely.

"...that would leave just Johnny...and Baby...together."

She looks at you.

Long.

One of those looks where you know the other person needs a little time to decide what the right thing to say next is. So you give it to her.

She speaks, finally. "Well, it's not that simple."

You say nothing. Not sure what it is you really feel.

She takes a sip of her wine, eyes you once more. Another long look. This one is meant to sway you, convince you, seduce you, convert you. And it's working. There is, there is no question of it, a power to her beauty. As you may have already mentioned. It's hard to withstand her overtures. You wonder, because she's drunk, does that mean it's more likely, or less likely, that she's lying to you? And are you both talking about the same thing here? Because you want to hear her say it. She's snuggled in real close now, breasts pushing up against your poor defenceless elbows. You want to know if all this is because she found out Johnny slept with Baby. Or is it more?

And then a scream tears through the house. An actual scream. Sounding just like Baby. And then another one. And it *is* Baby. Not as shocked the second time. More excited.

You tense and hold. Honey grabs your arm. You both look around. It's a bit eerie, as though Baby has been listening to you or something. Or everyone was. You hear people scrambling, up the stairs, into the house, dashing towards the living room. Stacy and Graham rush past. Maureen and Aaron. Johnny. Baby's red-headed friend, the Freckle King. What a face, like someone threw coffee in it. Even Cuz, you notice with dismay, is still here. Along with cohorts Sanderson and Dane. What dupes. Somehow they joined in when you weren't paying attention.

You and Honey ease in at the back of the room. In time to see Baby standing in the middle of it, pointing at the TV.

At your image.

Your head and shoulders fill the screen. The camera wobbles, the light against your face is harsh. You see yourself smile and say, "*No, but I've seen him throw up so much beer on the street that it flowed twenty feet until it found a sewer.*"

They cut back to reveal Liz Hunter standing beside you. Henry's apartment building can be seen faintly in the background.

She sighs, looks at the camera, and says, "Clearly, no answers are immediately at hand."

The image holds for a second and then dips to black.

A commercial comes on.

fourteen

The rest of the evening is, of course, a classic. For you. You float from back clap to handshake. A welcome smile greets you at every turn.

You are a star. Baby is in awe. Johnny is jealous. Aaron is amused. As is Stacy, and to a lesser degree Graham. Maureen seems the least pleased. Henry has eased into the background. And the red-headed kid is still, well, so relentlessly freckled.

Baby clues you in on what you missed. Her friend, Tim — his name is Tim, it turns out, a very speedy guy — helps. What they saw was short clips of you along with photos of Darlene and faraway shots of Henry. Plus parts of an interview with Darlene's mother, and Darlene's friend, the girl with the permed curls named Naomi Byrd. Both extremely distraught. Pleading with the public.

And then you came on, right after them. Leering, smiling.

Joking up a storm with Liz Hunter.

Oh.

You smile at them too, now. *Ah, but that's what you wanted to do,* you explain. *That's* how you were showing how ridiculous it all was. By acting that way. Part of the plan.

Tim nods fervently, eager to agree. "Well, you did sound stupid."

"*Very,*" Baby says.

They tell you what else Liz Hunter said. That she thinks the problem is no one follows a story like this because it's just some girl from the streets and there are so many. And there's no clean hook. No one really knows what happened. And the police don't have time. But she, Liz Hunter, has time. She won't give up. Something just doesn't feel right. Hers is just a small show, Tim says, a local specialty channel thing. But she thinks it's with causes like these that you can break through.

"Causes?"

"Cases."

"Wow. She said all that?"

"Tim's majoring in Communications," Baby informs you. "He might work in news when he gets out. But maybe movies instead."

"Wow," you say. "How vitally important."

"It's how they edit it," he explains. "They shoot you like crazy but use just the smallest bits of it. Cut up and juxtaposed against other bits. And then they bridge it with snippets of narration — *he seemed on edge, eager to confuse me* — and mix in quirky music, until what you meant to say and what comes out aren't the same thing."

"I see," you say, looking around for a means of escape.

"It's all ratings. That's what you have to remember. It's numbers. The story matters only if viewers decide it matters. It's not a system designed to mete out justice. It's strictly interested in what's new. What's hot. Or what's *old*, as long as what's old involves a degree of celebrity. As long as we remember you from the last time. To the point that just being on TV can be a guarantee you will be on it again. Because it's about itself, in the end."

"I see, sure." By now you're barely hiding the fact that you're no longer listening. Yeesh. All that red hair. It must make you break out in blotches and opinions. *It's all ratings.* Ooh. What an expert. How many people have you heard say this in your life? It's All Ratings. Simpletons. As though with this one sweepingly obtuse statement they've pronounced their understanding of all things television. Given us their expertise. Like people who say, It's Just Business, or, It's All Connections. Or, Everything's About Money. These people, of course, always turn out to be the people who understand things *least*.

Baby and Tim turn and look down from the balcony to see Henry, who has come into view. Aaron's backyard spotlight has detected motion and suddenly lit the area up. He's near the trees at the side, alone on the grass. He looks up at everyone, a forlorn figure. It's hard to know if he was there the whole time or saw the broadcast and then retreated. You realize you should go down to him.

But before you can do anything, you — and everyone else — hear Maureen bawling out Aaron. "No. He has to go, Aaron! *I don't care.*" Down the corridor to your left you can see Aaron doing the 225-Pound Pussy-Whipped Man's dance, hopping from foot to foot, circling her with his arms straight out in front of him, pleading, trying to convince her to relax.

"Now!" you hear her shriek, even louder. You're guessing it's not working. He looks desperately around him, sees you watching. "I don't want him here!"

You move out of view. There's not much that can be done. Maureen, everyone knows, is a mother bear. She gets out of bed each morning convinced that something terrible is sure to befall one of her little girls that day. She is on guard about it, on the prowl over it. Paranoid about it. And so now: a missing girl, Henry, your kisser on TV. These events send seismic shivers down the spine of someone like her. This should not be in the vicinity of Gabrielle and Danielle.

Maureen is harsh this way. She doesn't talk to her sister anymore, for example. Ever. Not even a bit. The sister's name is Pamela. Six years ago, when Maureen and Aaron had Danielle, Pamela had her son Ivan. They were buddy mothers, always doing everything together, absolutely everything, including making a pact to have a second child right away. Well, fifteen months later Maureen had Gabrielle, and Pamela had, um, second thoughts. At first she made it sound like it just wasn't happening, but eventually Maureen learned the truth. That they'd decided against it. Pamela's husband Howard had received a promotion but would have to start travelling more and they'd changed their minds.

Now, every month, Aaron and Maureen scramble to settle their bills, slapping down eleven hundred dollars a month to live in a place they don't even like much, raising their two little girls, exhausted at the end of each day, sliding a little deeper into debt at the end of each year. While Pamela and her husband just bought a pretty little house in a very safe neighbourhood and go on a vacation to the Caribbean every year. And this doesn't sit well with Maureen.

You walk down the stairs into the backyard. The spotlight has gone off. Henry eases over to the other side of the grass, in your direction. He looks pale, even in the semi-darkness. With the exception of the golf, Henry's barely left his house in the past few days. Stayed away from everybody, cameras and friends alike. Now tonight he's ventured out, as though to find out if there's still room for him. Held his breath and mingled. You saw him all night, on his best behaviour. Chit-chatting, though he never chit-chats. Sipping, though he never sips. Smiling and nodding, sniffing the wind.

And now this.

Aaron comes to the edge of the balcony. Hesitates before coming down the steps, enough for you to hold him back with a motion of your hand. He puts his own hands out at his sides, shrugs, brow furrowed. The international signal for just having gotten your ass reamed by your wife.

You look over at Henry. The truth is, Maureen's just saying what everyone's been whispering.

Others come to the windows to look down at him. It's evident on each face that no one really knows *what* to think about Henry and this sordid rumour. And so maybe staring at him now will help them decide.

You turn and lead Henry around to the right, towards the side gate. The quickest exit available. As another fucking spotlight goes on.

Man. What the fuck is Aaron so intent on protecting? A twelve-year-old van? He owns *nothing*. It's very annoying to get lit up like this.

From behind, you hear Cuz say loudly, "Good! Let them go."

"Freaks!" Sanderson calls.

You continue forward, open the metal latch of the gate.

"Get gone, boys!" Dane says.

"It's okay, Mo," you hear Cuz call over to her, as though he's some kind of close friend of Maureen's. "They're leaving. Goodbye, assholes!"

And so you stop. In your tracks. At the last possible step.

Turn to look at Cuz. Know he'll be looking back.

And he is. Staring at you. Teeth gritted, jaw clenched. Small animal snorts rumbling at his nostrils.

Sanderson and Dane lurking at his side.

You are aware that one word from you — one word — and Cuz comes barrelling down those steps and diving at your throat. With Sanderson and Dane right behind him. And you know that you'll have your hands more than full, and the beer and the wine and the joint won't help. And neither will Henry. For sure, Johnny will come to break things up, but not that quickly and maybe not until you've had a good number of your teeth kicked down your throat. You're doing all these calculations rapid-fire in your head, aware that time is running out.

Finally you scowl and turn away, waving your hand resignedly, trying to save face. But nothing more than that. Unwilling to risk it. And then you and Henry duck around the corner and out front to where his mother's car is parked.

41,695 career losses.

You get in the car beside Henry. Wait while he starts it up, adjusts his seat, fidgets, and fixes his mirrors. How could they have changed since he last parked? You feel yourself getting impatient. Angry. You remind yourself to relax, that blowing a fuse on Henry has never solved anything before.

You wait until you're out on the road and several streets away.

"Okay," you hiss at him. "Tell me the truth now. Do you know what happened to her?"

A pause. Then, "No."

"Did you hurt her?"

"No."

"Do you know where she is?"

"No."

He turns the corner, nearly side-swipes a city truck. Straightens the car out and aims it in the proper direction to drop you home.

"Henry, is she dead?"

"No!"

You sit back, stare ahead at the road. You pass several streets.

"Alright, forget it then," you say.

He nods softly, says nothing.

"I'm sorry," you say.

He nods again, stares straight ahead. Bites his bottom lip like he's fighting back tears. Won't look over at you. Good. Best he keeps his eyes on the road anyway.

fifteen

Sam Spayed wakes you, chirping her way down the stairs. It's a week later. You realize you forgot to close the door to the roof again. Left it open all night. Not that anyone would come in really, but your rooftop does border several others. And there's a metal staircase that is accessible from the ground. But how else would that dumb cat ever get in if you didn't leave the door open sometimes?

Now she jumps up on the bed and picks her way across the bumpy-legged comforter, making her way over your bodies and up to your face. She sniffs your nose. Negotiates her way over to Honey. Sniffs her. Honey lifts a lazy arm to stroke her behind the ear where she likes it.

Sam. Best cat ever.

She leaves and you both sprawl out, spread yourselves across the bed. Honey throws off the comforter with one leg, folds her arms behind her head. Her other leg traces its way over the sheet and up across your body, comes to rest on your stomach.

You take it in your hands, kiss the lovely full calf. "Hon…?"

"Mmn…"

"If we were on a desert island, let's just say…you know, imagine you and I were stranded on a desert island, all alone…"

"Mmn…"

"And there was nothing. Like no civilization. No food or shelter or huts or anything."

She's listening. She's half asleep but she's listening. You're still kneading her gorgeous calf, running your tongue lightly along the soft underbelly.

"And we're on this hot, sandy, tiny desert island," you say again.

"Right…"

"Just the two of us."

"Mmn." She gives you a dreamy little smile.

"Well, I just thought…I just wanted to say…"

"Yes…"

"…that…"

"…yes…?"

"…you'd be delicious."

And you give her calf a big fake bite. She squeals, laughs, tries to pull away. But you have a firm grip.

"That's sick."

"It's not."

"It is!"

"But sweetie, there's no food on the island…"

You cook her breakfast, watch her from the kitchen. She's reading your newspaper sitting cross-legged on your bed, perched above the dust and disarray. She's found the one place here that's not overrun with the physical litter of your life.

You'll tease her over with a three-cheese omelette. You have only one kind of cheese but you'll put in three times as much. One of your rare domestic skills. Cooking eggs. Making a killer spaghetti sauce. Plunging a toilet no matter how backed up. There aren't many others.

You stand at the stove cracking eggs, wearing only a pair of jeans. Bare-chested, bare feet. How daring of you. Exposing your body this way. Even your toes are skinny. You sense her watching you. It makes you feel good. Sam pads over. You crank open a can of her food and plop it into her dish, still in the shape of the tin. You go to the sink and run the water to wash out what's left so you can recycle it. Feeling hip the whole way. You recycle. Isn't that cool of you? Honey got you doing that. You soap your hands. Rinse them. Dry them, smell them. Wash them again, really work them, until they smell fresh and clean. Finally go back to the eggs. You're aware that Honey has monitored every step of this without appearing to. Either you scrub your fingers like a surgeon or she won't come within ten feet of your omelette, this you know. Chicks are touchy that way.

You eat the eggs. You have one smoke the whole morning. Pretty good. Excellent, really. You're smoking a lot less. She has, like, eight. It's starting to smell a bit gross in here to you. You eat and read, mostly silent. Usually when you start seeing someone it's a bit scary when no one speaks for any significant period of time. You've known Honey for far too long for this to be the case, regardless of what's changed. And so, what a couple you feel like. What a feeling. Every fifteen minutes or so it hits you what's happening. Honey Zamner. And you. After all. In the end.

It's too much.

Imagine they came to your door one day to tell you you'd won the lottery, except you'd already stopped buying tickets. That's what it feels like. And it seems even more real here at home, the two of you doing absolutely nothing. It's so boring, it's exciting. It's so relaxed, it's intense.

You eat and shower, dress and go out. It's a beautiful day. You don't have her car because Johnny still has it. It seems like Johnny always has it. It doesn't matter, it's better this way. Walking. It'll take longer to get wherever you're going.

Honey's hand reaches down to find yours, her fingers snaring your fingers, tangling them up. She wears big rings. The kind of rings that look plastic and toy-like, silly in the store, until you see them on a girl like her. She bounces when she walks. Just a little bit, up and down. It's fun. It's cute. You have to check yourself sometimes to make sure you're not bouncing along with her.

What day is it? Thursday. What to do? She wants to go to the cinema. The cinema. It's fun the way she says it. The Cinema. Who says that? It's cute. It's fun. Everything she does is cute. She's gorgeous. She has a tiny overbite and ever so slightly crooked front teeth. They look even more fabulous today. The way they push her top lip out ever so slightly. That's her thing. Everyone has a thing. Henry had a strangled father. Honey, it's those teeth. The girl with the million-dollar overbite. It sets her apart from everyone else the first time you meet her, and every time after.

She tells you the movies she wants to see. They're all stupid. You tell her so. She laughs, insists anyway.

"But why can't it be a romantic comedy? Why can't it ever be a romantic comedy? I *like* them."

"It just can't."

"One day I'm going to find a boy who likes romantic comedies."

"Yes. And he'll be dating your brother." This is a dumb thing to say. And she doesn't even have a brother. "Anyways, I'm sorry. I just can't do the romantic comedy thing. I can do the Shop-With-You-All-Day-If-I-Have-To thing. And even the Slightly-Change-The-Way-I-Wear-My-Hair-For-You thing. Or the Throw-Out-Half-The-Furniture-In-My-Place-And-Buy-Everything-From-Ikea thing. But not the Pretend-To-Like-Stupid-Movies thing. I just can't."

She punches you in the shoulder. It hurts. You wish she wouldn't do that. Johnny punches you in the arm a lot. She gets it from him.

But you don't end up at the cinema. You don't do much of anything really. Except stop for coffee. And rent a video that you might watch later. And buy bagels that no one wants to carry. And all the while you've got this chick on your arm, and you're loving it, man.

Eventually you end up in Old Montreal. Her mother has called and asked to meet for lunch. Her mother rarely comes into the city, it's hard for her to say no.

"Will you come with me?"

"I'm not sure I want to sit in a restaurant for the next hour with your mother and you," you say.

"Don't then."

"But I'm not into leaving either." You peck her on the top of the head. You've been sneaking each other kisses all day. "I want to be with you every moment."

"Then stay."

"Call your mom back instead. See her another day."

She brushes the hair from in front of her eyes. "No, Lee. Today."

Honey's family has money. It's one of the reasons she's so sure of herself. She's very cocky. They're from Europe. The Zamners. She's actually Hanni. And her sister's real name is Babette. Honey says having rich parents isn't why she's so sure of herself, but you know it has a lot to do with it. People with money never admit that it's because they have money.

In Honey's case it is a bit different. Honey's father is already very old and very cranky and he says he won't give them any of it until he dies. He believes the later in life they get it the more it will benefit them. The wiser they'll be with it. This drives Baby nuts but Honey doesn't seem to mind. Honey says she sort of agrees with him and you have to believe her. She says that knowing it's there brings her more peace than having it — and none of the problems of doing the right thing with it. Honey's father says he doesn't want them to have anything until both he and Honey's mom die, actually, but you're pretty sure that Honey's mom has already told him he can go fuck himself about this. You know she already funnels the girls bits on the side.

Baby, on the other hand, believes there would be no problem having the money right now and deciding what to do with the money right now because the right thing to do with the money is to, um...spend the money! This would be a fairly typical Baby way of seeing things. Baby's usually wrong about things and Honey almost always isn't.

You're walking on St-Paul. It's quaint and touristy but mostly just touristy. The traffic is barely moving because everyone's following a calèche toddling its way down the middle of the street. A horse pulling a buggy with big wooden wheels is not your most modern form of transportation, not to mention that this horse is about the same age as Mr. Zamner. You've got to be a masochist to own a car in this part of town. And if you're not stuck behind a horse, they've blocked the street because they're shooting some shitty American movie here. Set, undoubtedly, in Europe. The skinny cobblestone streets and old buildings make it a dead ringer for Paris or Moscow or any number of nineteenth-century sites. The architecture is remarkably intact. If you squint your eyes you can almost see the peasants peddling fruits and furs on the banks of the St. Lawrence River. Well, if you squint your eyes and smoke a big fattie.

Honey tugs at your wrist while a car horn complains in the background. "Give me a bagel."

"You had a bagel. Good God, woman. How much do you eat?"

"Let's pick up another coffee then."

"Another coffee? It's not night shift. How can you possibly want another coffee?"

She lights a cigarette. Doesn't even offer you one. Rude.

You take her hand again. "Tell me why," you say abruptly, whispering it into her ear.

You reach a corner. Walk across the cobblestone. A man wearing a ridiculous beret is waiting at the opening of a vendor lane. He's sitting on a stool next to an easel with his caricature sketches on display behind him.

"Nice hat," you say to him.

He looks at you quizzically. Like he doesn't understand. Is this possible? After all, almost the whole city speaks French. *Français.* You anglos are a decided minority. So while it *could* be that he doesn't speak English, of course it isn't. Not by a long shot. Not down here. Not with all the American dollars to be had.

Honey has been quiet this entire time.

"C'mon…" you prod her.

She ignores you. You walk a bit more.

"Okay, tell me *one* reason," you say. "For me. Or against him. Your choice."

She rolls her eyes but you know she will.

"What I will tell you," she says eventually, "is how you're the most different. What makes you so different."

"How we're *so* different? Me and Johnny?"

"Yes."

"Uh, no. Thanks."

"I'll tell you that you're softer. That Johnny's harder and rougher. And when you're together a long time, that's a *long* time, you know? Softer is not a bad thing. Rough is a bit much all the time."

"Rough?"

"I don't mean rough. I mean gruff. Harsh. Always having to win. Rough on people, even weak people. Everything is to the death. Even a conversation. I never see you do that, keep pushing at someone even when they've already lost."

"I do that. Everyone does that."

"No. You're softer. I think you care more when you see someone who's hurt. You're a more vulnerable person and that makes it harder for you to be mean."

"Johnny's not mean."

"You have a soft part to you. A feminine side."

"Okay please, don't…" You croak this out. You can feel your balls actually crawling up inside you. In fact you can taste them too. "I don't want to be Soft Vulnerable Guy."

Together you step up onto a last stretch of sidewalk. At the end of this block are the good restaurants.

"You're different, Lee. You're sad and desperate and always trying to figure everything out. In a good way."

"In my soft way."

"Johnny doesn't try to figure anything out," she says.

"Johnny doesn't need to. Everything's figured out."

"He thinks so, doesn't he?"

"What's wrong with that? Exactly?" You take her hand again. "I'm not trying to be sarcastic. Is it so bad? It bugs you, I guess."

A motorcycle pulls out of the jam, accelerates past the horse and its passengers. Its tires sound fat and wet against the hot stone.

"Maybe you're right," she says. "Do you think you're right?"

You say, "He doesn't have time to stop and calculate things. He's just one of those guys who's always sort of moving forward. Instinct and adrenalin. I don't have to tell you. "

"I guess so. That's what everyone says." She squeezes your fingers in her hand. "But it's difficult to find room around Johnny sometimes. There's so many people there. His brothers and his mother and his father all the time and all the guys from the sports teams. And you guys." She gestures around her. She means you and Henry and Aaron and all. "But not with you. You're sort of always off to the side. I guess because you want to be. I think everyone knows this about you. Nobody thinks they know you well at all, did you know that? Yet I feel like whenever I came to see you, you always had time for me."

"That's us effeminate loners," you say. "Our schedules are usually open."

You think, Time for her? Who wouldn't have time for her?

A man carrying two briefcases and wearing an earpiece passes, talking in a language that can't possibly exist. Honey waits until he is out of earshot before continuing her thoughts. Unnecessarily, you feel, seeing as neither of you is speaking Zorgon.

"Come on." She takes your arm. You're in front of a bistro that serves big salads and pressed veggie sandwiches and you just know this is the place she's meeting her mother. "You want to know exactly

YOU comma Idiot

145

why. I can't tell you why. I can tell you things and you can decide if they are the things that can help you figure out why. And if you figure out why, you can tell me too."

You see her squinting though the glass to see if her mother is inside.

"Are you going to eat with us or not? Maybe you should just, you know, not. Or maybe you should. It's up to you. Hey, want to know another one?" She looks you square in the eyes. "Another difference? You're a better kisser."

You don't know what to say. Who would?

She waves through the window to her mother. "Are you coming in or not? There she is."

Honey's mother is standing at a small reception bar. She is, as they say, a handsome woman. As Honey will one day be. She is expecting to meet her daughter for a quiet lunch. It seems an obvious moment to be on your way.

sixteen

So instead you follow Honey inside. The maître d' leads you through to the giant terrace out back. Mrs. Zamner doesn't seem to mind at all that you join them.

Honey lights a smoke. Her mother lights a smoke. You light a smoke, what the hell. They smoke like chimneys these people. Haven't they heard of lung cancer in Europe?

"Mom," Honey says. "You know Lee."

"Of course," Heidi Zamner replies.

"You remember him. Doesn't work. Janitor of the building he lives in. Does nothing all day. Johnny's friend since high school."

"Yes. Certainly. How's that working out?"

"What? Not having a job?" you say. "Or being Johnny's friend?" You glance quickly at Honey. Despite yourself.

"Having no job."

"Oh. Well, it's not easy. You never have any money."

"I guess not."

"And it's not very exciting."

"Right."

"And it's humiliating. When people ask you about it." You smile at her.

Mrs. Zamner smiles back. "I imagine it would be."

"I'm going to stick with it, though."

"Lovely then. Make us proud."

Honey orders the salmon. Her mother orders salmon. The two ladies at the table next to you are having salmon. The waitress looks like she would order the salmon if she were sitting with you. For some reason you're reminded of an old line you used to hear a lot at the Elbow Room: there are two things in life that smell like fish and one of them is fish. You order a big salad that also promises bacon and cheese and little pieces of chopped-up egg and probably those freakishly tiny corn cobs. The waitress wants to know what dressing you want. You ask for a thick meat sauce. With a grin. Settle for ranch and no smile back.

"You were on television," Heidi Zamner says now. "Was it as much fun as you pretended?"

"No," you admit. Dash your cigarette out.

"Were you nervous?"

"Yes." Strange. That you would choose to answer this honestly.

She takes a second to gather you in. She's studying you for signs of sincerity. "You don't want to talk about it?" she asks.

"I don't," you say. And you mean it.

And so she stops. She's good that way, Mrs. Zamner.

You talk instead about Honey. Her job. Mrs. Zamner asks Honey a lot of questions about the hospital and nursing, but mostly it's about whether Honey *likes* doing it. You're pretty sure Honey's mother knows Honey isn't exactly super committed to being a nurse. But she can't come out and say it. She can't say negative things. Mrs. Zamner says only positive things. She has a great smile. She's the great encourager.

And Honey has been in it a long time now, actually. Over five years. So maybe she will stick with it. She's hard to pin that way. You don't think of a nurse as someone who loves clubs and dancing and drinking and getting loud. Or as someone who can be out until four in the morning and then do a twelve-hour shift on two hours' sleep. But that's her. Back when Honey was in nursing school you remember her going to class stoned more than a few times. And now at work she always seems to be in search of the lightest floor and the easiest shift. She likes drinking coffee and gabbing with the other girls. Joking with the boys. She has no interest in promotion or additional training. She maintains a popular profile with Nursing Office mostly by never complaining about what schedule she's given, quietly accepting all the nights they book her. There's less to do at nights, less to be sloppy at. She's shown a recent interest in the psychiatry ward but that's only because nurses get to wear their own clothes there.

As you watch Honey and Heidi Zamner talk, you wonder if the man at the table behind them is listening in. The way he's leaning in. He's extremely thin, like you. Unattractive, like you. But in a different way. He's older. He has hair in a perfect steel-grey tone, everything in place, one of those men who will never lose a single hair on his head during his lifetime. Tight beady curls sewn to his head. Like a wire brush. A hairline an ape would covet. Full sideburns and a steel-grey moustache. He's all about his hair. With good reason, of course. His nose hooks forward in an almost violent way. His eyes have raccoon rims around them, only partially obscured by his tinted glasses. His skin is bumpy. You have a thing about spotting unattractive men. It gives you hope. Are you better-looking than this one? That's what you're always secretly asking yourself.

You watch him over their shoulders, casually spooning his soup and reading his paper. You can see also that he is a very tall man, again like you. He's wearing a beige suit with a colourful shirt and a colourful tie. Flashy shoes. You've seen this sort of guy before. Many times. Throw a stick at the auto show or a school board meeting and you'll hit ten of him.

You switch gears, aim your spaceship back towards the table. Honey and her mother are discussing gay people now. Or gays in hospitals, more specifically. It seems. Apparently Heidi knows a doctor who's brilliant and gay and also works at the Royal Victoria. Heidi Zamner always knows people who are brilliant. Everyone is brilliant.

Honey interrupts, launches into a story about her and Johnny and a trip to Barbados they once took. When they were first dating. It catches you by surprise, hearing her suddenly describe this, and you're not sure why she's doing it.

"And so we go to Barbados. Which is, like, expensive. But Johnny had some money saved, and his brothers — or just George, I can't remember — gave him, or lent him, some. And I had some from you and Daddy, so I put in that. And so we go and it's crazy expensive but we have this really awesome time. Beach, beautiful water, always sunny. Always sunny. Beautiful people. And this is years ago and we're kind of still just dating even though it's serious and everything, but he's trying to impress me and get me to officially fall in love with him — I think the whole trip was his idea to get me to decide that I really loved him — and anyways, we're having this great time and of course Johnny's meeting everybody and we're always with these other couples, smoking *Bob Marley* all the time because there's a lot of grass down there if you get to know the guys from the beach.

"But there's also these two guys from Britain at the resort too, and the sight of them is just driving Johnny crazy. One of them is maybe twenty-two and seems like a kid, and the other one is, I don't know, maybe sixty. And they both have their hair dyed identically blond. So you can imagine what they looked like. But — and this is hilarious — at the end of the first day, and believe me you noticed them right away, they were very loud and overdone and especially the young one had a shrill voice and actually ran everywhere, but Johnny somehow didn't get it right away that they were gay, I think maybe he thought they were just really excited to be on vacation, so after dinner we were all just sitting around and Johnny suddenly asked everybody if 'the English man and his son' weren't completely bugging the shit out of them. Like they were doing to him. The English man and his son. And people just spit up! Were they laughing! I was killing myself!

Because, especially *him*, not to get that. And then he got it, and it was so obvious, but somehow he missed it at first and me and the other couples just pissed ourselves thinking about Johnny watching that little English boy spread lotion on his father's back…"

Honey stops, gathers a breath. You look at her mom. She seems thoroughly enchanted with the story so far. Honey looks at you. You look away again, fish around the table for another smoke. You know you've heard this story before but don't really remember where it goes. Johnny ends up a hero or something. You study her mom again. To you, so far, this is not the kind of story your average daughter tells your average mother, and it's certainly not the kind of story a mother would enjoy hearing. Is it? Can anybody be this encouraging?

"So now these two poor gay guys are really making Johnny mental for the next few days. Just the sight of them. Oh, you had to see it when the young one would come over at the pool bar and sort of worm his way onto the older man's lap. Johnny would get completely bug-eyed. And they were always talking too loud with all the old ladies they'd become so friendly with, and they had big flowery towels that they tucked into themselves at the waist, like skirts, and a bright yellow air mattress shaped like a phone that they carried everywhere. Johnny couldn't help himself. He was always trying to look at them and not look at them at the same time. I actually felt sorry for him, he looked so miserable. I said to him once, 'They're ruining your stupid trip.' And then he starting getting kind of mean whenever they were around and really just giving them awful, awful looks. And saying a few things. And so they started getting uncomfortable too, because until then they were having just the most wonderful time.

"Then we end up one night at a reggae place, Johnny and me and a few other couples plus some Bajan guys. And the two English guys are there too. And I don't remember but Johnny's being pretty shitty to them, when he's not out back smoking up all the time, and then eventually I wanted to leave because it's very late but he didn't want to, and so somehow, even though I shouldn't, me and this other girl end up in a cab — you go everywhere there by cab — and Johnny and her boyfriend will come later. And like I said, I don't want to take a cab back to the hotel with just this girl and this big black taxi driver that I don't know, but Johnny lets me go, I guess. Though to be honest, I don't even know if he saw me when I left. I was kind of mad. So finally we leave and then doesn't the taxi driver stop halfway to the hotel to let his friend in and then we all end up going a different way, of course, not straight to the hotel but through this fish market instead, where there are these restaurant shacks and music and tables where you can buy things. But everything's closed up because it's so late and there's just lonely music playing from one speaker on a pole and then they stop the car there and they want us to get out and dance with them and there's almost nobody else around. Especially no other girls."

"Oh my," says Mrs. Zamner. But calmly.

"And the other girl and I start to freak out. We're trying to be calm and be cool and not be scared but that hasn't worked at all and so now we're going to scream if they don't start the car back up. Which they finally do, but then there's always a delay and a reason why we can't leave right away and they try to get us to smoke with them, which we don't, and the other girl — Meredith — screams a few times, she's starting to really lose it. But it's amazing how nobody responds. Nobody! And then that's not even true because these other guys come over, and these other guys are even worse news than the cab driver and his stupid idiot friend who started everything. These new guys are scary and mean. We're starting to look at the first two assholes to protect us, that's how scary these new guys are."

And again you look at Mrs. Zamner, who is still smiling and sipping her wine and following the story with perfect aplomb. Maybe she's heard the story before. Maybe Honey doesn't remember she's already told dear old mom the bit about how the black guys almost gang-raped her all night at the fish market. There's only two things that smell like fish. But you would think that, even so, every time you heard this story about your daughter you'd get a little more rattled than this fifty-year-old woman with the nerves of an assassin seems to be getting. What is it about Europe?

"And then what?" Mrs. Zamner asks sweetly.

"They killed you?" you venture.

Honey doesn't even glance over your way. "Meanwhile, the two gay men have left the club not much after us and they've taken a taxi back to the resort and the older one somehow thinks to ask around and check if we've returned, and we haven't, and he waits a few more minutes and asks around some more and somehow — I swear I don't know how — figures out that something's wrong, and they take a taxi *back* to the club and find Johnny. And Johnny actually smartens up and grabs this local guy, Carson, who's a pretty heavy guy and who was getting all the dope for everyone, and somehow Carson — I don't know how, again — figures out where to look and so he and Johnny and the two English ones get back in with the cabbie and the five of them go speeding through the town and out to the fish market where we are!"

Heidi Zamner's eyes widen a millimetre.

"And the cab has very bad brakes and actually slams into the pole with the speaker when it tries to stop in the parking lot. But we're not far from there and we hear this, and the music stops when the speaker gets smashed and so then you hear nothing except this guy Carson who's holding a handgun in the air and running towards us and then Johnny who overtakes him and comes roaring up and plows into the two guys we were with first. And he starts smacking the cab driver in the head and then kicking the guy's friend in the ass over and over and over — which I did too, a few times — and the other meaner guys have all taken off by now, and Carson puts me and the girl and finally Johnny into the cab they came in, and gets himself and the English guys into the other cab, and we peel out of the fish market and back to the hotel a million miles an hour in a car which, I'm thinking the whole way, basically has no brakes."

The waitress brings the salmon and your big salad.

There's a silence while everyone fingers their cutlery and tinkers with their food. Heidi Zamner contemplates her daughter's harrowing tale, hears in it the potential treachery of youth. But also the mercy of fate. She looks into her daughter's eyes, deeper than you or Johnny or anyone else on God's earth could ever do, to see the daughter who has spoken, safe now, retelling the episode with a tiny laugh from the safety of a stylish wrought iron chair on the sun-splashed terrace of a restaurant many years later.

Honey's thinly disguised pleasure at being able to shock her mother, the quick licks at her lips betraying her childish pride, is evident. And to her — you're watching now as she hacks a manly swatch of salmon for herself and drowns it in a pool of computer-beige sauce *circa* 1996 — it's really just a story, the subject was gay people and so this was her story with two gay guys right smack in the middle of it. And the main point for her, the fun part, was how Johnny more or less had to eat shit the whole rest of the trip. The way he had to tiptoe around the English guys after that.

But to you the story has a different meaning. To you it's different.

It's simpler. It's precise.

It's Honey remembering the time that she did, in fact, fall in love with the boy Johnny Karakis.

It's that moment.

The stupid salad is good. You dig into the heaping bowl with a sudden appetite. Honey tears another strip off her fish, plunges it into the sauce. Mrs. Zamner dips delicately into her brown rice, raises her fork to her mouth.

You remember Johnny recounting his version of this same incident to you back then. He talked about how sick it made him feel to make nice with these two *malakas poustis*. But he had to. And that he found the older guy, the guy who saved Honey, to be an all right guy in the end. But not the boy toy, Conrad. And he also found them, despite their girlish shrieks and hands forever in the air, to be just another sad couple from England, no happier or more fulfilled or gayer than anyone else.

Mrs. Zamner glances over at her daughter then over at you. Gathering the two of you in. Together. She won't even ask. She's too polite. Too positive. She scoops up another tiny mound of rice.

Honey's mother knows, you think to yourself.

You watch the ugly man in the background. If he was interested before, he no longer is. His paper is folded up and he looks to catch the eye of the waitress, seeking the bill. You look around, spot her standing over by the windows. Watching you, actually. You wonder vaguely if she recognizes you from the Liz Hunter thing. She shrugs herself away from the wall, makes her way through the tables over to him.

seventeen

Sunny, golden. Again. What a summer. Too hot, but you like hot. Some people sweat like pigs but not you. You freeze in winter instead. It's all in the legs. Skinny legs, no body heat. In summer you can tolerate oven-like conditions. In winter you wear long johns like other people wear windbreakers, slipping into them at the slightest chill. It's the only way you can talk yourself into leaving the house.

You're walking The Boy in his stroller. Not even ten minutes ago Cuz and Sanderson passed you in Sanderson's ridiculously souped-up Honda Civic. They blasted you with a series of long honks and loud laughs. With your sunglasses on and music in your ears you made like you didn't notice. It's unlikely they were fooled but at least they didn't stop.

You decide to get off the main drag, wheel Ack! into the park. Scan the grounds, shimmering in the heat. Your park. This park. Tremendous amounts of time have been spent here. Still are, though less so now. You think of days and nights gone by when you were younger. All of you. Whole summers, and more. Past Labour Day, past the return to school for some, everyone still gathering every night. Trying to hold on to the feeling. Autumn evenings with their cooler air, the bunch of you shivering stubbornly in T-shirts. Lighting cardboard on fire from empty beer cases and pizza boxes when it got past midnight, then huddling close for three minutes' warmth. Nobody going home because it was fun and crazy and you didn't want to miss anything. Didn't want to hear the next night that something wild or hilarious had happened and you weren't there. Aaron brought his boom box every night, and if he wasn't coming, someone else brought it for him. And so each wondrous evening would be set to music and dope and tossed footballs and absurd conversation, watching the sky go from day to dusk to the black of night, ambient light floating over from the street lamps to brighten you up, shiny molecules dancing in the air. The air flecked with floating bits of magic. People forever dropping in, friends of friends, guys who knew they could score here, the brazen overtures of girls looking for somewhere to belong. The kind of girls that are full-blown women by fourteen, peaking at seventeen, fading at twenty. Done like dinner by twenty-five. Guys from parks all over came by, brought their friends and their girlfriends. You can remember silly nights when you laughed and screamed so hard that even by then you had begun to think of these as legendary moments, already fading into the past. Sepia-toned and thoroughly stoned. Sun-bleached summer memories tumbling one after the other in a seemingly endless montage.

You steer The Boy along the paths, aim towards the kiddie part. Stacy's gone to a — hold your breath, everyone — job interview. So you've got Ack! again. Whose little keester is already back in his stroller even though you've only been out ten minutes. He's not a big long-distance walker, Ack! He likes to give it his all for about forty feet and then taxi the rest of the way. You don't have much in the high-hopes department for him with respect to carving himself out a career as an Olympic medallist.

The park is nearly deserted today. Too hot, too muggy. Some days there's afternoon ball games. Good games. Hardball, not softball. Softball is for agfays. Come any later than one o'clock and the teams are liable to be filled. A great thing about Sherbrooke Street West, this. All the good players. With all that free time. The unstated goal of everyone here is to slide through life doing as little as possible. If not, they'd already be in Toronto. Maybe it's a displaced anglo thing. The choice to live life in English within a French city. To steer west of everything unfamiliar. Eschew the east. Celebrate Canada Day but stay home and pout on St-Jean-Baptiste. Read the *Gazette* and listen to CHOM and watch American TV shows. Or local English crap like Liz Hunter. Bitch and moan but never venture very far outside the hood. Cutting themselves off from all the gorgeous French chicks, too. Maybe worst of all. It's retarded but so many do it.

And so you play in the ball games sometimes, with Rocco and Boiler and Ace and Weemer and all the other cartoon characters, just showing up with your glove and bat in time to get picked for a team. There's always been a lot of serious players in this area. Half drunk before the game even starts maybe, but talented. Snagging ground balls amidst the pebbles and bottle caps and bits of broken glass, cigarettes dangling at their lips, cut-off jeans, bare-chested, even barefoot some of them, and at a glance you can tell there was potential here at one time. Some of these hombres connect on a fastball and they can still take it 275 feet into the trees that protect the parked cars.

On game days the stands are dotted with girlfriends and friends sitting in clusters, yakking away, only occasionally watching, perking up maybe if an argument or a bout of shoving erupts. Games are twenty-five innings long some days, suppertime and beyond, and by then everybody's totally wasted and getting stupid. You never get involved in the pushing-around stuff, leave it to the alpha males. Just because you're not a lover doesn't mean you're a fighter.

This is where Johnny wooed Honey. It's where Aaron met Maureen. It's where Henry first started to really lose touch. It's where Cuz showed up a little later on, a strange boy, intense and competitive, dancing at the edges of the group, jabbing at all of you from the outside, bobbing and weaving and finally insinuating himself into its core.

You pull up. The Boy wobbles cautiously over to the sand. As he does, the phone rings. Her phone, in her bag. Which she insisted you take. She's probably calling you now to remind you to give him water or give him fruit or put his hat on or put cream or check his fucking diaper. It's exhausting, the deeds you're responsible for. This is no job for you. You are in a sour mood.

You find the phone, flip it open. "What?" you say to her.

There is a silence on the other end. And then a decidedly unfeminine voice says, "Well, that's not the most pleasant greeting I've heard today."

You get to your feet and walk over near the fence, away from where Ack! is playing with two girls and their nanny.

You say, "Hey, how are you?"

"Busy," Your Dealer says. "With little time to talk. I have to go out. Sharon's already downstairs in the car."

"Great. Take care then."

"Ah, wit. Rare these days. The clever kind, at least. I just thought I'd check in. We might be out late tonight, Sharon and I."

You say nothing.

"Could be out all night," he repeats. "Miss the news."

Your antennae are up now. What's this about? You glance over at Ack!, make sure he's okay.

"Of course," Your Dealer says, "I usually catch the news. Most nights."

You say more nothing. Listen.

"I find it *frustrating* when I don't catch the news. I like to see what's going on. Do you know what I mean?"

Say nothing. Listen.

"*Who knows* what's going on? Fires. Floods. Accidents. Bombs. Threats of bombs. Bombs as threats. International. National. Political. I like pretty much everything. I'll even watch the local stuff if there's a bit of intrigue to it."

YOU comma Idiot

159

Say nothing.

He says, "I enjoy a little homegrown story once in a while. If it's on the quirky side. Like your friend Harry. He's quite the diversion."

"Henry," you say softly.

"Right, Henry. I know. Henry Miller — The Quiet Killer? Isn't that what they said? Isn't that the cute little catchphrase they wrote at the beginning of the story? He's your buddy, isn't he?"

"It's just one stupid reporter," you say. "And a couple of newspaper stories at the beginning."

"She seems interested enough."

"It's a specialty channel. No one watches it."

"You think so?"

And now you hear another phone ringing. You hear it through his phone, and then you hear him answer it and listen and grunt and listen some more and then say to Sharon, "Well, I know you're in the car and I know you're tired of waiting but I don't see how you're going to leave without me since *you don't even know how to fucking drive*, so just stay there, I'm coming…" and close the phone, turn in, and direct his heavy breath at you again.

And he waits, and waits. But this time you're not going to bite.

And so he sighs and says, "Believe me, Lee, please, when I tell you that once you reach a certain age almost all of life's joys become muted with the overexposure of time. Just about all of them. And life's sorrows too. And most of life's curiosity. Nothing can ever be new again, and nothing can ever really be fresh again. Have you ever thought of that? Or maybe you're still too young."

"I—"

"Because it's not the experiences that have become old. Really, it isn't. Some have, but that's not it. There are always others you can seek out. No. It's your own emotions that have become old. Too familiar. Your reactions. There is almost nothing you can do that will deliver *a brand new sensation*. Sex and drugs and love and even money have long ago ceased to stir anything even remotely resembling what you felt for them in your youth. Even pain, to some degree, no longer enjoys the notoriety it once did."

He allows a pause here.

"And yet, there's one exception. One. Do you know what it is? *Frustration*. That feeling, that gut-wrenching, chest-tightening motherfucker, hasn't lessened one bit. In fact it's worse. It'll rip you to shreds. If left unchecked. That emotion somehow becomes more powerful and insidiously destructive with each passing year. If ever I kill, it will surely be within a rage of frustration. It's the only thing that can still overpower me, and make me lose hold of my senses. I still can't control it. And it drives me more insane than ever before that I *can't* control it. Do you understand? Isn't that interesting?"

You gulp silently. Wait the appropriate beats. Then say, "Alright, so you're upset."

"Upset? Why would I be upset?"

"You're not upset?"

"No. I would think it would be *you* who would be upset."

"Me?"

"Yes."

"Why?"

"Well," he says, "how good for you can it be if things are not well between us?"

Which you have to think about for a second. Which sounds like he's saying things are not well between you because he's upset, and yet he's saying he's not upset.

"So you're angry?" you say.

"I'm not angry."

"Unhappy?"

"Not unhappy."

"Displeased?"

"I'm never very pleased to begin with."

"Maybe you're unsatisfied?"

"I'm satisfied."

"Disturbed?"

"No."

"Perturbed?"

"I'm not turbed of any kind."

You see Ack! looking around suddenly, panicked that he doesn't see you.

"But you're frustrated," you say.

Your Dealer pauses. It sounds like he's drinking. Likely a throatful of wonder juice.

"I am frustrated," he allows.

"I'm sorry," you say quickly.

Your Dealer clucks his tongue a few times. You know he's formulating his thoughts, about to pronounce his next and — you hope — final words on the issue. You're grateful for the light at the end of the tunnel even if, as they say, it is an oncoming train.

"You know what the worst part of going bald is?" he asks you now.

Good Christ. Here we go again.

"I imagine there would be many worst parts."

"Well, it's — fuck you — it's realizing that it's been happening to you five years after everyone else has. You're still combing and fluffing and puffing and behind your back your friends are all rolling their eyes and snickering. And then one day you see a picture or a reflection in a mirror *or a DVD at your friends' anniversary party* and you realize what everyone's known for years, that your hairline is at the top of your skull."

"Wow," you say, for lack of options.

"I have a friend named Michael that I've known for years. You know what he used to call me when I first started getting a bare patch on top?"

"No, I don't."

"Ozone."

You laugh politely.

"You think that's funny?"

"No," you say. "Of course not."

"Certainly it's funny."

"Right."

"It's very funny."

"Sure."

"And you can understand that it's also frustrating. No?"

"Uh, yes?"

"Very frustrating? Right?"

"Sure."

"No, not really," he corrects you.

"No. Of course not."

"Not really, you see, because I can't do anything about it. Do you understand? There's nothing I can do about it."

"Well, there's operations and pills —"

"*There's nothing I can do about it.* And so I accept it. And with that realization, knowing that, my frustration fades. It has to, and so it does."

"Okay, good then."

"But not when there's something that *can* be done. That's different. That's a different situation. And sometimes, something can be done. Oh yes. And it kills me, it tears me apart, to think that I wouldn't do whatever I had to do to stop whatever was happening from happening. If I had to. Do you get me?"

You don't answer.

"Do you understand?"

"I do," you say. And it's true.

"Of course you do. So then, how should I deal with it?"

"Well —"

"Swiftly," he says. "Immediately."

"Wouldn't that be more the answer to *when*?"

"No. The answer to when is now. This call."

The Boy is at your knees. He has found you. He burrows his head affectionately into your crotch. You put your free hand on his forehead, gently remove him.

"I would prefer," Your Dealer says now, in a curious mixture of delicacy and finality, "to never turn on my television and see your face again in my lifetime."

You are desperate to change the subject. "Where did you get this number?" you ask him.

"Are you listening to me?"

"Who would tell you I'd have this phone?"

"I don't even know whose phone it *is*."

"Cuz? Did Cuz give you this number?"

"Now you're asking me something you know the answer to."

"Why're you so friendly with him?"

"Am I?"

"I definitely think so."

"Really? Well, then it must be true."

"Why do you let him *see* you? It used to be just me."

"You sound like a jealous woman," Your Dealer says, and you know this reminds him that Sharon is waiting. "And now I have to go. Already it's been too long. She's blown a gasket by now, I'm sure."

"Every time you let him come see you, that hurts me," you say. "I know you know that."

You hear shuffling through his phone and what you recognize as the closing of a door. You can picture Your Dealer walking down his corridor towards the elevator. He sounds increasingly distant.

"You know we've spoken about this before, Lee. First off, I'm hardly going to talk about it with you now. Secondly, and once again, I find myself having to remind you about a recurring problem with perspective you seem to have. Thinking that what matters to you matters to me. Which, of course, it doesn't. You need to understand this. And I have to go. This is all she's going to talk about at dinner, you realize. She doesn't let go of things like this easily."

You hear the elevator bell ding through the static.

"Can't you tell Cuz he has to go through me?" you ask loudly.

The line is warping, getting fuzzy.

"Remember!" he shouts, choosing not to hear. "Remember why I called!"

"*What?*" you holler back, looking to end on a note of confusion, hoping to absolve yourself for future transgressions.

It's funny to hear Your Dealer speak this way, but not entirely uncommon. He's a little guy, maybe five-six. Hardly a physical presence. But with a big baritone voice. In person he would never be aggressive like this, but on the phone he always sounds more severe. Goddamned phones. And email and Blackberries and iPhones and all that shit. The empowerment of the little man. You throw Stacy's phone into the bag, fold yourself down onto the grass, and pull Ack! with you.

"Little man. Be my friend. I need a friend."

Ack! gladly collapses on top of you, happy to be of service, slurping his gratitude onto your neck and down the front of your T-shirt.

You squeeze him tightly. What a buddy.

eighteen

The whole story, it seems to you, is a big joke. As far as you can tell. You've caught her updates a few times over the last two weeks. *Liz Hunter*. Her stupid little montages. Voice-overs. With nothing to say. Hardly any new developments, no sign of the girl. A pair of running shoes tied together by the laces found hanging from a phone wire down where Upper Lachine Road and St-Jacques Street split. Nobody's even sure if they belonged to Darlene or not. Even the newspapers run only the tiniest blurbs. Only Liz keeps flogging it.

There's a guy on the radio who talks about these things every once in a while. He says girls like Darlene Dobson drop out of sight all the time. He says people don't have the time to care. He says maybe it's sad to say it but you read about something like this and it really seems bad until you see a story on the next page that's twice as revolting and then you don't even remember the first one anymore. There's too much going on to even bother trying to keep up. He says if she'd just turn up *dead* it would be a lot simpler. Something for us all to get behind. He also says that if she is fine, alive and well, that will probably be even more disappointing. When you think about it. Who'll give a fuck then? Another white-trash chick back on the streets. Great.

He's very opinionated. People enjoy that.

It's all ratings, you see.

=

Camera Guy is talentless, by the way. Utterly devoid of any acquired skill. To a stunning degree. You've seen yourself replayed in various clips by now. He's got the top of your head cut off half the time and you're always too far off to the side. While Liz Hunter, that she-weasel, cheats forward during every shot. Looking for added presence. Effectively stealing what little light there is, leaving part of your chest and one shoulder draped in shadow. It's true. You can see it if you really watch. It's only because you're a foot taller than her that your head is in any proper exposure at all. And so you are a gleaming face, straw hair pointed in so many different directions, perched atop what comes across as only a fraction of your already rail-thin body. You look slightly alien.

Liz Hunter, by contrast, could never be mistaken for anything other than from this planet. Liz Hunter is a woman with curves. Gentle face, gentle shoulders. Gentle hands. Not the hard-bodied lioness typical of the genre. Physically at least. Soft and blousy. Surely closer to forty than thirty, but with a casual sexuality that comes across. The camera paints her as fleshy and alive while you appear sallow and brittle. Emphasized by Camera Guy's poisonous lighting. When you see him next, he will hear about this.

You run into Cuz outside the banking machines off Cavendish. There are other people walking nearby. A good thing. It keeps everything civil.

He calls out, "Hey, Superstar! You so cool!"

People look over. You say nothing.

"TV star! Hey!" he leers at you through blue wraparound shades. "Wow! I saw you on TV again, man. A few times. Very amazing! Very erudite! You know what I mean? So cool."

"Really? That's what you thought?"

"Oh yeah."

"Cool?"

"Yeah."

"And erudite?"

"Sure."

"That's a strange way of describing it," you say.

"Well, I don't know what 'erudite' means."

You never could trust Cuz. You knew that from the beginning. You feel stupid now, not to have foreseen that this day would come.

He says, "One time when I saw a clip of you I was with Dane and Sanderson. Fuck, was it funny. We were pretty *gone*, you know?"

"Great," you say.

"You sure made us laugh."

"Terrific."

"You were always standing *on the edge of the screen*, man. Sanderson was going hysterical!"

"Sanderson's a fucking jerk."

"Hey, did that chick talk to you after?" He winks at you, as if you're buddies. "I'd like to do her. Wouldn't you? And don't say no. Did you, like, smoke a big bone with her after?"

"Oh yeah," you say. "We *smoked a bone.* And then we rolled some more *doobies*. And then we, like, *got destroyed*, you know?"

His eyes narrow through the tinted plastic. "You bug me," he sneers. "Did you know that?"

"You dump everything cheap," you say. "You front everybody. You front *anybody*. You don't have any clue what you're doing. You're just screwing everything up."

"I know what I'm doing."

"You're a little punk."

"Better stay out of my way, Lee."

"*Your* way?"

You watch Cuz's eyes dart left and right. See him sizing things up. His fists tighten. Teeth grind. It's broad daylight. Lots of people around.

Witnesses. He already has a record for this sort of thing. He can't afford it, and you both know it.

Henry's mom is tidying the lobby when you arrive, gathering stray flyers and discarded mail. She folds her arms in front of her when she sees you. She owns the building. She bought it with the money from the insurance. There are eight units inside. She lives in one, Henry lives in another. They survive nicely on the proceeds of the other six.

"I'd like to see him, Mrs. Miller."

Mrs. Miller says nothing. You know how hard this is for her. After all the years of looking out for him, now *this*. You could drop a kind word here about that but know she would only lash out at you. Sympathy makes her angry. She's all skin and bones and piercing eyes, a tiny, tired woman leading a selfless life but in the most selfish manner. Defending the error of her son's ways. A lifetime of denials and rationalizations. Misgivings.

You all took the same drugs in the beginning, she knows that. Experimented with the same things, graduated to the heavier scenes. Every one of you. But only Henry got damaged. The rest of you walked away. The rest of you, she believes, got off scot-free.

And she resents you for it.

"Not today, Lee."

"Please, Mrs. Miller."

"Come back tomorrow maybe."

"Let me talk to him, Mrs. Miller." You push the buzzer to Henry's apartment, several stabs with irregular punctuation. "I'd just like to see him."

She waves a hand at you frantically, shushing you to stop. You push the button again. She glowers back at you.

"Just take me up," you say. "I won't be long, Mrs. Miller."

You include her name with each sentence. Why, you're not sure. You raise your finger to pin down the buzzer again if she doesn't relent. It seems to work. She scrunches up her face and turns away, mutters, and leads you up the stairs and down the hallway and up other stairs and down another hallway and then finally into Henry's apartment simply by pushing open his door and walking in.

Henry is not at all surprised that it's you.

You look around. It's not how you expected it. Or maybe it is. Henry's eating raisin bread that's shiny with butter, nibbling on it like a rabbit. Toast crumbs are everywhere. Dirty plates. Half-full cups of tea. Newspapers and magazines. He's wearing a T-shirt and sweatpants you're sure he slept in, and a housecoat over that.

Instead of leaving, Mrs. Miller goes over to the kitchen and begins rinsing the dishes strewn there.

Henry smiles at you through stained teeth. He says, "Hey, you know what happened?"

"No."

"The police came by this morning."

"The police?"

"They wanted to look around."

"*This* morning?"

"They left twenty minutes ago. They just left. You just missed them. They've come before. Twice. With a search warrant. Today they didn't have one. My mother let them look anyway."

"Really?" Like a moron you scan the apartment looking for signs of their search. "Where do they look?"

"On my computer."

"Your computer?"

"And today at my shoes."

You look over at his shoes. They're lined up at the door.

"They ask you questions?"

"Not many anymore."

"What do you say?"

"I say the same thing every time," Henry says. "I ask them if they're going to arrest me."

You're fascinated by this interplay, this intrigue. You hadn't realized.

"And what do *they* say? Do they answer you?"

"Sure. They're very polite. They say, 'Not today.'"

Again, you had no idea. It seemed like the whole deal was fading away. You thought Liz Hunter and the buffoon with the camera were the only ones still paying attention. You thought it was all dying out, sort of.

Abruptly, Mrs. Miller leaves the kitchen. Gives Henry a long look as she passes by, doesn't even glance your way. Walks out the front door, clicking it closed behind her. Leaving the two of you alone.

Though it's you who has come to visit, you have nothing urgent to say. You lean back in your chair, watch him.

It's Henry that speaks. "No one comes much."

You shrug. "Well, you know."

"No one comes *at all*."

You hold back a grimace. "People call."

"Not many."

"Sure. Your mother answers. You're hard to reach."

"She tells me who calls. Not many."

You nod, say nothing.

Henry says, "Aaron calls. Almost every day. Aaron and me were never really such great friends. I was more friends with you and Johnny and Honey. But now I speak to Aaron more than I ever did."

You nod again.

"I'm not sure why," he says.

You run a hand through your hair, rub an eye. This is the part where you tell him you're sorry. Tell him you'll call him tomorrow too, and the day after. Where you're supposed to say you'll come by more. Every day. See how he's doing. But you just can't say it. You're not that into it. Too bad, but it's true. What can you say? You've been distracted. As rare as it is to hear yourself say this, you've been — wait for it — *busy*. There's a few things going on. After all, you're fucking

Honey. And fucking *Johnny*. And Cuz is fucking *you*. And you were on TV, and that was fucking weird. And so you haven't really followed how it's all been working out for poor Henry. This is also the part where you wonder if you're a bad person.

You do a head count in your head. Who thinks he did it, who doesn't think he did it. Johnny, no. Probably. Honey, yes probably. Baby, yes. Maureen, yes. Cuz, yes. Sanderson and the other finks, yes. Aaron, you would have said yes before, but now that he's calling all the time you're not so sure. Though it's not like Aaron not to think what Maureen is thinking.

Henry says, "You remember when we rented that house up north that time? That chalet? And everyone left on Sunday night and I was the last one and I was supposed to lock up and drive back with the key?" He takes a tiny bite of raisin bread. "But then somehow I burned the front porch down instead?"

"Yeah."

You eye him. Nod one more time. What's this about? You've talked this through with him so many times before. Is there some new angst? Something he's never told you before about his role in it?

"Well, everyone was mad then too," Henry says. "But not for that long. After a while everyone forgot about it."

And now Mrs. Miller comes in again. With bedding and other clean laundry that she makes a big deal of straining to carry across the apartment. Her teeth are clenched and her forehead is so furrowed you'd think the basket was made of cast iron. She seems engaged in some private, medieval game of torture.

Henry tips back on the hind legs of his chair. "Ma, can you make Lee a coffee?"

"Lee doesn't need a coffee, Henry. He's leaving soon."

"Well, I'm hungry."

"Don't worry, I'll make you something in a few minutes." She heaves the laundry up on the counter while at the same time squeezing off, you're pretty sure you hear this, a quick fart. "Right after Lee goes."

Neither of you say a word. The TV is on in the living room; you can see the commercials going by out of the corner of your eye. You half expect a news report to come on and Henry's face to appear. You both listen as his mother opens and closes drawers, placing her items.

Henry says to you, "I saw a girl I hadn't seen for about ten years last week. She recognized me at the drugstore with my mom. She spit at my feet. She said she hoped I died. She said even that would be too good for me."

You glance at Mrs. Miller. She's pretending she's not listening.

Henry says, "She said when people like me kill themselves, it's not even suicide."

You blink. "It's not?"

"No."

You wait for him to explain. He doesn't. Naturally. Funny how even when you're feeling sorry for him here like this, you could still slug him. That's how annoying he is.

"Well, what is it then?" you ask.

"Insecticide."

"Insecticide?"

"Yeah."

"She said that?"

"Yeah."

You consider this. He watches you.

"Insecticide?"

"Yeah."

"That's pretty good," you say finally.

"It's not bad."

He grins at you. You smile back. It's nice to see him happy.

Mrs. Miller looks over, clears her throat.

"I guess I will go," you say to Henry.

"Alright."

"I'll come again. And I'll phone you. You want me to phone you?"

"Okay."

"When does Aaron call?"

"Lunchtime usually."

"I'll call you at dinnertime then. So you'll have a call at each meal."

You stand up. Take several steps towards the door. Mrs. Miller is already there, waiting.

You stop, turn back towards him. "Henry, there's *got* to be something you can tell the police. Something you know. Something you can tell somebody that makes sense. So you can get *out* of this shit."

Henry's eyes dart over to his mother's. You can see Mrs. Miller is getting antsy.

"Oh, I'm not telling them nothing," Henry declares.

You are taken aback. Say, "You can't? Or you won't?"

"Right-o, baby."

"What?"

"I wouldn't tell them a thing," he repeats, just as defiantly, until he sees his mother glaring at him. He slumps back against his chair, the belt of his housecoat brushing against the floor, sweeping against the crumbs there. "If I knew something, I mean."

Mrs. Miller's face is pinched, her fingers drumming at her sides. "I'm asking you to leave *again*, Lee," she says, though technically this is not true, it's the first time she's actually asked.

You take a few more seconds to stare at your friend, puzzled at why he is saying this, at *how* he is saying this. Does this mean something, or is it just you?

But Henry looks away. And Mrs. Miller opens the door wider.

"Lee, go. Please."

nineteen

And so you do. You make your way out the door and along the hallways and down the stairs and through the lobby out onto the street. Turn and walk up towards Sherbrooke Street. Realize you're being watched.

Stop. Pivot to face Camera Guy, who's aiming at you.

"You've *got* to be kidding…" you say.

He floats you a wry smile from behind the lens.

You ask, "Where's Liz?"

He points behind you. You turn and spot her. At the corner, waiting. She moves forward.

"What do you want?" you say.

"What were you talking about in there?" She gestures towards Henry's building, moving in closer.

"Nothing."

"Darlene Dobson?"

"No."

Her eyes narrow dramatically. Camera Guy is catching all of this, swish panning from one face to the other.

She says, "Did he tell you what he did to her?"

You let out a long sigh, rub your eyes. "Can't you just give it a rest?"

"Tell us," she says. "Obviously you know something."

"Yeah, obviously." You turn to Camera Guy. "Hey, Hopeless. Your Uselessness. Am I in focus? Are you awake? How much of my head is lopped off right now? Can you even *see* me?"

You wave your hands in front of him. Like he's Helen Keller. That'll be a hoot when it gets on TV.

Liz says, "Oh, no. C'mon. You did this last time. *Talk* to me. Talk *with* me. You can't just ignore what's happening."

"*Nothing's* happening."

"Listen, people were upset with you last time. Did you know that? They wrote in. We got a lot of response. We got emails. About how little it seemed you cared. His best friend. People wondered about you. Some were incensed. Do you know what that means?"

"It's when you burn incense."

"It means people were angry. But it also means there's *hope*. That people care. That something can be done. It's not too late. People still care."

"Sweetie," you say to her, slowly, condescendingly, your lips moving in exaggerated motion, mugging for the camera, "*no one's watching*. Your little reports. Your five-minute slot at the end of the half-hour. 'The Hunted.' What *is* that? Could you be more trite? Everybody else has moved on, doll. You've got the wrong guy. You've got the wrong angle. You've got the *wrong story*, maybe even. Right now, Darlene Dobson is probably lying on a mattress, skin-popping herself to heaven and back, for all you know." You start edging away, stepping backwards. "You're just wasting everybody's time."

"Wasting *your* time?"

"Especially mine."

"Oh, I don't think so." She comes after you, stealthily, like a stalker. "You seem pretty into it."

"Ha! I—"

"Do your friends think you're a big shot because you were on TV?"

"No, they—"

"What about Henry? Does he buy it that you're defending him — or does he know how much you enjoy it?"

"Why are you —"

"You look good on TV. Have you noticed? I'll bet you have. I can see it in your eyes. You look *better*. Broader. Not as skinny as in real life, right? I bet you like that. So tall. With that big head. Tell me, do you see a cooler-looking guy in the mirror now when you get up in the morning?"

"Look, I —"

"There's a seventeen-year-old girl that nobody's seen in *weeks*, Lee Goodstone. Do you understand that?"

"Don't —"

"Her mother is *frantic* with worry."

"So —"

"But you don't care. You don't —"

"Hey! Darlene Dobson lived *on the street* some days, doll. You've said it yourself. You *reported* it. She lived with anyone she could. She crashed anywhere. She stuck needles in her arm and slept with men she hardly knew. What does that have to do with my friend Henry, and why the fuck wasn't her mother frantic *before*?"

Liz holds the microphone in front of her, suspended in dramatic pause. "That's your answer?"

"That's my answer."

Her eyes narrow once again. "You *know* something…"

You throw your hands up. "I know nothing!"

"Give me something good" — her eyes twinkle now — "and I'll put you in the opening montage."

"Something good?"

"Yes."

You look around. Glance at the camera, ponder the question. Notice several bystanders drifting over. Turn back to her.

You say, "Okay, fine. Once, when Henry was younger, three dogs on his street were killed. All in one week. All three got their throats cut. And Henry hates dogs, right? Can't stand them. He likes snakes. Though that's another story. And so anyways, he knew every one of those dogs; they were the pets of neighbours; and each dog died with a knife stuck in its chest, left behind in the body. And Henry owned a big collection of vintage knives, everyone knew that. He was very proud of it. Except later, when they checked, exactly *three* knives were missing."

"Really?" she says, eyes wide.

"No. But you remember a bunch of years ago, when it was in the news about someone putting powder into envelopes and packages, and then mailing them? To people's offices or homes or government employees? Really vile stuff, laced with shit that could kill you? That would poison you in seconds? Make your skin fall off and your lungs explode? Well, the person that *some* people believe mailed those packages was Henry."

"Really…?"

"No. But when he was a teenager Henry used to babysit these two little kids, Marshall and Morgan. A boy and a girl. Nice. I knew them too. Very cute. Henry watched them many, many times. Their mother really trusted him. He was, like, the number one babysitter she would always call. The kids loved him. And then one day, boom, he never watched them again. That was it. She never called him again. *Never again.* You know why?"

She sighs. "Why?"

"Well, they moved away."

She looks at you. Blankly.

"Yeah," you say, nodding. "Like, far. To Detroit or something."

And then suddenly, right there at the next corner — miraculously, wondrously — you spy Honey sitting in her car. Idling at the light. Waiting for it to change. Sunglasses on, radio blaring. Her fingers keeping time against the steering wheel. Only the Deadhead sticker and the Cadillac are missing.

You start towards her. She looks up, smiles uncertainly.

Liz says, "Lee, stay!"

"I've got to go."

"Stay and talk. Say something *honest*."

"I'm leaving. I've already left."

You wave, she glares back.

"Well, keep watching the news then," Liz calls after you, with some anger. "You'll see. Something's going to give. And soon!"

You give her the finger, hold it an extra beat to give Camera Guy a chance to focus. You feel taller than you've ever felt in your life. Chin held high. You congratulate yourself on your quick wit. Your great reflexes. First-class anecdotism. Excellent fibbage. Made up right on the spot, in the spotlight, just like that. Now *that's* quality TV.

You lope across the street with a last look back at Liz.

Watch the news. The nerve of her. Why should you watch the news? Does she think you have time to watch the news?

Of course you're going to watch the news.

You *love* watching the news.

You look *great* on TV. She's right. That gorgeous wide screen just flattens you right out, puts on all the pounds they say it does. You've never looked better. And the glances you get simply walking down the street sometimes. People sneaking looks. You've noticed. What a gas.

You pull at the car door. With a big creak, it opens.

Honey is pleased to see you. Leans over and gives you a sweet, sloppy kiss. Hugs you, kisses you again. Runs her hand through your long hair, then guns the two of you through the intersection, the growl of the old Firebird resonating against the pavement. A stylish exit indeed. You wonder if Camera Guy can see this, if his lens is powerful enough, but don't dare sneak a glance back.

twenty

Of course, *where* she was headed wasn't something you'd thought to ask. She pulls up minutes later in front of Johnny's parents' place. Johnny comes out, obviously anticipating her arrival. Yours, not so much.

"What're you doing here?" he says to you.

"My lift…" You smile, bow, and gesture to the beauty beside you. "You remember the lovely and talented Miss Zamner?"

But Johnny doesn't have much smile to him on this day. He walks over to Honey. "I don't want it," he says.

"Well, I brought it," she says, moving the opposite way, around to the trunk of the Firebird.

She lifts the latch, lets it spring open. She pulls out Johnny's guitar and two hospital laundry bags filled with folded clothes. Retrieves a pair of his boots and his rock magazines. And his second-best leather jacket. Arranges them all on the curb.

"Sweetie, just hold on to everything," he says.

"Even your *guitar*, John?" Her tone drips with sarcasm. Johnny's always going on about his guitar. Where's his guitar? He better bring his guitar, he's got to practise his guitar more. As if somehow, someday, that guitar's going to *mean something* in his life, is the insinuation, the charade you're all guilty of letting him get away with, the private joke among you, the nudge and the wink, the pretence that he is a true musician. "Surely you must need your guitar."

"Sweetie…"

"Don't."

"Honey…"

"Don't."

"Babe…"

"Don't" — and she lifts her finger directly in front of his face — "say that name to me."

Jesus. If it was you she was addressing you'd have wet yourself by now. But Johnny just shakes his head, looks like he could almost laugh.

You edge away, in the direction of the Karakis house.

You hear him say quietly, "It was three years ago, Honey. We've talked about this every single fucking day now. I can't change it. I can't explain it. Let's just *get over it…*"

Johnny lives in a bachelor pad carved out of his parents' basement, accessed through a door at the side of the garage. An okay place, bigger than you'd think. Dark, though. And always cold. Anyway, he's rarely there. And whenever he is home, he's upstairs eating at his parents' kitchen table.

You stop walking. Look up, see Mrs. Karakis looking out their front window. At Honey and her son. And you. See Mr. Karakis come up behind her, trying to peer over her shoulder. He's shorter than her. It occurs to you what this scene might look like to them. You being here. Johnny and Honey arguing. It could almost look like, well, like what it is. Although today is by accident, the truth lurks nearby.

You've been best buddies with Johnny since forever. You survived high school together. You even *lived* with his family for the last year of it. Johnny's mother doting on you like a son. Johnny's brothers beating on you like a brother. Johnny's sister Voula yelling at them to leave you alone, trying to protect you, like a big sister should. Only Kostas, Johnny's dad, couldn't bring himself to see you the same way.

He could never give you a hard time. He would growl and bark and threaten his boys every time he lost his temper, but not you. He kid-gloved you from day one. He just couldn't do it. You weren't Greek. And you weren't his son. And you weren't Greek. Three reasons. He seemed to like you enough, though. He never spoke a word against you. But only you knew and he knew that he didn't really trust you.

It was a strange thing to come and live with another family, but there were few options. Your parents' marriage blown to smithereens, your sister following your mother to Florida. Your father unable to care even for himself. For a boy your age it was hard to imagine a more unnerving turn of events. And so, the Karakis family came to your rescue. Who can ever know whether they would have been willing to take you in under less dire circumstances? It hardly matters. You were, and will forever be, grateful.

Kostas backs away from the window but Johnny's mother stays. More intuitive than he, perhaps she senses that this is not just another tiff between her son and his girlfriend. She peers down at them, nostrils sniffing for signs of trouble. It makes you wonder what it's been like over the years when they've gotten together, Mrs. Karakis and Mrs. Zamner. They're so different. Two very different flavours of Europe. You wonder too whether Johnny's mother doesn't ask herself when Johnny and his gang will finally grow up. To her you must still act like children. Or teenagers. Breakups and beer, parks and pot. Henry, for example, will be thirty at Christmas. And the rest of you aren't far behind. Come to think of it, when *will* you all finally start to grow up?

You remember when you and Johnny were fourteen and you used to go down into the Karakis basement and sneak through Kostas's stack of vintage *Penthouse* magazines. Dust them off and stare at those hairy bushes and natural breasts. And read the crazy sex letters. You loved those letters. You thought they were real. They were the best letters ever. There were letters from bushy, large-breasted housewives who picked up fourteen-year-old boys in department stores and took them back to their stylish homes to fuck their brains out.

This left you *frothing*. You got all twitchy. You spent entire afternoons ready to go off like a pair of cocked pistols. Eventually it also made you warped enough to actually go downtown together and walk aimlessly through department stores when you should've been in class. You would split up and stroll through the Bay waiting to see which large-breasted housewife was going to pick you up. Shuffling through lingerie aisles, ambling through housewares, standing unnaturally close to women at linen displays. Asking innocent questions. Adding playful little glances. Fourteen-year-old innuendo. It didn't go well. There were some angry looks. Some nasty replies. You cringe thinking back on it. You actually cut school to do this. It *never* worked. Once, you remember, it got so hopeless you didn't even bother meeting up with Johnny at the end of the day. It was so futile. You went by yourself to see a movie instead. It was pathetic. And yet you did it over and over. What a pair of clowns you were.

You watch Johnny still making his case to Honey. Glancing over at you, too. See Honey backing away, drifting over to the door of the car, still open. She handles him so coolly, tight smiles and soft gestures. His responses are also measured, equally restrained. You feel like a kid, peeking over at them. Obviously he doesn't know yet. And it seems almost amazing that he doesn't — that no one knows — except that everyone is so used to you and Honey hanging out like pals all the time, all those years, killing the hours together while Johnny was off on one kick or another, that it's just not that different than it was before. On the outside. But when Johnny *does* find out. Hoo boy.

Four years ago Johnny's brother George finally got married to Christina. After the dinner, while everyone was dancing, you, Johnny, and his brother Peter sneaked into their honeymoon suite and plastered the ceiling with gay male porn. Absolutely covered it. Dicks and asses and oiled-up bods, engaged in *very* specific acts, Scotch-taped into the most horrific collage of swashbuckling erotica, oddly stimulating, you wince remembering this, pasted right above the bed. The final destination for that evening's festivities. A splendid prank. *A classic.* All Christina would have to do was look up and freak out. Maybe George would freak out too. For twenty incredibly nervous minutes you cut and taped and giggled and cracked jokes while Peter videotaped the whole thing, narrating it in a low voice like he was standing next to a green at Augusta.

A great night. A great memory for you. An actual sense of family. And the thing is, Johnny and Peter could have done this to their brother on their own. They didn't need you. None of Peter's or George's friends was invited. But Johnny brought you because he knew how much it would mean to you. He knew how cool you thought his brothers were and how you looked up to them all, what a great story it would be once everyone heard what you'd done. And Christina *did* freak out, shrieking and scrambling out of bed exactly on cue, as you all listened through the door, and it *was* great. A fantastic success. Someone even threw a quick website together afterwards where you could see footage and post funny comments.

You knead your fingers against your forehead now. Don't know what to think about yourself at this particular moment. You are careful to keep your eyes low to the ground, away from Johnny's parents' front window. You can't bear to think what a woman like Mrs. Karakis would say if she knew what was going on. Or a man like Kostas. *Hopa!*

Honey gets into the car, eases her thick door shut. Looks over at you. "C'mon, Lee…"

You've known this moment was coming. Decided already that this time you are not going to wuss out. And so you trot over, passing in front of Johnny. You give him a big smile, at the same time hoping he's not figuring this out too quickly.

"Sorry, man. Gotta run."

"Where're *you* going?" he wants to know.

But you are too busy to answer properly.

"Have your people," you say to him, never delaying your forward progress, hopping into the passenger side of Honey's car, all the while making the international sign for phone call with your extended pinky and thumb pressed to your ear, "call my people."

Honey's tires grip the ground once more and catapult you forward. You hang on to the door to steady yourself. She can be an unpredictable driver. Still, you are along for the ride. You're willing to keep moving, press ahead, surge forth, careen from one fleeting idea to the next, secure in the knowledge that God can't hit a moving target.

Somewhere in the distance, a dog is barking.

At least, statistically.

twenty-one

Of course, there's Ugly You. It goes without saying. At least in your mind's eye. Though maybe you're a bit harsh on yourself sometimes, it's been suggested. But still, you're no lead singer, that's for sure.

And then there's also — occasionally, sometimes, rarely, but it happens — Eerily Attractive You. The you that, in the right light, seen from exactly the right angle, with maybe just the right shirt on and a tan and the right hair if it holds well that morning and there's no real wind, can be an attractive you. A different you. Rock Star Ugly you, even. The bassist, say. Or the keyboard player.

You're looking at that guy now. On TV. Your latest interview. Shot just two days ago. They sure work fast. Your Dealer's going to shit himself. And the screen does indeed flatten you out. Adds a few pounds and softens your edges. You're not complaining. When a nifty little graphic that says LEE GOODSTONE, FRIEND OF HENRY MILLER slides into position, you have to admit, it gives you a woody. Camera Guy, despite his awkward framing and questionable focus, has done a better job this time. He should be commended.

You're watching along with Honey. You titter together as they film you coming out of Henry's building, startled by the camera, quick to deny Henry's complicity. Acting silly. Hamming it up for the lens again. Pushing back at Liz.

People were incensed. Do you know what that means?

It's when you burn incense.

Ha! Honey cackles. You smile over at her. Love it that she gets you.

You're at your place. Kicking back in the afternoon. Honey bought a big slipcover that fits over the couch, sealing in the cat hair and keeping you free of it. You're sprawled across it. She's in the armchair a few feet away, similarly protected. In general the place is much cleaner since she started crashing here some nights. She has brought order. She has simply blustered into your scene. You've never talked about why Johnny did what he did with Baby, and maybe never will. You just moved right past it. It doesn't matter how it began. All is right, now. In your world. You dig it that every moment spent with her feels stolen. You get a rush just thinking about it. You're not a person who's had much experience at this. In fact you've never actually done the cheating thing before. Never been the cheater, or the cheatee.

You had no idea how *exciting* it is.

It's not heavy. You'd think it would be heavy but it's not. It's fleet-footed and light. It's trippy. You're more like a pair of bank robbers than a duplicitous duo. Honey and Clyde. It's breezy, superior. Buzzing from activity to activity, every meeting fuelled by clandestine urgency. What a rush. The ugly are not supposed to experience this. This is the other side of the tracks, the other side of the lake. This is the rich man's summer cottage, so luxurious it makes your own home pitiable. This is the peasant in the fancy restaurant, too busy looking around to taste the food. The drunken pensioner splurging at the cheap-metaphor sale.

She tells you to turn off the TV. The feature hasn't even ended yet. You do it anyway. In the short span of several weeks she has quickly established herself as the man in the relationship. This is new for you. Usually you're so busy bouncing around the room trying to be funny and slick and entertaining — anything to take a girl's attention away from the fact that she has agreed to be alone with you, lest she reconsider — that you dominate every sentence and fill every silence.

Instead, Honey has the situation well in hand. It's entirely comforting. There is less pressure to perform like a trained seal.

Later, and she's napping. Shift people sleep a lot. You remember how this used to be you. You're walking through your apartment. Though it's built as one vast open space, you have subdivided it into zones over the years. A good-sized kitchen, an eating area with a picnic bench in the middle, a bedroom area, a giant living room area, and a general junk area where you throw sports equipment, old exercise equipment, bicycles, books, and boxes, anything else.

The divisions have been made by neatly stacking beer cases atop one another to form thick walls. They range from three feet high at the edge of the kitchen to six feet high on the two sides of your bedroom. The empty bottles have all been meticulously washed and dried before going into their cases, and the cases are in the finest shape. No banged-up boxes accepted. Johnny and Aaron and Henry and Cuz and you put up the first walls many moons ago, the year you moved into the place, cordoning off a couch, a TV, and a stereo area. It takes a full season of drinking to put up a decent wall. The Junk Area's still not completely sealed off. Production diminished when Aaron began his first overtures towards a life of sobriety. It's hard to hold on to a good employee.

You climb the short set of stairs that lead to the rooftop door. Open it and step out onto the shabby wooden deck. You whistle for Sam Spayed. Look around. Climb back down, leaving the door open for her.

You walk into the kitchen. Go to the fridge and open the freezer. Reach in past the prop foods there, looking for the bars of hash buried at the back. Feel them. Count them. Reassure yourself that they are there. Close the freezer back up. You do this several times a week. It makes you feel better.

You hear faint noises now. Through the wall, on the other side of your fridge, a real wall separating your kitchen from The Old Man's. He's in there at this same moment, you can hear him rattling through his cupboards. You used to know him better than you do now. Before his wife died. Of a heart attack, right on the front steps. Poor thing. It was so embarrassing. You used to help them sometimes back then. Carry things up, try to fix shit for them. They'd have you in there once a week at least, on one pretext or another. They were sort of a cute couple. She'd go along with everything he said even though she knew he was half batty. After they'd gone shopping they'd come back and he'd spread all the groceries on the counter to put everything away. She'd just watch him. He'd put all the jars to one side and crack each one open, seal it back up, and then stick it in the fridge. With those big hands. Jams, pickles, mustard, relish, olives. Anything you could name in a jar. He'd pop them open then close them up again and put them in the fridge. One after the other. You saw him do it on several different occasions. Why? Why'd he do it? You asked, of course. Because — and here he'd point at the label with one of those knobby fingers, smile at you like you were daft — because it was clearly written, *Refrigerate After Opening.*

After she died you thought he'd give up, but that's not what happened. He held on good. He's a tough bird. He rallied. But he's mean now. And bitter. It's just how it is. People live long enough, they get mean and bitter. It's not their fault, just what happens.

And now things are tense between the two of you, too. He refers to you openly as "the drug peddler." Says it to anyone he sees in the building. And mutters under his breath whenever you meet in the elevators. And if you leave quarters at the machines in the basement for your laundry, he steals them. He leapfrogs your loads, too.

It makes you nervous that he hates you so. He's old and probably harmless but it feels like a bad omen. Of course, what it also points to — and this nags at you much more frequently — is that if The Old Man knows, and if most people in your building know, and if all your friends know, and if even strangers who have simply heard your name know, then you can't help but ask yourself — and this is not really about the cops or anything, because you long ago made your peace with *that* — you can't help but wonder about the thoughts in the minds of all of them, and more specifically, precisely, disconcertingly, whether anyone ever bothers to think a thing like this through for more than two seconds.

Because if they did, there's one question they might ask themselves. Where's all the money?

After all, how could you sell all that dope for all those years to all those people and not have a whole lot stashed away? A whole lot. And yet, of all the people you hang with, no one's ever really asked you.

You don't have a car. You don't have a house. You don't go on trips. You almost never have a girlfriend. You hardly spend anything on clothes. You just spend a bit of money on food. And beer. And the odd movie.

There just has to be a whack of money around somewhere. Has to. It's not like you've been paying rent with it. Or taxes.

So where is it?

In the bank?

Not bloody likely.

With a friend?

Yeah, sure.

Who?

All right. So that's not it.

Then it must be right here. In the building, no?

Okay, yes. It is.

Where?

You're not telling.

And that's it. That's what you worry about most. That's what makes you most nervous. How long it will be before one person, one day, seriously asks himself that question. The wrong person.

It would weigh on anyone.

"Take me to dinner," she says later. Awake, showered, gussied up. She is radiant.

"You take *me* to dinner," you say back. "For once."

"Oh, but you're my man," she says, collapsing against you, forcing you to wrap your long arms around her. "A man like you *always* knows what to do. Think for both of us, darling. Pick a fine restaurant. Where we can dine. And wine. You have money. You have means. I'm just a country girl, with simple needs."

"And yet a fan of expensive restaurants..."

"There are more of us than you'd think."

"But I have no money."

"But you have lots of money."

"I can't possibly afford it."

"How can you not afford it?"

"But where could we go?"

This easily, you have already given in.

"Oh, I don't know," she says, though undoubtedly she has three or four places dancing around in her head. The truth is, you've spent more money indulging the two of you in the last few weeks than you spent feeding yourself the last three months. She places the back of her hand against her forehead. "*It's just so complicated.* Surely you can whisk us away to somewhere private and perfect."

"I can't. But please keep calling me Shirley."

"Somewhere exotic and erotic. Exquisite and pristine."

"You've been staying up late," you murmur into her ear, nuzzling against her porcelain skin, "reading your thesaurus."

"Oh *think*, Lee — it's too much for me." She paws your chest. "I can't bear it."

"But I don't know."

"Think!"

"Wait —"

"Yes —"

"I might —"

"What —"

"Do you — ?"

"Yes —"

"Do you like Scottish food?"

And she ponders this, still wrapped in your arms, at first smiling, pleased, intrigued, then her brow slowly furrowing, wondering what you are up to, until suddenly she elbows herself free with her trademark move and whirls to face you.

"I am *not* eating at McDonald's again."

twenty-two

Sorry is a board game. Henry had a T-shirt once that said that. You're nearing his building. Once again. The intention this time is to get him out and into civilization for a few hours. Maybe go downtown. Play video games or something. He likes that.

But as you are about to make your way down Madison you suddenly stop. Several vehicles are parked at the bottom of the street. Bodies are milling and equipment is strewn about. You can see the Hunter Films production van, Liz and Camera Guy, and others you don't recognize. You watch from a safe distance.

Is Henry being arrested? There are no cop cars anywhere. Yet. Or maybe they're already gone. You're not sure what to think. Only one thing is clear: there's nothing intelligent to be accomplished by staying here. You should leave. And quickly, before one of them turns and trains a telephoto lens on you.

And then you hear a small sound, a polite horn beep. It comes from behind you, someone with a practised touch.

You turn, surprised to see Cuz sitting behind the wheel of a shiny Lexus.

"Get in," he says, elbow resting on the edge of the window.

You walk over. Can't help but keep staring at the car.

Cuz motions to the passenger door. "C'mon, get in. He wants to see you."

You glance down at the car again. Of course. It must be His.

Your Dealer wants to see you. And this monkey has been sent to deliver you.

In some ways, this is the more alarming development.

You get in. Let him drive you out of the neighbourhood, quickly onto the highway, and then down to the bottom of Atwater. Next to the market, where the bike paths follow the canal. To where Your Dealer is waiting, standing next to his racer.

He's wearing a crimson and gold stretchy top and matching shorts, skin-tight, complete with gross little testicle bulge, leading down to bone-white knees and frightfully hairy calves. On his head he has one of those huge shell helmets with the pointy fronts that make grown men look like six-year-olds. His racing gloves match the suit, fingers poking out and gripped around the handlebar of a three-thousand-dollar bike that probably weighs nine ounces. His wrists are taped. His huge wraparound sunglasses are wrapped around his shrunken fifty-five-year-old face. His skin appears pale and parched in contrast to the rich plastic moulding covering his eyes.

"You look sort of scary," you greet him. "Like a big bug."

"It's a biking uniform, idiot. Do you know how long I ride for? Do you know how fast I can go?"

"You look like you have a giant rock taped to your head. I wouldn't stop near young children. It could get screechy."

"I drive *over* children," he says, "if they're not going the proper speed."

Next to you, Cuz makes a motion. Your Dealer looks over at him.

"Fine. Good. Go park the car."

Cuz turns and walks away.

Your Dealer says to you, "Do you know how hard it is to stay in shape?"

"I haven't the faintest idea. Truly."

"It's a mindset. It's the only way. To keep death away."

"Death is coming just the same."

"I'll outlive you."

"Be my guest."

Your Dealer purses his lips and frowns, like he's bitten into something sour. "I'm giving him a route," he says.

Your eyes bulge halfway out of their sockets. "You're *what*? You can't!"

"I'm giving him a route."

"It's like taking mine away."

"I'm *thinking* of taking yours away."

A route. Your Dealer had a newspaper route when he was young. Back when Ben Franklin was inventing the car. So now whenever somebody who works for him manoeuvres himself into a strong enough position to merit big quantity, bulk pricing, additional credit, and most of all a stake in everything that arrives, meaning that even when things go dry — and they do sometimes — that person is entitled to a share of whatever's still around in order to keep his key people happy, no matter what, he calls this getting your route. It's a wonderful moment.

You can also lose your route. For a variety of reasons. Like non-payment. Like being careless. Like professional misconduct, say, being stupid enough to end up on TV or something. Though that would require a lack of judgment of Herculean proportions.

"This is why you brought me here?"

"Yes."

"It's why you got him to bring me here? That little prick?"

"It was important that we speak."

"I'm going to kill him."

"Do, and you're done."

"I'm going to punch him right in the face as soon as he gets back."

"If you do, you're finished."

"This is so full of shit. That fucking Cuz is a weasel and a cheat and most of the people he sells to now are people I used to sell to. And other guys buy less from me now because he's selling them on the side too. I know it. I used to take care of everyone at the Elbow Room before he and Sanderson and Dane moved in there. And the gym and the bowling alley. And other places, the new spots on Monkland."

"Yes, that's how it used to be."

"He throws product at everyone. He fronts anybody. He discounts everybody."

"Well he's not getting a discount from me, son. Perhaps it's time you adjusted your end."

"Give him Walkley Avenue instead. Let him get his goddamned head blown off."

Your Dealer winces. No one likes to talk about Walkley.

"How many years have I been with you?" you ask him. "It's not fair. There used to be something known as my fucking territory."

"Then I imagine now you'll want to work harder at what's left. And conduct yourself more appropriately."

"I asked you not to let him meet you. From right at the beginning. Didn't I? I knew it was a mistake."

"It wasn't a mistake for me."

"I'm going to attack him!"

"Then you'll be done. Wrapped."

"And if I don't care? Maybe it's worth it. Then what're you going to do? Maybe I'll just teach that fucker a lesson and you won't have either of us hawking for you. Then what?"

He stifles a laugh. "Please, must we? You're, what — really going to hurt him? And bluff me? That's your plan? You're going to put the Big Hurt on him? Please. You might as well kill him, Lee. You better, in fact. Because he'll hunt you down like a dog, that one. If there's even one breath still left in him. Please. Don't make me laugh."

"What do you know about him? Fuck off."

"You know I'm right."

You spit on the grass, tramp around for a few seconds while you try to think.

He warns you. "Lee, be careful what you say. Don't make this more than it is."

"It's bullshit, is what it is."

"Sometimes in life there's bullshit."

You spy Cuz cutting across the grass.

You turn back to Your Dealer. He's antsy to get back riding, you can tell. People are whizzing by in the background, jogging over the bridge. He's got bottles of water and a whole mess of sandwiches peeking out of the unzipped top of his tiny backpack. All ready to jam himself back down on that hard little bicycle seat and pedal the day into submission. No wonder his ass is always so sore.

You give it one last go. "Don't do this. Reconsider. I'm sorry."

"Some things you can't ask."

"How many years have I been with you?"

"It's not about you."

"I'm begging."

"You can't ask some things."

"Please?"

Cuz is close, less than twenty yards away.

He says, "Ask the government if it's okay if you don't pay tax. Ask the mayor if you can park your car anywhere you want. Come back and tell me what they say. Do you understand? Don't ask me this. It's done."

"You're a fucker to be this way. I've known you a long time."

"You're saying you and I are close?"

"Why can't I say it?"

"I'm closer to many others."

Cuz arrives. He looks from one of you to the other. He knows everything, the sly toad. He's just trying to gauge how deep into the pleading you've gotten.

He allows himself a faint grin. "Everything cool?"

Your Dealer looks at you. Warns you.

You shrug. There's nothing to say. At this moment.

You see Your Dealer and Cuz exchange their own look. What a complete screwing this is. You don't sell as much as you used to, it's true. But you don't feel like it as much. And you don't have to, to tell the truth. You've had a lot of very good years. People don't realize.

Your Dealer says to Cuz, "Okay, go get the car."

"Go what?"

"Go get the car."

"But I just got back."

"Go. Get. The. Car."

"You're kidding."

"No. Drive him back."

You hold up a hand. "I don't want to be driven back."

"He doesn't want to be driven back!" Cuz says.

"Go get. The car."

"Screw it," you say. "I'm going to walk back."

Your Dealer stops you with a finger on your chest. Though you tower over him, he has you entirely in his control.

His eyes are slits as he addresses Cuz. His voice is barely above a whisper. "Go fetch the car. Come back. Pick up Lee. Drive him back. To where you found him. Begin now." He waves him away.

Cuz slinks off. As he goes, an extraordinary sight replaces him on the horizon. It is Sharon. Undoubtedly Sharon. In the same stretchy gold and crimson bike suit, much more stretched in her case of course. Same matching pointy-headed helmet, gloves, and glasses.

Sharon weighs close to 160 pounds and stands maybe five-five. She has arms and legs like massive Gaelic sausages. Though you don't really know what that means. And she is, at this moment, moving at a decent clip. Like a giant bullet. A heaving and grunting, pumping engine of clammy flesh and dense bone. She is, you see as she weaves past the slower riders with grim determination while others simply move aside at the mere sight of her, a weapon.

She veers off the path and bumps over the grass to where the two of you are standing. She pulls up, removes her sunglasses and helmet. Sweaty hair tumbles out. Her cheeks are crimson like the suit.

She waits to be introduced, though you know she knows you.

"This is Lee. You've met him before, Sharon."

She nods at you. You nod back.

"I didn't know you guys were back together," you say. "Officially and all that."

Sharon studies you, nods again. Barely.

Your Dealer says to you, "We're so close, you and me. Are you sure I didn't tell you?"

He lifts a bottle of water from her backpack, gives it to her. She immediately begins swilling it, throat muscles constricting in large, audible gulps. There are linebackers that don't have necks like this.

Your Dealer is a slight man and looks frail next to her. For the first time you can appreciate the strange attraction he feels for her. She is strong and always prepared to fight, something he's always respected. And although her face is wide and fleshy, the features are not unappealing. She has a petite nose and the greenest eyes. Her ass is huge but so are her breasts. You've known other guys who dig this combo too. You picture fucking her from behind, quickly banish the image.

It's sad for you, what he's done today. You're angry, but you are hurt too. You did think you were kind of close. You've known him for almost ten years, from when you first met his son.

His son's name is Matthew. You hung with him for a while. One summer. An okay kid. A forgettable kid, really. The forgotten son of a reasonably famous father. Your Dealer was once a very well-known man around town, a voice on the radio. A Morning Man. A personality. A time when Your Dealer never slept. On the radio in the morning, in the bars at night. Wheeling and dealing all day in between, shilling himself around town for cash and cars and meals and free leather coats. No time for his wife. No time for his kids.

You and Matthew worked together that summer, punching tickets at a mini-putt and keeping the machines filled with balls at the batting cages. Spent other time together, weekends and nights, at his house. Through him you got to know his father. Who liked you. Who took a shine to you. As they say. He seemed to like the way you always asked questions, listened to the answers. Your Dealer was still something of a star back then, but already fading. To you, though, he seemed hip and happening and you loved the way he let you hang around as long as you wanted to, at their big house, eventually whether Matt was there or not.

It wasn't long before he let you start selling some of his hash on the side for him. He wasn't as established back then, just dabbling. Over time, however, his career continued to slide and the money dwindled, and so he made his move towards trafficking in the copious amounts of drugs he knew the people above him — stars who hadn't blinked out yet, unlike him — would be willing to pay for.

It proved a timely decision, executed in a wily, calculated way. Plus he had charm, Your Dealer. He put that personality to work. That voice. Success was quick. Expansion was aggressive. It's how you got your route — along with several others — once he really made his mark, helping him carve out a sweet niche for himself in the city and then slink back into the shadows to let his underlings continue the grunt work.

Sharon says, "Shouldn't we go?"

Your Dealer nods. He eyes you warily, zips up the pockets of his backpack and puts it on. Tightens the Velcro on his space-age shoes. Sharon fits her helmet over her broad skull and slides her sunglasses into place.

The Lexus honks from the curb. On cue.

Your Dealer looks at you sternly. "I don't want any trouble on this," he warns you. "I'm telling you right now. Again. If you do, you're done. I've told him too. The same thing. You guys better listen."

You look over at Cuz. The car is waiting. You nod goodbye to

Sharon, who gapes back at you. The narrow stare of a bully, the bovine expression of one of life's dupes.

You say goodbye to Your Dealer with hardly a glance. Dissing him with a last subtle gesture.

You trudge back across the grass to the car.

As Cuz drives, you are at first in a bit of a daze. You forget where you're headed. Then remember it's back towards Henry's. You recall also the warning from Your Dealer. No trouble. From either of you.

And so you say, "Just drop me at the park, you little prick. That'll be good enough."

Cuz turns and looks at you. Like you've gone crazy talking to him this way.

You say, "You heard me, you sad freak. You ugly turd. You fucking pig."

Cuz squeezes the steering wheel, sorting out his thoughts. The Lexus purrs along. His eyelashes flutter. He's wondering, can you say this? Are you allowed? Why are you doing this? You can see him calculating each progressive bit of logic. He's thinking, I got what I wanted. I got my route. Now I'm driving him back. And he wants to fight! Can he do this? Can I fight back? Can I fight with Lee?

No, I cannot. I can never fight.

Now I have the most to lose.

You watch this realization arrive.

"You were always a stupid dummy," you tell him, "though I guess you've gotten a bit smarter lately. But we always thought of you as a dimwit. Did you know that? We laughed at you. Johnny and me. Honey and Baby and Aaron and Mo. Even Henry. We all laughed at you. Always. When you and my cousin broke up, I took her out to dinner. It was a celebration. Irene and I drank to your sad little life and toasted your unhappy future. We joked about the clothes you wear. Honey thinks you always look dirty and smell funny. And Maureen doesn't like it when you're near her girls. You scare them, with your ugly face and bad teeth. Did you know that?"

Wow, all these things. You can say anything. This is *sick*.

Cuz can only keep driving.

"You're a fucking leech. No one ever liked you, you piece of shit. It was a drag just to see you each day. No one ever wanted you around. But you wouldn't leave so we used you and ridiculed you. Even he" — you gesture around at Your Dealer's car — "is just pissed at me because of the whole Henry thing and it's not about liking you or trusting you, you sad little piglike runt of an ugly beast."

This last bit leaves you out of breath. Takes the last air from your lungs.

"Just pull over here," you wheeze as he turns off Sherbrooke back onto Madison, and you realize that you will soon be dangerously close to the small media scrum that's still gathered in front of Henry's mother's building. "Park here, you little putz."

But Cuz shows no sign of slowing down. Instead he has aimed the two of you right at the scene waiting at the end of the street. He will deposit you right in front of the cameras.

"Park, fuck!"

He is, you're realizing rapidly, perhaps somewhat less stupid than you may have alluded to in some of your earlier remarks.

You scream *"Park!"* a last time.

He clenches his fists around the steering wheel, arms rigid.

You will arrive in front of all of them. They will swarm you. You will be shot. It will be more news with your face on it. It will not be a good thing. Your Dealer will not understand.

He will take away your route.

You reach across Cuz's legs with your left foot and mash down on the brake pedal as hard as you can. He tries to stop you. At the same time you grab for the steering wheel. Instinctively he jerks it away, throwing the car into a tight turn.

But there is no room to manoeuvre. The front end of the Lexus takes a hard left and crumples directly into the long nose of a Volvo station wagon parked next to the sidewalk.

The noise is deafening.

As the front windshield shatters, the back end of the car slides across the pavement and slams against the side of a second parked car. More noise. More glass.

The airbag blasts Cuz in the face. You fling yourself backwards through the space between the front seats, into the back seat, narrowly avoiding the thrust of your own bag. You feel something slice your cheek as you land, your head rattling against the seatbelts and the door.

You pull yourself over and flail at the inside door handle to release it. Crawl face first onto the pavement and roll onto your knees.

You stay down. Crouching, spying through the windows of the battered Lexus. You see heads turn your way, a cameraman begin to run, someone else jump into a van.

Cuz is covered in plastic and glass. You can't tell if he's badly hurt, can't even see his head. There is no time.

You whirl and run. Low to the ground. For you, anyway. Across the nearest lawn, straight through a set of bushes, and down a long driveway that slopes alongside an apartment building. At the bottom is a three-step staircase attached to a pathway that opens to a series of fences and hedges, all of which you vault easily. You could jump over a house, the way you're pumped.

This gets you through to West Hill. Good. You look around. Same options. Again you cross quickly and pick your way through a lane wedged between buildings. There's garbage everywhere. You dodge and dart and climb over another fence, cross the street and scurry onto Benny.

Here you turn without even pausing to catch your breath and run like a bastard back up to Sherbrooke Street. You pass an ugly little strip of stores where you buy your cigarettes sometimes. Though you could certainly go for a calming smoke, this might not be the time to stop and buy. Another relapse avoided. You sprint on, up Benny, cut onto Godfrey and aim yourself towards Grand Boulevard, which will lead you to Honey's.

There you stop. Bend over, hands on knees, panting wildly, shaking, blood rushing through your head.

No one seems to have seen you. No one seems to be chasing you.

You check yourself in the side mirror of someone's bright red Jeep. Your cheek is cut but not deep. It's just some blood. And your forehead is nicked. That's all. Lucky. Two little scratches.

You stumble away in the general direction of Honey and Baby's place. You're seriously out of breath. You remember when you used to be able to do a run like that and hardly break a sweat. Ten years ago. Time flies, the rest of us have to drive.

twenty~three

When you arrive, you ring from the lobby. The intercom cackles and the door buzzes open. You climb the stairs. It takes all your energy. Baby opens the door. It's a drag for you that she is at home. Similarly, her eyes lower at the sight of you.

Honey is in the bathroom, Baby tells you. Busy at this moment. It is loud behind her in the apartment.

You follow her in, realize Aaron is there too, but without Mo. And Tim, The Freckle King, is here also. Making sangria for everyone. Why? The TV is on and the stereo is playing as well. It's like being at Stacy's house. You check the furniture for milk stains.

Everyone coos at your appearance. The cuts on your face give you a certain cachet, of course. You realize also that your shirt is ripped at the shoulder, one sleeve hanging loose. Your best shirt. And you're limping. And there's blood seeping through the fabric at your elbow, a previously undetected injury.

Honey comes out of the bathroom, gasps. Ushers you back inside to dress your wounds. You sense that she wants to talk to you. Wants to tell you something. Your heart is still doing a drum solo in your chest. You picture the accident in your head for the tenth time. Replay the sensation of impact. The bone-jarring impact. The way the windshield cracked like lightning and the back window blew out into a thousand gummy shards.

You want to throw your arms around Honey but someone is always hovering. It's difficult even to speak. First it's Baby and Aaron, then it's Tim, then it's Baby again. Everyone wants to know what happened. You're undecided what to reveal. It seems easiest just to tell them that you and Cuz had a fight in the street. So you do. You describe it in vague terms, invent a passerby that broke it up. Leave Your Dealer's car out of it. No one believes you entirely. You exit the bathroom, brush off further questions.

The door rings from below. Once more Baby works the intercom. You worry that it's Johnny. You eye Honey again. You want to ask her what she's done in the hours you weren't together. You want to know how she spent every minute. Was she thinking about you? You were thinking of her.

Instead it's Stacy. As well as The Boy.

"Why Ack!?" you want to know.

"Baby watches him sometimes," Aaron tells you.

"I watch him on Tuesdays and sometimes Fridays," Baby beams, walking into the middle of the crowded living room.

"Really?"

Baby nods. Honey and Aaron and Tim nod. Everyone knows this but you.

Stacy lets Ack! loose. He bolts directly for Baby. You find yourself in the dubious position of watching him gurgle and squirm in the arms of Auntie Baby. He slobbers all over her cheeks and neck, slobber that is rightfully yours.

"It's just because he knew we were coming here," Stacy whispers to you. "He gets excited to see her. What *happened* to your face?"

You tell her. Or some version of it. She has no comment. Eventually she draws The Boy away from everyone else, leads him to you. You wrap your long arms around his little frame, careful not to crush him.

Reluctant to let go once he starts squirming loose. But you know that he is like a puppy, anxious to sniff at everyone else in the room before he can settle in.

Tim, The Sangria Servant, puts drinks in front of everyone, a 7UP for Aaron. People settle back. Honey turns the music down. Aaron puts his feet up on the table, Maureen is not here to swat them off. You see him checking out your face. Catch Stacy and Baby doing the same. A silence has settled in. Everyone is staring at you.

Aaron says, "So, you're okay?"

"I'm okay."

"You're alright?"

"I'm alright."

"Good, then." You notice a wry twinkle in his eyes, an almost malevolent twist to his smile. Strange for Aaron to act this way. Uncharacteristic.

You gulp some sangria. Not bad. You nod a thank you to Tim, look around at the others. They're still watching you.

"What…?" you say.

They look at one another. Except Honey, whose eyes are on the floor.

Baby gets to her feet. Walks over, picks up the remote.

Aaron says, "You didn't hear?"

"Hear what?"

"You don't know?"

"Know what?"

Again he's got that grin. "What they're saying."

"Aaron, I'm going to shove this fucking glass down your throat sideways," you say to him, which is absurd because you could never do it and he could pound you out in a minute if he ever got aggravated enough, "*with* the liquor still in it, if you don't stop it and just tell me what's going on."

Tim answers for him. "Baby has it recorded."

You look over. The TV pops on. Liz Hunter fills the frame, frozen in mid-cliché, microphone in hand. She stands in her usual spot, Henry's building hulking in the background. You'd think Camera Guy could find a new angle every once in a while, the lazy arse.

Baby looks over at you then lets it play.

"And so," Liz Hunter intones, making sure everyone understands how important it is to keep listening, "police have finally arrested Henry Miller. The move was made just moments ago, removing the twenty-nine-year-old from his apartment and placing him in custody."

Footage of Henry. Head down, wrists cuffed. Escorted into the cop car. Terrified, you can tell. Trembling. On the verge of tears.

"Madeleine Miller, his mother, was also taken in for questioning. No statement has been issued."

Footage of Henry's mom. The camera pushing in tight each time, clearly looking to exploit the shrewish nature of her features.

"Meanwhile the young girl's mother and friends expressed their satisfaction. They've held the belief from the beginning that Henry Miller was involved."

Footage of Darlene Dobson's mom. Sober for once, wearing her Sunday best. She seems to have cleaned up in recent weeks. Weeping now. And footage of Darlene's friend Naomi Byrd, who had been the most vocal in her accusations of Henry.

"Reaction in the community has been mixed. Many question why the authorities took so long to act, while others are asking what caused them to proceed now. What new evidence has surfaced?"

Older footage from the Sears warehouse Henry worked at, his boss, Mrs. Fernandez, his co-workers, and then a shot of you from the first interview that night, grinning like a moron. And then the second one. Including walking away from Liz, seeing Honey stopped at the light. Getting in her car.

And, of course, the kiss.

Ulp.

You look over at Aaron, then the others. Look over at Honey.

All watching you.

You look back at Baby's TV. The Firebird pulls away. They throw it into ultra slow motion, adding a cheesy synth soundtrack as it fades to black.

And then Baby's show comes on. Her soap. The one that she never misses. Which is why she has this recorded in the first place. *Lovers and Other Strangers.* With its paper-thin sets and flimsier characters, off-screen tragedies and paint-by-numbers plots. Handsome people continually walking in and out of rooms. As though it were all actually a parody, a satire of some kind. Is it?

No one says anything. Instead you all watch until Baby clicks it off.

Then you look around at everyone, throw your arms out wide, warble, "They *arrested* Henry? That's not right. That's not fair!" You say it with far too much enthusiasm. "What're we going to do, gang?"

Predictably, there is no response.

You put a finger to your chin. "I know. Let's put on a show!"

Another intolerable silence.

Finally Tim says, "Sangria? Anyone?"

Slowly, Baby and Stacy hold out their glasses. So does Honey. You too.

Not Aaron. Instead he says to you, "Christ, Lee. What are you *doing* on TV anyways? How is that helping? Why didn't you just leave Henry to his own mess?"

"I didn't audition for it, Aaron. They just come out at you from out of the fucking blue."

"Well, you sure look like you're enjoying it enough."

"That's true," Tim agrees.

"Well, I'm *not.* Don't worry."

Dubious looks all around.

"It seems to me," Stacy says now, looking from you to Honey, "that there's another question here. Don't you think?"

Honey turns to her. "What is it exactly you want to know, dear?"

Baby answers in her place. "How long it's going to be until you tell Johnny. Is that fair to ask? Or is that going to *upset* you?"

Her sister's eyes flash at her. "What's going to upset me? Is that what you're worrying about?"

"Oh, look. She's already upset."

"You should just stay quiet."

"I'm concerned about Johnny."

"I'm sure you are."

"Is that wrong?"

"Johnny and I have split up."

Small pause.

Then Baby says, "Well, he still has to know."

"Maybe *you* should tell him then."

"Fine, I will."

"How considerate of you. How selfless."

"Sangria?" Tim says. "There's still a bit left."

When the buzzer from the lobby goes, you jump up along with the rest of them. Only Ack! seems unfazed.

It's Johnny. You recognize his voice coming through the speaker, hear his heavy boots arrive a half minute later, impatient outside the door.

Baby lets him in.

Johnny takes several steps, stops in his tracks when he sees you all. "Whoah! The whole fucking neighbourhood is here."

You watch as Ack! immediately runs over to him. What's *that* about?

Johnny takes him into his arms. Gives him a big hug and looks at you. "El Gee," he crows. "What're you doing here, bro? I been trying to reach you. And *nice* face! And look, Aaron's here too. Baby, Stacy, and the heavily freckled guy. Everyone's here. Wait a minute, is this a party? Huh? Is this a surprise thing for me?"

He lowers The Boy. Looks at you once again.

"Man, you look like shit. How can you go out like that? Honey, why don't you say something to him? Hell, if that was me out with my shirt half torn off, she'd be all over me. You're an embarrassment, dude. And you're all cut up. Where'd you get all those scratches? A badminton tournament? Is this a shuttlecock-related injury?" He looks over at Baby. "He doesn't even play badminton. I just love saying *shuttlecock*. Don't you? Say *shuttlecock*."

He goes over and kisses Honey. On the mouth. Everyone flinches, not just you. He pulls back up and walks into the kitchen.

"Who wants a beer? Me, Lee, Honey, Baby. That's four. Anybody else? Tommy?"

Tim says, "We're having sangria. Have a sangria."

"First I'll have a beer. I'll have sangria later. As soon as my cock falls off and I grow tits."

He comes back with two beer.

"Hey, you know what? Guess what?" He grins at all of you, spreads his arms wide, handing you off your bottle in the same motion. "*Golf pro!* That's right. Me. Part-time, the rest of the summer. At the driving range. Silvio hired me. I get the kids and the old ladies when Silvio and Dave Kirkwood are booked. Thirty fucking dollars a fucking hour. They charge seventy. For my services. I get half. *That's* money, thirty bucks an hour. And it's easy."

Aaron slurps the last of his 7UP from between the icy gravel at the bottom of his glass. "People are going to pay seventy dollars an hour to get taught by you?"

"Listen, these are fifty-year-old women holding a club for the first time in their lives. And teenage kids with cheques from their parents. I already did one today. See, the idea is that Silvio and Dave Kirkwood can actually do two people at one time because mostly you're just showing someone something and then telling them to hit a thousand balls. But of course they can't look like they're doing two people at the same time, so they get me to do one. I show them a grip or straighten their left arm, make them bend their knees. Try to get them to transfer some weight. Then Silvio comes by, watches and adjusts things, makes sure I'm not fucking anyone up. It's not hard. And I'm pretty good."

Aaron says again, "Seventy bucks? To get taught by you?"

"What's wrong with that?"

"You used to give me tips for free and I still wanted my money back."

"Actually, *you* should come by. Sometime when we're not busy. When there aren't many people around. Tell them you know me. Come on out and we'll take some swings together."

"Really?"

"Sure!"

"Just come out? With my clubs?"

"Yeah. Well, and seventy bucks." He grins at Honey and Stacy. "I'm also the assistant sales manager."

You get to your feet, start across the room. The Boy puts down the coasters he's fiddling with, reaches up for your hand. Toddles beside you. He likes to walk with people, anywhere they're going. It's very cute.

You get to the door, turn back to look at them. Look at Honey.

Johnny says, "Where you going, man?"

"I'm going."

"But I'm telling about my golf job. And I got a good story. And I need to *see* you. And what happened to you anyway?"

"I got in a scrap with Cuz. Look, I just dropped by. I have to go. Call me later."

The Boy takes a last look up at you, hobbles back to Auntie Baby. She gathers him in her arms.

"Okay, but wait." Johnny shrugs his shoulders and looks all around, as if being begged to continue by the others. "So get this. This morning this pretty big guy and his sexy girlfriend come in. The guy said he just wanted to hit some balls and have someone watch. Silvio gave him to me. I thought I was just going to show off in front of her a bit, and maybe I could correct a thing or two with the guy. Just explain some basics. I even said, to the girl, walking out to the mats with our balls, *Okay, here's my first tip,* I said to her, *those pants you're wearing* — they were skin-tight, she had a fantastic ass — *wear them as much as possible. They're dynamite. That's my advice.* I told her that. Is that beautiful? I was trying to be funny. Even her boyfriend laughed."

He smiles at all of you. You all smile back.

"Anyways, I tell the guy to go warm up awhile and he takes out an iron. Well, you know what? He starts blasting rockets 230 yards right down the pipe. With a four-iron. You had to see them. Straight? Turns out he's an amateur looking to get his card this year and just needed someone to watch his hands, tell him if they were too fast or getting out too far in front. Well I immediately go fucking running for Silvio or Dave. Haul Silvio over. I think the guy knew. So Silvio had to come and watch him. Then hit balls with him. And I had to get the hell out of there. Right away. The girl was laughing. She knew for sure. Even Silvio was laughing. My first fucking guy. Later I came back and watched the guy hit for a while. What a swing."

You're leaning against the door frame. Johnny winks at you. You nod at him. Smile warmly again. You do like this guy.

You will miss him.

"Henry got arrested," you say. "Did you know that?"

Johnny's grin vanishes. "I *thought* I heard that. Is it true? That's why I came over."

"They took him downtown."

"Did you speak to him?"

"No."

"Is there, like, proof or something?"

"I don't know."

"They showed it on TV?"

You look around at the others. They're staring at you. Even Honey. Especially Honey.

You say, "Baby has it recorded. She can play it for you."

Johnny looks over at Baby. Baby retrieves the remote once more. The TV blinks on. You slip out the door and down the hallway before anyone can say anything.

twenty~four

Your Dealer called your place six times the first day to say you were cut off and to pay him everything you owed and to not even think of ever calling or coming by again. Then he called the next day to tell you that they finally figured out that Cuz's wrist had been broken in the accident—and what did you have to say about *that*? Another time he called to tell you they'd given him a Pathfinder to drive while they fixed his car, and you know what? They weren't so bad. He could see himself buying one someday.

Once, early in the morning, he called to tell you that they were going to diagnose him with cancer one of these days, he just knew it. Just like that, in some bare-walled little office, they were going to name one of the cancers and tell him he had it. Skin, ass, bone, lung, brain. Something. And this of course was going to drive him *out of his head with frustration*, the bitter, unrelenting unfairness of it all, coupled with its audacity at having singled him out, the gnawing thought that he would be forced to shrivel away while someone much less deserving was allowed to live on. In fact the sheer idea of that could kill him even before the cancer did.

But if it didn't, and if he X-rayed and chemo-ed and cocktailed and held on by his fingertips and lasted months, maybe years, and *survived it*, living a reasonably long and satisfying life afterwards until finally one day the natural moment of reckoning came and he had no choice then but to confront death once and for all, the end, his impending death, the pure terror of drawing his last breath, the *feel* of it, to finally have to face it and accept it, look his life in the eye, how would he react? How will any of us react? And so, therefore, after considerable deliberation, he'd decided that, whichever way it goes, he would invoke the memory of John Lennon. Not for the first time in his life, rest assured. He would remember John. Bless his soul. And thus have no choice but to accept his fate. *John Lennon.* Did you understand? John Lennon died when he was forty. John Lennon was shot by a complete fucking idiot. John Lennon was younger than Your Dealer is now and at that time he was rediscovering himself and embracing the change and rising up to meet the challenges of the second half of his life, which is a lot more than Your Dealer could say for himself. John Lennon gave more to people than anyone else he could think of. John Lennon had so much more to live for, and deserved to live so much more than anyone else. He had a *young child.* John was the hope in all of us. And still God let him die. Imagine. Of all the people. Living life in peace.

Now, what could Your Dealer possibly say in the face of that? If he looked at it in this way, could Your Dealer feel unreasonably treated? No. So John Lennon is who he would think about.

He called another time to say that his preoccupation with death was due to the fact that he couldn't stop looking back on his life and marvelling at how little he'd accomplished. He said that at its most basic level his complaint with dying was that it was just so humiliating. You come off as such a loser to everyone else staying behind. He said that death robs you of your *potential.* It takes away the minuscule possibility that you might have been destined for something great and wondrous. Instead death stamps your file closed and brands your life pointless.

A couple of times he called absolutely ranting and raving and — though you would have sworn previously that he didn't drink — awfully drunk-sounding. Did you have any idea how much trouble he was having with his car insurance? Did you understand the hassle involved? Did you have any idea how long it's going to take *until the whole thing is settled*? What could you have been thinking? He never would have believed you capable of something so irresponsible. How wrong about you he'd been! And then he reminded you that you were cut off and to pay him everything you owed and to not even think of ever coming by again.

Once, in the middle of the night, he woke you to tell you that John Lennon was, without question, The Greatest American Ever. Bar none.

Though partly asleep, you'd been able to correct him. "John Lennon wasn't American."

He'd just scoffed at you. "Everyone's American, pal."

The last time he called you was to tell you that you can break people down into three basic categories: Those who worship Money. Those who worship Pleasure. Those who worship Time. Everyone is a slave to one of those three currencies.

He, of course, worshipped Money. Naturally. Because he was intelligent. And knew how to earn it. So did his friends and a lot of other successful people. It was only logical to worship money.

Most people worshipped Pleasure. Drinkers, druggies, adulterers, fatsos, actors. Drama queens. TV addicts. Including the Liz Hunters of the world, who worshipped adulation.

And then there were those who worshipped Time. People like you. Just looking to stretch the whole thing out. Lazy, with no true ambition. No potential. Unwilling to assume responsibility. Whose only goal is to prolong the experience of existing. Quantity over quality. Who resent any demands that life makes upon them. And, as such, unpredictable, undependable people.

Then he reminded you once more that you were cut off and to pay him everything you owed. To not even think of ever coming by again.

For once, you hung up on him.

After all this time, all these tirades, this was the first time you'd ever hung up on him. The only time. Even though he'd crashed the phone down on your ear plenty of times before. But this time he'd made it abundantly clear that he was through with you and that you were not about to get any product from him ever again.

So why waste your precious time?

twenty~five

You can see a field from here. From up on your roof. From your *terrace*. Which is a plastic patio chair and an old golf umbrella set into rotting grey wood. From up high like this you can see the field across from the train tracks where the young kids like to play. Filling their plastic pails with dirt scraped up from the long, skinny bare patches that have been trampled through the grass. It's early evening and a few are still out. You watch as two boys and a girl chase after another boy who's carrying what looks like the handle broken off a wagon. The boy with the handle is bigger and faster, more agile, feinting and darting away from them easily, the way he's seen the older boys do. You listen to their little yelps, both excitement and frustration. Suddenly one of the chasing boys stumbles around a turn, loses his balance, looks like he's about to regain it but then abruptly pitches forward, screeching elbows first into the dirt with a cruel skid.

The boy with the wagon handle stops, doubles back, leans in with genuine concern. It strikes you that you feel somehow reassured by this. That no matter what else is going on in this city, on this night, at this moment, whatever other incidents and accidents and arguments and beatings and cheatings might be blindsiding other unsuspecting victims, here this bigger boy has stopped to help a smaller, fallen one. Almost nobly, he bends down and extends his hand. The instant he does, of course, the little clumsy one senses the drama of the moment and lets loose with a series of wails.

You turn away. Crying children is not your thing. You pull hard on your joint. Notice other people in the dusky exposure. A woman hurrying, pushing a baby stroller along a narrow path. Two men talking nearby, giving her the once-over as she passes. Another neighbour gets into his car, cranky and rusted. It's seen better days but they were a long time ago. The car lumbers out into the street, slowly rocking over a pair of speed bumps and then accelerating around the corner. You follow it with your gaze until it's out of sight. Then panning and tilting up like a camera, your eyes widen their scope to frame the blots of hulking apartment buildings, and the more distant office towers beyond them, this hazy grey backdrop, row upon row of rooftops, a big-city mountain range presiding over all you village idiots.

A mother's voice calls out. Bath time, bedtime, beckon. The Wagon Handle Bunch react with typical disregard, pursuing their game until she calls out again, more insistently. Now the chasing turns half-hearted, the yelps are fewer. Reluctantly they begin to gather their toys and leave.

The boy who took the fall stays behind and talks briefly with the older one, then he too makes his way towards the apartment buildings at the other end of the field. He's a grimy sight, his pants brown and green and baggy at the knees, his elbows and little chest painted with even darker dirt marks that his mother will surely shit herself over when he gets his sorry ass home. Soon only the older one, the noble little dude, remains. He's tossing pebbles up in front of himself, swinging at them baseball-style with the handle as they come down. A lone batter in a deserted field, trying to connect.

You stub your roach in the ashtray. By now the balcony is half draped in shadow. Cooler air, night air, is creeping in, driving the humidity up into the sky. It takes only a few tosses until the boy loses interest. Soon he begins to shuffle off as well. Away from the apartments, towards the tracks, a direction none of the others took.

You have to strain to keep a proper focus, trying not to lose sight of the small receding figure. You think, *What about you, noble one? Where are you off to? Home? A warm bath? Or to roam the streets some more? In five years, ten years, where will you be? Will you be noble still, and kind? If it's me lying there one day in the dirt, will you kneel to help? Or crack me a good one in the head with your stick and take my money?*

You go back inside. You're alone. Honey has a run of evening shifts going on. You're so used to being with her you're forgetting how to be without her. Ah, young love.

You listen to music and read for a time, eventually heave yourself up and walk over to the bathroom, start the shower. You run it super-hot, always have. Even in summer. It's one of the reasons your hair has the texture of old straw. Your scalp is hard and burnt and like the Mexican desert. Does Mexico have a desert? Under the water you feel suddenly tired. Showers usually wake you up but this one's making you sleepy.

After a long while you get out. Your apartment is dark, only a single lamp is lit. You dry off, put on your hospital bottoms, and brush your teeth. You take your book with you into bed. You'll crash. You were going to stay up and watch a movie but not anymore. All around is evidence of Honey and your new life. Clean shirts, new pillows, the oversized T-shirts she sleeps in. Her aroma. Yummy. You'll read a bit then maybe jerk off and go to sleep.

Almost instantly the book is heavy in your hands. You feel yourself dozing off. Once, twice. It's hard to tell how long you're out. Then something stirs you. A noise? You blink your eyes open. Glance around you, quietly place your book on the floor. Click off the light. Darkness. You remember that you never went up on the roof to let Sam Spayed in, who must be hungry. Is the door properly closed? You can't remember. You're tired. You want to stay in bed and sleep.

Instead you hear it again. What was that? Was that outside?

It didn't sound outside.

It sounded inside.

And it's not a cat.

You leave the light off. Don't move.

Barely breathe.

You listen harder. Maybe it was nothing. Something that was nothing, really.

Except now you hear a rustling. Is that a door latch?

Holy McFuck.

You lift your head from the pillow, crane your neck, still trying not to breathe. This is unreal.

Is there someone on the roof?

You angle your ears to squeeze every last decibel of sound from the air. Instead you hear your own heart beating. You hear the space between your ears, the air flowing through the tiny canals, internal microphones turned up so high the ambient hum of your own existence is deafening.

Now you hear another rustling. *Another one.* Not even from the same direction.

Then silence. Absolute still.

You strain to see in the darkness, afraid to move too much lest you create your own rustling. It's as though you can hear the walls listening back at you. You try not to panic, try to calculate instead. What are your options? What should you do? Quality answers are not at hand.

You sit up. Your bed creaks. You cringe. Listen for reaction. Nothing.

You sneak a breath, try to think. The neurons in your brain finally come to a consensus.

There is someone in your apartment.

That's what you heard. Not the sound of the door to the roof, not the latch up there or even the stairs that lead down. No. It was sound on this floor. Near. Not far.

Mother of God.

You'll get your throat slit. You'll be shot in the face. Beaten with a bat in the darkness, unable to ward off the blows.

It's somebody already inside. Trying to get *out*.

Someone who came down those stairs when you were in the shower. Or was here before you even got here. Or came in after you fell asleep. Goddamned door up there.

You can't help it, suck in a deep breath. An audible one.

Listen back. Again, nothing.

You want to call out. You would, if you knew what to say. Hello? Go away? Don't hit me in the face?

Whoever it is knows where you are.

Whoever it is saw you turn off your light.

Whoever it is…is whispering.

Oh God.

To whom?

And then a mad scrambling screech of feet and limbs, falling boxes and toppling furniture. Bottles smashing. Running. Crashing. It sounds at first like a thousand wildcats but then you pare it down, your eyes squinting into the shadows, picking out one, two, maybe even three clambering bodies, silhouettes moving quickly from behind a wall of empties to the staircase and up through the door and out and then across the roof, thundering above you. Is that laughter? Your hands actually rise in the air to clamp your ears shut. You are actually trembling. You are that scared.

Seconds pass. You stand rigid in the darkness. You glance upwards. The door to the roof has swung half open and moonlight seeps in.

Once again you hear only your own heartbeat.

You click on the lamp on the table beside your bed. Shield your eyes until they adjust. Venture forward. Scout the huge floor space. See the beer cases that have fallen, the boxes lying on their sides, flaps open. Little brown rocks of glass lie out front in spray formation, the bigger shells of the broken bottles still trapped inside.

You walk into the kitchen. Drawers and cupboards have been flung open, the refrigerator and freezer doors as well. The door to your oven is open. The microwave. Even the lid to the garbage bin. You check at the back of the freezer and see immediately that the bars of hash that were stored in Baggies there are now gone. You cross the floor, check inside the pantry for other small stashes among the soup cans. Also gone.

How long were these fuckers here?

You cross back through the apartment taking long, nervous strides. Past your bedroom, past the untouched drawers of your bureau. Avoiding the glass. To the living room where the cushions of your sofa have been uprooted and your DVDs and CDs are in a state of upheaval. The rug has been pulled up. A chair is on its side. An old chest you use as a table has its top open, contents strewn about the floor.

You go up the stairs. Immediately lock the door, not even venturing onto the roof. You're about to go back down when you hear Sam Spayed scratching, feel the tiny weight of her paws against the door. You unbolt it and open the smallest sliver necessary then lock it back up again, all within the space of two seconds. Give her a little kick in the ass on her way down the stairs.

She dances across the floor. You follow her for several yards then veer over to the far wall, to the Junk Area, where you stow anything that doesn't belong somewhere better.

Whether this room has been rummaged through or not is anybody's guess. It's always such a mess. There are old golf clubs and skates and bicycle seats and boxes of dishes. There are ten-year-old phone books and pieces of lawn mowers. You kneel down beside a tattered hockey bag stuffed with old equipment. Take a breath. Unzip it. Your hands search inside until they pull out a suede bag, brown and soft with a gold drawstring. You open it. It's crammed full of bigger, thicker bars of dope and packets of hundred-dollar bills.

Your fingers fumble over the bills, rifling the edges, rubbing the texture. You're thankful that it's all still there. Over six thousand dollars. Again you breathe in deeply, this time savouring the sweet aroma of money not stolen.

Later, you've done a fair job of cleaning up, now you're falling asleep again. Or trying to. It feels like it's been hours. You've been twisting up skinny cigarettes from your rolling tobacco and smoking them until you're about to puke. You've clicked over more TV channels than the world can possibly need. Now you've lowered yourself back into bed and feel ready to try again. You let yourself go. Let yourself drift. Slowly it comes.

And it's only then, slipping away, receding, that you can properly replay the movements in your head, slowing them down, picturing them almost as sports highlights, seeing the silhouetted figures with greater clarity, not so hurried, not so panicked now, finally seeing it again — that the third one, the last one up the stairs, the one holding his arm cocked at a curious angle, queerly thick at the end, confirms in your mind's eye what had been gnawing at you from the beginning, that he was wearing what could only have been a cast on his wrist.

twenty~six

The next morning, Stacy and The Boy rap at your door. Wake you up. It's noon. She called hours earlier but you barely heard what she said. Can't recall what excuse she'd provided for saddling you with Ack! yet again.

Still, you're glad to see him. You squeeze him once, twice, three times. You could go on with this kissy stuff forever. His thin, hot chest pressed against yours. Adorable little ball of love. He struggles away from you, begins exploring your place. He loves your apartment, all the wide open space.

You're sort of glad to see her as well. Ferocious, snarling ball of love that she is. She too is sniffing around. You can read her confusion. Her radar knows intuitively that a woman's presence has established itself here and yet the general disarray suggests the opposite. You make no effort to enlighten her.

Stacy seems in no rush to go. For someone who has quote unquote *an absolutely infernal amount of things to do* — she actually talks this way sometimes — she doesn't seem to be leaving any time soon.

You play with Ack! on the floor, using a couple of your hockey sticks to whack a bumpy ball back and forth between you. You're using one of Sam's chasing balls, strips of aluminum foil wadded together. The Boy looks adorable holding your heavy, oversized stick. That you are a goaltender makes it even more unmanageable for him. Still, he has skill. He has game. Very professional-looking spittle clings to his chin.

Stacy makes sandwiches for you and her, pasta and veggies for The Boy. You watch her, busy in your kitchen. She nukes Ack!'s little portions from the tiny Tupperware containers she carries in her tote bag. She has everything in there.

You have to admit, it's nice not to be alone. It's nice to have company. She looks good today, too. Better and better all the time, really. If you weren't so heavily, absolutely, passionately, overwhelmingly involved with Honey in this new lifelong, eternal, till-death-do-you-part commitment, you might just…well, it's hard to say. Sometimes Stacy seems to have a sexy-mommy allure to her that's more inviting than any single-chick vibe.

"I thought you were trying to quit smoking," she calls over.

"I am, mostly."

"It stinks in here. More than usual."

"It's Honey."

She doesn't answer. Though you can't see her you know she is displeased with this answer. You get to your feet. Crack open a window, the only one you can. The rest are factory-style glass panes, sealed shut, old and stained with dirt. You go over to the stairs, climb them. Unlock the door and open it. Step out, scan around. Check for interlopers. Come back in and down the stairs, leaving the door open above you. It's the only way to air the place out.

You know it was Cuz. It had to be Cuz. With Sanderson and Dane. Come to rob you.

You return to Stacy and The Boy at the kitchen table.

"You know what I've always wondered about?" you say to her now, seemingly out of nowhere. "You've never asked me to lend you any money. Not even once."

You study her reaction. While eating your very tasty bacon and tomato sandwich and watching Ack! devour his wagon wheel–shaped pasta, hamster-like, stuffing one after the other into his already milky-fat cheeks.

She says, "You don't have any money."

"Well, I have *some*," you say carefully. "But you've never asked. Me to lend you some, I mean."

"Yes I have."

"When?"

"I asked you once if I could borrow two hundred dollars. When Zachary turned one."

This is true. You remember now.

"Well, I didn't have it then."

This is not true.

"I *have* seen you with money," she allows, thinking about it. "I guess the money to do your little deals."

"My little deals."

"You know, your" — and here she mouths the word *drug* — "deals that you do." She looks over at The Boy as though checking to see that he's not monitoring the conversation for inappropriate content. Instead he's monitoring the gobs of mashed sweet potato on his fingertips.

You swallow a big hunk of sandwich. Delicious. Really, really good.

"But that's not my money," you say.

"I know. You have to give it to that man."

"Yes." She's never met him.

"So it's not yours." She takes her own bite, tiny and polite. "Lee, is that what you want? To lend me money?"

She looks at you with the sweetest, most earnest expression. She really is a doll sometimes, Stacy. Innocent and honest. Such a good mother.

"I would," you say, surprising yourself. "Yes."

You get up and walk over to the Junk Area, behind the wall of empties where she can't see you. Ack! toddles in after you seconds later. Some days he has to follow you wherever you go.

You dig into the brown suede bag and take out two hundred dollars, press it into his little hands. Send him back. "Here, go give this to Mommy."

After lunch, she still doesn't leave. But she does tell you why she came. She has to go shopping. To buy outfits. For her new job. She got a job.

"Can you watch Zachary? A day a week? Two days a week? Please please please."

You run your hands through your hair. Rub your eyes. Get up from the table. In lieu of answering. Take Ack!'s glass with you into the kitchen to refill.

Why does she need a job? Why does she need a job and what about Graham? He makes money. And what kind of job? What the hell can she do?

"I'm doing telephone sales," she explains. "In an office. But it's good. It's a salary not a commission, and Jeffrey, who's the boss, says he doesn't think I really have it for sales but if I do it for three months then I can manage the office after that. Because he doesn't want to do it anymore and people come and go so much that no one's ever around for too long, so really it's a job about placing ads and hiring people and then training them and I like training because it's like teaching, which is what I really like to do."

It's not as scattered as it sounds and you follow it and even understand it. Perhaps even more than she realizes.

"You're leaving Graham?"

She looks at you with an actual smidgen of respect in her eyes. You're standing at the fridge.

"I guess so."

Shit.

"Are you still with him now?"

"Oh, I am. And don't you be going and saying anything! I'm not planning to do anything right away. I want to be a manager first."

"But you're leaving. For sure?"

"For sure."

"Wow."

"Yeah."

"I'm sorry."

"I can understand."

You ignore this shot. Give The Boy his milk. Sit down. Finish your sandwich. Very, very tasty. Listen to her explain that Graham is not right, Graham is not who she needs to be with, Graham is not in love with Zachary. Graham is probably not that happy either, in all likelihood. Graham's career is really starting to move. He wants to go on calls at night, go to bars with the other planners, hold sucker seminars on weekends. Graham's about to start making a lot of money and Graham's not going to stick around forever, there's no sense pretending about that.

"So it's defensive," you say. But not maliciously. "You're getting ready for when he leaves you."

"No, I'm not." She says this with no hesitation. Looking you right in the eye. "I told you what I was doing. I told you what I've decided. On my own. But I need help. And from you this time. I need you to watch him. Two days a week."

A thought occurs to you. Unrelated. You get up. Cross the length of your place to reach the stairs. Ack! doesn't light out after you this time. Once again you climb the steps to the top. Get down on your knees. Examine the lock. Angle it against the sunlight looking for scratches, signs that it has been picked. Maybe you didn't bolt it from the inside last night but you sure didn't leave it unlatched either.

You see it in the light. The tampered edges on the inner metal, and then the splintered wood along the edge of the door frame where it was pried open.

You close the door, set the bolt, come back down. That fucking Cuz. You walk back to the kitchen, exuding as casual an air as you can. Check the clock above the sink.

"Can I go out for ten minutes?"

"Out?" She looks at you.

"Yeah, ten minutes. Can you stay until I get back?"

"Where you going?"

"One of those, you know, deals." You mouth *drugs* at her in an overly dramatic manner. "You don't want to know. Do you? So can you?"

"I guess."

You walk quickly to the Junk Area, retrieve the suede bag once more. Ack! arrives just as you're finishing. You cross him as you leave, going back over to the kitchen drawer where you keep all your sets of keys. Find the ones you're looking for. Again Ack! arrives just as you slide the drawer closed and leave. Now you walk to the front door and open it.

"Okay, bye," you say to Stacy.

"Lee?"

"What?"

"Why aren't you taking your sunglasses?"

Everyone knows what a sunglasses freak you are. You reach back in and take them from atop the little table.

"I didn't know it was sunny." What a dumb thing to say. Sun has been trying to fight its way through your grimy windows all morning.

Ack! arrives once again, almost out of breath by now. He really needs to do some roadwork, this kid. You reach down and scoop him up and give him a big kiss on the belly. He's giggling as you set him down and close the door between you.

twenty~seven

The elevator grinds down to the basement. You exit, reach back in through the door, and send it back to the top floor. You walk down the damp corridor, past the laundry machines to where the locker rooms are. Conveniently there is no one around. The Old Man goes out to lunch every day at this hour. Every single day. Amazing. He's like a machine. A soldier. As for the rest of the building, most of the students are probably still asleep.

You open your locker. Walk inside. Clear a path to the boxes of books in the corner. You slide them out of their spot to get to the flat stones underneath. One is easily pried loose. There is a tiny hollow space ten inches by ten inches by four inches deep. You reach into the suede bag and remove only the wedges of hash. Place them in the shallow opening. You have to put a few of them in lengthways and a couple sideways, like a kid's puzzle. When you are finished the fit is snug, there is room for nothing more. Hidden but accessible. You have done this before.

You replace the stone, slide the books back, and close the caged door, lock it behind you. Leave with a suede bag that contains only money now.

Next you climb the stairwell all the way back up to the fourth floor. Purposely don't take the elevator. The stairs are metal, you try to make the least noise possible. When you finally make it to your floor you must tiptoe past your own apartment on your way to The Old Man's. You hear Stacy and The Boy inside. It's her turn to play aluminum-foil ball hockey now.

You listen at The Old Man's door. Nothing. You take out the set of keys you've brought and gently open his door. Inside, you nudge it closed and quietly lock it behind you, creep across the floor. Unlike you, he has big ugly rugs placed everywhere covering the beautiful old floors, and Gyproc walls have been erected. The paint is old and flaking and marked with bruises in many areas. The apartment smells of curry and stale socks. The furniture is even older than yours. Long, thick curtains have been mounted over the windows to keep out the light. There are spiderwebs in almost every corner and you can pick out the scent of mould in areas. It's a bit of a fixer-upper.

You walk quietly to the back. You know your way around. You've been here before. Spent time. He has papers and magazines and other junk stored here, like you. In addition there are many cardboard Bankers Boxes filled with accounting records from long-forgotten, less than successful business forays.

You take out the boxes from a stack almost completely hidden at the rear. They're marked *Murray's*. It was either a hat store or a bicycle shop, you're not sure.

You select the one marked *1990-1995*, lift the top.

Inside is a thin layer of faded financial statements. You pick them up and remove them to reveal the wads of cash stored underneath.

Your cash.

You recover this box and move it down to the floor, open the one below it. It has *1985-1990* scribbled on the front. Inside it's the same story: you remove the top few papers to reveal the large sum of money that lies beneath.

You heart races at this sight and yet at the same time you feel easier breaths escaping. Not that Cuz and Dane and Sanderson or anybody else would figure this one out in a million years, but thank Christ everything is still here. This is your life's work.

You push '85-'90 to the side and pull '81-'84 towards you. Open it and lift the top papers. Empty your sack on the floor.

Two four six. Six thousand dollars, give or take, is what you are about to deposit in this cardboard box in this stranger's home. Along with the other dough, a helluva total.

All told, a bit over one hundred and ten thousand dollars.

Can you dig it?

It's the safest place you can think of. You can't just put this stuff in a bank. It's not that easy. Or smart. So this is what you do. You've got to hide it. From everybody. You've been doing it for years. Sheer genius. The Old Man has no idea. It's right here. Imagine. It's insane. And to think how much he hates you. Imagine if he knew.

At this moment the sound of the elevator suddenly groans through the wall. It's being summoned to the lobby.

Oh, great. Of course. Of fucking course.

You quickly begin placing the packets of bills inside the Bankers Box. The fit is not great. You stack and stuff and shift the money, trying to get it as flat as possible. It's questionable whether there will be room for it all. But what other option exists? This is not the moment to start '77-'80! There's no time to hollow out a new box, pull out the thick wads of statements that you must take with you to dispose of later, leave everything looking just right, as few handprints as possible left in the dust that coats everything.

You stick with it, packing and placing and finally managing to cram everything inside. Then you close up, re-stacking and sliding all the other boxes back into position, straightening and re-straightening for what feels like an eternity. Next you hurry across his stinky rugs to the front door. Only to arrive and realize that you've left your suede bag on the floor beside the boxes. Dolt! There is no choice. You must return and retrieve it.

And so you do.

Then you're back at the front door once more with your ring of janitor keys out. Your fingers are trembling and too many of the keys look alike. Usually you have no trouble picking out the right one, but this isn't usually.

You hear the elevator arrive and creak into position. You fumble. Fumble some more. These keys used to have little stickers with numbers on them but a lot of them fell off and were never replaced and so you've gotten used to just eyeballing it every time.

You hear the doors open. His footsteps. You jam the keys back into your pocket, retreat into the apartment. Cursing yourself, beginning to sweat. You look this way, that way, your decision-making abilities evaporating with each frantic second. Finally you dash into his bedroom.

What a choice. What a mess. And what a smell. Your eyes dart left and right. The closets are flimsy pressed wood creations that could never camouflage a frame as long as yours. You look behind his two bureaus, then behind a large wicker hamper. Still not large enough. Finally you drop to the ground and stuff yourself under his bed, slithering to a spot in the middle, just beneath the sagging box springs.

You hear the door bang open. You hear him wrestle it closed. You hear a bag being placed on a counter, water running in the sink, cupboard doors opening and closing.

You hear a kettle come to a boil and tea being prepared.

You hear a radio crackle on and a talk show in progress.

You hear the TV come to life and another talk show begin.

You hear other noises you can't put a definitive action to. What sounds like a newspaper being read. What sounds like coupons being cut from circulars. What is unmistakably a shit being taken.

You hear grunts and groans and shuffling from room to room. You hear the clumsy roar of old age and the silent screams of solitude. You hear constant heavy breathing.

You hear snoring. Snoring from another room, The Old Man asleep in his chair in the living room. You presume. Thank God he didn't come in here to flake out. You picture The Old Man in his ugly living room, splayed open-crotched in front of the TV. His chin digging down into his chest. Shock of white hair. Huge hands. Bony wrists. Ash-white skin, creased and paper thin, like air-dried meat.

He scares you, this living skeleton.

You can't will yourself out from under his bed. Instead you dither and waste opportunities. You give yourself deadlines, letting them pass and then making new ones. Two minutes. Or thirty more snores. Next commercial. Or after this interview.

Someone from below summons the elevator. It grumbles to life. You hear him stir. Mumble. Hold your breath to see if he will go back to sleep. Think of Cuz. That motherfucker. The reason you're here now. Minutes pass. The Old Man doesn't rise but the breathing is not as rhythmic as before. The snores come like bursts of gunfire.

You lose your will entirely. Let your head slowly collapse down against your fingers. Lie there, still. Very still. Until, incredibly, you feel your own eyes closing and your own nap coming. Ah, fuck.

The telephone jangles loudly. You awaken with a start, knocking your head on the wood slats above you. You hold your breath, listen, gauge The Old Man's reaction.

It takes him forever to get out of his chair. Five rings at least. You catch a view of his bony ankles and big, bumpy feet crossing in front of the bedroom doorway, disappearing around the corner. Four more rings.

Finally he picks it up. "Yes hello what?"

You hear a mouse squeal coming from the receiver.

After a time The Old Man cuts in. "Fine then."

You hear him click the phone off and put it down.

=

He runs a bath.

Gulp.

You know what's next. Naked Old Man. In this room.

You're starting to despise yourself.

He takes his bath. With the door open. Which you'd have to pass in front of in order to leave. Which means he'd see you. And hear you. You're certain of this. His apartment is the mirror image of your own. Which means you're still trapped. Sigh.

He gets dressed again in the same clothes. At least it's a development. He has another tea. He watches more of his show. And then, you can tell, he's really getting ready to go. He shuts off the TV, the radio. Rinses his dishes. Puts his shoes back on.

You hear him making his way towards the back of the apartment. You listen as he climbs the stairs that lead up to his door to the roof. One. By one. By one. It's arduous work. The breathing is always heavy. You've never noticed before how laboured his movements are. You think of scenes you've had with him in the laundry room and the lobby. He hadn't sounded as bad as this. You listen as he checks and double-checks that the door is locked. Good man. Wouldn't want some thief to break in one night and make off with boxes of old bank records.

He comes back down and begins walking back. Painstakingly. It's forever to you. But you know you're only a couple of minutes away from liberation now.

And then suddenly his steps become erratic and you hear him tumble and you don't know if he's tripped or just lost his balance or is having a bloody heart attack and then he comes into your view through the bedroom doorway, you see him collapsing and tumbling and finally falling to the floor not more than fifteen feet in front of you.

Bang. Just like that.

Well, sort of bang. Maybe more like *ugh gunhh grrr uhnff* and then an odd sort of crumpling to the floor.

And he's lying there. For a seemingly awfully long time. Without moving or making a sound. Except for his breathing. Still wheezing, very forced. But alive at least.

You don't know what to do. Reveal yourself? Call 911? Call out to him? Help him? Wait a bit more? Another nap perhaps? As usual, the plethora of options renders you inert.

And then he moves. Mercifully. He groans. Turns. His head lolls in your direction. He opens his eyes. For a heart-stopping instant he is looking at you.

It looks like he's staring right under the bed, right at you.

But he isn't.

He's simply groggy but alive, and then slowly, defiantly, getting to his feet. And then moving out of your sight, over to the bathroom where you hear the water running in the sink for what feels like an hour. And then it shuts off and he comes out and you hear him walking — wait for it — *away*, yes away, towards the front door!

And it opens and he exits and he locks it carefully and then the elevator arrives and its doors open and close and it begins its painful voyage downwards.

twenty~eight

You let yourself into your place. You go straight to the bathroom. Piss like mad. Splash water across your face. Soap your hands into a frenzied lather.

You expect Stacy to be cross with you but she is uncharacteristically unballbusting.

"Boy, some ten minutes…"

"I'm going to take a shower."

"Zachary's reading. Go give him a kiss."

"After my shower."

"Just go see him fast."

"I really have to shower."

You enter the bathroom, close the door behind you. Drop your T-shirt to the ground, peel off your pants. Turn on the water.

"Thank you for the money," she calls through the door.

"You don't have to pay me back," you say.

"But I will."

"Look, just keep it."

After you towel off and get dressed, you hang out playing cars on the floor with The Boy. Then you order pizza while she fries up tofu for him. Later you give him his bath while she cleans up. She says it'll be good practice, you'll be watching him more from now on. You let it pass. It's not the night to argue. You're going to stick with the good vibes tonight.

Stacy keeps a pair of pyjamas in her magic bag. You put them on him. Is there anything cuter than a boy in pyjamas just a little too small for him? You tackle each other onto your bed. He pins you, he's always pinning you. He's undefeated. You snuggle up to him as you read in bed. A wonderful thing. A great book. In the history of all mankind, there has only been one Dr. Seuss. Still, you do that thing where you try to skip a few pages in the story. Some of those books are pretty fucking long. You're getting drowsy again. So when you get to how Thing One and Thing Two are in the house freaking out the kids, you subtly fold several pages into the next flip and then suddenly The Cat is already cleaning everything up with his gizmo. A deft move. Neatly done. He catches you anyway. He always catches you. You go back and read the parts you tried to skip. He is delighted.

The Boy is beautiful. The Boy is sweet and innocent. The Boy spreads joy wherever he goes. The Boy For President.

Stacy's mother is supposed to pick them up. Of course she's late. Now Stacy's phone rings and she listens as her mother explains that she's going to be even a teeny bit *later*. Stacy clicks her phone closed and gives you a look and then you all read more and talk more and play more until eventually he starts getting wobbly and Stacy turns down the lights and you carry Ack! over to your bed. You lay him down, give him nuzzles, return together to the living room. Turn the TV down lower there too. Sit silently, watching the show. Occasionally you turn to Stacy, give her a good long look. Take her in. Occasionally she turns towards you, does the same.

Thoughts flutter in and out of focus. Many of them revolve around how you wish you could get high. Or rather you *can* get high, but what if you do? Will she freak? She gets squirrelly about it sometimes when The Boy is nearby. You think also how cool it is that Honey is your girl now. Your *girlfriend*. Have things changed for you or what? Too bad you can't bring it up with Stacy, talk about how cool it is this happened. You used to be able to talk to Stacy about anything. But you can't talk to *anybody* about this. It's just that kind of subject. No one's giving you grief but no one wants to hear you babble on about it either.

You think of Stacy too. How great she is. What a tough gig the single-parent thing is, and how good at it she's turned out to be. How it's ironic you're sitting beside each other right now, looking probably just like a married couple. How you liked her instantly, Stacy, the very first day you met her. All that honesty and vulnerability on display for anyone to see. She was moving into a new apartment, a recent friend of Maureen's, that was the connection. And she needed help. You, Aaron, Aaron's brother, Johnny, Henry, and Cuz. Recruited on a day's notice. Her place was an absolute mess, nothing properly packed, not even enough boxes to go around. She was so nervous. Yet happy you'd all come. Incredulous almost. Watching the bunch of you, complete strangers, killing yourselves moving all her shit up and down the stairs. Just because Maureen and Aaron had asked you to do it. It was a weird day. Hot and stressful but packed with energy and humour. Stacy seemed to be either laughing or crying all afternoon long. All the boys flirted with her, just because she was new. Just to see how she'd react. And in fact it was you she preened back at hardest, wasn't it? Yes, it was. Not Johnny. You. This was a few years ago, of course. Before she was a mom. Back when she first came to the neighbourhood. Back when Johnny and Honey were solid, the king and queen of Sherbrooke Street West.

You reach over now, put your hand on hers. Stroke it fondly. Think how you're never as nice to her now as you were back then. That's the truth. Think how pretty she is, actually. That wide face, wide smile. Big frame, strong frame. Tall, like you. A well-muscled girl. Athletic. In a *good* way. You like her. She's a genuinely good person.

She turns in your direction now. Presses her palm against yours. Wraps her fingers around yours.

Her eyes flutter subtly. A soft smile appears.

Uh-oh.

That's not what you meant. You meant…something different. You were expressing your…friendship. Your fondness. For her. Was that not clear? Perhaps not. Yet what about Honey? She knows about Honey. How could she not think about Honey? You and Honey just *started*. Can she really think you'd be thinking about cheating on *Honey*?

What are you, a big slut?

Gently, you try to extricate your fingers. Loosen your hand.

At first she misunderstands. Tightens her hold on you, thinks you're playing. Then gets it. Allows you to draw your arm back, her eyes clouding in embarrassment, colour inking into her cheeks.

You try to make it seem casual. You try to make it mean nothing. It doesn't matter. It's too late. You feel her stiffening. Feel the couch growing cold.

She stands up, flustered. With no clear destination.

Goes to check on The Boy.

You watch her. Pad down the hall, duck into the room.

When she returns she is collected. She is calm, resigned. Accepting of what has just transpired. A familiar expression for you, this suffering angel.

She sits down in the armchair. Sighs. "Just let me know if you can help out, okay? A couple of days a week?"

Instead of your sense of charity being stirred, instead of kindness being elicited, resentment surges forth in its place. That she forgives you so quickly makes you angry. Why is that?

You say to her, "Well, for how long?"

"Well, for now. I don't know for how long."

"How can I say then?"

"You can say okay for *now*."

"But how long *is* now?"

She rubs her eyes, tired as only a mother can be tired. "Are you doing this on purpose?"

You say, "You know, don't you think Graham should pitch in with this whole thing too? I mean, he's got responsibilities as well."

"Lee, I told you. I'm *breaking up* with him." She smiles sweetly.

"Still."

"Still what?"

"Well, I might not always be available, you know."

"Lee, Graham works. Anyway. He can't just leave his job."

"He's always working."

"Well, he has to. He's building his business."

"Right. Like a big sellout. Like a big suck. He sure traded in his jeans and long hair in a hurry."

"Oh, so what? What's so great about long hair and jeans?"

"They're great. Don't worry."

"To you."

"Yeah, to me."

"And Graham's doing what he thinks is right."

"Boy, you sure don't *sound* like someone planning to break up." Why you're goading her, why you're picking this fight, you're not sure. You're not even sure why you're ragging on Graham. He's not such a bad guy. "Admit it. He just gave up."

"Gave up?"

"Yeah. I just think Graham gave up too easily. It's like, shrug, shrug, the whole world's about money, I guess I have no choice but to become a big fink and suck cock like everybody else."

"Oh, right. *You're* the good one to be talking about who gives up easily."

"I'm not sure in what way you mean that exactly," you say, give her a sly smile. "Or maybe I am. Is Graham what I'm not?"

"Graham's trying, I think."

"As a financial planner? What is that? It sounds like so much bullshit. Investment counselling. Fund management. Mister Two Percent. You know, there was a time when you didn't suffer financial planners so gladly either."

"Geez, really? Would that have been, uh, before I had a baby? By any chance?"

"You know, you always bring it back to that."

"Because it has to come back to that. *Moron.* Stop pretending you're so clued out."

"I'm not saying let The Boy starve. I know you have to eat. Just that you don't have to suddenly just sell out and go right over to the other side. You can see first if there's other ways of working things out."

"What other side? Are you living in a movie? There's no time to see if things work out, Lee. If this is what it costs to have you watch Zachary a couple of days a week, forget it then."

Which of course is what you want her to say. But you don't leap on it just yet. You let it slide. As her phone vibrates to let her know that her mom is downstairs.

She packs up her bags and heads over to your bed to get her son.

You trail after her. "How come Graham never watches Ack!? It just seems funny that you do it and I do it and your mother does it but he never seems to do it."

"I do it. And my mother does it. You do it *occasionally.*" But again she averts her eyes from yours. "Anyways, he does it. When I have to go out for a bit. If I ask him. And how do you know when he watches Zack? And how much do you think you actually watch him? Please. I don't think you have a good grasp on how much time is involved raising a child."

She's wrong. You do. That's the problem.

You say instead, "Is that what it was? Time? You had a baby, so there was no time to waste, better hurry up and grab yourself a financial planner with bad skin and thin wrists who can't even buy a suit that fits him right?"

"Oh, really. Look who's talking again. Graham's wrists are too skinny for *you*? I'll have to tell him you said so."

"Tell him I said they're faggy skinny, like he couldn't throw a ball across this room. Or make a real fist."

She scoops up Ack! He hardly stirs. You take a last long look. So beautiful.

You follow her back out. For the record, you have a pretty accurate idea of how stupid you're sounding right about now. Very. You're always ragging on Graham behind his back yet never say anything to his face.

"A financial planner," Stacy hisses at you, "just helps people save the money they've earned. It's not a dirty thing. It's his job."

"Yeah, well," you whisper back, "why doesn't he just go earn his own money?"

"Like you, you mean?"

"No —"

"Sell hash, you mean?"

"No."

"Maybe that's what he should do. Sell dope. I'll tell him that. I'll tell him that's what you think he should do."

"Don't bother. He'd never be any good at it."

"You don't think so?"

"Oh, I know so."

"He'll be so disappointed."

"And he wouldn't get to wear those smashing suits anymore."

She gives you a sharp kick in the shin. Makes you step backwards, lean up against your front door.

"When are *you* going to do a little earning and saving? Huh, Lee? A little financial planning. When are you going to get a job? How long has it been?"

"Ah, I don't think so."

"You're too special, I guess."

You move to one side. Away from the door, and her feet.

"I'm no mutual fund peddler, Stace."

She gives you a hard look. Can't sustain it. It fades slowly, in the end just a sad gaze. "No, I guess not," she says.

"Everyone knows that."

She sighs. "That's true."

"It's how it is."

"Yeah, I guess. Except."

"Except? Except what?"

"You know. Except."

You sigh. "Except... Ack!?"

"Call him Zachary, please, when you're talking with me."

"It always comes back to this," you say.

"To what?"

"To this."

"Say it. What?"

"To Zachary," you say.

"To Zachary Who?"

You give her a look now. "Haven't we been through this so many times? What else can I say? Is there something new you expect to hear?"

"No, of course not. Except that it works out just perfectly for you, doesn't it? How do you feel after you've babysat for an afternoon? Like you've done something special? Do you feel grand? Is it a grand feeling?"

She's got The Boy in one arm, with her purse, her baby bag, and the folded-up stroller in the other. You carry nothing, of course. She's waiting for you to open the door but you have no immediate plans to do so.

"It just feels like I've helped out a bit. A little bit, that's all."

"Liar!"

"It does."

"I don't believe you. You feel all good about yourself."

"I don't..."

"And then off you go. Over to someone's house. Over to see *Honey*." She spits this out.

You say nothing.

"You have no idea how hard it is," she says.

"But you wanted a baby."

"It's not a question of that!" she hisses.

Abruptly she shifts her cargo down to the floor while still holding Ack! almost perfectly aloft, twists the door handle open herself, and reclaims her load in one fell swoop.

She says, "Can you imagine how much I worry? Yes, it's about time. And not just about now. It's about how things will be later. And you have the nerve to stand in front of me and tell me how you can't go out and work like everybody else? Because it's just not for you? *I'm no planner, Stace. Everyone knows that, Stace.* Like that changes a single goddamned thing or makes it one bit easier? What if I didn't have my mother? Have you ever thought of that? Then what? All you have is time, Lee. Why shouldn't you at least share some of it? And I'll tell you something else. If anything ever happens to my mother, *it's your scrawny neck*. Understand?"

You lift a hand, dab one side of your head. Then the other. "Sorry," you say. "I'm just cleaning the blood trickling from my ears."

"Answer my question."

"I don't know what your question *is*," you growl at her.

"Please don't be an ass."

"What do you want to know?"

And you can tell by the way she doesn't rattle something right back at you, how she pauses and lets her eyes wander for an instant, that she isn't entirely clear about what it is either. And then in a quieter, smaller voice she says, "Don't you think you could change?"

It's a peace offering. An overture. A last-minute chance for you to make nice.

Instead you say, "Geez, I don't know, Stace. Could I? I guess there was a time maybe when I could have. I mean, there was a time I remember, right around the same time I slept with you *one single solitary night* for reasons I don't altogether remember anymore, when you said you were on the pill and I didn't have a condom but you said you were on the pill and how the hell we could be so unlucky I don't know but you turned up pregnant and then you had Ack! and the very first thing you let me know was that he was yours and by that you meant *not mine* and that I should shove off while you gave him the right home and no druggie was going to be a part of that, and so I did shove off just like you wanted, and I guess that was around the time I might've *changed…*"

And it is a speech, granted. More or less the one you give to her in your head every few weeks or so. Designed to get Stacy to back off and to let you off the hook. Truth be told.

But she says, "You know, that you actually remember it that way makes me feel better that you're not around, you know that? Because then Zachary is actually safe from a certifiably insane person, even if it is his father, and it actually makes me sure I made the right decision, and it wasn't that way at all, you liar. Like you were — what? — going to stop getting high all the time? Stop going out? What I remember is that for like maybe a week, *maybe* a week, you hung around and pitched in and mostly slept, actually, and after that you and Johnny and Aaron and Henry and everyone else went out more than ever, and there were times when you pounded your fists on my door at five o'clock in the morning —"

"No, there were times you wouldn't let me in at five o'clock in the morning, and that's why I had to pound my fists —"

"— because you are —"

"— because if you had just opened the door —"

"— so utterly —"

"— it wouldn't have been such a big deal —"

"— childish —"

"— and we could've all gotten some sleep —"

"— and self-centred —"

"— instead of Zachary crying all fucking morning."

"— that I'm ashamed I know you sometimes, Lee Goodstone."

And on this shitty note, she goes.

twenty~nine

The thing about Johnny is that he's clever. You have to remember that. He's not an idiot. Racing over to your place and pounding the shit out of you is the *obvious* thing to do. It's what he's *dying* to do. It's what his brothers are *urging* him to do. And it's what, ultimately, he's going to do. One day.

But not right now.

Johnny has his eye on the prize. He fucked up when he slept with Baby, he's not going to make a mistake again now. Kicking your ass is what Honey expects him to do. Humiliating you in front of her is precisely what she's waiting for him to do. Then, once it's done, Honey can hold it against him forever. It's crossing the line. And he knows it.

So no, Johnny's playing it cool. He's showing he can be patient. Mature. Considerate even. While you live a little longer.

Why can't you fight back? It's a good question. You're certainly big enough. And yet also a chicken. As in, A Big Chicken. You've spent your life ducking scraps. You're a coward. What you know about fighting you learned from watching movies. And it doesn't translate well. In the movies one guy throws a punch then the other guy gets to throw one. Then the first guy comes back with a couple more. It's well choreographed and designed to see-saw back and forth.

In the few bouts you've been mixed up in, the other guy came at you with such a spastic flurry of fists and fingers, punching and gouging and tearing off pieces of your face, spitting at you and trying to knee you in the balls all at the same time, that you barely had a chance to defend yourself. There was, let's be clear, no counter-punching of your opponent involved.

In every instance observers intervened, breaking it up within twenty seconds. A good thing. Though you are tall and look as though you could easily conk down on your opponent's head, a single fist delivered to your ribs or stomach and your body instantly shuts down. Your arms turn to spaghetti and your hands to jelly. And spaghetti and jelly, unless you're six years old, don't go well together. Meanwhile your face is turned high and away the whole time, with your chin back as far as it can humanly go, straining to get away from the whole fiasco. Refusing to identify the incoming blows and insisting that everywhere else bear the brunt of the assault. Until finally your guts can stand it no longer and you are forced to double over in agony. At which point the other dude unloads on your big, crooked, and suddenly available nose like a mallet pounds in a stake.

When Johnny comes looking for you he will meet with little resistance, you know this. He knows this. Oh, you'll try, of course. Stare him down at first. Dazzle him with a bit of unlikely footwork. Who knows, maybe you'll even land him a good conk on the head before he begins pulverizing you, a saving grace when you're forced to explain the cuts and bruises that will adorn your face all the weeks afterwards. The public spectacle of it all being the most daunting, naturally. Over time your face will heal, but the whispers behind your back will dog you the rest of your days.

Years have passed since you and Johnny first became friends. A million things have happened. Yet something in the yin and the yang of it all kept the two of you tight all through. Others came and went. Girls. Schools. Jobs. You and Johnny long ago made a pact not to bother asking much of life. Unspoken but clear. The road most travelled. Johnny would cruise his charm and good looks right down the middle of the highway as far as it would take him. You would ride shotgun, sneering alongside him. That's all changed now.

You arrive at Honey and Baby's place. It's the rare Friday evening Honey doesn't have a shift.

Baby answers the door. She's in a dour little mood. You can tell the minute she opens her mouth.

"What?"

"Can I come in?"

You say it pleasantly, refuse to be drawn into her darkness. She knew you were coming by. You called ahead.

"Well, I just cleaned. You'll have to take your shoes off."

"Hey, no problem. Hell, I'll take my *socks* off if you want."

She makes a face, goes.

You flop on the couch beside Honey. The two of you are going to a movie later on. She pecks you on the cheek. You give her a big, sloppy kiss back. She punches you in the thigh with her fist. Ow. She can really hit, this broad.

Baby's got her own plans. Within minutes she has her purse and jacket and is heading out the door. The two sisters rarely talk anymore.

Later, Honey is ready and you are about to leave. You're still treading lightly. She's touchy lately. Quick to go off on a pout, not want to talk to you for long periods. You have to watch it. She holds a grudge like a longshoreman.

You're on your way to an overly expensive dinner and then *the cinema*. There will be wine. Much wine, if you have your way. There is hope for good loving. You'll go back to your place tonight. The hell with sleeping in this museum. You'll sleep together in a bed Johnny's never touched. Sort of. Of course he has, naturally, technically, *touched* it. Over the years. He's passed out in it even. Loads of times. And barfed on it once. *So* gross. But still, it's different.

You ease in behind her at the door, knead her exquisite shoulders. Breathe softly. Crane your neck in, lower your lips to her ear.

"Later, when we get back to my place…"

"When we get to your place…"

She is ready to play along. You are grateful for this.

"I'm going to run the bath…"

"You're going to clean the bath…"

"I'm going to clean the bath, and then fill it with the softest, soapiest water…"

"…ooh, a nice bath…"

"…and we're going to get undressed…"

"…undressed…"

"…get in the water…"

"…warm water…"

"…and soap each other clean…"

"…mmmn…"

"…until we feel so soft and lazy…"

"…yes…"

"…and then I'm going to take you right there and turn you over…"

"…and then we're going to towel off and go into the bedroom…"

"…where I'm going to take you and turn you over…"

"…where we'll put on fresh new sheets…"

"…and I'll take you and turn you over…"

"…and you'll take me and turn me over…"

"…and have my way with you."

"…and have your way with me."

=

But somehow when the evening's done with and by the time you get back up to your apartment and put your stuff away and feed Sam and then snack again yourselves because you're both still hungry even with all the popcorn and chocolate you had after dinner, by that time a bath seems like a lot of unnecessary effort and it's already so late and before you know it she's in her least sexy nightshirt curled way under the sheets with her magazine in her hands and the evening has come to a screeching goddamned halt.

You're worried. You know that in some way, somehow, you are becoming a disappointment. But you aren't sure how. And so you snake your way in beside her and a cool silence ensues as she tries to read while you toss glances at her.

And finally she lowers her magazine and lies back against her pillow and sighs and then, pretty well out of nowhere, starts reminiscing about meeting you and Johnny all those years ago in the park, and at first you're pissed that she's talking so much when you wish you could just be screwing but then she starts talking about you and him and how you used to compete with each other even though you pretended like you weren't and then revealing that, yes, Johnny was gorgeous, but you were sweet and funny and the decision to be with him was not as easy as you probably thought it was all these years.

And you are suddenly interested. You say, "But you went with him anyways."

"I did. Yes."

"So what, then? So you *almost* went with the ugly guy. But in the end didn't. Big deal."

"Oh, but it wasn't like that."

"How was it then?"

"I didn't know what to do. You were both so fun. I was excited when either of you was around."

Your heart rate quickens. They *were* heady days. Everything moved fast then. You were all free. Time was free. Love was free. You remember the arrival of Honey and Baby in your and Johnny's world. Direct from Yurp. As that idiot Dubya would've said. This was glamour. This was excitement. Every guy around wanted one of them.

She says, "So do you know what I did?"

"No."

"I decided that the one who wanted me most was the one I'd go with."

"Wanted you most."

"Yes. Tried the hardest."

Ah, yes. Effort. Not your strong suit. You search for a rebuttal. You want to reply. You rack your brain for the argument that will prove she was wrong. There is none. You *never* try hardest.

Busted.

She laughs sweetly. "You seemed so nervous, Lee. It was that too. Johnny was good at knowing what to say at the right time. You got pretty anxious when it mattered. You weren't exactly *clutch*."

You don't know what to say. What are you supposed to say? People don't understand what it's like to be Johnny's buddy, the weight carried by knowing you are always number two. To everyone. Less colourful. Less popular. Not handsome. Not strong and not great at every sport. No cool brothers. No gorgeous girlfriend.

And once again a realization strikes you. What you will answer the day Johnny asks you. And that day will come. Sooner or later. You and Johnny will come face to face and it'll be the moment and he'll say to you — hopefully without too much malice, without complete hatred — he'll say, "Why'd you do it, Lee?"

And you'll have to explain to your best friend that *you just had to find out*. What it felt like. For once. To be a winner. To walk down the street with a girl like that on your arm. To be him. You'll have to tell him that.

Ugh.

Uh, maybe not. Maybe that's the kind of thing you keep to yourself.

She leans over, turns the lights out. You lie back. Listen to her breathe, wait for her touch in the darkness. It never comes. Instead she's off on another stroll down memory fucking lane. *Another* one. After a long introductory sigh and a tiny laugh. This time it's about when she made Johnny tell her how he lost his virginity. How he didn't want to say. But she made him. And it was a funny story. He told her about his father's old *Penthouse* magazines. And you, of course. And those sexy letters. And about how the two of you would go downtown to try to pick up horny housewives and how it never worked out.

Except for him. One time. When for some reason you didn't show up at the end of the afternoon. And so he was waiting to take the bus home alone and then he helped this woman put her bags in the trunk of her car and the next thing he knew he was being driven home — not to his house, to *her* house — and into her bed and her arms and between her legs, and that was it. Virginity lost. She gave him cab money for the ride home. He pocketed it and walked instead, an hour through the falling snow. High on the experience. Finally fell asleep. When he woke up the next morning, he told no one. Didn't even tell you for the longest time. She's not sure how long. Didn't tell anyone. Kept it to himself. Saw her again a few more times after that even. That was Johnny, to be quiet that way. He knew how devastated you would be. And he even went back downtown to the stores with you a few times, when you insisted. Cruised through the aisles. Until you finally gave it up. Of course his own thirst for it wasn't what it had once been. Mission accomplished, and all that.

Yes, she says to you, he was sweet in that way, Johnny. Wasn't he? Never threw it in your face. Not a bigmouth. She's getting a bit groggy, you can hear the sleep in her voice. She says, we think Johnny's so selfish, but he isn't always. Not always.

Right?

You say nothing.

"When was it you finally found out he met that woman?" she asks thickly. "Were you jealous? Or did you think it was nice that he didn't want you to feel bad?"

You say nothing. Again. Pretend you're also falling asleep.

thirty

"Two what?"

"Two heggs."

It's a week later. You're downtown. You're standing in line in the food court at the train station. *Gare Centrale*, as they call it. The man ahead of you has just ordered breakfast. He has ordered two eggs facing the sun.

The accent is from France. The clothing is from France. The pinched expression and caffeine-soaked breath are from France. The way he says *heggs* comes out as one giant exhale. There is an odour.

The kid taking the order leans back to get away from it. He says, "And they're doing...um, what?"

The Frenchman knows he's making an error, he's just not sure what. For some reason he has chosen to order in English. Sometimes here, right in the centre of town, in a place like this, it's hard to know which to lead with. The dominant tongue can be fuzzy. And now, having committed, he seems unwilling to switch.

He says, "Facing de sun?"

Once more, the big exhale. On *suh-hunn*. The kid's head bobs back as though dodging a jab. He wafts his hand in the air. Glances at you, next in line. Making sure you're getting all this.

You watch the man squirm. You are in no rush. You have nowhere to go. You're killing time. And time is killing you. It's seven-thirty in the morning. You are less than fully awake. There are people everywhere. It's amazing how many people are up and about at seven-thirty in the morning.

The man says, "And a *rôtie*. And coffee. Please."

You hear a lot of different languages here. See lots of different faces. There are many kinds of food to be bought here, many blends of coffee. People sure like their coffee. They walk around extremely busily carrying their coffees. They're just basically on their way to do their jobs like they do every day, but they're very busily going about it. Stern, focused. Maybe it's the need to show they belong. Because here, at this time of the morning, one must belong. Not belonging invokes the thought that one might be *up to no good*. One might even be a terrorist. You look at the man to see if he is a terrorist. No, he's just from France. Waiting for the kid to decide if he has enough information to go on.

But the kid is still jerking him off, pretending not to understand. "What's that again?"

You step forward. Speak up. "*Rôtie* is toast. And he wants his eggs sunny side up."

The man smiles in your direction.

But the kid frowns, annoyed at you. "Oh, gee. Thanks. Like, I didn't know. Hey, *I know* what 'facing the sun' is with these guys. Trust me. You think I don't know? Are you stupid?"

You look at him straight on. "You're treating *him* like he's stupid."

"He *is* stupid."

"I don't think that's right, man."

"Oh, you don't?" He looks at the Frenchman. "You want two eggs facing the sun? Is that what you want?"

"Yes…"

"Well, what do you see behind the counter here? What's behind this glass?" He jabs at it with his young finger.

The man blinks. "Muhh-ffins?"

"And over here?"

"Muhh-ffins?"

He points upwards. "What does the sign on the wall say, above the prices?"

"Muhh-ffins?"

"And the name on my shirt?"

"Muhh—"

"*We don't have eggs!* Understand? Do you see a grill? Do you see me wearing an apron? Or a fucking hairnet? There's no eggs. Nobody's facing the sun. How many times a day do you think I tell people we don't make eggs?"

The man blinks again, turns to look at you. You blink back.

He reaches down, lifts the handle of the briefcase lying at his feet. Straightens and pivots briskly away. Like an extra in a movie. His scene over. No *rôtie*, no coffee. Unless they cut to him later, strafing the food court with an Uzi.

The kid looks at you. You don't know what to say. You turn in the direction the Frenchman went, start away.

"Hey," the kid calls after you. "Where you going?"

You pause, though you shouldn't. Turn to face him.

"I'm not really mad," he says. "I was just fucking around."

You say nothing.

"My name is *Stéphane*. I speak French. I just don't *like* those guys. Guys like that. Where you going? You don't have to go."

Ah, but you do. You never should have turned back.

The kid motions for you to return to the counter. "C'mon. Tell me what you wanted. I'm not mad. What did you want?"

You pause. Freeze. Stall a few seconds. There is no use. You have nothing else prepared, can answer only the truth.

"Well, eggs…"

=

You come to the train station the first Monday of every second month. Early in the morning. To meet a guy. To take care of a guy. Sometimes he arrives, sometimes he doesn't. You have to show up and stick around anyway. To find out. Every time. That's the deal. You never know ahead.

You've never spoken to this guy on the phone in your life. Always in person. If he comes, he meets you at the same gate every time. You barely exchange a word. Then you walk together to where you've got his shit waiting for him, usually in a big envelope in a locker. Then he takes off in a cab. What he does and whom he sees afterwards, you have no idea. You met him through Your Dealer years ago. He's a heavy hitter.

Today is the first Monday of the second month. You have nothing for him. For the first time ever. Nothing hidden in the locker. You don't know if he's coming or not, but if he is, you'd better be here to meet him just the same. Explain it to him.

You're staring at one of the TVs on the wall. You're dying to go back home, back to sleep. You can feel yourself rocking slightly from side to side. Shapes go by. Your eyes and ears are on autopilot.

Suddenly you snap alert. Read a graphic that says BREAK IN THE CASE. Then it slides away and quick-scrolling text appears, white against the black captioning box. You follow the words of an announcer.

He's telling you that Darlene Dobson has been found. Alive. She was admitted to the Royal Victoria Hospital a couple of days ago. She was not immediately recognized because she arrived with virtually no identification. She had her hair dyed green. She had various new facial piercings and a large tattoo on her throat.

She is heavily medicated. She was also treated for several minor injuries. It's suspected that the seventeen-year-old is currently suffering from post-traumatic stress suffered at the hands of an ex-boyfriend slash ex-convict, released from prison only months earlier. They had previously been involved in a volatile and occasionally violent relationship. He was a twenty-five-year-old petty thief and part-time pimp who had recently been incarcerated on a conviction for home invasion, sentenced to eighteen months, but let out after only six. It's reported that he had returned to the area less than two weeks prior to Darlene's disappearance.

They switch to Liz Hunter, live outside the hospital. She's looking good today. Extra sultry. In her un-sultry way.

Liz lets you know this is going to be an *in-depth report*. She assures you she *has the scoop*. And reminds you this is *breaking news*. As Camera Guy zooms uncertainly in, Liz reveals that the alleged assailant has been identified as one Teddy Lewis Jr. He had been following and watching ex-girlfriend Darlene Dobson for several days. It is possible he'd already approached her and she'd rebuffed his initial advances. On the morning she disappeared he stalked her as she left the apartment she sometimes shared with friend Naomi Byrd and made her way to meet with Henry Miller. And then at a point later that morning Teddy Lewis Jr. approached her on the street, persuaded her or forced her — it is still unclear — into the car he was driving. He then drove out of the city. To his father's house up north. Liz gives one of her famous eyebrow moves on *up north*.

It was there, she continues, that the relationship eventually soured into one of intimidation and manipulation. While she may have arrived willingly, when Darlene asked that she be allowed to leave, Teddy Lewis Jr. refused. Ultimately she was given no choice but to live as his girlfriend, his cook, his housekeeper, and his sexual partner. They "married" in a ceremony conducted by his father. In her ninety-nine days as his hostage she left the property five times, always accompanied by Teddy. With her baggy clothes and coloured hair and piercings and the grotesque tattoo he'd forced her to have stitched into the side of her neck, Darlene was close to unrecognizable.

And then, on the one hundredth day, Teddy Lewis Jr. and his father accidentally locked themselves in the basement. They were sealed in behind two-and-a-half-feet-thick cement walls, from where no scream could escape and no cellular phone signal extend, a heavily secured barracks they had built underneath the house, used to sort, package, and distribute marijuana they grew on the property.

They were trapped for twenty-six hours.

Darlene Dobson escaped by simply walking off the property in the middle of the night wearing only a T-shirt, underwear, and a pair of men's slippers. She followed the roads in the dark until she reached the fire station in the middle of the nearest town, sat herself down on the front steps, and waited to be found. Freaked out and barely able to speak.

All righty, then.

They end on a long shot of the Vic. Inside the building, it occurs to you, Honey is beginning her day shift.

You rub your eyes, get to your feet. Feel the rush of blood to your head, lift your fingers to your temple. It will pass. Or it won't. You should sit back down. Or stay up. It's hard to decide. You keep picturing Darlene Dobson walking down a country road in her panties in the middle of the night. You're a sick puppy.

You try a few tepid steps. Stop. Spy a familiar figure rounding the corner, coming towards you. Within seconds you are face to face.

Your client?

No.

Your Dealer?

No.

Johnny then?

No.

It's just the Frenchman from the muffin place. He has what looks like bits of dried yolk at the edges of his mouth and a wiped egg stain smeared onto the bottom of his tie. He brushes past you on his way over to the escalators, takes hold of the rubber rail, and lets the mechanical stairs do the rest of the work.

thirty~One

Naturally, the police release Henry. Immediately.

There is much celebration. Jubilation. The gang reunites. For a while there it was looking like this would be the big goodbye, the summer everyone parted ways. Now Henry is back and he's a star, proving to be more of a glue than anyone suspected.

You're at The Q on this sunny Sunday afternoon. Everyone is there. Everyone. You. Henry. Honey. Your friends. Johnny. Johnny's brothers. Everyone.

Henry is genuinely elated to see all of you. It's touching but sad, given the whisperings that have gone on about him these past months. The doubts of his innocence. The all too quick acceptance of his guilt. Everyone hugs and tugs and tousles Henry's hair. Aaron gives him giant noogies. Maureen hovers with a frozen smile on her face, pretending to be thrilled. Baby flits from table to table carrying a blue martini. Tim, The Ferociously Freckled Phenomenon, is always by her side, but so is some other young guy from their school. Man, with her you need a scorecard. Unlike Tim, this new one is covered with thick black hair. He sports a huge mane, fierce eyebrows, a furry beard. There is hair gnarled at the stem of his neck and surely a forest of it on his chest and back. He is The Hairy Wonder. She sure knows how to pick them.

And yet, for the first time ever, you feel that it's actually true when you say you don't care who she's with. You no longer care. The fever has passed. Meanwhile, on Baby's end, being with Johnny no longer seems to matter much either. She seems oblivious to him. You watch Honey alternately watching Baby and watching Johnny, evaluating. Baby is careful to steer clear, stays with her own kind. She sits and listens and plays with the rim of her martini glass as The Hairy Wonder lectures on how all music today is shit and controlled by big corporations and the radio stations just play what they're told to while we all listen, and it's *immoral* and goes against the spirit of music in the first place and we're all just lemmings. We have to stop, we have to stop listening to these same songs and these same old singers and force a change and think for ourselves.

Baby nods, considers this. You can tell she's taking it all rather seriously. Finally she asks, "Yes, but what if it's just *dance*?"

You look over, notice Johnny overhearing, smirking. You want to laugh too. With him. *Dance music.* Ha! All she thinks about. It makes you want to go over and drape your arm over Johnny's shoulder, snigger with him, and make Stupid Baby jokes the rest of the afternoon. But, of course, you can't.

Stacy arrives. Late, of course. Without Graham. She too is genuinely thrilled to see Henry free. She has tears in her eyes. She wants to know *everything*. She wants to know how did it feel, did he know Darlene was alive, what was jail like, what did the police say, did he wonder why no one believed him?

Then she asks what everyone is thinking.

"Are you mad at us?"

Henry smiles. Cautiously. He says no, he's not mad. He says, anyways, what do you mean? Everyone trusted me. Right? He smiles again. He's joking. Henry's actually making a funny.

He seems changed. But then, shouldn't he be?

Everyone looks around uncomfortably. You, however, stand a little taller. You came out on Henry's side early on. Didn't you? You even went on TV and said it.

Stacy says, "But why weren't you more mad at the police? Why didn't you just tell them? They kept acting like you were with her that day. And like you did something to her."

Baby and Tim nod, look to Henry for his answer. Aaron and Mo as well. Breath, as they say, bated.

"Well, I did see her. I mean, I was *with* her. That day."

There is a recoil. You, especially, are taken aback.

"That morning?"

"Sure."

All eyes are on Henry.

"Sure," he says again. "She came to see me. I asked her to. She promised she would. I told her I had something to show her. Something she had to see."

Even Johnny's brothers have stopped to listen. The music, it seems to you, has been lowered.

"I took her with me to an apartment building my mother owns part of. A new one. Across the tracks. All the way down on Upper Lachine Road. We walked there. We crossed over the walkway at Grand. It's far. Like twenty minutes. I wouldn't tell her why. She kept asking. We were laughing. She was so curious."

There is a joy in Henry's eyes remembering this.

"My mother let me have a two-bedroom place on the second floor. Until they rent it. I had it all decorated up. I mean *all*. Appliances and furniture and everything. And I painted it. Colours I knew Darlene liked. Lots of black. Everything I picked, I picked because I thought she would like it. I put shag carpeting in the living room. And the bedroom. Because I knew she liked shag carpeting. I couldn't wait for her to see it."

He pauses for a couple of chips, a sip of his drink. Iced tea. Like Aaron, you realize for the first time, he's not drinking. And he's semi-articulate suddenly. Quasi-intelligible. Pseudo-lucid.

It strikes you now that he's probably rehearsed this. All those hours spent hiding in his mother's building. Eating raisin bread. All that time to mull over his version of the events. He's played it over and over in his head. He knew one day he would have this story to tell. Probably in this bar, to these exact people.

Henry's *prepared*.

"I brought her there," he says. "I showed it to her. I said, 'This is for us. Live here with me.'" His eyes go wide when he recalls her reaction. "Boy, did she hate it! *Hated* it. Not the colours and stuff but just *hated* the whole idea. I mean, she flipped. She got *very* agitated. Yelling. She said, who did I think I was? Was I a freak? She kept saying she was only seventeen and how creepy it was. And I thought, *But we've been fucking for months.* You'll be eighteen at Thanksgiving. You've slept with about a *million* other guys. What's the huge gigantic stupid deal?"

He continues, "I just wanted to make a safe place for us to be in and spend time together in. You never knew where she would be sleeping. I kept thinking, Why is she getting so angry? I kept saying, I can change it. I can paint it different colours. *I thought you liked shag.* We can take all the furniture back and start again if you want. I kept talking but I didn't know what to say."

Henry looks around at everyone. Settles on you. You have trouble returning his gaze. You don't know how he does it. How he bares his soul to people like this.

"And then all of a sudden she took off down the hallway toward the front door. I chased after her and got there first. Blocked it. I just couldn't let her leave. I'd worked so hard to get my mom to let me have this place — I just couldn't believe that she wanted to leave. After only five minutes! For weeks I'd just kept thinking about the first time we were going to get undressed and get into bed in our new bedroom. How great it was going to be. I kept thinking about that exact moment. And I'd thought about it and thought about it and now she was going to leave...and I just couldn't...handle it, you know?"

He munches another few chips. Chugs some more soda.

"So then all of a sudden she grabs an umbrella that's leaning there and *plunges* it into my stomach. As hard as she can. And man, I go down! She goes out the door down the stairs of the fire escape. I get up and go after her, holding my gut and not moving very fast. It's early morning and there's like no one else around, as I half walk and half chase her down the lane."

You glance around. Everyone is riveted. It's almost as if they've forgotten she ends up alive.

"So the funny thing," Henry says, "is that we're both outside in our socks — because of the new shag, I'd insisted — but I'd somehow remembered to grab her shoes as I went out the door. So we go along for a bunch of streets, shouting back and forth in an awful kind of conversation. She kept a good distance between us the whole time. Walking in our *socks*. We looked totally stupid but there really was no one around. Then I calmed down for a bit and started trying to save anything I could, but she wasn't into any of it. I said everything I could think of. She wasn't even listening, I don't think. Then I lost my temper again and took a last dash at her but she just ran away from me. She was laughing at me. I chased her again. Eventually I threw her shoes at her. I had tied them together while we were walking, and I just grabbed them and threw them as hard as I could. And I told her to fuck off, she was a whore, and other things I didn't mean.

"So she stopped, and looked at me, and I realized she wasn't laughing. She was crying, her eyes were swollen. Though I don't know why she was so sad. *I* was the sad one, you know, with a big umbrella gash in my stomach and a black apartment and all that fucking shag carpeting everywhere. Then she picked up her running shoes. I thought she would take off with them but instead she just stared right back at me. Then she swung the shoes by the laces as hard as she could and flung them up in the air — so high — until finally they came down, hooked over a telephone wire running between the buildings. Like, thirty feet in the air. On St-Jacques. Where they found them. We both just stared at them swinging there, without saying anything."

You notice Honey now, somehow moved a tiny bit towards Johnny. And Johnny just a shade closer to Honey. Or are you just imagining this? Everyone is standing, leaning against the tall island tables. It's hard to tell. No one is seated. Still, you're pretty sure. You steal another glance while Henry continues.

"Then she took off her socks and threw *them* away too. Turned around and started walking. I didn't go after her. I just watched. I saw her go all the way down to where the Mazda place is. Where you can grab the highways. And there was a car idling there, like maybe it had been waiting. Watching us. She walked over to it. I could tell she knew who was in it. After a few seconds she opened the door and got in."

Baby's eyes are bugging out of their sockets. This is stuff straight from her soaps. "A white Gran Torino?" she asks breathlessly.

"Yes."

"Teddy Lewis Jr.?"

"Yes."

"You knew that?"

"Yes."

"You saw him? She'd told you about him?"

Pause.

"Yes."

No one speaks for several seconds. Allowing you to once again scope out Honey and Johnny. If someone would run and get you a measuring tape, you're sure you could prove they've moved closer together.

Baby says, "Still, I don't get it. Why didn't you tell the police? Or say it on TV? You could have told them what you knew. You could've proved you were innocent."

"But I *was* innocent."

"You could have told them."

"Why?"

"To *tell* them. To make them go away."

But Henry just looks off. He shakes his head the tiniest bit. And you know what he's thinking. You can tell just by looking at him. What he's thinking. That it was more noble like this. That Darlene would be somewhere watching him on her TV and see what he was going through. For her. The suspicion. The questioning. He could tell the cops, he could clear his name *any time*, but he wouldn't do it. If she didn't want to come back, he wouldn't force her to. If she wanted to run away and make a new life, he'd let her. If she wanted him to wait for her, he would wait for her. And if she wanted him to suffer, he was suffering. Just look. Henry always made a good martyr.

You watch him pick up a chip, hold it, forget to bring it to his lips. Look off again.

He's still in love with her. Even now. The dummy.

thirty~two

People mill about. More shots go down. There is talk of going outside. Getting out in the sun. To smoke a few bones. Maybe walk towards the park. It's the end of September, the days are shortening, and there is an urgency in the air, a sudden need to snatch the warmest and best hours of each day and hold them against your chest.

You've had a bunch of drinks. More than you're used to. On the house, *naturellement*. You've got to love these Karakis brothers. You push away from the main bar and start patrolling the room, weaving between pool tables, scanning for Honey. The two of you agreed to be low-key tonight, not push anything in anybody's face. Not be too out there about your relationship. Which made sense, of course. At the time. Now you could use a hug. And some tongue. You wonder where she is. Your girl.

When you're with her, you glow. Still. Every day feels new and fresh, proud and bold. At least for you. With Honey on your arm everyone looks at you differently — friends and strangers. No matter what they may say to the contrary, this gorgeous chick digging you has changed your life. From here on, glory reigns. You are so fucking cool now it's sick.

It's crowded. You pick your way past the restaurant part of the bar to more spacious grounds. Enjoying the vibe. Friends everywhere. On your way to find your lady. Until suddenly you stop. Straighten. See her. Your lady. Face to face with Johnny. Their noses almost touching. Talking. Quietly.

They see you too. It's too late to turn away. You can only press forward, your legs carrying you there while your head tries to process.

Honey's eyes greet your arrival, Johnny's stare stonily ahead of him. She says, "Hi, sweetie."

"Hi," you say to her. Tentatively, in case there's a crushing punch-line coming.

But there isn't. You see her smile. She leans away from Johnny, takes your arm in hers.

"What were you talking about?" you ask.

Honey smiles wider. Likes you more for asking this question.

"Well, I was just asking Johnny how my sister is," she says. "Now that there's nothing holding him back, I was asking Johnny if he's enjoying his unlimited time with her."

Johnny twitches. Wants to answer, doesn't want to answer. You wish he'd at least look over at you. It's nerve-racking the way he can't seem to even look at you.

Finally he says, "And I was saying... how I've spent *no* time with Baby... never intended to spend any time with Baby... and I fucking *said that* from the start..."

Honey says, "Um, from the start? I don't think so. From the start it was all lies. That's what I remember."

"Which was *three years* ago... which is not *now*... which is what I *thought* we were talking about..."

"Ah, but you see," and here Honey turns directly to you, still addressing him through you, and you're not at all thrilled by this, saying, "that's what Johnny thinks, but that's where Johnny's wrong. Johnny doesn't see that then *is* now."

Johnny snorts. Keeps his gaze straight ahead. "And what the fuck does that mean?"

"It means now is too late."

Johnny takes this in. You watch him. He stares at her. Looks past her. Looks around the room. Looks everywhere but at you. He is defiant. Another guy might plead with her. Or be embarrassed. Or get real angry. Johnny will do none of these. He sees Honey as an individual who is simply making a mistake. It just needs to be righted. You know him well. His patience is rooted in the belief that he can repair absolutely anything, given time and the right angle.

"Just be careful," he says evenly, "that it doesn't become too late for *you*."

Honey tries to suppress a gasp. Tenses with the effort.

Slowly she lets go of your hand, allows her fingers to untwist themselves from yours. She takes a step back. Looks the two of you over.

"I'll leave you boys now, let you talk. You two can *chat* a bit."

She turns and glides away. You try subtly, desperately, to catch her eye before she moves out of range, you want to give her a hard look, ask her, with your expression, *Where on God's green earth are you going?*, but she disappears into the room.

And you are left alone with Johnny.

For the first time since — well, you know.

The song changes. It's one from a few years back, catchy and cute enough to still get played, about a girl who kissed another one.

Johnny makes no effort to speak.

You don't either.

A verse goes by. The girl wonders if the boyfriend will mind her little dalliance. Uh, probably not, darling. If only just for the fresh jerk-off material.

Neither you nor Johnny move away. You glance at him from time to time. His stare stays committed to the other end of The Q, where a few bodies dance loosely. He works on his drink.

Eventually, when it seems there is no other choice, you say, "Fucking Henry. He kills me. Only he could sit at home, surrounded by the cops. Say nothing. Think he's doing the right thing. Think he's being noble."

You peer over at him to see if he agrees. But he doesn't appear to feel strongly either way.

It occurs to you this is maybe closer to home than you need be. Fickle females and all that. Silent nobility. You switch tack. "Or maybe he was just scared of Teddy Lewis. Maybe he was scared to say anything to anyone. Which isn't that dumb. If you think about it. Did you see the clips of that guy? He looks like a wild bastard."

No response. At all. A face of stone. Technically he still has not acknowledged your existence.

Abort. Is what you should do. Of course you don't. You've got to know. You need to find out. Is this it? As in, forever? Is there even an inkling of a chance of a possibility of a hope for forgiveness? One day, maybe?

"John," you say in a low voice. "I'm sorry. Why'd I do it? *I don't know.* I'm really sorry. I'd like you to know that."

Johnny's eyes are still fixed in front of him. He says nothing.

"You know, I wanted her too," you say, close to a whisper. "From the beginning. Not just you, man. Me, too. You remember, don't you?"

No answer.

"You *got* her. But I loved her too."

No reply.

You peel at the label of your beer bottle, trying to think of something else to say. But before you do, Johnny eases himself away from the table, scooping up his drink as he glides off. Without ever seeing you. As if he'd been alone the whole while.

And there's your answer.

You sway towards the can. Your brain is still thick with drink. You spot Stacy, who wants to talk. And Tim and The Hairy Wonder, with goofy-little-boy smirks on their faces. You brush past all of them with perfect aplomb. You have, after all, been on TV a number of times.

You have an understanding of the commoners, and the importance of making them wait.

You aim yourself down the narrow corridor that leads to the stalls. You are looking forward to this moment alone, just you and your urinary tract relief. But just as you get there Peter Karakis pushes open the door and comes out. Stands before you. In this narrow corridor. There is no avoiding him. He's right in front of you.

You say, "Hey."

He says, "Hey."

Your heart races. You can feel the alcohol draining from your brain. Replaced by dread.

"I love your club," you say generously.

"You do?"

"I do. It's the best."

He nods, as though considering your words. Stands perfectly still. Looks at you. His eyes are dancing.

And then, in the quickest instant, the flex of his neck, the clench of his teeth, you see it coming. You don't even try to move. You don't dare react.

His fist drives into your chest.

Unhh.

A second pounds into your stomach.

Hunhh.

You retch for air.

He laces you across the ear with his forearm. A second time. A third. Your head bounces against the wall with each blow. You try to catch your breath on each rebound.

He raises a leg, pounds viciously down on top of your foot, pulverizing the small bones there.

Now you are gasping and hopping.

You still haven't lifted a hand to defend yourself. And there's been hardly a sound. And he hasn't left a mark. Despite the searing pain, this occurs to you.

He moves his thick fingers to your face, pinching your frail jaw. Squeezing with an almost unbearable pressure, digging his thumb and forefinger into you so mercilessly that the flesh of your cheeks meets in the hollow of your mouth. He holds you this way for several seconds, forcing you to look at him. Your knees buckle. Finally he pushes you back, rubbing you against the wall like a mosquito he's crushed. You ooze down to the floor, gasping for breath once more, but quietly and only once he's a safe distance away, lest this upset him somehow.

You struggle to your feet, hobble into the washroom. Piss gingerly, steady yourself against the sink afterwards. Squint into the mirror, study yourself. There's not much to appreciate. Unbridled fear. And a lack of dignity. Minutes pass before you make your way back to your friends at the tables. There you wait several more minutes, pretending to sip at your beer until you can finally ooze out the front door and down the stairs, once you're sure no one is watching. You'll call Honey later, Henry too — you can think only of getting out of there.

The glare from the afternoon sun is intense. You reach for your sunglasses that hang from a chain around your neck, realize it's broken away and that they're lying crushed somewhere on the beer-soaked floor of the hallway to the washroom at The Q. A place you'll never see the inside of again.

thirty~three

Camera Guy has the three of you neatly framed. You can see the shot on the monitor. Honey is to your left, Henry is to your right. You are standing on the waterfront where the Lachine Canal approaches Old Montreal, beyond where the sugar refinery used to be, next to the guardrails that line the paths. Near where they once dragged for Darlene Dobson's body. And not far from the Hunter Films studio offices, you've since discovered.

It's late afternoon. Like young children you wait dutifully for Liz Hunter to turn her attention your way. Finally she stabs her phone closed and slips it into her back pocket. Picks up her microphone from the back of the van, tests it quickly, walks over to where you are posed. She sports a Cheshire cat grin, wears a snazzy little cardigan over a tight black top.

She glances at Camera Guy then turns back your way. "So, you ready?"

You answer for the three of you. You are, after all, media savvy. And standing in the middle.

"We're ready."

"Great."

And she reaches out for Henry's hand, waits until he takes it gingerly. Shyly. Then leads him away. Out of the shot. Glances back at you with a smile once they're a safe distance along. She did it on purpose, you know, faking you out like that. Leaving you behind.

You stay back with Honey as they walk and talk, stand and talk, sit and talk. Watch as Camera Guy sets up each angle with blazing speed, a different background each time. You realize that by shooting it this way, twenty minutes of work will look like they spent an entire afternoon soul-searching with Henry.

When he returns, Honey says to him, "So, how was it? What did she ask you?"

"I don't know. Everything, I guess."

"Why you never came forward?"

"Yes."

"What did you say?"

"I said, now I wish I had. "

You give him a look.

Honey asks, "Was she mean to you?"

"She said I could have helped the police. Which could have helped Darlene. She said I should have thought of that. But no, not mean. I mean, she's *right*."

You give him another look.

"She said no matter what other people think, all she's ever interested in is the truth. And that shouldn't be something that scares anybody. Especially if you didn't do anything wrong, like me."

Honey says, "What did you say?"

"I said I realized that now. I said I didn't know Darlene was in trouble. I thought she just wanted to go away."

Honey nods.

"I said I was sorry," Henry says.

"You said you were sorry?"

"I *am* sorry."

You give him *another* look. You're running out of looks.

Honey asks, "Was she surprised?"

"Maybe. Yes, I guess. I think she expected me to defend myself.

I told her I didn't want to. I wasn't going to. I told her I didn't want to fight. I wasn't going to argue or say insulting things to her. But I think she was waiting for me to."

For some reason all eyes turn towards you.

"*What?*" An idiotic grin escapes. "Couldn't you at least give her a couple of zingers? Or make fun of the camera dude? The Prince of Darkness? The Poster Boy for the Focus-Challenged?" This stuff's gold, Jerry. Gold.

In the background a taxi has pulled up and Liz Hunter climbs in. You check to see if she will glance your way, meet your eyes, acknowledge the moments you've shared together. She doesn't. The vehicle pulls away, the last you will see of Liz Hunter.

Camera Guy is twenty feet away, wrapping her audio pack. *He* looks over instead, winks at you. As though he knows what you're thinking. That in a year she probably won't even remember your name.

Honey asks Henry, "Did she ask you about Darlene Dobson?"

"She did."

"If you miss her?"

"I told her I think about Darlene less now. Some days."

"What else?"

"She wanted to know if I was disappointed. That Darlene's never called me. Never tried to see me since then. She wanted to know if I would contact her."

"Will you?"

"I don't know where she *is*. But no. I won't. I told her I understand. I understand now, I know I was wrong."

Yeesh. You roll your eyes. Are you the only one that doesn't turn into a big pussy as soon as the camera clicks on?

Honey gives you a harsh look, knows what you're thinking. Turns back to Henry. "Did she ask you what you were going to do?"

"I told her, good things only. That I'm not going to get my mother upset anymore. I'm not going to get in any more trouble. For starters."

"Those are good starters," Honey says.

Henry smiles. "I think so."

"Did she?"

Henry thinks about this. "I don't think she was really listening anymore. By then."

Camera Guy calls over to you. All of you. To come over. For some last shots. It's called B-roll and they need a bunch of it to cover Liz's last bits of narration. You guys walking, talking. For the epilogue. So come on over.

Camera Guy is the one who contacted Henry. A few days ago. Asked him to come out, just this once. A last time on camera. Willingly for once. For a few words. Before they put the whole thing to bed. His side of things, now that it was over. They were shooting their final coverage, the last episode.

Henry had made you promise to come too. And you made Honey agree to come. You wanted Honey everywhere you went — especially if there was going to be a camera. So you could show off. But it didn't turn out that way. It turned out the opposite. You feel petty and shallow in her eyes.

A couple of girls are walking by. On the path where Liz and Camera Guy interviewed Henry. They look over now. You recognize one of them. Red hair, blazing red. Heavy, a bit. Nice face, soft green eyes. Who *is* she? You're sure you know her but it won't come to you. You glance quickly at Honey and Henry to see if they recognize her. Nothing.

The red-haired girl is getting closer, still chatting with her friend but looking over more and more. At Henry. At you. As though she recognizes not just Henry but you too. Which of course is entirely possible. You had your ugly mug up there on the screen enough times.

And then you get it. It comes to you. That naked girl, the red-haired girl in front of Blockbuster that day, it seems so long ago, teasing the crowd, the cameras filming. That's who she is.

She stops. Your eyes meet a final time. Two has-beens. A pair of fifteen-minuters. Chewed up and spit out, of little use to anyone now.

You look away. She walks on. You turn back to Henry and Honey. Take Honey by the hand, tap Henry on the shoulder. And then it's you this time, finally, leading everyone away, away from the camera, in the direction of home.

"Where you going?" Camera Guy calls after you.

You don't answer. For once.

thirty~four

You walk the short blocks to Honey's car, get everyone inside, take the wheel, and pilot the growling Firebird away from the curb, through the bumpy, stumpy streets of Griffintown, and then finally over to University Street and up the hill, a smoother ride, windows down, the afternoon wind tossing everyone's hair about. Honey is in back, behind Henry. Henry slid in shotgun. Which is not how it should be, you are aware of this. Not the plan. Your sweetie should be snuggled in beside you and your snakebit friend ought to be in the back seat, where he belongs.

The traffic quickly becomes heavy. You change lanes, join a faster one, only for it to grind instantly to a crawl. You glance at Honey in the rear-view mirror, searching her for expression, she still seems upset with you, then over at your side mirror, eyeing a return to your previous alley. Right in front of the same black Jeep, who already hates you because you cut in front of him less than a minute ago. There are vehicles lined up in every direction you look. Everyone is trying to navigate the same narrow routes at the same time. Jobs finish, offices let out, the sudden influx is too much for the tiny downtown core. The problem with living on an island, as you once wrote in a garbled grade ten geography essay, not one of the finer moments in your illustrious academic career, is that you tend to be surrounded by water.

You fight your way to the front of the Vic, finally glide into a No Stopping zone where other cars are already idling, blinkers on. You push your heavy door open and hop out, cross behind the car, make sure you're already standing there when Honey's first gorgeous leg slithers out. You take one of her hands in yours to steady her, adjust the purse strap on her fine shoulder with your other hand. You watch her straighten, feel her brush against you. The way her jeans are painted to her thighs never fails to stir you.

You glance quickly around, to see who's watching. Even now, here, in front of the hospital for the umpteenth time, you've hustled over so that everyone sees the two of you together. You hate the idea of pulling up with Henry plopped in the front seat beside you. It's still vitally important that everyone understand Honey is your girl, despite the sub-par seating arrangements. Is that so wrong?

You creak her door shut behind her. "Are you mad at me?" you ask softly.

She doesn't answer right away. Looks around. You see that, like you, she is scouting the sidewalk and benches to see who might be lurking. Though surely not for the same reason.

"If I was mad at you," she says coyly, "it would be like admitting you were capable of doing better."

You gaze at her, try to read the intent. "And we wouldn't want that…?"

She takes your hand, a wonderful feeling. "No," she says, squeezing it. "We wouldn't."

"Because…"

"Because there's no hope. For a boy like you."

Ah, nice. You smile, lean in for your kiss.

"I'll come get you tonight," you promise her. "At twelve-thirty."

"Mmn, okay. Thank you."

And then she looks suddenly up at you, forces you to lock eyes. Studying you. She's done this before. She's searching for something.

You're sure of it. Though you're not sure *what*. Is she trying to identify what it was that attracted her to you in the first place? Trying, once again, to capture that feeling?

She opens her cigarette pack, removes one for each of you. You wave yours away.

She frowns. Lights hers, slides yours back in the box. "You don't want a smoke?"

"No," you say. "I don't. I've quit. Actually. As I've said before."

And you have, it's true. It's been weeks since you've smoked a cigarette. Miraculously. The desire has abruptly, amazingly, wondrously left you. Even the suggestion of it now sends waves of nausea rippling up your throat.

Honey pulls her smoke from her lips, careful to allow a portion of her tobacco exhaust to waft into your face. You step back, only a little too late.

She smiles, mocking you. "Nobody likes a quitter."

You give her a lopsided grin, grind the heel of your boot against the sidewalk. This is the third, maybe fourth time she's used this line on you. You let it go. You'll let *anything* go. And have, recently. The more you sense her edging away, the more desperate you are to keep her. You have to keep her. After all you've invested. Her little tuna melt. Her little rotator cuff. You picture yourself on her arm now, see it in your head when you fall asleep at night and when you wake up in the morning. *You've seen it on TV, for chrissakes.* You can't imagine yourself any other way. Not after everything you've risked.

"Still love me?" you ask. You know she doesn't like this, your continual need to hear it. You shouldn't do this. You know. You do it anyway. "Still crazy about me, sweetie?"

Ugh. Is this really you?

"It's okay, Lee," she says calmly. "Everything is fine."

"Is it, my love? My precious?"

"You're trying too hard."

x

YOU comma Idiot

"You would too," you say, "if you were me."

There is silence while she takes another drag. "A lot changed this summer," she says.

"Is that bad?"

"I don't know if it's *good*. It was fast. There's no doubt about that."

"It had to be. Maybe. No? It was fate."

"There's still dust settling."

"Let it. It's all worth it."

"Is it? What we did to Johnny?"

"Yes."

"Your dealer? Your drugs, your money? Gone now."

"Worth it."

"What about Henry? They put him *in jail*, Lee. And that girl, she could've died. Still worth it?"

"Yes. All for you."

She shakes her head. "All of us, every one of Henry's friends — even *you*, you liar — thought he killed her. At some point."

"At some point. Maybe."

"Me. My sister. Johnny Aaron Maureen Cuz Stacy Graham. My mother, my father. People we barely knew and people we didn't know at all. We all thought he took that girl's *life*, Lee. Our Henry. Can you believe that? That's not a normal thing. That's a thing to think about. When you think that about someone. A friend."

"Yes."

"Of how many years?"

"Many."

"Yes." She stamps the butt out. "And so, this was a good summer?"

You hesitate, but not for long. "Yes."

She looks at you. The dreaded eyebrow lifting once again.

You feign innocence. Hold your palms out. "You want the truth, don't you?"

She frowns.

You say, "I can't help it. That's how I feel. Don't you give any points for honesty?" You give her a hopeful smile. "I'm *crazy* about you. I've always been crazy about you. So yes. It's all worth it. Everything. I'm saying it. Even Johnny. Even Henry. Would you rather I lied?"

You catch your breath. Hold your tongue. Stop speaking, boy, for one blessed moment.

Her eyes leave yours.

And then you hear Henry say, "Well, maybe *I* would."

You turn, look over at him. Honey turns, looks over at him.

Henry, of course, is not even ten feet away. Still sitting in the passenger seat, elbow perched on the open window frame. He holds his expression, keeping the suspense alive for a few seconds until finally the cracks show through.

Then he breaks into a grin. "I'm *right here*, you know. I can *hear* you."

You grin back at him. "You know what, dude? You're getting funnier. Did you know that? Hon, am I right? Henry's *funnier*, no? Since he came back."

Henry says, "Hey, fuck you. I shouldn't even be talking to you."

"He's still dumb," you continue, to Honey. "Still the dimmest of bulbs, don't get me wrong. But he's more clued in now. Don't you think, Hon?"

"I'm *right here*," Henry says again. "I still *hear* what you're saying."

Honey shifts her purse to the other shoulder. Walks over, touches Henry's arm. "Henry's beautiful," she says quietly. "Henry's sweet."

She turns to go. Blows you a kiss. "And I'm crazy about you too. Don't worry so much. Okay? Believe me?"

"Yes."

"Trust me?"

"Yes," you say again.

The smell of tobacco, since you've quit, makes you feel sick. Thankfully you've developed no such aversion to the sound of lies.

You power up the Firebird and drive Henry and yourself away. There are several paths you can follow from here. If you forgo the expressway, go down and turn right on de Maisonneuve instead, you can snake through the leafy, lower Westmount streets and avoid a good portion of the traffic. Counterbalanced, unfortunately, by a stop sign every seven feet.

You do it anyway, aware that this will bring you within pissing distance of Your Dealer's place.

"Where we going? Home?" Henry asks you. He still has the remnants of a smile on his face, so happy is he to belong again. He won't dwell on what was said. Today, or all the yesterdays. He'll accept it. Already does. More readily than Honey, or you. If his dearest friends thought him capable of something so shocking, so heinous, Henry can only assume he must have been deserving of it. Such is Henry.

"No," you say. "Or yes. But just you."

Your heart beats just a little faster, your fingers knead themselves a little deeper into the leather grip of the steering wheel. You knew the instant you turned this way there was only one reason for it.

You make the rights, the lefts, and double-park in front of Your Dealer's building, impressively recessed from the street. First time you've ever pulled up in front like this. But what the fuck, there's hardly a risk anymore.

You get out as Henry slides over.

"Thank you, man."

"No problem," he says.

"Drop it and I'll get it later."

"Righto."

You watch him prepare to ease back into his lane. Not rambunctiously, like before. Not carelessly, as he used to. With caution instead, and concentration, attention to detail. Brow furrowed, eyes checking in all directions. He couldn't possibly do it more deliberately or responsibly. It takes forever. It's *too* careful. And so, before he even moves five feet, a woman in a rusted Hyundai roars up behind him, leans impatiently on the horn. Henry stomps on the brakes, nearly jumping out of his skin, then backs up shakily in order to let her pass.

You leave him there. Readjusting his seat now, fixing his mirrors, fiddling with the belt. You march up the walkway to Your Dealer's building and go in. Smile to yourself as you think of Henry. Is that it? Is that the legacy of this whole ridiculous episode? That Henry actually changed? Became *responsible*? You feel a warmth. Could that be it, wouldn't that be cool? The cobwebs in Henry's head finally swept out?

You cross Your Dealer's lobby, stab the code to his luxury condo into the panel encased by glass.

It takes a while before a voice crackles through the intercom. "Lee?"

"Let me up."

Another delay.

"Uh, why?"

"Just for a minute."

You hear an awkward rustling behind him. Either he's not alone or he's stoned.

"Not be happening, son."

He's stoned.

"I want to explain," you say. Nicely.

"Not be necessary."

Oh, good. Jamaica-speak the whole way. He must've just finished blowing a huge one.

"I just want to...say I'm sorry. About your car. About the TV stuff."

Silence.

"It won't happen again," you say.

"Be irrelevant. Be of no interest. Position occupied by Lee be coming with certain restrictions, certain commitments. Broken now."

"Just let me up."

"Be denied."

"I still owe you some coin, I think."

"Be in the past."

"Please…"

"Be time to shuffle off, son."

You put your hands on your hips and look into the camera on the wall, try to look friendly but as though you still mean business, try to picture how you look in the monitor in his front hallway. "I'm going to stay right here," you say. "Wait for you to buzz me in."

Which you do. For a full minute. And then another one. And then a third, and you're starting to feel kind of stupid, you don't even know if he's still *aware* of you even, he might have forgotten by now, it feels so long, until his voice finally comes crackling out again, flatter this time, stern.

"Be time for *Rocky and Bullwinkle* to start, Mr. Goodstone. Then *$100,000 Pyramid* and then *Get Smart*. Be starting now. Be hearing song already. Missing opening. Understand?"

And there are no more non-negotiable words Your Dealer could utter. You know this. Your Dealer has access to every retro TV station signal broadcast on the planet and, when high, adheres to a rigid schedule of mindless diversion.

You leave the lobby through the side door, go down into the basement and out the back exit, along the spotless streets, past the greystones and brownstones and luxury apartments. Like The Q, a destination you realize now you'll never return to. Make your way back to your hood, to get Honey's car, to kill the hours of the night waiting until it's time to pick her up. Only, as it turns out, to receive an eleven o'clock phone call saying she's staying to work a double. Without — you're pretty sure of this — a modicum of actual remorse in her voice that the two of you will be apart.

thirty~five

But in the morning she is late as well and dead tired and wants to go right to sleep so you don't really get to talk to her much and then it all bleeds into the next few days and then eventually a barbecue at Aaron and Maureen's that at the last minute neither of you go to because of a tiff over Johnny and would he be there and would she be speaking with him and, if so, why the fuck would that be? Of course, sadly, you get the feeling she's *dying* to, but you're too chicken to actually accuse her of it, and she tries to scuttle the whole issue entirely, pouting behind one of her magazines at the other end of your huge space. So instead you're both at your place and grumpy and letting the drone of the TV apply the soundtrack to your lives when you hear the familiar strains of Liz Hunter's news theme come floating out, whereupon you both drift over from different directions until you each have a view of the screen.

And it's the final instalment of THE HUNTED, airing a full week from when you last saw her, and it's more of a post-mortem than anything else, summary statements set to a montage of older footage. Little of that afternoon on the canal survives. She doesn't even bother including you and Honey, edits in only the parts where Henry acknowledges his regrets. The piece just sticks to the facts, like Liz promised. As it should. It recounts what happened and tallies the score. It documents the beginning, middle, and end. A seventeen-year-old girl's life will never be the same. A twenty-five-year-old man will go to prison for the third time in his young life. And Henry was simply a distraction, inconsequential. You, even more so.

And it's almost over and you're reaching for the clicker when suddenly the camera is tracking the Firebird on its way to drop Honey at the hospital immediately afterwards, up University, everyone's hair billowing in the wind, and then following you all the way down to Your Dealer's building, watching as you park, get out, Henry sliding over. And you can't figure out why they're even showing this — and why there's no voice-over, no music even, just the ambient street sounds — when you feel the camera abruptly lurch and hear the van door open and suddenly it's walking hand-held across the street, Camera Guy's point of view, step by step towards Honey's car, still double-parked with Henry fidgeting in the front seat, an eerie suspense to it all, the lens getting closer and closer, Henry utterly oblivious, still putzing around with every button and lever on the dashboard, you long gone, until we see his head jerk up and hear Camera Guy's voice — not Liz Hunter's, you realize she's not even with him — say, "Hey, Henry! Buddy! Whatcha doing there, man?"

And Henry gurgles and swallows and looks around for your help and finally looks back at the camera.

"I'm not doing nothing."

"Where's Lee?"

"I don't know."

And all you can think of, watching Henry squirm, riveted by his panicked face trapped on the screen in such close-up as he says this, is, Uh-oh, better drive away, dude.

Camera Guy swings his lens over now towards Your Dealer's building, refocuses until your outline can be made out through the reflection in the glass, talking into the lobby intercom. Then he turns it back to Henry and asks his next sinister-sounding question.

"What do you mean, you don't know?"

"Don't know."

"Well, he's in that building."

"Don't know."

You can barely watch as Henry's thumbs begin rubbing the steering wheel, his sideburns sweating, licking at his lips, not knowing where to rest his gaze, trying so hard not to glance over at you, call out to you, run over to you, while all you can think again now is, Drive away, dude.

The camera moves in a bit closer. You hear Camera Guy muse, "Hey, don't I *know* that building? Isn't that a building that's...been...on the news?" And he swish pans over to it again, this time widening and framing it top to bottom all at once, with his signature awkward flourish.

And then immediately tightens back up on Henry again.

"Or am I wrong?"

And you take a deep breath and beside you Honey takes a deep breath and you look at each other but it's nothing compared to the helpless look in Henry's eyes and his stunted breathing and his incessant fidgeting and all you're thinking, you want to shout it at the screen now, is, *Please, drive away, dude.*

"Wasn't there...an investigation...there? For drugs? Wasn't that on the news — that they had that place under surveillance? Just last year?"

The camera pushes even tighter on Henry.

"What's Lee Goodstone doing in there, Henry?"

And, oh Lord, if this is the new and improved Henry, clued-in Henry, you can't even begin to imagine how the old Henry would have held up, because Camera Guy's stunning little nugget of in-depth, behind-the-scenes, beyond-the-fucking-call-of-duty fluky reporting has Henry close to *hyperventilating*, perspiring profusely and tugging at his chin and nose and ears and hair, not to mention you, who could jump out the goddamned window right about now, the feeling of panic in you is so urgent, and Honey has lit a nervous cigarette now, so that's making you feel even worse, like throwing up on your way *out* the window, and you're still watching Henry stammer and squirm until finally he shakes his head a few times and croaks, "I don't know…" in the hoarsest of confessions, and then you can't help it, can't control yourself, you scream at the TV at the top of your lungs, "Drive *away*, dude!"

At which point, mercifully, he does.

thirty~six

They're almost finished. You can tell. Two of the cops are still poking around up on the roof but they've been up there for twenty minutes already. Another pair is in your kitchen, mostly just talking now. Low enough that you can't decipher more than a few words, but you know they're not happy. And the last one you can see in your living room, looking mostly like he's sifting through your music collection. What's he going to find there? Van Morrison bootlegs? Sam Spayed is curled on the couch not far from him, watching, licking her paws. You get the feeling she'd make the best detective out of the whole crew.

From where you are, on a chair they provided you with by the front door and told you not to move from *for any reason*, with your tea and your sports section, you can tell by the way these guys are looking at each other that they're just not into it anymore. Which is just as well. They're not going to find anything.

You knew they were coming, of course. You'd been warned by Your Dealer, and then even forewarned as to exactly when they'd arrive. Now *that's* connections. Somebody knows somebody downtown. Of course, Your Dealer never spoke with you directly. What happened was that once you saw Henry on TV you immediately knew two very specific things: one, that you had to warn Your Dealer; and two, that you had to clean your apartment of every chunk of hash and bale of cash in the place. And three, that some serious shit was on its way.

And getting rid of the money wasn't so hard but cleaning out all the dope was. It was fucking *everywhere*. Grams and grams of it. Big pieces, little pieces, broken pieces, dust. Tons of dust. You wiped down so many surfaces you're pretty sure you're developing Hash Dust Wiper's Elbow. The dope itself you moved through a guy to another guy who eventually sold it to Cuz, of all humiliations.

Getting through to Your Dealer proved to be more difficult. You couldn't call him. You've never had a direct line for him, ever, only a number you could leave a numeric code on so that he knew to call you back, which he certainly wouldn't now. And you couldn't risk a return to his building, nor was it certain he would even answer you if you did. In fact, probably not.

So someone had to go see him for you. Immediately. And the only person who was right for it was, of course, Johnny. The only person you could trust to do it intelligently, in the proper light, explain that this was serious and bad but also not your fault and not to get angry at you. Because Your Dealer was a serious dude, you suspected, when it came down to issues like this. A potentially aggressive individual, you were convinced. You'd met a few fellows that took care of these sorts of messes over the years, thugs whose paths you'd crossed at his apartment coming or going at the same time as you. Scary guys.

The problem here was that Johnny wasn't likely to be all that into it. Which you could hardly blame him for. Not that Johnny had issues with Your Dealer. He didn't. They'd met a few times, got on fine on every occasion. Johnny's issues would be with you, naturally.

You realized you needed Honey to help.

"I need you to help."

"How?" she asked. "Even though I won't, by the way."

"You have to get Johnny to go tell him."

She rolled her eyes. "Are you kidding me? There's nothing I could tell him. He would never help you. There's absolutely nothing I could say."

"Tell him it was *your* car they saw. *Your* licence plate."

And at this point she squinted at you, wondering where this Mensa moment had come from. "Except that, of course. Yup. That would work."

Sigh. And so what happened was, she did go see Johnny and he did agree to go warn Your Dealer. Who *was* angry and who did realize how serious it was. But who did have friends and did know how to handle situations like this and it was just a shot of the building, after all, although things like this weren't hard for a narc division to make an issue of, if they were so inclined.

And so — and this is Honey talking here, relating to you what Johnny had told her, and doing it just a little too smugly and a little too condescendingly at points, which you didn't like the vibe of *at all* — what seemed to upset Your Dealer most was not that there was any imminent danger but that he would have to call in a favour to make sure there wouldn't be. And how lightly he would need to tread for the foreseeable future. And how that might make him look to certain others. *That* seemed to upset him.

And *then* what happened was, you didn't see much of Honey for a while. You kicked yourself for sending her over to Johnny but knew you had no choice. And you could've gone looking for her in the days that followed but knew if she wanted to be with you she would be. Of course, you remembered how emphatically she'd always assured you she would never return to Johnny, but also knew this was no longer to be relied upon.

Instead, you kept busy feeling sorry for yourself. Stayed holed up in your place waiting for this very moment, this visit, two weeks to the day after that last broadcast, exactly as Your Dealer had gotten word to Johnny it would be. You knew it was coming, knew what questions would be asked, knew they wouldn't haul you back to the station with them, knew there would be no charges laid as long as they found nothing. After all, there was no other evidence. Your Dealer's own place wouldn't even be visited. Neither would Honey's. As related to you by her, and then you didn't hear from her again. Or Johnny, of course. Or Baby or Aaron or Mo. And you couldn't reach Henry no matter how many times you phoned. You didn't even know if he *lived* there anymore. Only Stacy and The Boy had come by, on a few occasions. For which you were grateful.

The five cops split, one after the other. Two uniforms and three plainclothes out the door in single file. Leaving your apartment decimated in their wake. As though they'd known all along this would be the sole punishment they could inflict upon you.

"Don't worry, boys! I'll just clean it all up myself, you fucking pricks!" you don't call after them, because that would, after all, be retarded.

No, you don't utter a word. You know this much. Even when the last one spits right into the centre of your front door, a bubbly gob of saliva drooling its way down the flecked paint, you say nothing. You'd taken your sweet time opening up when they first came pounding and they hadn't liked that, thrusting the warrant right up into your face and pushing past you, fanning out, attacking your place with a vengeance.

And now, an hour and a half later, they were leaving empty-handed. Which makes you, among other things, a fortunate guy. Better than Lucky. So you can appreciate their frustration. You can understand their ill will.

thirty~seven

You make your way over to Henry's apartment that same afternoon. It is not warm. There is very little summer left. You huddle behind the turned-up collar of your jean jacket, staking out his building. And then, before you even have to summon the courage to face her, you see Mrs. Miller exiting the lobby, coming down the steps. A happy miracle. She glances suspiciously around her property then makes her way down the street towards her car. Her walk is pained and furtive at the same time.

You wait several minutes then scuttle across the road. Enter the lobby and ring every buzzer but Henry's. Someone lets you in and you climb the stairs to your friend's door.

You knock.

You hear shuffling.

You knock again.

More shuffling. Though it doesn't sound like it's getting nearer.

"Henry," you hiss.

Quiet.

Then, weakly, "Lee...?"

"Yes. Open."

"No."

"What?"

"No."

"Open!"

"No…"

Okay, what *is it* with people unwilling to let you in these days?

You plant a sincere look on your face, can see from the shadow that he's watching you through the peephole.

"Henry — listen to me. This is *serious*. I need to see you. I need to speak to you."

"Go home. I'm not opening."

"Henry. Open up. This is something important. This is something you have to do. Understand? This is something that could be… dangerous. To you. Are you listening? I have to see you."

And then you hear movement. Soft, tentative. His slippers against the floor, the handle turning. You see the door pull back.

Henry stands framed in the doorway. In his bathrobe. Looking at you.

His face is swollen in every possible direction.

He is bruised. He is stitched. He is bandaged. His lips look too swollen to speak. His eye sockets seem too swollen to possibly see from. He is hunched over, moves like an old man.

Someone has put the beats on Henry.

You catch your breath. Say, "When?"

"A few days ago. Nights ago. It was at night. I was coming home. Lee, I never even saw *who* they were."

"Why? Why did —"

And then you stop.

You know why. You know who. Of course you do. After all, what had you come to warn him about?

Henry says nothing now. Just looks at you.

The humiliation in his eyes is unbearable for you. He looks as though every ounce of self-worth has been pummelled from him.

You look away. Can't stare at him any longer. His eyes drop to the ground at the same moment.

You think, It was Henry's fault. It really *was*.

So why does this feel like it's on you?

You turn and flee before Mrs. Miller comes home and catches you bothering her son.

Four days later, Henry is gone. Out west. To Vancouver, Stacy tells you. Mrs. Miller has family there. The plan is that she will sell her buildings and join him as soon as she can. Henry Miller will never set foot in Montreal again. She wants you all to know this.

The Boy watches cartoons in the background. The sounds of Bugs Bunny and Yosemite Sam fill your apartment as Stacy quietly tells you about the last time she saw him. Her eyes, you are surprised to see, are wet. You lean in close to hear her say that the last time she saw Henry his cuts were healing but his eyes were scared and confused like a child's.

You spoke to him. You didn't tell Stacy this but you did. He called you from the airport with five minutes left before boarding. It was nine-thirty at night. On a Friday. You could tell his mother was standing right there beside him.

"I can tell your mother is standing right there beside you," you said.

"My mother's not interfering."

"She's standing next to you."

"She's a few feet behind me," he said, "actually."

"Ha! See? You're funnier," you said to him. "Have I told you that?"

"Yes. You have."

You were walking around the apartment cradling the phone against your neck. Hands jammed into your pockets. Kicking a balled-up piece of aluminum foil along the floor with each step. Which had your cat's undivided attention. Not a hard thing to get.

"Vancouver?" you said.

"Yes. I'll stay in at first, until my face is better."

Kick.

"I'll get an apartment and my aunt will get me a job and then I'll start to learn the city."

Kick. Kick.

"It rains a lot there but it's warmer."

Kick.

"After a while I'll make a couple of friends, I guess. From work, probably. Which'll be good."

You'd given the foil ball a last boot, watched it skitter off the base of the stove, behind the fridge. Watched Sam trot her way over, begin sniffing around. Devising a plan to root it out.

"Just put down the phone, Henry," you'd said suddenly, in a kind of loud whisper. "Leave there now."

"I can't."

"You can."

"I won't."

"You don't have to go."

"I *want* to."

You'd taken a long, sad breath. Decided to try one last angle.

"There's nothing there for you, Henry. Pay attention to me. You'll have to meet people. You won't have your friends. There'll be no one there who knows you. Your friends are all here. There won't be anyone to *help*."

And here Henry addressed you as though you were somehow incapable of understanding a very simple concept.

"But I think that's the idea," he said.

thirty~eight

There are civilizations in South America where the East represents the past and the West is the future. If someone from the tribe leaves the village walking into the forests of the East, he is seeking to go back in time. If the person leaves towards the West, he is in search of a new beginning. A new life.

They build their homes with this in mind. Place their doors, angle their windows. Plant their headstones. In their culture you are either one who looks backwards or one who looks ahead. Over time, everyone chooses.

Personally, you're not sure which way you would go. You've never been much of a Western walker, preferring the soft, nostalgic footpaths of the East. And yet events seem to be leading you West recently. The past holds less attraction for you now.

It's hard for you to contemplate this. You've always resisted change, always needed the comfort of how things were before. And you don't know whom to talk to. There seems to be no one left. You wonder if you have the courage to move forward. You're unsure if the strength to embrace a new world is within you. Know how easy it is fall back to where you once were.

Ah, fuck that noise anyway. There's no tribes of Amerindians walking East. Or West. Or anything like it. Making life decisions that way, positioning their stupid little huts. You just made it up. You're just fucking around.

You go to see Honey at the hospital. Once, a hundred years ago, she blamed you when you didn't come fast enough. This time you'll go see her right away.

She's working in the psychiatry department this evening. You haven't walked through Psych since you used to do shifts here yourself. It's cleaner here, smells less like shit. That's the first thing you remember. It has a different feel. Shinier, too. Sterile. Also scarier. Like a smack in the head is never far away.

Honey's working four to twelve again this week. You used to hate that shift. No time left to live, you're always on your way to or from work. Get home late, sleep in, go back. Of course, you didn't like day shifts either. Wake up too early, crazy busy all day long. Nights were the only scene you could hack.

You are careful to arrive at eight-thirty. A good time to show up if you want to drop in on someone's evening shift. Supper's over, everybody's winding down, looking forward to their drugs. It's hard to say who's more enthusiastic about the meds, the patients or the nurses giving them out. A few employees nod at you or raise a hand as you go by. TVs play softly, last visitors make their way out. No one speaks. It's all about staying calm and quiet.

You find Honey in the common room with a pair of patients. She is wearing a top too gorgeously tight and white jeans. Only the security card clipped to her belt identifies her as staff.

When she sees you, her eyes go sad, teary.

It confuses you at first. You want to rush over, hug her. Even more, you wish she would rush over, hug you. It's okay, you want to hear her say. It's not what you think.

You watch as she gathers her composure, hardens her face.

Behind you the shuffling sound of paper slippers makes you turn. A patient, an older man, slithers past you over to the set of green vinyl couches that line the wall. He collapses into one, his metal cane clanging along with him. His hair is pure white, thick and curly. Long in back, like a grown-out perm. His eyes are a brilliant blue though he is well into his seventies.

Behind him, seconds later, a young Filipino orderly glides into the room. He's quietly shadowing the man, leans against the wall now, maintaining presence.

Honey turns to the orderly. "Thank you, Santos."

"Iss okay."

"You can leave him with me."

"Iss okay." Santos stays where he is.

"When's your break?" she asks him.

"Pipteen minutes."

You look over at the patient again. You know him, recognize him easily. A lifer. He's been in this ward since before you ever worked a shift here. Harry Something. Bloom. Or Feld. Maybe Bloomfeld. A crazy dude. Okay, obviously. But more than that. A strange man. You recall him now, conversations you had. A funny dude, too. Everyone knew Harry. Wild, screaming family visits. Obnoxious daughters with impatient husbands. Poor Harry. Senility, some Alzheimer's, some schizophrenia too, as you recall. Delusional. Decades ago he ran a very lucrative group of companies. Now they do it all for him.

Harry barks out at Santos, "Get me a juice."

Santos smiles. Winks at Honey. "You can get jooze yourself, Harry."

"I want a juice!"

"Get one den."

"Get me a fucking *juice!*"

"Harry, don't yell."

"Harry, don't swear." This from Honey.

Santos says, "Essercise your legs, man. I toll you."

"Get me a juice!"

Man, the noise he's making. It's a wonder no one comes running. You look at the fridge, not even ten steps from him. Stocked full of juice, you know. You could walk over and get him one yourself. Just to shut him up. They're all juice freaks.

"Alright! How much you want?" Harry fixes his glare squarely on Santos. "What? Five? Five thousand?"

Santos ignores this. A good strategy.

"Ten? Twenty?"

Santos says nothing.

"ONE HUNDRED THOUSAND DOLLARS??"

"Harry...ssh!" This is Honey again.

"For a bloody juice??"

Santos's gaze stays even. He doesn't reply. Doesn't move. The picture of calm.

This makes Harry crazy. He cries, "Get me a fucking juice, you fucking Jew!"

Weird. Harry is Jewish. Someone shushes him from down the hall. Honey straightens, leaves her two patients. She walks over next to Harry. Makes like she's going to sit down but then stays standing.

"You want a juice?" She looks down at him. "I'll get you a juice, Harry. For a million dollars."

Harry gasps. "A million dollars?"

"That's right."

His eyes light up. "I have it, you know." He scans the room, eager for someone to challenge him. His eyes stop on yours. You search them for a flicker of recognition. Would get a kick out of it if he remembered you.

He doesn't. He doesn't even remember what he had for supper, the poor bastard. He looks back at Honey.

She says, "I know you have it."

"I made so much money, you wouldn't believe."

"I know."

"You think I'm stupid?"

"Never, Harry."

"One million?"

"Yes."

"Too much. Ten thousand."

"No. One million."

He looks at her. Stares at her. And then suddenly he is beaming.

"Okay…I'll do it! *Done!*"

Wow, master bargainer. You grin at Santos as Harry searches frantically for the little pad he always carries with him. Checks the pockets of his housecoat, his lap, the seat next to him. Doesn't see that it's fallen to the floor beneath him.

Honey bends down, picks it up. Hands it to him.

Harry says, "I'll write it up. Watch. Take this to any bank. You'll see. Say my name at any bank."

Chortling, he fidgets into position, putting shaky pen to paper, the result instantly unintelligible.

Santos pours juice into a Styrofoam cup, brings it over.

Harry looks up, accepts it. Drinks greedily, spilling half down the front of his gown. They all have shaky hands and drymouth, the poor souls. From the bad dope.

He thrusts the cup back at Santos. "More!"

Santos looks back at Honey.

Harry turns to look up at Honey.

"Two million," she says to him.

Harry's cheeks bulge. Jaw tightens. His skin reddens, his eyes shine brighter. He looks around with a sputter.

You remember him even more now by this. So familiar is this reaction. As though he's decided to hold his breath then forgotten he's done it.

Finally he exhales loudly. And glares again at Honey. At you too, and then Santos. Then once more he cries out. *"Deal!"*

He lifts his pen into the air, hands trembling, beaming at you all. Loses his grip. The pad clatters to the floor a second time.

Harry immediately loses interest. Looks at Santos once more. "Go! Jew Nip! Get my juice!"

Santos, bless him, walks calmly back to the fridge.

You turn towards Harry, address him. "Two million dollars, Harry? That's a lot of money. Why don't you just suck the front of your shirt instead?"

Harry turns slowly, stares at you, incredulous. "Suck my shirt?"

"Yeah."

"Do you know who you're talking to?"

"Yes."

"Suck my shirt?"

You're trying not to laugh. God, you remember him now.

"Yeah…"

"Okay, *you're out*!"

Honey is startled by the outburst. Santos too. He spills juice at his feet.

You say, "Harry, no…"

But Harry wipes his mouth with the sleeve of his gown and glowers back at you. "That's it. Out!"

"Please…"

"You heard me!"

"Harry…"

Meanwhile Honey is looking at you like you're the one who's lost his mind. "Out?" she says to you.

You nod sadly. "Looks like it."

"Of what?"

You look at Harry. "His will."

Harry nods. "That's right. Out!"

"Out," you say to him, "of the will. Again! I can't believe it."

Honey says, "As in, you've done this before?"

"We have."

She smiles. "Is that true? Harry?"

Harry nods again. Smug, imperial.

You say, "We go back a while, me and Harry. Right, my man? From when I used to do nights here. We've had these negotiations before, Harry and I. Many times. Right, my friend?"

"Don't beg," he says. "It's pathetic."

The lights in the corridor flicker on and off in quick succession. Pills at the front office, this means. For those on the list. Which is, of course, everybody.

Harry struggles to his feet, refusing Honey's arm. He shuffles away as quickly as he came, cane swinging from side to side, its tip not even bothering to touch the ground.

Santos tosses Harry's cup in the garbage and follows him quietly up the hallway.

You look at the clock. Five to nine. That hasn't changed in years. Same time, pretty well the same drugs. Same result, that's for sure. Knock everybody out until morning. For some people there is no option. Sad as that is to say. That's just the way it is. You remember a boy who was raped when he was twelve. Horrible, just horrible. He was here for years. You used to let him drink all the juice he wanted. Couldn't bring yourself to say no. Couldn't imagine him ever getting better either. You wonder, maybe he's still here? You remember other people who just absolutely had other people in their heads. Real voices. You had to see it to believe it. How do you escape that?

You look at Honey. "Eight pipty-pive," you say.

She nods. Her last two patients are shuffling off to Buffalo.

There's just you and her now. She turns off the TV. It's extremely quiet.

You say, "I was sure, once I got here, I would know what to say."
She just looks at you.

"But of course I don't."

You stand in front of her. In all your slender. Looking for a little understanding. Maybe just a little sympathy. A little *feeling*. You grow more uncomfortable with each second that passes. She knows what you want. Can't give it to you. That much is clear. Of course, you shouldn't have come. And of course, you had to.

Honey glances down towards the ward office. There is nothing pressing, others will cover for her. You know this, she knows this. But it's a signal of her desire to see you leave. Never that much of a talker, this one.

It's time. To say the most honest thing you can think of. Do that. You can't regret that.

Now if only you could figure out what it is.

Honey starts towards the office. Ever so gently. Careful not to insult you but clear that she is officially in movement. It's up to you to follow.

It's time to speak.

"I don't think what you did to me was fair."

She keeps moving. "You knew what was going on, Lee. The whole time."

"You were mad at Johnny."

"You knew that."

"You were mad at your sister."

"And you knew that."

"Johnny took away your sister," you say. "So you took away me."

She catches her breath, her step falters. "I didn't mean it. That way."

"I think you did. I think you must have."

She sighs. Takes your hand in hers. You tingle at her touch. Allow her to guide you forward with her once again. She gives you her big eyes. A sad smile. The tiny overbite on her bottom lip that says, Believe anything I say. Squeezes her palm against yours.

She says, "Lee, I just still love Johnny. Okay?"

There. That's it. What can you say to that? By this point you've reached the big doors that lead out of the ward. Time to go.

thirty~nine

You're the kind of guy who ends up alone. You're the kind of guy who will never win the lottery. You're the kind of guy who leads off the ninth with a base hit but then gets nailed trying to stretch it into a double. You're the kind of guy who needs a Plan B.

Trips to the grocery store are done alone now. Of all the shopping you have to do alone in life, this is the hardest. When you're buying bread and milk and frozen egg rolls and giant bags of ketchup chips, you should be doing it with somebody.

You loved grocery shopping with Honey, the way she knew her way around every aisle and every shelf. You miss her for it. Now you pay your bill and walk outside to the bus stop with your bags. This is how you travel. No more Henry's car, no Honey's car, no Aaron's van. You're on your own. No more taxis. No more dope money.

It doesn't bother you that much. So you have to take the bus with the plebes. Shit happens. You'll have to get a job at some point, too, you suppose. Hopefully nothing too strenuous. You're not too into the physical labour thing. Unless you can get work like Camera Guy, a cushy gig like that. Maybe you should talk to him. Flexible hours.

Good pay. You've seen those audio guys on shoots sometimes. Holding the boom. You'd be good at that. You're tall and have long arms, you could position the microphone in just the right spot.

You saw Camera Guy not long ago. Up on the mountain. At the tam-tam. You were alone. He was alone. He wasn't working. The drums were pounding. He came over to chat. You shared a joint. You have no hard feelings. He asked what you were up to. You answered nothing. He didn't push it. You asked him what he was up to. He said he was taking his gear down to the coast of Florida the next day. To hook up with Liz. To where that plane went down.

That plane. It changed everything. Seventy-nine people blown out of the air for all to see. Just after takeoff, into the Gulf waters. Half of them celebrities. Singers and actors and athletes. Baseball, football players. Three out of a starting five in basketball. Movie stars and TV stars. Producers and directors and technicians and journalists. All attending the same event. Ignited at three thousand feet. Pieces of them falling into the ocean. Shot live by six different cameras. A cruise ship sprayed with falling debris. It was a media orgy. It still is. The biggest story ever. Since the last one. Until the next one. It's the most significant mass celebrity death in history. There are rumours that it wasn't an accident. Stories persist that terrorism is linked. There will be investigations and reports, tributes and memorials, from now until the end of the decade. And beyond. On every anniversary. It will become a mini-industry unto itself. It will be a *Where were you?* moment. It's wiped the slate clean and trivialized everything that came before it. Henry Miller and Darlene Dobson are just footnotes now from a bygone era.

You told Camera Guy you regretted getting involved with him. You told Camera Guy that Henry had to leave *because* of him. And Liz. And you. All of you who fed the machine. You told Camera Guy you were ashamed because you got excited by something as small as being on TV. You lost your focus. You should have had your friend's back.

He didn't say much. He seemed to understand.

At home, you sort through the sad array of grocery items. For some reason you've bought three jars of pizza sauce. You've never made pizza in your life. What will you do with these? Refrigerate after opening? Which reminds you — the Old Man's not next door anymore. An ambulance took him away a few weeks ago, all tubed-up and clinging to life. The apartment's empty while they wait to see if he'll be back. It's eerie not to hear him through the walls, muttering about. Of course, as soon as everything calmed down you let yourself in to get all your money. And tidy up his place a bit, as it turned out. You had to. It was embarrassing.

Your own place is cleaner than it used to be too. That's something from Honey you've held on to. Now that you've stopped smoking for good you've been able to air the place out. You've organized as well. Thrown things away, cleared out the Junk Area. After the raid you gave a lot of things to Stacy. A lot. Just dumped it all there on a day when her mom was babysitting. All kinds of good stuff you thought she might need, even some things from when you were a kid for Ack! to play with when he gets older. Told her mom to tell Stacy to make sure to go through everything, keep what she wants. That was a while ago. You haven't heard back.

And then, doesn't she go and call?
"Lee?"
"What?"
"What're you doing?"
"Nothing."
"Are you alone?"

YOU comma Idiot

"Yes."

She asks if she can drop by. She asks if she can bring The Boy. She asks if you need anything at the store.

You say okay, sure, and no.

And then, just as you put down the phone, there is a knock at your door. Geez, whirlwind afternoon. You don't get many visitors anymore.

You walk over, open up. It's Your Dealer.

You haven't seen him since way back when. He's never been inside before. Once, you met him out front.

You usher him in. "Beer? Coke? Lemon ginseng pulverized root juice?"

He smiles politely. Acknowledges your attempt. Sips from the bottle of water he's brought with him while walking through your apartment. There is a slight hitch to his step that wasn't there before.

He says, "So, what are you doing with yourself now?"

You don't answer immediately. Watch him instead. Is he angry? Pleased? Is he here to give you your route back? If so, you want to play it cool.

You say, "I'm thinking what to do."

He nods. "You're thinking what to do?"

"Yeah."

He stops, looks around at the half-filled boxes. "You're moving?"

"No. Just cleaning stuff up."

He scans the rest of the place. More piles, more boxes. Everywhere you look. He eyes you again. "Because you're moving?"

"Uh, maybe."

He nods, limps across the room. "You leaving the neighbourhood? The city? Or just the apartment?"

You don't answer. You don't know.

He wipes the dust off a box with a cloth from his pocket, sits down. Your Dealer says, "Your friend, Harvey —"

"Henry."

"I know."

"Can't you just say it then? Henry."

He sips from his bottle. Lets a few seconds pass. "You want me to explain?"

"No."

And it's true. You don't. Henry's gone and it's for the best anyway. You've come to this conclusion. The cuts and bruises have probably all faded by now.

He peers out your big grimy window. Turns back towards you. "How old are you?"

"Twenty-eight. Which you know."

"Twenty-eight. And you've done exactly what so far in your life? Fuck all?"

"About that."

You wish you still smoked. You'd light one now. Just to make him crazy. Through the wall you hear the elevator being summoned back down to the lobby.

He says, "You know, I remember the year I was forty-nine. Everyone kept asking me if I was upset that I would soon be turning fifty. Was I depressed? Was I worried? And so I thought about it. A lot. Fifty. Half a century. All that bullshit. And then I realized that no, I wasn't. I wasn't upset. I was *okay* with it."

He looks at you. That same blank stare. The one you never know what to do with.

"That's good," you say finally.

"Good?"

"Good for you."

"Is it? I'm not sure."

"Why is that?" you sigh. Why are you even asking?

"Because" — he takes another swig — "I also realized that I was absolutely terrified of turning *sixty*. Petrified. Horrified. That in ten years I'd be sixty. Do you understand? Fuck fifty. What about sixty? There's *nothing* left to do at sixty. I realized that. Nothing. You better have done it all by then."

"Right."

"Sixty. That's very old."

"Sure."

"Not much is going to happen after *sixty*. If you're not rich by then, it's unlikely you ever will be. If you're not popular, if you're not funny, if you're not the kind of person that everyone wants to hear what he has to say about things, it's not going to start happening once you turn sixty. If you're not a ladies' man. If you've never helped people in your life. If you haven't left your *mark*. You're not going to do it after sixty."

"I guess not."

"Lee," he says suddenly, crinkling his eyes at you, "how old do you think I am?"

Ah. So that's it. You give him a jaunty look. Feel the confidence swelling in your chest. This one time, this once, you know the right answer. You get it. See where he's going this time. That he's the exception. He's special, the one who can do it anyway. Who can still do great things at *any* age.

You take your time. Savour it. It's not often you find yourself a step ahead.

And then you answer. "Sixty."

His pasty face goes all red. "*Sixty?* I'm not *sixty*! I'm fifty fucking seven. Jesus Christ! Weren't you even following? Weren't you even *listening*? How dumb can you be? You can't *wait* until sixty, I said. You have to do things *before*, I said…"

"I thought you meant —"

"I'm making all the changes *before* sixty," he says, regaining some control. Lowering his voice, taking another gulp. "I'm not *waiting*.

How can you not get that? Wow. Like a bag of nickels, I'm telling you. I made *moves*, I'm still making moves. I'm doing what I have to do. I've got it in *gear*. By the time I'm *sixty*" — and he shoots you another hateful little glance here — "everything will be done. I'll be sitting pretty. Right where I deserve to be. You understand?"

You get up from the couch, walk towards the kitchen.

He gets up, limps after you.

"So what's the plan, Stan?" he says to you now, a sudden change in tone. He's a nut, this guy. "What's up, Sport? Any actual thoughts? Or is this just another aimless move, a symbolic gesture? A pretend-to-look-inward. Your typical reply. A shallow examination of your life with no real intent on changing anything. Hold on, let me guess. You'll find a new place, smaller and cheaper. Find a hapless job, shut yourself in, smoke dope, and watch the years go by. No money, no future. Spend everything you earn buying the same hash you used to sell to everybody else. Who's your connection going to be? Cuz?"

Wow. A mean thing to say.

"You haven't thought about it for even half a minute, have you?"

You scowl, turn from him. Who comes to a person's house and talks this way? And fuck him all the same. First of all, you've stashed away more money than he would ever expect. So he can just kiss your skinny white ass on that. You weren't so stupid. And second, now you know why he came. He's come to give you another chance. He's going to let you deal again. So you're not so stupid *twice*.

You say, "Yeah, well, why don't you just get to it then? If you came to tell me I can work again, let's hear it. What's the pound of flesh, man? Make up my mind."

He turns to face you straight on. A queer look on his face. "You — work for me?"

"Yeah."

"Again?"

"Yeah…"

"I hardly think so."

"No?"

"No."

"Oh."

Your Dealer leans back against a counter. Lost in thought. The sheer absurdity of the idea seems to have momentarily paralyzed him.

You stay quiet. Try to gauge your level of disappointment. In a way you've become rather comfortable with this side of the law. The idea of getting out of the business. Truth be told.

Your Dealer sips at his water. You hear the elevator arrive at your floor. Hear its doors clang open.

Stacy.

He continues, "What I'm saying is, take some time but then get over it. Get past it. Move on. This happened, that happened. Things changed. Okay. A lot changed. *Things change, Lee.* Don't take too long. Don't take forever. Don't be the kind of guy that takes forever. Don't be the kind of guy that *wallows* in it. You're going to be sixty someday too. Grasp that. What will you look back on then? Anything? It does get to be too late at some point, son. You *do* realize? Too late. To accomplish anything. How long do you think you can go before you at least try to do something useful? Did you think you would deal forever? For how much longer? Did you think you were going to one day become *me*? Do you have any idea what's involved? Trust me, you're not cut out for it. I'm doing you a favour. You don't even realize that. *I'm doing you a favour.*"

And you do get it. Actually. That he's doing this for you. Today. You realize he's come for this reason. To tell you this. That there's no route ever coming back. He's taking the time to *explain* this to you. And he's thanking you. In a proper way. For services rendered.

"It's not the life you think it is, Lee," he says. "It's not for you."

The door pushes open, you'd left it ajar. Stacy enters. Along with The Boy. She stops, surprised that you are not alone.

She's had her hair done. Coloured it a bit. And gone shopping.

Wearing a white blouse and new jeans and shoes with heels, for the first time in a couple of years probably. She looks, there is no other word for it, *attractive*.

Your Dealer gives her the once-over, turns back to you. "Alright then, I'm going." He scoops up his water bottle, starts towards the door, still favouring one leg. "Think about it, boy. It's your move."

You watch him walk awkwardly across your space.

"Hey, are you okay?" you say to him. "I hope it's not something serious."

"What? No."

"You're sure?"

"Just too much time on the bike. My knee swells up. This time it doesn't seem to want to go away."

He's getting closer to the door. Stacy seems unsure what to do. Move away? Hold it open until he arrives?

"Or maybe it's cancer," you say. Give him a big, goofy grin. "Could it be cancer, do you think? Like maybe bone cancer? Sometimes it starts out that way, no?"

Your Dealer stops dead. His eyes snap wide open. Like you've just slapped him in the face. Or called Jesus a big homo. You just said the C word. You're jinxing him. And yourself. He waits to see if you will be struck by lightning.

You wink, look over at Stacy.

Your smile fades.

You see that she is clutching your brown suede bag in her hand, golden sash wrapped around her wrist. It had been strategically hidden among the items you dumped at her place so she wouldn't find it right away. Inside there was also a note addressed to her and Ack! It was only a matter of time until she came across it. Now she's brought it back with her.

"Lee," Stacy says, coming forward, waggling the bag in the air, insanely choosing *this* moment to do this, "could you please explain something to me?"

"Later."

"No, now."

"After."

"No." She drops the bag onto the kitchen table in front of her. And Your Dealer.

You watch the two of them look at the bag, look at each other. Realize they've never met. And that this is not the time to introduce them.

"Stace, we'll talk later."

But she's riled up. "What's this all *about*? You scared me half to death."

"Stacy—"

"Where did you get this?"

"But we'll—"

"Is it yours?"

"Yes. No. Yours."

Your Dealer has been watching all of this. He reaches over and lifts the bag.

Stacy moves to stop him, looks at you.

You nod at her. It's all right.

As if on cue, The Boy runs over to you. Demands that you pick him up, hold him. You do. Watch together as Your Dealer unties the sash, tugs it open, and begins thumbing through the tightly wrapped bundles of bills.

You know that inside the bag is exactly $66,300. Exactly half. Of everything you ever saved. You know this because you counted it ten different times before you put it in there.

Stacy says, "What am I supposed to do with this? Is this *legal*? Did you know you scared the hell out of me? I almost fainted. Did you know that? And what are you trying to say, Lee?"

You don't answer. Continue watching Your Dealer. Replacing the money now. Retying the cord, setting it gently back on the table. You make out a faint smile on his lips.

Stacy watches him too. And at this instant, suddenly gets it. Who he is.

"Do whatever you want with it, Stace," you tell her. "It's for you and Zachary. Put it down on a house with a big backyard for him to grow up in. You're always going on about it. So do it. Whatever you think."

Your Dealer gives you a last look. Turns and lets himself out. Wordlessly. For once, not wanting to disturb.

Stacy looks around at the apartment.

The boxes. Piled everywhere.

You turn away with The Boy, veer towards the living room where you can throw him down against the carpet and let him wrestle you into submission. Pretend not to hear her following you. Begin battling Ack!, pecking him with kisses, making him squirm and giggle. He's a good kid, this one. A toddling two-year-old tribute to All That Is Right And Meaningful In The World. He is an honest soul. Zachary is goodness, and you need some goodness. Zachary — you still can't get past that fucking name — is beautiful. Truly. You've stared at him. For hours. Sober drunk straight stoned. From every angle. He is gorgeous. He has skin that is so smooth it's *polished*. For such a tiny thing, he *understands*. Way more than you'd ever think he could. Deeply, instinctively. And he has a *sense of humour*. He might even be a *goddamned genius*, you think sometimes.

She comes up behind you, kneels down. Puts her hand on your arm. You can feel the warmth of her breath at your neck.

"Do you want to live in that house with us, Lee?" she asks softly. "Is that what you're trying to say?"

You don't answer. Can't speak. Concentrate instead on your son. He is part you. He is skinny. He will be tall, surely. He already has no ass, just like you. He is ultra blond in that way kids are before they get older and it begins to ebb away, and he will end up with a straw-textured head of hair like yours one day. Will he be ugly too? It sure doesn't seem like it today. He is gorgeous, perfect. He has her eyes.

Her manner. Her way of thinking carefully about something before doing it. Her staunch belief in right and wrong. He has such long eyelashes. He has her bright smile but your athletic gait, more and more. Your arrogance. Your love of lounging around doing nothing, watching people. He is developing into a fine young man.

You will have to look out for Zachary. It's a complicated, unpredictable world out there. Until he is big enough and smart enough to take care of himself, this will be your job. Basically forever. You couldn't be happier. You have a purpose. And when the time comes, you will tell him about decisions you took and mistakes you made. You will try to explain this to your son.

Orty

You look over at the scoreboard as the final seconds tick down. The buzzer goes. With your blocker hand you push your mask upwards until it sits on top of your head. Sweat escapes from your hair and drips down your forehead, making your eyes sting. You wipe your face with the sleeve of your jersey as your teammates skate over to your net, alternately slapping you on the side of the head or whacking you on the pads.

A line forms. You join the end of it. When it comes time to shake hands with Sanderson, Dane, and ultimately Cuz, you make sure to meet their eyes. Straight on. You were a bit nervous they might try to run you out there, but nothing happened and by the last period you weren't even thinking about it. You haven't seen any of them in a while, since all the different shit went down.

Everybody skates over to the boards and off the ice, clomping like clowns through the corridor to your respective dressing rooms. Inside, you plop down into your stall, strip off your sweater and shoulder pads. Lean back against the cool cement. Twist open a beer. Glance around at the others. The mood is high though you got spanked 16-11.

Every year around Thanksgiving, a game is held. It's a memorial match organized by the family of a guy who died when you were all much younger. The James T. Reilly Memorial Hockey Game. They do a dinner afterwards and raise money for research into brain cancer. It's a big event in the neighbourhood.

You sit there, drinking, listening to everyone blabbing at the same time. This play and that play. Who was good, who wasn't. Who sucked. You catch yourself grinning, always enjoy this part most. The score, you don't give a fuck about. The hockey, *feh*. You come for the conversation. The insults. The searing indictments. Here, if you don't have skills, you're exposed. If you're too slow, you're exposed. If you never pass the puck, exposed. Always pass, exposed. Clumsy, dirty, mouthy, chicken. Exposed. Fat, skinny, too hairy, not hairy enough. Big ass. Small dick. Exposed. Unemployed. Divorcing. Still living with your mother. Exposed exposed exposed.

You're a goalie. Not a very good one. So you've heard your share. Johnny's a centre, a very good one. The best one, usually. Today he certainly was. Aaron played too. And Tim and The Hairy Wonder. And others, guys you see only once a year. Plus a few fresh faces. Friends of friends, pitching in to keep it going as the older players fade away. Henry used to come every year. He was a surprisingly fast skater for such a stocky dude. A great forechecker. Relentless.

You miss him.

Most of the room is listening as Johnny rags on Aaron. Before the game there was a speech at centre ice and then a moment of silence was held in memory of James Reilly. And Anna Nicole Smith. Then the puck dropped and within the first fifteen seconds Aaron lost his balance along the boards and absolutely levelled the referee. Pasted him headfirst into the glass. It was harsh to watch. The ref was super pissed when he got up. He gave Aaron four minutes for Being Such A Fucking Klutz. The other team took a two-goal lead right off the bat.

Aaron protests his innocence now in the room. "I didn't do nothing. That's not a *penalty*. I don't know why he made such a big deal. He's getting paid."

"He's going to need *dental work*."

"He's the *ref*. Get out of the fucking way!"

"You're a train wreck out there, man."

Aaron looks down, drops his elbow pads into his bag one by one. "Hey, you know what? Screw you. I played good. Get away from me."

"You played good?"

"I got two goals."

"It was 16-11. *Everybody* got two goals."

"I got four points."

"Big fucking deal. Honey was up in the stands reading her decor magazine" — Johnny throws his own elbow pads into his bag — "and *she* got four points."

Aaron looks away again, starts rooting through his gear for some imaginary item. "Okay. Talk to somebody else."

Johnny laughs, reaches for his beer. "I'm kidding. You played good. Everyone played good. Mikey, you played good. Roscoe, you played good. Travers, very good. Marco…"

Marco looks up. "Yeah?"

"Not good."

"I know."

"You played shit."

"I know."

A guy named Debrofsky says, "Well, maybe he —"

Johnny whirls to face him. "Hey, *you* played shit too, Debrofsky. Don't worry. I'll get to you. With that wooden stick. And those ankle guards. Who're you, your father?" Johnny turns back to Marco. "I'm just saying, dude. You were really bad. That's all."

"Alright. I know."

"The other guys are thinking it too. But I'm saying it."

"Okay."

"You were complete shit."

Marco nods.

"I don't know if anyone was worse," Johnny adds.

"I'm sorry."

"Maybe one guy. That's all I can think of."

"Debrofsky?"

Johnny stops. Stares at Marco. Shakes his head slowly, milking it. A sad expression on his face. Then he turns back to the rest of you. "Can you believe this prick? Plays like shit and then does my Debrofsky line?"

Several guys laugh. Even though this makes them the next likely targets. Marco grins. Debrofsky grins.

You sneak a look over at Johnny. Wanting his attention. Not wanting his attention. Careful not to draw his ire. But Johnny looks down at the floor instead, begins unlacing his skates. You turn away before someone catches you watching.

You'd better get undressed, you remind yourself, and into the shower. Stacy is waiting for you. She came to watch with The Boy. You are together now, the three of you. Officially. So did things turn out so horribly? Maybe they turned out *better*. It was a blast to see them in the stands this afternoon. Even though you let in so many goals. They were seated in your end, close enough for you to hear their cheers. Hearing him call out for you, it was weird. Zachary sure has a pair of lungs on him. It made you feel good. It made you feel great.

Honey was at the complete other end. Sitting off by herself the whole time, you noticed. Engaged, finally, to Johnny. A ring and everything. And Baby was there too. Rooting for Tim, who finally seems to be her boyfriend, ultimately, though she applauded anyone who did anything remotely positive. What a fan. The two sisters never acknowledged each other. Instead, Baby sat yakking with Maureen and her girls, Danielle and Gabrielle, the four of them sitting together, a strange grouping.

You sigh. Reach for another swig of your beer, put the bottle down gently on the bench beside you. You feel suddenly, strangely, almost comically, sad. Instantly nostalgic. Nothing is the same anymore. You'll walk out the door today and it'll be another year before you hear sounds like this. It's just too weird how everything is now. The endless summer vibe is gone. Johnny and Honey keep to themselves.

You and Stacy too. Baby is always off at school. Aaron and Mo see all of you, but always separately. No more barbecues. No more park. Henry is gone. No more picking up the phone just to jabber or argue with somebody. It's all changed.

A voice snarls, "Hey, Goodstone!"

Your head jerks up. Cuz is standing at the doorway. Suddenly arrived from the other room. Already in his street clothes. Glaring at you. You can see Dane and Sanderson standing in the corridor behind him.

"I'm waiting outside for you, asshole. Let's go!"

And with that he disappears, taking the pair with him.

Instantly you feel yourself break into a brand new sweat. Your heart begins to thunder.

There is a silence in the room. All eyes fall upon you. The pause is long and uncertain. Five seconds, ten. And then an eruption of hoots and whistles and a flurry of that clever banter you enjoy so much.

"Whoah! Listen to Cuzzie! Throwing down the gauntlet…"

"*Somebody's* wrist is better…"

"Hey, Goodstone! You're fucked, man…"

"Boy, you give up sixteen soft ones and they lose all respect…"

"Goodstone, you fucking sieve! What're you gonna *do*?"

You glance at Johnny. But his head has stayed down, fingers still fiddling with the laces of his skates. Purposely taking his time. You look quickly over at Aaron. See his eyes averted as well, pointedly kept from looking at you. Okay on you too, Aaron.

You look around at the others. Still watching you. In this crystal clear moment you can read every one of their opinions. Who likes you, who never did. Who you've always annoyed. Who couldn't care less about you. Who simply enjoys watching someone take a good licking. This is your fight — no one else's — but in a gleaming burst of understanding you know exactly who will be pulling for you and who will not. Some of them just because you fucked Johnny's girl, of course.

You begin fumbling with your equipment. Your fingers are trembling. Your tongue is instantly dry, frantically searching for even the faintest signs of moisture. You can hear it ripping itself from the roof of your mouth, over and over. You pull your beer bottle to your lips but only drops remain. Your breaths echo in your skull. Blood gushes in and out of your eardrums.

You picture the minutes to follow, until you finally walk into that back parking lot. You will have to strip off all your equipment. Pack it away. Shower. Should you shower? Get dressed. Hoist your bag over your shoulder. Get your sticks. While everyone watches. And eggs you on. Making. You. Even. More. Nervous.

And so, instead, you pull off one skate. Then the other. Find your boots. Dig your feet into them.

Strap your shoulder and elbow pads back on. Pull your sweater back over them.

Pick up your mask. Slip it on.

Put your glove on. Your blocker.

Grab your stick.

And then, without a word to the others, you leap up — inasmuch as a person wearing seven hundred thousand pounds of sopping wet hockey equipment can leap up — and lurch out of the room.

In the corridor you are blocked by a group of giggling girls. You grunt past, squeezing yourself against the concrete wall to get through. Hobble along the rest of the way towards the door to the parking lot. Throw your arms at the metal release bar, fling it open with a satisfying thrust.

Cuz is there, standing hands on hips. Dane and Sanderson lurk nearby.

Prepared to watch. Or help?

And then suddenly you get it. Can't believe you didn't figure it out until now. That it was Cuz. And these boys. Who put the beats on Henry that night.

You charge at them, nailing Cuz right off the bat with a stick to the ribs. His breath leaves him as he doubles over. A sweet sight. A goalie stick is fucking *heavy*. Dane grabs at you, trying to tear the mask off your head. You blocker him neatly to the face but Sanderson wrenches the stick from your hands at the same instant. From behind you now Cuz tears at your shoulder pads, trying to haul you to your knees. You flail away with arms and legs but the equipment is heavy, more hindrance than protection. Dane tackles you onto your side. You lie beached, like a whale. Someone goes for your mask again. Sanderson. You gouge at his eyes with the rough lacing of your trapper, trying to stave him off. They are all around you. On top of you. Rabid beasts. You are keenly aware that you are flailing on borrowed time. You can hear only heavy snarls around you, closing in.

And then, suddenly, *crack!*, you see Cuz's head snap to one side, recoiling from the strike of a gauntlet. He topples over, howling and clutching at his ear. You look up to see Johnny standing over him, hand still in the air. Like you, he is in full gear minus skates.

Now you watch Johnny swivel around, take his stick, and hook Dane's feet out from under him. *Boom*, down he goes. Sanderson immediately rushes over but Johnny cross-checks him in the shoulder, smiling, pitching him to the pavement almost with ease. And when Cuz tries to get up, Johnny slashes him on the ankle, eliciting a new set of wails.

You rise, lumber over beside Johnny. Look at him, look at the bodies on the ground. That's at least eight minutes in penalties lying right there. And probably a misconduct too. Dane and Sanderson get to their feet, slower now. So does Cuz, with even less enthusiasm. Dane lunges at you. You clothesline him with your forearm pad. Two minutes for interference. A frothing Sanderson grabs at Johnny but he dances out of reach then turns and smacks him in the back of the head. *Ooh.* Unsportsmanlike conduct. The ref will call that every time.

At the back door of the arena you catch a glimpse of the boys arriving in just their jeans, barefoot and shirtless, jostling for sight-lines, cheering lustily.

Cuz takes a last run in your direction. You and Johnny elbow him in the chest with simultaneous blows, knocking him backwards into a sitting position. More minutes in the box. And more cheers. Dane and Sanderson attempt a final charge. You stop Dane with a gauntlet to the mouth at the same time Johnny gives Sanderson his own face wash of tough, sweaty leather. And while they're still within range Johnny gives them both hard kicks in the backside. Each staggers about with a hand on his face and the other on his ass.

This brings more howls of laughter from the gallery. You see Marco and Debrofsky pumping their fists in the air.

Cuz retreats, limping towards the cars.

You and Johnny back off, allowing Dane and Sanderson to follow.

You watch as they pile into their cars, scatter off.

The boys applaud. You pull off your mask. Try to contain the rush of adrenalin still coursing through your veins. Relief, joy. Johnny takes off his helmet and tucks it under one arm, pushes back a handful of sweaty black curls. Then he straightens his gear and, after a slight hesitation, taps you lightly against the pads with his stick, no different than if you'd just made a nice save.

The boys file back inside. They cross other spectators, arriving now, making their way outside. Spilling out onto the pavement. Milling about. Parents, kids. Grandparents. They heard about a brawl. Hockey fans love a good brawl, even if it's not on the ice. Especially if it's not on the ice.

They stare at you and your friend, still in your equipment. In your boots. In the parking lot. They're asking each other what has happened, what it is they've missed.

You ignore their stares and start back towards the arena along with Johnny, walking side by side.

Somewhere in the distance, a siren is wailing.

No, really.

THANKS to my sister Cindy, my earliest reader and perennial supporter, in so many ways. Thanks to my wife Véronique and my mother Anna. To Mark, Michael, and Gabrielle. To Bruce, Lisa, Olivier, Trevor, and Julie K. To Peter and Brian for such great feedback. To Bethany, Milena, and Lorin for challenging me. Thank you, Penn, for being cool and taking me on at the Ann Rittenberg Literary Agency. In appreciation of Akou, Corey, John, Julie, and Susanne of Goose Lane Editions. And a special tip of the hat to Felix Rebolledo for his invaluable help, as always.